THREE
BULLETS

THREE
BULLETS

R.J. Ellory

ORION

An Orion paperback

First published in Great Britain in 2019
by Orion Fiction,
This paperback edition published in 2020
by Orion Fiction,
an imprint of The Orion Publishing Group Ltd,
Carmelite House, 50 Victoria Embankment,
London EC4Y 0DZ

An Hachette UK company

1 3 5 7 9 10 8 6 4 2

A CIP catalogue record for this book
is available from the British Library.

ISBN (Paperback) 978 1 4091 6316 9

Typeset at The Spartan Press Ltd,
Lymington, Hants

Printed and bound in Great Britain by Clays Ltd,
Elcograf S.p.A.

MIX
Paper from
responsible sources
FSC® C104740

www.orionbooks.co.uk

Prologue

November 23, 1963

Ed Conroy stood at the fifth-floor window of the Texas School Book Depository and looked down toward the junction of Houston and Elm. Fifty-six years old, insomniac and irritable, he wondered how much longer he could hump boxes for minimum wage. From where he stood, he could clearly see the precise vantage point he'd taken up on Dealey Plaza three or four hours before the president and the first lady were even due to appear. He remembered how they'd looked. That pink suit she wore. So elegant, so beautiful. She'd smiled as she looked in his direction, and even though there was a throng of people, he'd wanted to believe the smile was just for him. Foolish, because Jackie smiled for everyone, but what the hell?

'Ed?'

Ed glanced back toward the stairwell. Larry Furness appeared at the other end of the room.

'Did you see 'em?' Ed asked.

'Sure I did.' Larry joined him at the window.

'I was right down there,' Ed said, and pointed toward the plaza.

'I was over on Elm,' Larry replied. 'A little way before the underpass.'

'Hell of a thing.'

'Sure was. But now they're gone and we have to move all that stuff upstairs.' He glanced at his watch. 'Two hours. I wanna be out of here on time.'

Ed closed his eyes for just a second. He recalled that unmistakable Jackie Kennedy smile, and then he turned and followed Larry.

'What the hell is this?' Larry said as he emerged from the stairwell and surveyed the sixth floor.

Ed looked over his shoulder. Boxes had been moved, dozens of them, and stacked a good four or five feet high in a makeshift wall between the end of the room and the window.

'Who the hell did this?' Ed asked.

'That new kid works up here,' Larry said. 'The skinny one.'

The two of them walked to the far corner and turned left around the long line of boxes. A couple more boxes had been pushed up against the wall, and there were signs of someone having attempted to conceal themselves.

'Looks like someone wanted their own picture show of the motorcade,' Ed commented.

'Least he could've done was put everything back where it came from.'

'Hell, no big deal. We gotta move everything back toward the stairs anyway.'

They started work, hefting the cartons of schoolbooks one after the other. It was tiresome and repetitive work. Each new semester required a different catalog of texts, and they had to be located, organized, accessible and packaged for delivery to the different educational districts.

Fifteen minutes in, making good progress, and then Larry stopped.

'What the hell?' he said. He leaned down and picked something up from the floor. 'Ed ... look at this.'

Ed came over. There, in the palm of Larry's hand, was a single bullet.

Ed picked it up. 'Jesus,' he said, his voice a whisper.

Larry looked back at the remaining boxes that sat between the stairwell and the window. 'You thinkin' what I'm thinkin'?'

Ed held the bullet between his thumb and forefinger and inspected it more closely. 'That's a six-point-five-mil round,' he said. 'Definitely for a rifle.'

'Let me see again,' Larry said, and reached for the bullet.

Ed saw it fall from Larry's fingers. The bullet bounced once, and then started rolling back toward the stairs.

They went after it, not a single word between them, chasing it as it skittered across the floorboards. Ed instinctively kicked out with his foot, trying to stop it before it reached the top of the stairwell. He skidded awkwardly and lost his balance. The bullet kept rolling, and then seemed to hesitate for an instant in its progression.

Larry lunged forward as it disappeared, grabbing at the space between the floorboards a split second too late.

He heard it bounce against the secondary layer of boards beneath the floor, and then it was gone.

He leaned back on his haunches. Ed was beside him.

They looked at one another.

'I'll get some tools,' Ed said.

For an hour they worked, carefully prying up the boards for a good six feet in each direction. They found mouse droppings, endless handfuls of thick dust, wood chippings, even spent cigarette butts, coins and a couple of keys. But the bullet could not be located. They looked through every inch of that space, and it was as if the thing had just vanished into thin air.

Finally, reconciling themselves to defeat, they replaced the boards, finished moving the boxes, and then stood at the sixth-floor window overlooking Dealey Plaza.

'What are we going to do?' Ed asked.

'Nothing,' Larry replied. 'That's what we're going to do.'

'Should we say something to the kid? What's his name?'

'Harvey,' Larry said. 'I think it's Harvey … Harvey something-or-other.'

'You think he had something to do with this?'

'With what, Ed?'

Ed didn't respond. His expression was distant and pensive.

'With nothing,' he finally said, and then the two of them walked back toward the stairwell in silence.

I

July 3, 1964

Judith Wagner lay naked on the bed. For the past few minutes she'd done nothing but stare at the ceiling, a single thought running through her mind.

How long can I keep doing this to myself?

Jack was in the bathroom. Judith could smell his cologne on the pillow. She could hear him opening pill bottles and taking one after the other – Librium, Ritalin, codeine. God only knew what.

How many other girls are there? Does he treat them all the same? Do they all lie there afterwards and ask themselves such questions?

In the moment, she was everything. Afterward, she was nothing. As if what they shared had never happened at all.

His attention was like a spotlight, and there she was, center-stage, and that attention was heady and intoxicating and addictive. I mean, who wouldn't be captivated, even overawed by such a thing?

I would, she thought. *And so many others too. Of that I am sure.*

Judith rolled over, sat on the edge of the mattress and reached for her cigarettes. She lit one, stretched toward the chair and tugged at Jack's shirt. It slid to the floor, and just for a second she was tempted to leave it right where it was. *How much would that annoy him?*

Instead she lifted it, put it on, slipped a couple of buttons, and then walked barefoot to the window.

A pill bottle clattered into the bathroom sink. Jack cursed.

He appeared in the doorway, looked to the chair, then across at Judith. He scowled and clicked his fingers at her. 'Shirt!' he snapped.

Judith undid the buttons, took the shirt off, held it by the collar between her thumb and forefinger and walked toward him.

He snatched the shirt from her, blind to her nakedness, and said, 'And put that thing out ... I told you not to smoke in here.'

Judith slid by him and dropped the half-smoked cigarette into the toilet bowl. It hissed. She flushed, but still it floated there obstinately.

Jack closed his eyes and sighed.

Judith wanted to smack him hard. She wanted to leave a welt on his face that wouldn't disappear for a week. She wanted to hit him so hard her fingerprints were indelibly etched into his skin.

Bastard.

But she didn't hit him. She didn't say anything. She walked back and sat once more on the edge of the bed, now pulling the sheet up around her, hiding herself, and she felt quiet and lonely and awkwardly ashamed.

I'm an attention junkie, she thought. *I need him so much more than he needs me, and yet I know I can never have him. No one can have him. No one owns Jack but himself. And he plays with that. He plays with my mind and my emotions and I love him and I hate him and sometimes I just wish he would die.*

There was a gentle knock at the door.

It was time.

Judith got up and put on a robe. She opened the door and Walter was there. Walter was a good man. He gave a damn.

'Hey, Walter,' she said.

6

'Hey, Judy.'

'He's coming now.'

'Okay.'

'You want to come in?'

'Sure.'

She opened the door a little further and Walter glanced back down the corridor each way before stepping inside.

Walter could stand anywhere and be invisible. He never looked nervous or uncomfortable. He was some sort of Buddhist, she thought. He was tough, no doubt about it, and would not hesitate for a moment to take a life, but still – somehow – his eyes possessed a depth of kindness that seemed rare in any world Judith knew.

Jack walked out of the bathroom. He had on his tie and his jacket. His hair was immaculate.

'Walter,' he said.

'Sir,' Walter replied.

'They outside?'

'Yes, sir.'

'Let's get going. Can't be late for the TV people.'

Jack didn't even look at Judith, didn't pause to smile, to kiss her, to even touch her hand as he strode past and left the room.

Walter did pause. He reached out to straighten the collar of her robe, and then he brushed a stray lock of hair over her ear.

Judith closed her eyes. She wanted to cry.

'Take care,' Walter said.

'You too, Walter,' she replied.

He closed the door silently behind him.

Judith could hear their footsteps disappearing down the hallway. She walked back to the bed and lay down. She closed her eyes.

If she told anyone, they wouldn't believe her.

The greatest defense against exposure was disbelief.

After he'd gone, she felt worthless. Same as always.

But she knew she was no more worthless than any of the others.

Even Marilyn Monroe fucked him, and she was as far from worthless as you could get.

Judith had made this bed. She knew that. And now she was consigned to lie in it as long as he allowed.

One day he would let her go, and there would be no coming back.

After all, he was Jack Kennedy, President of the United States of America, and once he let you go, it would be as if you'd never existed at all.

2

July 4, 1964

Perhaps we all share the same fear: to walk the earth unseen, unknown, unrecognized, unremembered.

The thought – errant and unexpected – arrived amidst a number of other unrelated thoughts. Mitch Newman sat and stared at the bourbon in his glass and considered it. Was it something he'd heard, or did he really believe that?

Loneliness is very rarely a matter of being alone. A lonely human being is just as lonely in a crowded room.

He raised the glass and emptied it. He nodded at Tom, the barkeep, and Tom headed down with the bottle.

'It's Independence Day, Mitch. You don't have a place to go eat dinner? You got no party to go to?'

Mitch smiled sardonically. 'I'm not a party kind of guy, Tom.'

'Everyone's a party type of guy. They just need the right kind of party.'

'I'll keep on looking then.'

'I'm going to put the television on in a little while.'

'Kennedy?' Mitch asked.

'The civil rights thing, sure,' Tom replied. 'You wanna see it?'

'Why the hell not, eh? We voted for him, we might as well listen to what he has to say.'

'It's a big deal, wouldn't you say? I mean, Dr King, the

Freedom Riders, all that stuff. Election time again in November, and this is surely gonna count for something.'

Mitch took a drink. 'I'm a journalist,' he said. 'I've been listening to these people my whole working life. What they say, what they mean and what they do are three very different things.'

'You are way too cynical.'

'And you are way too trusting, my friend. If they really do start repealing segregation laws and giving colored people the same job opportunities as whites, then there's gonna be someone somewhere making a great deal of money as a result, believe me.'

'Hell, man, how did you get so bitter?'

Mitch shook his head. 'It was a lot easier than I thought, Tom ... a lot easier than I thought.'

Kennedy looked good. Even Mitch Newman had to agree. Midway through the speech – aired right out of the Oval Office – there was an edit jump, so the thing wasn't live, but what better day to make such an announcement than Independence Day? The Democratic National Convention was little more than six weeks away, and who was going to run against Kennedy? Nixon again? Goldwater from Arizona? Getting the president's face on television between *Fanfare* and *Gilligan's Island* with something as potentially significant as the Civil Rights Bill was a clever move on the part of Kennedy's special assistant, Ken O'Donnell, and the press secretary, Pierre Salinger. Mitch had met Salinger. Smart as a whip. The Kennedy brothers ran their own little Irish mafia, and Salinger was a good *consigliere*.

Mitch lit a cigarette, reached down the bar for an ashtray.

'In July of 1960, when I accepted the Democratic presidential nomination, I spoke of America and all Americans facing a new frontier. I spoke not of promises, but of challenges ... challenges that would face us as individuals and as a nation in the years ahead.'

Kennedy paused for effect. The previous year had been a tough one for the administration. The Republicans had been chasing a vote-rigging allegation. Rumor had it that some kind of House Ethics Committee under the chief justice, Earl Warren, might be convoked to investigate. With sixty-nine million citizens having their say, Kennedy had crept under the wire in 1960 by a margin of little more than 110,000 votes. It was the closest election for nearly a century, and already questions had been raised regarding the way the votes had been counted in Alabama. Nixon had carried four more states, but Kennedy took the Electoral College vote and thus the White House. Robert Kennedy, using all his influence as both attorney general and the president's brother, had been concocting every delaying tactic possible. No one in the administration wanted an independent investigation ahead of the new election. Still, November edged ever closer, and the more Robert tried, the more it fuelled the Republicans to dig the dirt.

Mitch took a refill, asked for a couple more ice cubes.

'My fellow Americans... tonight I want to tell you that one of the most fundamental liberties a man possesses – the liberty of equality with his fellow man – has been carved indelibly into the very bedrock of our great nation. Just two days ago, on July second, 1964, the Civil Rights Bill – a bill for which I have relentlessly and tirelessly fought since I took office – was signed into law. Let this day – American Independence Day, July fourth, 1964 – be forever remembered not only as the day we acknowledged our anniversary as a self-governing and independent nation, but also the day we became free from the last vestiges of injustice in America. Let us close the springs of racial poison that have infected our land. Let us demonstrate to the world not only our progressiveness, but also our devotion to decency, to honor, to truth, to the very foundations upon which this great nation was built: life, liberty and the pursuit of happiness...'

'Enough,' Mitch said. 'Shut it off would you, Tom?'

'Cynical,' Tom replied. 'Cynical, unpatriotic and friendless on Independence Day. It really couldn't get any worse, could it?'

'Oh, let's not tempt fate, shall we?' Mitch said. He swallowed the last double in one go, slid off the stool and steadied himself. He'd lost count of how many he'd had. Enough, that was for sure. 'I'm outta here,' he said.

'You take it easy, my friend,' Tom said.

'I doubt it,' Mitch replied, 'but I'll give it a go.'

Perhaps some people go crazy because crazy is the only place left to go.

That was the thought in Mitch Newman's mind as he sat at the table in the small kitchen of his Washington DC apartment.

Considering his life, the events in Korea that had broken him, he'd often wondered how everything might have changed had he made one different decision. Wasn't it the case with all lives, at least the lives that had failed? With some, there was a shattering cataclysm, tectonic plates colliding suddenly, the entire world buckling under the pressure. For others it was an accumulation of small shifts that culminated in collapse. Where had it really begun, and – more importantly – where would it end?

West Haven, Virginia: the small-town boy gone bad. That was the crux of it. The aspirations, the dreams, the diligence with which he had applied himself to his passions – writing, journalism, photography – had all been so energetic and focused, and yet here he was, thirty-five years old, eking out a living reporting the second-hand microcosmic reflections of a far bigger world. DC, capital of the continental US, capital of the world's greatest superpower, and Mitchell James Newman, unacknowledged journalistic genius, failed hack, mediocre photographer, was taking call-outs from the PD to shoot corpses in Georgetown when the official crime-scene snapper was sick.

There were days when he woke believing this day would be his last. And then it came to a close, the light faded, and he knew he'd made it through. Sometimes he felt a sense of relief, other times a strange disappointment.

What would he give to turn it all back and replay it differently?

Everything, that was what he'd give.

Everything.

The phone rang.

It rankled him, aggravated the edge of patience already frayed. Someone calling to invite him out. *Come on, it's July fourth, you miserable son-of-a-bitch!*

Mitch sat for a further thirty seconds. They would quit, surely.

The phone kept ringing.

Finally, resentfully, he got out of the chair.

'Mitchell? Mitchell, is that you?'

Mitch Newman stood for a second, and then he stepped back and leaned against the wall.

That voice. It came at him like a slow-motion bullet from the past, and it cut a swathe through more than a decade of darkened history; a history that had left him hollowed out and broken up.

'Alice?' he said, scarcely believing that he could be right.

But he knew that he was, and before she said another word, he was overcome with the most certain sense of dread.

'Oh, Mitchell,' she said, and her voice came apart at the edges, and there were a million tears contained in every syllable.

Mitch knew. He knew without a doubt.

'She's dead, Mitchell. Jean is dead. And they're telling me she killed herself, that she took sleeping tablets and killed herself. It's a lie, Mitchell... it's a horrible, horrible lie...'

'Dead?' Mitch asked, as if saying the word would somehow dispel it, make it disappear, wake him from this awful dream.

'She's dead, Mitchell... my baby girl is dead.'

3

Jack Kennedy stood in the doorway of his wife's bedroom. She was fixing her hair, and though he knew she could see him, she made a point of ignoring him.

'Did you hear the speech?'

'I did,' she replied.

'What did you think?'

Jackie hesitated. She closed her eyes for just a second, and then she turned and faced her husband. 'I think it was wonderful, Jack. I think it was perfect and beautiful and eloquent and that you are the greatest man that ever walked the face of the earth, and please don't come any closer because I can smell cigarettes and perfume on you and it just disgusts me.'

'Jackie...'

'No, Jack. Don't *Jackie* me. This time I don't even want to know who it was or where it was, or how many times you've seen her before. Was she a showgirl or a pretty journalist or some party contributor's daughter, or was she just some intern from the press office? You know what? I don't care, Jack. I really don't care.'

Jack took a step into the room. She could sense his anger. It was almost hateful in its intensity.

'I'm going to a charity fundraiser with Lady Bird. You can get drunk with Ken and Pierre and whoever else and congratulate yourself on your forthcoming landslide.' She glanced at her husband, made no attempt to conceal the disdain in her expression. 'Of course, you can't conceive of the possibility of losing, can you? To you, such a thing seems impossible, but then that just highlights your arrogance. You can't go on fooling the world forever, my dear.'

'There's word that they'll convene an investigation on the election result,' Jack said, not rising to the bait, sidelining the routine hostility that now seemed never to dissipate. He had long since reconciled himself to the fact that his wife would never fully appreciate the pressures he had to bear, nor the ways in which he had to alleviate those pressures. She had never fully recognized his needs, and he knew she never would.

'Bobby will take care of it,' Jackie said. 'Leave it to the Irish mafia, like everything else.'

Jack sighed and shook his head. 'This is breaking my heart,' he said.

'Well, sweetheart, when it's all good and broken, let me know, and you can join my club.' Jackie turned back to the mirror.

From where he stood, she looked amazing – fierce and beautiful and proud and defiant. She was a force of nature, this woman, a hurricane, a tornado, and yet again he'd stood in the way and been crushed.

He loved her. He knew that. He believed she knew it too. Yet he could not withhold himself from the addiction of other women; the allure, the seduction, those first moments so precious and perfect.

If only the world knew, he thought.

Jack Kennedy turned and left his wife's bedroom, his heart like a stone, his thoughts like cold rain.

4

Had his life's memories been wiped clean, Mitch Newman believed that the last to be erased would be that of Jean Boyd. From the first to the last word, that girl, that woman, had occupied his mind, his conscience, his heart; she had fuelled the highest highs and the deepest depressions.

He could, even now, recall the first moment he *really* saw her, which quickly became the first moment they spoke.

Saturday, April 19, 1947. Her uncle had thrown a birthday party for Jean and her friends.

Of course, Mitch knew Jean by name and sight. West Haven, Virginia was no sprawling metropolis, but until that day she was just some cute girl with bangs and barrettes and a bicycle.

The girls that interested him were those heading to the University of Virginia, where he himself was destined to arrive in just a few months. Prior to that day, Jean was just a small star in the vast cosmos of potential future romantic conquests. But that day, and then throughout that long, brutally hot and oppressive summer, she became the center of his universe.

He had been sent over to the Boyd house by his mother with a pitcher of ice cream. If there was one thing that Ruth Newman could do better than pretty much anyone else he knew, it was make ice cream, and she was often called upon to provide. He found the front yard crowded with Jean's friends, and there she was, up on the porch, looking directly at him as he came along the walk.

'I know who you are,' she said.

'And I know who you are,' he replied. He held out the pitcher. 'Ice cream,' he said.

'What flavor is it?'

'I have no idea. My ma made it, asked me to run it over here. I think you should put it in the icebox before it melts.'

Jean turned and hollered for her mother.

The pitcher delivered, Mitch shared a few courteous words, and then turned to leave.

'You can stay if you want,' Jean said.

'I wasn't invited.'

'Do you have a gift for me?'

Mitch shook his head.

'It's not right,' she replied. 'You know, if you don't bring a girl a gift on her birthday, then you probably shouldn't even be speaking to her.'

'I guess not.'

'Okay, Mr Ice Cream Delivery Man. You've done your job. Now you have to get off the front yard before I call the cops.'

Mitch started laughing. 'You're just a little bit crazy,' he said.

'Why, thank you,' Jean said, and curtsied.

From that moment, and with no clear explanation or rationale to back it up, Mitch Newman knew that life and all it had to offer would never be more than an arm's-length away. Jean Boyd made him feel that there was a lit firework somewhere, and at any moment it could easily explode.

With her beside him, he could swing the world by its tail with one hand, catching everything that tumbled off with the other.

Of course, she didn't feel the same way. Not at first. Getting her attention was tough enough, for it seemed to span every possible angle at once. Securing her undivided attention was something else altogether, and that took strategy and perseverance.

The day after the party, Mitch took a single flower and a cupcake to Jean's house. He knocked on the screen, and Jean's mother, Alice, came through from the back.

'Mitchell Newman,' she said. 'How's your mother?'

'She's just fine,' Mitch said.

'Well, give her my thanks again, would you? Tell her that the ice cream was just wonderful.'

'Sure thing.'

'I'm guessing those aren't for me,' Alice said.

'No, ma'am.'

'You know you're a day late.'

'Yes, I do.'

Alice turned, called Jean's name. 'There's someone here to see you.'

'Who is it?'

'Come take a look.' Alice vanished.

Footsteps along the upper landing became footsteps on the stairs. Jean appeared, dungarees, a red T-shirt, her hair tied up.

She looked at Mitch Newman, and did a double-take.

'Really?' she said.

'Really.'

'It's kinda sweet, but weird too.'

Mitch didn't reply. He stood there with the flower and the cupcake and he didn't care how it appeared.

'I'm not inviting you in,' Jean said. 'I don't even really know you.'

'I don't really know you either,' Mitch replied. 'Isn't that the way every friendship starts?'

Jean smiled. 'Is that a line from a movie, or did you just make it up?'

'I made it up.'

'You want to start a friendship?'

'Yes.'

'Why?'

'Because if I don't, then tomorrow will be the same as today, except that I'll be kicking myself for not coming over here and finding out if you really are who I think you are.'

Jean laughed. It was a wonderful sound, charming and infectious. 'Do you talk like this all the time?' she asked.

'Not usually, no,' Mitch said. 'I'm making a special effort for you.'

Jean stepped forward. She took the flower and the cupcake.

'Happy birthday, Jean,' Mitch said.

'Thank you, Mitch,' she replied.

They stood there for a moment longer, the silence between them as tangible as a third person, and then she said, 'Tomorrow, seven o'clock. Come and get me. You can take me to the movies.'

Mitch borrowed a car. He took Jean all the way to Culpeper. He paid for hot dogs and popcorn. He made her laugh so much she spilled soda on her skirt. When they got back, he opened the car door for her and walked her to the stoop. She told him she'd had a great time, and then she kissed him on the cheek. 'Let's do it again sometime,' she added, almost as an afterthought, and then she went inside.

For three years they were emotionally inseparable. Mitch went on up to Charlottesville and started his journalism studies in September. They spoke on the telephone every day, and he returned to West Haven every weekend to see her. By the time

Jean graduated, there was no way in the world she'd consider anywhere but the University of Virginia. She was accepted, and enrolled on the same course. A scholarship covered her tuition fees, and with some part-time work for both the Charlottesville *Daily Progress* and the *Richmond Times-Dispatch* – which doubled as an internship – she earned sufficient to rent a room in a house near the campus.

She cut her teeth on articles like 'Keswick Man Admits Stealing Two Cars' and 'Rheumatism Keeps Pope From His Daily Walk' on the same page as the transmission listings for WCHV. Most nights she stayed over with Mitch, all the while conscious of the fact that had their relationship been discovered, they might have been expelled from the university. They were discreet, they worked hard, they enjoyed what they were doing. It seemed that the life they were creating together could not have been better had they planned it. So much so that on New Year's Eve 1949, Mitchell Newman proposed to Jean Boyd and she accepted. They would finish their respective studies, they would make career decisions, find jobs, but as far as finding the person with whom each of them wished to spend the rest of their lives, that part was done.

The ground they shared, so very stable for so long, started to shift in the summer of 1950. As if there was some distant earthquake on the horizon, the tremors came in waves as Mitch tried to explain why he had to quit college and leave her behind.

'Korea,' he said. 'We are going to war in Korea.'

'I understand that we're going to war in Korea, Mitch. What I don't understand is why you have to go too.'

'Because this is who I am and this is what I want to do. It's opportunities like this that make careers.'

'All of a sudden you're Robert Capa?'

'Hell, Jean, Robert Capa was an illegal alien who got the

British attaché in DC drunk enough to give him an exit visa and sailed to England with no passport. He went ashore with the first beach landings in 1944 and took the most iconic photos—'

'And you're a twenty-year-old journalism student from West Haven, Virginia, and there's no way in the world that you're going to get leave to go.'

'If I have press credentials, I can go.'

'And where the hell are you going to get those?'

'I was going to ask Lester Byron at the *Dispatch*,' Mitch said.

'You were going to ask *my* editor to give you press credentials? I'll tell Lester that if he does anything to help you, then I'll quit his damned newspaper.'

'Jean—'

'What, Mitch? Would you just listen to yourself? You are two years and nine months into a degree, and you plan to drop out, fly halfway round the world, and get shot at in the jungle. I can't even take this seriously.'

So went the conversations, and those conversations soon became bitter and awkward, even accusatory. Jean never changed her opinion. What he was thinking was not only irresponsible and selfish, it was downright suicidal.

In mid June of 1950, Mitch Newman secured a valid press credential from the *Richmond Times-Dispatch* chief editor. 'If a twenty-year-old can go out and fight, then why can't a twenty-year-old go out and report on the fighting?' was Byron's viewpoint. Always matter-of-fact, always pragmatic, he was enough of a newspaperman to be undaunted by Jean's threat to quit. A reporter's personal life, unless it provoked something newsworthy, was none of his business.

The hardest sell was Mitch's mother, Ruth. Mitch's father had been killed in action in the Kasserine Pass in February of 1943. It was a clean headshot from an Afrika Korps sniper; he was dead before he hit the ground. His body was never recovered, believed to have been crushed into the ground beneath tank tracks in a last desperate assault by the Italian Centauro and Fifth Panzer divisions. Mitch had been fourteen years old.

After challenging every reason Mitch could give for his decision, his mother wanted to know what Jean thought. 'Surely she's not willing for you to go?'

'No, she's not,' Mitch said.

'And you can't understand why she feels that way?'

'Of course I can, Ma, but that doesn't change the way *I* feel. You start living life by everyone else's rules, meeting their expectations, doing what they want, and you might as well not live at all.'

'So like your father,' she said. 'Stubborn. Just so damned stubborn.'

'I am going as a press correspondent. I am not going to fight. I am not going to die. I am going to take photographs and send stories home for the newspaper.'

'You don't think press people get shot at too? Civilians get killed. Innocent bystanders get killed. You think a camera makes you bulletproof?'

Mitch didn't respond. All communication was now confrontational. Jean and his mother had one viewpoint, he had another. Those viewpoints would never be the same, and the more they tried to talk about it, the more intractable they each became.

On the last day of June, less than forty-eight hours before Mitch was due on a military flight out of Arlington Municipal, he and Jean sat up for hours. She was crying, and there seemed to be nothing he could do to allay her fears.

'I really thought we had a future together,' she said.

'We do have a future together.'

'But this was never part of any agreement, Mitch. I just do not understand why you can't see my viewpoint. You're voluntarily going to war. You're going to jump out of a helicopter and run toward something that everyone else is running away from, and the only thing you have for protection is a camera.'

'I think they might give me a helmet,' he said, trying to lighten the mood.

She glared at him.

'Sorry,' he said.

'You really are going to go, aren't you? You're just going to up and leave me here on my own, and you're going to be thousands of miles away and I'm not going to know from one moment to the next whether you're alive or dead.'

Mitch had no response.

'You are a thoughtless son-of-a-bitch,' she said, and she started crying again.

He reached out his hand toward her, an effort to pull her close. She slapped it away. 'Don't touch me, Mitch Newman. I hate you.'

'No you don't.'

She stopped crying for a moment and looked at him with that too-familiar fierce anger in her eyes. 'Read my lips. I hate you. H-A-T-E.'

He tried to explain. She did not want to hear any more of his reasons. She pleaded with him, she begged him not to go, but Mitch was unmoved. It was not stubbornness as his mother had said, but rather a sense of obligation and duty, not only to those who had sufficiently believed in him to not throw him out of the newspaper offices, but to himself. He owed himself something. What, he did not know. All he understood – and this he felt to the very core of his being – was that if he backed down now, he would never again be able to look at himself in the mirror without seeing weakness.

At 5.30 in the morning, July 1, 1950, Mitch Newman packed the last few items of clothing, two cameras, six dozen rolls of film, ten notebooks, a pint of bourbon and a dented aluminum Thermos flask that had belonged to his father.

Jean refused to say goodbye. She held him tight for a long time, and then she let him go without a further word.

Mitch took the train to Arlington. He would fly out to Seoul, and there join the 24th Infantry Division, to which he had been seconded with military correspondent status. He would be with the 24th when Task Force Smith became the first US military unit to engage with the North Koreans at Osan. What happened there, and during the rest of his time in Korea, would have far greater repercussions and implications than he or Jean or his mother could ever have imagined.

Jean went on to complete her degree, staying as a staff reporter at the *Progress* until May of '57. She took a permanent job at the *Times-Dispatch*, but moved to the *Washington Tribune* after only fourteen months. She had enjoyed her work, had learned a great deal from Lester Byron, but perhaps could never forgive him for facilitating Mitch's departure to Korea.

As a journalist, Jean Boyd was dedicated. When it came to investigative work, she was a firebrand. It seemed that in all she undertook there was a degree of commitment and perseverance. She was also opinionated, headstrong and forthright in her attitude. Write though Mitch did, and many times, she never replied to his letters.

The last time Mitch had seen her had been in the spring of 1951. Korea had chewed him up and spat him out after just four months. What had happened there had almost killed him. He came back with wounds that would perhaps never heal. He stayed with his mother, rarely leaving the house, and was racked with nightmares that did not fade for months. Of course, his first thought had been to contact Jean. He wrote to her care of the paper. He found her personal address and also wrote her there. He wrote every week or so for nearly three months. His mother told him that Jean had moved on, that she was now with someone else. No, she did not know who it was.

'You made your decision, Mitchell. You left her behind. She chose not to wait for you. You have to accept that and get on with your own life.'

Mitch just wanted to tell her he was back, that he was broken and sorry and was it too much to ask for forgiveness?

He drove to the university campus, parked up near her rooming house. Before he even saw her, he knew she was there. He did not question it. It was something of which he was just certain. Why she'd not gone home for Christmas he did not know. He sat in the car and waited, his mind quiet, his heart speeding up and slowing down. His thoughts were too confused to clearly define what he imagined would happen if she appeared. He wasn't even sure that he would be able to speak to her. He just wanted to see what happened within himself when he saw her. He hoped that he would feel nothing, but he knew that was impossible. One glimpse and it would all come flooding back, every word, every feeling, every regret, every broken promise.

Jean stepped out onto the porch. Mitch heard his own intake of breath. It was far worse than he could have imagined. In that second was every other time he'd waited for her, from those first thrilling moments when he knew that he was falling in love to the comforting familiarity they'd shared before everything started to fall apart.

She came down the steps and turned away. Mitch just watched her. He did not leave the car. He did not call her name. He did not follow her. More than an hour later, she came back with a young man. They were holding hands. They were laughing together. She looked beautiful and carefree and happy.

If his heart had only been partially broken before, it was now beyond repair.

It was not just the unwanted emotions that he fought; it was the anger and resentment at having to feel them at all. He had been the architect of this grand cathedral of ambition, and yet there had been no foundation upon which it could stand.

He had taken the wrong road, resolute in the belief that it would take him to the right place.

Without Jean, it felt as if life would be half of what it could be. Perhaps, in truth, it would be no life at all.

That had been more than thirteen years earlier, and now she was dead.

Suicide.

It did not work. It did not rationalize. It made no sense. But then what did he know? He had known Jean as a teenager, just nineteen years old when he'd last seen her. Tomorrow it would be exactly fourteen years to the day since the first US engagement in Korea, the first time he'd known what it was to be truly awestruck and terrified, the first time he'd realized that a life like that of Capa or Carl Mydans or Hank Walker was a naïve romanticized dream. While Hank Walker was shooting the picture that would win him the US Camera Prize, Mitch Newman was puking into a steel helmet and crying like a baby.

Almost as many years had passed since that day as he had lived before. Things changed. People changed. There was no moment that would ever be repeated. Not in all the broad span of time. The light, the emotion, the sound – all unique, not only in and of themselves, but for each and every human being. Everyone perceived through different senses, making judgments founded on singular and original experience. Jean had lived a life without him, and he would never know how that life had driven her to this end.

He had promised Jean's mother that he would find out all he could. He owed her that much at least. And he wanted to know. He wanted – needed – to understand.

Perhaps, in truth, he wanted to assuage the guilt he felt. He had to know whether his abandonment and departure had played some part in the drama now unfolded. Selfish, perhaps, but it ate at him like a cancer and would not be subdued.

Tomorrow was Sunday, but he would go anyway. He would find out where Jean had lived. He would learn the names of those who worked with her, those who knew her. He would search out all he could of Jean Boyd. He still loved her, had always loved her, and until he understood what had happened, he would never be able to let her go.

5

July 5, 1964

If he was brutally honest with himself – something that he tried to be as infrequently as possible – Mitch Newman felt that employing press credentials was a lie. A small lie, but a lie all the same.

After Korea, he had taken work in Charlottesville, Fredericksburg, a brief stint with Lester Byron in Richmond, even an abortive and frustrating eight months in Pittsburgh as deputy city editor for the *Post-Gazette*. From there it had been free-lance all the way, primarily photographs – crime scenes, public events, political rallies, society weddings, notable days and civic celebrations. He'd lugged his cameras and hawked his pictures throughout North Carolina, West Virginia, Pennsylvania, Maryland, even as far west as Illinois and Missouri. High points had included a project with *National Geographic*, but further work never transpired. There had been some reportage jobs, but nothing to elevate his career beyond the mundane. Cheap motels, endless driving, too much time alone, too much liquor, too many bad meals. Somehow more than ten years had dissolved quietly behind him. He was thirty-five years old, alone, exhausted, and the only girl he'd ever really loved had killed herself.

How long before you understand that a losing streak can keep right on going until everything is lost?

The phone book gave him Jean's D.C. address. It was fifteen minutes' drive from his own place. He had no idea how long she'd lived there. After the twelfth letter with no reply, he'd stopped writing, stopped looking, stopped waiting. That had been more than a decade earlier. He did not know if she'd married, had children, only that she worked for the *Tribune*. He caught her bylines every once in a while, but he could not bring himself to read her work.

For a short while Mitch sat in his car and chained cigarettes. He didn't want to go up there, but he knew he had to. How he would get into her apartment, he didn't know. Bribe someone. Force the lock. Maybe someone would be inside – a husband, a lover, a friend. On the one hand, he didn't want to see anything of her personal life, simply because he didn't want to be reminded of what he'd given up, but on the other, he had to find out as much as he could. The questions pulled at him, and he could not drop it.

A uniform was stationed in the apartment hallway. It was the uppermost floor of a two-storey brownstone, generous in size, an elegant building. With its own access and fire escape to the right-hand side, it would not have been inexpensive. Jean had established herself here in DC, and had seemingly flourished.

Mitch showed the cop his press card. 'Possible to get inside?' he asked.

'Why would you want to get inside?' the cop asked.

Mitch smiled, tried to appear unhurried and nonchalant. 'Er... no particular reason. I knew her. Worked with her. We dated as students. Her mother called me and told me she'd committed suicide.'

'That's right.'

'Officer...?'

'Garrett.'

29

'Well, it was a shock, as you can imagine. A real shock. I wanted to come over and see if I could find out what happened.'

'I can't help you.'

'And why are you here?' Mitch asked. 'Seems unusual to have a police presence at a suicide, unless there's some possibility it wasn't.'

Garrett seemed to relax a little. 'I don't know,' he said. 'Can't tell you what happened, or why. She was a reporter. I know that much. From what I understand, there's research material inside, stuff that belongs to whatever paper she worked for.'

'The *Tribune*,' Mitch interjected, hoping to give the impression that he knew a great deal more about Jean Boyd than was the case.

'The *Tribune*, right. Anyway, they're gonna send some people over to clear out anything that's newspaper property. That's all I know.'

'Makes sense,' Mitch said, and it did. Senior reporters were often in possession of notes, briefs, sensitive and confidential documentation. Scoops were scoops because someone kept it under wraps.

He was frustrated not to have gained access. Mixed emotions. It had not yet hit him. He knew that much. He kept expecting to break down and lose it, but somehow he kept it together. Delayed reaction, perhaps.

'Do you know how she killed herself?'

'Pills,' Garrett replied. 'A lot of pills. Beyond that I really don't want to say anything.'

Mitch was silent, inside and out. Overdose. Pills. A lot of pills. Like Marilyn.

'Sorry for your loss,' Garrett said.

'That's appreciated.'

Mitch left the building and went back to his car. He drove

half a block before he pulled over. He sat there for a while asking himself if what he was thinking was anything but crazy.

It was crazy, but he couldn't let it go. He had to get into that apartment. He had to see for himself.

From an odd assortment of tools he routinely carried in the trunk of the car, he took a screwdriver and a short tire lever. He had done this before, had believed he would never do it again, but as a reporter, the basic means of accessing locked rooms and entering buildings from fire escapes seemed stock-in-trade. Ironically, it was Lester Byron who had shown him how to open a locked filing cabinet with a bobby pin so many years before.

The rear of the building was unguarded and also far enough down the block for Mitch to be invisible from the street. He looked up, shielded his hand against the light, and could see precisely where the gantry gave onto the back of Jean's apartment. He hauled down the lower ladder, looked back toward the street once more, and then started up.

Had he possessed any second thoughts, they were dispelled quickly. The fire escape led into the apartment kitchen, and by working the screwdriver between the striker plate and the edge of the door itself, he secured sufficient leverage to wedge the tip of the tire lever into the gap. It maintained that gap as he used the tip of the screwdriver against the latch itself. He was out of practice. The trick was to keep a continual pressure against the latch and then flip it. The screwdriver skidded off the smooth metal surface a good six or seven times before he felt that point of no return. He leaned against the handle with a good deal more force and the latch snapped back. In the silence, ricocheting in the narrow confines of the high adjacent walls, it sounded like a gunshot.

Mitch stayed right where he was, the door unlocked, his breathing calm. After a good minute, hearing nothing from either down below or within the apartment, he drew the door open. He hesitated for one moment more before entering. It felt as if he was invading not only her apartment, but her life, somehow part of their mutual past, perhaps even bringing to the fore every emotion he'd tried to bury. Regardless, he had to know what had happened, and that meant confronting precisely how and where she had died.

After a moment, Mitch Newman was right there in Jean's kitchen, and it was as if she was still home. Unwashed crockery in the sink. A mug of cold coffee by the edge of the stove. The air was stale, and some sort of ammoniac taint invaded his nostrils.

Glancing down toward the trash can in the corner, he saw a litter box. It had been used many times. There were also two empty dishes. What had happened to the cat? Had someone taken it?

He looked around the kitchen, opened cupboards, even the stove and the refrigerator. There was nothing but the usual appliances and utensils.

In the small bathroom he found soap with strands of hair in it. There were bottles of pills in the cabinet above the sink. Aspirin, other painkillers, routine medicinal preparations, but there was also a bottle of imipramine with a few tablets left inside. Mitch was familiar with it, had once taken it after Korea in an effort to lift the very deep moods into which he fell. It was a powerful antihistamine and tranquilizer, but the doctor he'd seen had recommended it as an antidepressant. For Mitch, once had been enough. It made him feel like he was drowning in his own grief. To have been prescribed such a medication suggested that Jean had seen someone about how she felt. Had the drug contributed to even deeper depression, perhaps? There was no sign of sleeping tablets, however, though had she self-administered an overdose then the bottle would most likely have been with her, and would have been removed by the police.

Mitch went down the hallway to the living room. There were books, records, a packet of cigarettes and a box of matches, another half-empty coffee cup, a plate, and a pair of shoes on the carpet ahead of the TV. There were piles of newspapers, notebooks filled with her telltale scrawl, other documents and clippings. She had never been orderly, but there was at least some sense of orientation to the proceedings. A lot of her notes were to do with routine Washington business, the usual concerns of White House briefings, the *what we say can mean so many things* rhetoric of political life in the capital.

He looked through what was there, but nothing seemed striking or relevant to a suicide rationale. What had he expected? An overlooked note that explained why she'd had no choice but to take her own life?

He stopped.

A sound in the hallway.

Had the cop heard him, and was even now coming to check if there was someone inside the apartment?

His heart raced. He backed up to the wall beside the door and listened. He heard one more sound, a heavy footfall perhaps, but there was only one.

After a few minutes, he looked around the edge of the door and down the hallway toward the front door. There was silence but for his own breathing and the still-hurried pace of his heart.

He moved again, walking on eggshells. He came to the door that could only have been Jean's bedroom. Was this where she'd been found?

He closed his fingers around the handle. He exerted pressure and felt the latch release. Why he paused he did not know, but it seemed that here he was crossing a secondary and more significant barrier. This was where she had slept, where she had perhaps entertained other lovers, a boyfriend, where she'd shared those moments that they'd once shared together.

Mitch closed his eyes and took a deep breath.

He opened the door.

The cat flashed out between his legs. He lost his balance and stumbled back, caught off-guard, shocked and surprised. Grabbing the edge of the doorframe, he managed to stop himself from falling flat on his back.

Steadying himself, he went back toward the kitchen. A small tortoiseshell cat was up on the work surface. Eyeing him warily for a moment, it then came forward, perhaps overcoming whatever reservation it possessed out of sheer hunger.

'You must be starving,' Mitch said. He looked through cupboards, beneath the sink, but found no evidence of cat food. In the fridge he found a packet of ham. He opened it, tore strips off and fed them to the animal. It snatched them one after the other, devouring the entire packet and still wanting more.

'Christ... what the hell am I going to do with you?' he said as the cat came toward him across the counter. He held out his hand; the cat nuzzled him, starving not only for food, it seemed, but also for attention. The cat must have found a way back into the apartment, or – more likely – it had hidden somewhere until everyone had left.

'You want Jean, don't you?' Mitch said.

The cat paused and looked up at him.

'I knew her too,' he said. 'We both lost her, buddy.'

He left the kitchen, headed back to the bedroom. The cat followed, ran ahead of him, went right on in and jumped up onto the bed.

Mitch stood in the doorway.

The bed was unmade. He could see the impression of where Jean's head had rested on the pillow.

He closed his eyes. A wave of nausea overcame him, and he put his hand against the wall to steady himself.

The cat lay down and started cleaning itself.

Mitch could not stop himself. He took a few steps forward and sat down on the edge of the mattress. He reached out his hand and touched the pillow. The cat stopped what it was doing and watched him, didn't move a muscle, as if appreciating that this was a moment that should not be interrupted.

'Oh Jean,' he whispered. 'What the hell happened to you?'

The tears came, that all-too-familiar breathlessness, and Mitch sat there on Jean's bed with Jean's cat, and every question he'd asked himself about the past came back like a broken promise.

The memory of their relationship was like the dying sun. Jean had always been there, her silhouette angled against the fading light, a shadow that would stretch to the end of his life.

Had he actually believed that he'd possessed any real chance of winning her back? He did not dare ask the question, for to ask it would be to face an answer he did not want to hear. What more could he have done? So much more, of course, but there would never be a way of knowing if such things would have made any difference.

Now he would never know. Could never know.

Now she was gone for good.

He couldn't bear it any longer. He picked up the cat and held it close, left the apartment the same way he'd come in. Maneuvering his way down the final ladder with the cat inside his coat was awkward, but finally he stood in the alleyway. He looked up one more time at the building, and then returned to the street.

As far as he knew, no one had seen him arrive, no one had seen him leave, and that was precisely how he wished it to be.

6

Back in his own apartment, Mitch took a bowl from the kitchen cupboard and filled it with milk. What the hell had he been thinking? He had never owned a cat, didn't know the first damned thing about looking after one, but there was no way he could have left it behind.

Perhaps it was misplaced guilt. He had deserted Jean. He could not desert what seemed to be the only living representation of her.

The cat seemed content. It lapped at the milk, then found a corner on the sofa and curled up.

For a minute or two, Mitch sat beside it. He stroked it and it started to purr.

'What the hell, eh? Seems you got adopted, my friend.'

The cat looked at him, and then rolled onto its back and exposed its belly. It seemed content to have found a new home.

'Wish it was that simple for all of us,' Mitch said. 'Up and gone in a heartbeat. New place to live, new friends, new life, eh? That'd be something, wouldn't it?'

He had to call Jean's mother, but what could he say?

I'm sorry, Alice. Your daughter is dead. She overdosed. I don't know what happened. And even though I have to find out, it's based on selfish reasons. I don't want to discover that I might have contributed to her taking her own life. That scares me more than you can imagine.

I betrayed her. I abandoned her. I wanted her so much to forgive me, but now that will never happen. I am a coward, and that's the only truth you need to know.

He did not say that. What he actually said was, 'Alice. It's Mitch.'

'Mitchell. Thank you for calling.'

'I went over to her apartment. I couldn't get inside because they've stationed a police officer there.'

'Police? Why are the police there?'

'Because of her work. She was a senior reporter at the *Tribune*. She'll have had confidential material, research notes. Someone from the paper will need to gain access and ensure there's nothing that shouldn't be in the public domain. Then you'll be able to come up here and sort things out.'

Alice was crying. Mitch could hear her fighting it.

'I couldn't, Mitchell. I couldn't bear it. I don't want to see where she lived.'

'But you'll need to take care of her things, Alice. I know this is awful. I can't even begin to imagine how you must feel, and it's not something you have to think about now, but it will need to be done. You can't just leave her place empty.'

'Can you not help me, Mitchell?'

Mitch closed his eyes. He'd known it was coming.

'Did she own the place, Alice? Did she own it, or did she rent it?'

'She rented.'

'Did she not have a husband, a boyfriend?'

Alice was silent for a moment too long.

'Alice?'

'No husband. No boyfriend I was ever aware of. She used to say she was like a nun, but married to her work.'

Mitch didn't reply.

'At first, for a little while, maybe. She used to go out with boys at university. She dated another reporter when she worked in Richmond.'

Don't tell me, Mitch thought. *Just don't tell me.*

'She was never the same, Mitch. Not after—'

'Alice, no ...'

'You broke her heart, Mitchell. You know that. You can't hide from that.'

'Please, Alice, that was a long time ago. You can't tell me that what happened all those years ago had anything to do with what she did.'

'I'm not saying that. All I'm saying is that she loved you more than you could perhaps ever understand, and when you went away, she was devastated. It broke her heart. It broke *her*. It was a long time before she would even talk about it. I know you wrote to her, and I have no idea what you said, but every time she came back home she would—'

'Don't tell me anything else, Alice. Really, I don't want to hear anything else.'

Alice was silent.

'I'm sorry,' Mitch said. 'I just can't get involved in this.'

'What do you mean, you can't get involved? This is life, Mitchell. Jean's life, your life. She's dead, and I'm being told that she killed herself... and if anyone knew Jean, then they'd also know that she could never do such a thing.'

'Who ever actually understands anyone, Alice? I hadn't seen her for nearly fifteen years...'

'Are you really not going to come here, Mitchell? Are you really going to let me handle this on my own? Are you going to abandon me just like you abandoned my daughter?'

'Alice, I don't think that's fair—'

'Life isn't fair, Mitchell. Nor is death. My daughter, the girl you loved, the girl who never stopped loving you, is dead. Someone has to help clear up the mess that's left behind.'

Mitch Newman felt his heart swell. He closed his eyes and breathed deeply.

He could hear Jean's voice in his head.

I understand that we're going to war in Korea, Mitch. What I don't understand is why you have to go too.

He could see her face.

I really thought we had a future together.

He'd thought of her without respite. He'd tried not to, of course, but somehow she would always find a way into the spaces between his thoughts.

Read my lips. I hate you. H-A-T-E.

'Mitchell?'

Mitch snapped to. 'Alice. Yes, sorry.'

'So what are you going to do? Are you going to leave me to deal with this by myself?'

'No, I'm not.'

She started crying then, sobbing, and Mitch felt the emotion rising in his chest.

He had not been home for nearly four years, the last time for his mother's funeral in September of '61. Alice had been there, but Jean didn't show. Mitch and Alice had shared a handful of words. None of them had been about Jean.

'I'll be there tomorrow,' he said.

He put down the phone, walked through to the kitchen and fetched down a bottle of bourbon.

He sat at the kitchen table, and it wasn't long before the cat jumped up. It sat there looking at him, and he could not escape the feeling that it understood precisely what he was feeling.

'You need some proper food and a litter box, don't you?' he said.

The cat blinked, and then looked away, its attention caught by something Mitch could not see.

'I'll get them,' Mitch said, 'and I'll ask Tom to come feed you while I'm away.'

7

July 6, 1964

For Mitch Newman, it was hard to fathom that past and present
– so different, so estranged – were separated by little more than
an hour of freeway. I-95 was an artery between a broken heart
and a stubborn attitude.

He had escaped, this much he tried to convince himself, more
by state of mind than geography. West Haven was his childhood,
his anchor, his home. He had run away, just as Alice had said.
He had abandoned his mother, the girl he'd loved, everything
that had attached him to reality, and in exchange for what?

Ten miles from the outskirts of West Haven, Mitch pulled over.
He got out of the car and walked into a field. He kept on walking until the freeway sounded like a river, then like someone
breathing, and then until he could no longer hear it at all.

He sat down on the ground and pulled his knees to his chest.

*Keep running away and you'll inevitably find yourself on the road
back home.*

He closed his eyes and tried to remember what Jean had
looked like the last time he'd seen her. There was nothing. He
felt the loss, the sorrow, but the tears he'd expected did not
come. He knew they would, as well as he knew his own name,
but they would find him in their own time.

He lay back, looked at the sky, watched the distant trail of an airplane overhead, remembering vividly the moment he'd departed Arlington for the war. All that had happened had left him hollowed out and vacant.

Tomorrow is a new day. But it will be the same as all the rest.

He remembered his own bluff and bravado before he left:

People tell me this is wild and dangerous, as if I'm testing the will of God. I say, 'Is there any other way to live?'

What a naïve and irresponsible fool he'd been, convinced of his own rightness in the face of so much evidence that he was wrong. And he was still doing it even now, telling himself that the burden of regret had he not gone would be far worse. People never got to the end of their lives and shed tears for those things they'd done, only those they hadn't.

If he'd stayed, would Jean be still alive?

If he'd stayed, just as she'd begged him, would they have married, had a family, pursued their careers together, shared experiences that elevated and inspired and uplifted?

Perhaps. Perhaps not.

The airplane vanished. The sound of the freeway crept back into his consciousness. West Haven would always be at the end of the road, and there was no way he could avoid it.

For once, in as long a time as he could remember, he needed to keep his word.

'Oh Mitchell,' Alice said, and burst into tears.

She came out onto the porch to greet him. She put her arms around him, held him tight, and Mitch was aware of how old and fragile she appeared.

He stood there without a word. There were no appropriate words.

Once inside, they sat in the kitchen. For a little while there was silence, each of them perhaps remembering the last time they'd sat here.

'I didn't approve of you,' Alice said. 'Not at first. She was sixteen. She was just a child.'

Mitch smiled. 'Jean was never a child.'

'She'd lost her father, just like you. Too young to lose a parent. Children who are raised without a parent will always have things about themselves that they don't understand.'

'Maybe that's why we were so close. We had a lot in common.'

'I know, Mitchell. You became her life. I could see that.' Alice leaned forward. 'No, that's not right. Her life was never anything but her own. You became part of her life in such a way as to complement everything that she already was. I knew she was safe with you. When she was with you, I never worried.'

'Alice, please—'

'No, Mitchell, you need to listen and you need to talk. You need to know that after you there was no one in her life who meant even a fraction of what you meant to her.'

Mitch sighed. He leaned back in the chair. He would listen, but he would not speak.

'Those letters you sent to her after you came back.' Alice looked at him. 'I know you were trying to explain and apologize. I know you wanted to make things better.'

'I wanted her to talk to me. I was asking her for something, anything, but she never replied. After a while, it became too hard to think about it and I stopped writing.'

'She felt guilty.'

'Guilty? About what? What reason would she have to feel guilty?'

'That she didn't accept it. That she didn't understand why you had to go. When you came back, she told me how crazy it had all been. You were gone four months. You came back in November. She told me that four months was nothing, that she could so easily have waited, but she was even more stubborn than you, I think.'

'She had her moments,' Mitch said.

'She would never back down, never give in.' Alice looked up at him. 'And that's why this makes no sense. Even though she was under so much stress with her work, she would never kill herself. That was not Jean. Not ever.'

'What stress? What was going on?'

Alice shook her head. 'Oh, I don't know, Mitch. She was driven, always so driven. Her ambition was both a blessing and a curse.'

'Do you know what she was working on?'

'I asked her, but she never gave me any real understanding of what she was doing.'

'We can't always know everything about people, Alice.'

'We *always* know our own children, Mitchell. Certainly enough to understand whether they're capable of doing something like this.'

Mitch did not respond.

Half an hour later, Mitch stood in the doorway of Jean's room. She had stayed here regularly, coming back to West Haven for birthdays, Thanksgiving, Christmas, during vacations. It was the room of a woman in her thirties, but beneath it Mitch could see everything he remembered of her as a teenager. The paper was the same, the carpet, even the bed. The closet door was open. There were items he remembered her wearing when they'd been dating.

He saw a scarf. It was right there on a hanger. Blue wool, a bright, striking color. She wore it around her neck, but when the wind was bitter she would pull it up around the lower half of her face. He would move it to kiss her.

For a short while we were each the person we wished the other to believe we really were, and nothing more.

44

Mitch tried to feel nothing, but he knew he could not fight it.

He looked around the room. He could not cross the threshold. Images came – Jean laughing, Jean angry, Jean putting a 45 on the record deck and telling him he just *had* to listen to this.

The past rolled inexorably toward him with such speed and force that there was no chance to step out of its way.

He stood there for some small eternity, his body and mind torn apart with grief. He wanted to cry for her, but he could not.

Alice came and stood beside him for just a moment. She held onto his arm. He felt the pressure of her hand, and it seemed to be the only tenuous link to reality.

She looked at him through tear-filled eyes, and said nothing.

After a few minutes, he went back to the kitchen.

'I'll be back soon,' he said. 'I'm sorry... I just need to get out of here for a while.'

'Take whatever time you need, Mitchell.'

He walked to his car. He drove to the end of the block and turned left. Everything had changed, and yet everything was the same.

The pharmacy, the 7-Eleven, the realtor's office, the bank, the disused railway bridge where the kids used to play.

Under the bridge, over the track, run like fury, never look back.

It was all here, a stone's throw away from the here-and-now, but still it seemed like a life he'd never lived.

It was late morning, and the streets were busy with people's lives. Conversations, errands, grass being cut, the mailman delivering letters; garbage pails and flower beds and manicured walkways. All of this was going on as if nothing had happened.

But it had. Something important had happened.

A vast hole had been torn through the world, and Mitch was falling right through. He was in shock – he knew that much. He was dazed and speechless, and even though his heart had been torn out, that heart was still remembering everything it had once felt for Jean.

At the end of the freeway link, he pulled over outside the soda shop. He couldn't help himself, drawn as if by some irresistible force, much as he had been at Jean's apartment.

The awning was different, but inside it seemed as if nothing had changed.

The bell above the door rang as he entered, and the counterman looked up.

'Hey.'

'Hey there.'

'What can I get you?'

'You still do butterscotch malt?'

'We sure do.'

Mitch took a seat at the counter. He looked out toward the street. The jukebox caught his eye. It was the same. A memory returned.

Go put some music on.

It's a waste of money.

Well, Mitchell Newman, that is an attitude that is definitely gonna need to change.

How so? We're supposed to be saving for an apartment.

A couple of nickels isn't going to make a difference one way or the other, and whether you believe it or not, the simple fact that we can sit here and drink soda and listen to Ted Weems or The Harmonicats will be an important memory one day.

You are such a dreamer.

You don't believe me?

It had taken him more than a decade and a half to know she was right. Here he was, same seat, same butterscotch malt, and a memory of 'Heartaches' by Ted Weems seemed to be the most important thing he'd ever recalled.

The malt arrived. Mitch took one sip. He knew he wouldn't

drink any more. He left a bill tucked beneath the glass when the counterman went out back for a moment. He got in his car and drove to the end of the street. He sat in silence, smoked his cigarettes, tried once again to convince himself that Korea had not been a choice. For whatever reason – a reason he still did not fully understand or appreciate – he'd *had* to go. It had pulled and pulled at him. There was a magnet out there, and it would not let go. Yes, he would be Robert Capa. Jean would be his Gerda Taro. They would work together. They would take pictures and write stories. They would win accolades and awards. They would be recognized and acknowledged and respected by their contemporaries.

From the first moment his boots met the dirt of the Korean peninsula, it had been a trial by ordeal.

This was real. People were dying all around him. The view-finder through which he looked did not disconnect him from anything.

It took a week, perhaps two. He managed to hide how he felt, his thoughts, his horror at what he was seeing. His pictures were wired back home and published. He stayed four months, hanging in there and keeping it together until the day it all fell apart. A single event – seemingly no worse than any other – had finally tipped him over the edge. And then he shipped out. Nothing could ever have been the same again. Perhaps, had Jean forgiven him and taken him back, he might have found sufficient memories and reminders of his previous life that he could have recovered himself. But she did not forgive him, and she did not take him back, and the life that he'd once possessed was a distant illusion.

Mitch had continued to work. He'd continued to take pictures. He drank too much and got fired. He went freelance. He made the barest of livings, took a three-room apartment on the very outskirts of DC and just existed. That was how it felt. He just existed.

The only thing that had brought him back to West Haven was the death of his mother. Fifty-one years old. Cancer.

And now this? There were those who went home for Thanksgiving, for Christmas, for birthdays and celebrations. There were those who were pulled back by tragedy and loss.

What was he going to do? What choice would he make? Stay and deal with it, or run away again?

Flip a coin, Mitch thought. He laughed at his own stupidity, his own irresponsibility. Did he not actually care about anything anymore? About anyone? Jean Boyd had been his first real love, the girl he should have married, the girl with whom he should have raised a family and grown old.

Did he not owe her memory enough to see that her affairs were taken care of?

Did he not still love her enough to be there for her mother?

No one should have to deal with such things alone.

He drove back the way he'd come. No sooner had he searched the stoop than Alice opened the door.

'I need to go into her room,' he said.

'Yes, of course.'

Alice followed him down the hallway. He paused for just a moment ahead of the threshold.

She reached out and placed her hand on his arm. 'I'll leave you alone,' she said.

8

Ken O'Donnell, special assistant and appointments secretary to the most powerful man in the Western world, stood silently at the window of his bedroom and looked into the street. He could hear Helen downstairs. Twice already she'd asked if he was going into work. It was Monday. Kennedy had made his civil rights announcement. The whole world wanted details. Pierre had called four times. Each time Ken had not taken the call.

Finally she came upstairs again. The kids were gone. The place was silent.

'What is it, sweetheart?' she said. 'What's eating you up?'

Ken turned and smiled at her. Seventeen years of marriage. She could see right through him, read him like a map.

'There's gonna be a storm,' he said. 'I feel it coming.'

'About the colored thing?'

He shook his head. 'The Civil Rights Bill is a smokescreen. It's new paint on a rusty fence. If anyone thinks that'll change the world, then...' He shook his head resignedly.

'So what is it?'

Ken walked the few steps to the bed and sat down. 'You put a man like that in the White House... hell, you put anyone in the White House, you gotta make some deals, Helen.'

'I know, honey, I know. I've been a politician's wife for long enough to understand at least a little of what you do. What is it you always say? Whatever has to be done for the greater good, right?'

'Right,' Ken said, but there was hesitation in his voice.

'You think you did the wrong thing?'

'No,' he said. 'Not the wrong thing putting him there...' He looked up. 'But the man I helped put in the Oval Office is not the man who now occupies it.'

'What do you mean?'

'It doesn't matter. Decisions were made, rightly or wrongly, and it's too late to go back.'

'Is it the investigation thing? About the election?'

'Yes, and other stuff too.'

'Will they have a hearing?'

'The hearings have started. They're already asking questions. Bobby is firefighting, but I don't know if he'll succeed. You remember Earl Warren?'

'Chief Justice Warren?'

'That's him. He's the one lighting the fires, and if ever there was a man who won't back down or quit, it's Warren.'

'It'll be fine,' Helen said. 'We've seen it before. We'll see it again. No one will remember in a month's time. Today's newspapers clean tomorrow's windows.'

Ken O'Donnell sighed. He felt a war coming, and it was a war he did not have the energy or motivation to fight. The simple truth was that they needed another four years, not just to fulfill the promises they'd made, but to cover their tracks. And there were a great many tracks.

There was no guarantee Kennedy would make it. November might very well bring the collapse of the House of Camelot. It was not just a pessimistic slant; it was a very real possibility. Integrity had been tested, and found wanting. If Kennedy didn't kill it stone dead at the Democratic National Convention, then they were all done for, and in more ways than just being unemployed. Whatever he got up and said in August had to not only reinvigorate the voters' belief in their president; it had to reinvigorate his own people. He had done it before. He had charmed the world. But now he needed so much more than charm. And then they would have just three months to convince America that the present administration deserved another four years.

Kennedy was Ken's friend, his boss, the man in whom he had invested his faith, his trust, his political future. He was obliged to believe in him, but his belief was weakening. He had heard too much, seen too much, and now there was a chance he would be subpoenaed for what he knew. And he knew he would not withstand an inquisition.

Sometimes the price you paid for your ideals was the compromise of those very ideals. This was not how it was supposed to have been. Not at all.

He had nailed his flag to the Kennedy mast. If the ship went down because the captain was drunk at the helm, then they would all drown with him.

'Okay,' Ken said. He got up and put on his jacket. 'I may be back late.'

'That's fine, honey.'

'You might get tired of hearing me say that.'

Helen walked forward and placed her hand on her husband's face. Her touch was warm and reassuring, as always.

'You do whatever you have to do,' she said. 'And no matter what happens, I'll be here when you get home.'

He looked right back at her, but she knew his mind was very much elsewhere.

9

Jean was far more organized here than she had been in her own apartment. It seemed that her childhood home had become the archive for her career. Papers were everywhere. Boxes, files, folders, bundles of handwritten notes tied with string. There were journals, old notebooks, photographs of people, places and public events. Everything was dated and correlated, and it seemed that she'd kept her research and records for every story she'd ever written.

By all accounts, she had become the journalist she'd always intended to be.

Mitch went through as much as he could absorb. Sanitation crew strikes, graft and bribery in the construction industry, backhanders to civic officials, payoffs to lobbyists, state conventions, political rallies, and two boxes of material relating specifically to the 1960 presidential election. From what he could gather, it appeared that Jean had had no love for either Nixon or Kennedy. A telling comment read, *The only good thing about whichever candidate wins this election is that the other one won't.*

Perhaps, for all her years in Washington, she had become as bitter and cynical about politics as he himself had.

What Mitch experienced as he went through the collected memories of her professional life was a combination of respect, admiration and envy. She had kept it together. She had graduated, interned and secured a foothold in an ever-so-competitive profession, and she had worked her way up. Add into the equation that it was still very much a male-dominated arena, and Jean Boyd had done some remarkable work.

Then there were her personal effects. She had a box of mementoes, and it was a few minutes before Mitch realized that it contained keepsakes of their time together. Movie theater ticket stubs, a necklace he'd bought for her, a barrette, an empty perfume bottle, a handful of stones they'd collected on a long-forgotten walk.

Look at this one, Mitch. Like a cat's eye.

And then he found the letters.

All of them.

Every single one of the twelve letters he had written, all of them opened, preserved in their original envelopes, held together with a rubber band in date sequence.

They *had* been received. She *had* read them.

He told himself not to look at them. He told himself it would do nothing but fuel further upset and regret, but he could not withhold himself.

November 27, 1950. December 5, December 11, December 19 ...

The letters went on, one after the other, until the last week of February 1951.

He was young, naïve, sorry, heartbroken. His spirit was broken too, his war experiences having devastated whatever sense of rightness and purpose and motivation he might have possessed.

He wrote how much he loved her. He sent her lines of poetry.

No other time or place, no other person will ever feel like this.

The arrival and the departure. The holding and the letting go.

Mitch Newman read just a few of his own words, and everything he could remember feeling at the time, every wretched moment of self-pity and loathing, came back at him a hundred-fold.

Whatever mechanism and machinery he'd managed to build in defense against the truth fell apart like dust and shadows.

The sound of voices and the silence.

The things we knew, and those of which we were ignorant.

He put the letters back where he'd found them. He could not read any more. He would come back to them, if not in reality, then in memory.

He returned to the notes Jean had made back in the run-up to the election. Names were there, including that of Dean Rusk, someone with which Mitch was all too familiar. Rusk had been Assistant Secretary of State for Far Eastern Affairs. It was he who'd advised the split of Korea into north and south at the 38th Parallel as early as 1945. He had been made secretary of state under Kennedy in December 1960, sworn in at the start of January '61. Alongside Rusk, Jean had written the names of Stewart Udall, Secretary of the Interior, C. Douglas Dillon in the Treasury, Pierre Salinger, Kennedy's press secretary, and the White House chief of staff, Kenneth O'Donnell.

Irish mafia, she had added. Alongside this was a note that must have referred to the Alabama vote count. *How did they buy AL? Gov. Patterson. Support of KKK in gov. campaign. 1959 Patterson/CIA agree AL Air National Guard can train pilots for Bay of Pigs invasion. Advised JFK to postpone Cuba until after election.*

Kennedy had won by little more than a hundred thousand votes, a margin of less than a fifth of a percent. There had been a great deal of controversy about pledged and unpledged votes in Alabama. Had the unpledged votes been split equally between Kennedy and Nixon – as many believed should have been done – then Nixon would have taken the state. He would also have taken the election and the White House, and with a greater margin than a fifth of a percent.

Had Jean, like so many others, suspected that the infamous

Joseph Kennedy – bootlegger, anti-Semite, serial adulterer – had bought a place in history for his sons? Was this what she'd been looking into?

Even now this issue was newsworthy. Robert Kennedy was attorney general, not only the chief law enforcement officer, but also the chief lawyer for the United States government, seventh in the presidential line of succession. The president's own brother, subject to summary dismissal by the president, impeachable by Congress, was being asked questions about vote-rigging and electoral corruption. The questions were coming from the Republican camp, of course. Nixon's supporters had not taken his defeat lying down. They leveled accusations of vote fraud in Lyndon Johnson's senatorial seat of Texas. Fannin County had registered over six thousand votes from fewer than five thousand registered voters. Dead people had voted for Kennedy in Chicago. Attempts had been made to overturn results in Texas, Illinois and nine other states. Nixon's campaign staff had lobbied to challenge the validity of the final count, but Nixon did not pursue it.

Was this where Jean was going? Playing hardball with the White House?

She had always been impulsive, hot-headed sometimes, but she was anything but stupid. Her impetuosity and passion were balanced with a pragmatic eye. She knew what she could say and when she could say it. At least that was the Jean he'd known.

Mitch paused. He was thinking of her in the past tense.

The beginning and the end. The impulse and the restraint.

He looked around the room, a room he'd known so well. He needed something, anything at all, to point him in the direction of why she'd taken her own life.

Maybe she'd become increasingly obsessed about something. Had something happened at the *Tribune* that had put her under pressure? He would have to talk to Lester Byron. And there would be others who'd known her, worked alongside her, perhaps had some understanding of what might have driven her to such an extreme and desperate solution.

It had happened in Korea. Men had committed suicide, or attempted to self-inflict wounds of sufficient severity to warrant an immediate return to the US. But that was war. That was in the presence of a real and terrifying threat of immediate death. But Jean? A newspaper reporter?

Mitch was without anchor in this raging ocean of emotional reactions, and he desperately needed to understand, if for no other reason than his own peace of mind.

There was a sound in the hallway beyond the door. Alice appeared. She looked awful.

'I'll not be long,' Mitch said.

She hesitated for just a moment longer, and then disappeared back toward the kitchen.

It was amongst the last few notes about Kennedy – the pre-election rallies, newspaper clippings of speeches given, events attended – that Mitch found an envelope, right at the bottom of a box. In it was a ticket stub for a flight to Dallas in November of the previous year. She'd gone out on the twentieth, but there was nothing to say when she'd returned. There were also a few sheets of notebook paper upon which were dates, telephone numbers, the initials *JR*, the word *Carousel* and the names Joseph Civello and Carlos Marcello. The names meant nothing to Mitch. The initials HW kept reappearing. *HW at C 10/63. Where did HW go after 11/22? Did JR know about HW?* He looked over the pages one final time, and then put them back in the envelope and returned it to the box. It was as he was doing this that he saw the corner of a business card lodged beneath the flaps in the base of the box. He took it out. *Dallas Metro PD. Detective Nelson Shaw.* On the back, Jean had written *Rubenstein* and *Holly W.* Were HW and Holly W. the same person?

Mitch made a note of the detective's name and telephone number. He put the card in the envelope with the other Dallas paperwork, replaced everything where he'd found it and left the bedroom.

He closed the door, stood quietly in the shadowed hallway.

The certainties and uncertainties.

He took several deep and silent breaths,

That you were there and that you had to leave.

He closed his eyes and clenched his fists, fighting the un-stoppable wave of emotion that rose in his chest and tightened his throat.

The promise and the betrayal.

The life and the death.

It was the end of an era for him as well as Alice, the end of any hopes or dreams he might have had concerning Jean's forgiveness, the possibility that one day she would call him up and say, 'A lot of years have passed, Mitch. Let's meet. Let's talk. Let's see what we can salvage from the wreckage we made...'

That call had never come, and now it never would.

Jean Boyd was dead, and there was nothing he could do to change it.

IO

'I'll tell you something right here and now, my friend. If Nixon'd had the guts to fight that result, he'd be in the White House now instead of that drug-taking, weak-minded, adulterous son-of-a-bitch. Nixon won that election, and Kennedy money stole it from right under our noses. Alabama, Illinois, Texas. It was a fiasco. It was a goddam joke. I ran Nixon's campaign straight and true, and we won it fair and square.'

Donald Finch stopped shouting for just a moment. He paced back and forth across the hotel lobby. It was late. There was no one there but himself and his old campaign buddy, Murray Chotiner. Chotiner himself had put Nixon in the Californian Senate seat back in December of 1950. Despite the late hour and the absence of clientele, the desk clerk seemed agitated. People shouting at one another in the lobby of the Los Angeles Biltmore was just not acceptable.

Finch – an ex-Marine who had served in both Europe and Korea – was a tough, no-nonsense political tour de force. Chotiner was a strategic genius. Between them they should have put Nixon in the Oval Office, but they had failed. It had left a sour taste and a deep and abiding resentment for the 'Democratic freak show' that was now running the country.

Finch took Chotiner by the arm. He steered him out of sight of the reception desk and spoke in hushed tones.

'My new guy, George Murphy. Okay, he's an actor, a goddamn

actor. He's done more than forty films. Could you ever have imagined an actor in the Senate? Well, it's going to happen. He's a good man, a good Republican, and there's no way in the world I am having Nixon's old senatorial seat taken by a goddam Democrat—'

'You need to calm down, Don,' Chotiner said.

'Calm down? When the hell did any situation improve by telling someone to calm down, Murray? You know what's happening. Senator Engle had surgery in August last year. He had surgery again in April, just three months ago. He can't speak, he's as sick as a dog, and he's going to die. The Democratic senator for California is going to die. And who's in the running? Pierre Salinger. You understand what I'm saying? Jack Kennedy's press secretary, as Democratic as they come, a man who was instrumental in stealing the White House from Nixon four years ago, could very well succeed in taking Nixon's old seat in California. It makes my blood boil. Talk about adding insult to injury. And it's not opportunity, Murray. It's goddam calculated. Jack and Bobby Kennedy are running their show just the way they want it. You think Jack Kennedy wouldn't let his press secretary go to the Senate? Of course he would, just so he could stick one more knife into Nixon. They're that malicious, Murray, they really are. Their father was a gangster and a thug, and he's raised them in his own image.'

Finch leaned closer to Murray. 'You really think I want to manage a senatorial campaign for a goddam Hollywood song-and-dance man? Honestly? Well, I *am* doing it, for no other reason than to stop that pair of bastards from driving this country into the worst political and financial minefield since... well, since history began.'

'Okay, Don, okay. So what do you want me to do?'

'We're going to ruin them, Murray. We're going to ruin them before Kennedy has a chance to get up at the Democratic

National Convention and persuade everyone, once again, that he's not a back-stabbing, lying, cheating son-of-a-bitch. He did that before, and I believe he can do it again. I want him thrown to the lions before August. You understand me? I want to ruin him before he has a chance to sweet-talk his way back into the hearts and minds of the American people, the same way he sweet-talks his way into the beds of God only knows how many girls. I want to drag the entire Kennedy circus through one senatorial hearing after another, and come what may, I am going to get that bastard impeached, so help me God.'

'Then you need something substantial, Don, and I don't mean rumor or hearsay or whether or not he might have known about misrepresentation in the vote count. You need to get him on something that could see him impeached, even jailed.'

Don paused. He looked intently at Murray. The question was unspoken, but it was there.

'You need someone to talk. You need someone to give us a real-life, honest-to-God felony that we can hang him for. Anything less than that, we're pissing in the wind.'

'Then we better get looking,' Don said, 'and fast. Whatever it takes, Murray, we need to derail this fucking circus train before it gets to the DNC.'

II

July 7, 1964

'However good Jean might have been at making friends, she was better at making enemies.'

Mitch Newman had not spoken to Lester Byron since Korea. Back then, simply out of courtesy, he had returned to see the man who had given him the credentials to go, the man who'd received so many of the photographs he'd taken. Soon after, Lester had started working for the *Washington Tribune*. Now he was city editor. Ironically, it was the very same paper that Jean had wound up working for, and whatever investigative work she had undertaken, Byron was the man who would perhaps know more about it than anyone else.

Seeing him again was difficult. They'd shared a history of war, and now they would share a history of loss.

'Enemies, how?' Mitch asked.

'You know the beat, Mitch. You're familiar enough with DC to know that this is no ordinary town when it comes to the news. Even though it grieved me to do it, we had to let her go.'

Mitch looked up, surprised. 'Let her go?'

'From the paper. Her... well, let's call it her resignation.'

'I'm sorry. I don't understand what you mean. She resigned from the paper?'

61

Byron paused for a moment. He looked squarely at Mitch. 'You didn't keep in touch with her.'

'You say that like you already know.'

'We were pretty close, Mitch. She told me that you wrote to her. She also told me that she never replied. That doesn't mean she told me everything that happened between you.'

'Did she say why she didn't reply to me?'

'You don't need me to answer that for you.'

Mitch knew he was right.

'You've been out to see her mother?' Byron asked.

'Yesterday.'

'And she didn't say anything about Jean no longer working here?'

'Not a word.'

'Well, perhaps she didn't want to say anything, you know, considering the circumstances.'

'Circumstances?'

Byron shook his head resignedly. 'I guess it does no harm now she's dead. We called it a resignation, but we really had no choice. Had it been anyone else, she would have been publicly fired, but I respected her far too much to disable her career prospects to that degree.'

'What happened? What did she do? And when did it happen?'

'Back at the end of May,' Byron said. 'Last day she was here was the twenty-ninth. I had her desk cleared, and she just went out of here with no ceremony at the end of the day.'

'So what happened?'

'She broke the cardinal rule, Mitch. Get a source, confirm it twice.'

'Concerning?'

'Ken O'Donnell, Kennedy's special assistant.'

'She wrote about him.'

'Oh yes. Jean very definitely wrote about him.'

'And said what?'

'That he was an alcoholic, that he had been complicit in vote-rigging in 1960, a whole bunch of things.'

'But those rumors have been around for a good while,' Mitch said.

'There's a very significant difference between unsubstantiated rumor and actually putting it in print, even when the consensus is that it is indeed a fact. You know that, Mitch.'

'And the *Tribune* ran it?'

'Hell, no, of course we didn't run it. You think I'm suicidal...' Byron stopped mid sentence. 'Christ, that was thoughtless. I'm sorry, Mitch. I wasn't—'

Mitch raised his hand. 'It's okay, Lester. It's just an expression.'

'Anyway, no, we didn't run it.'

'Then how did it result in Jean's dismissal?'

'Because she was a hurricane. You did know her, right?'

Mitch smiled. 'Yes, Lester, I knew her.'

'Well, that's just as good a description as you could want. She was fierce. Determined, resolute, industrious, all good things, but a complete nightmare sometimes. I refused to run it. She and I had a shouting match, and not our first. She threatened to leave. I called her bluff. She backed down. That might have been the end of it. I was insistent that she find corroborative evidence of what she was saying. I told her to drop the alcoholic thing. That was a losing game. On the vote-rigging, I told her to get some more facts, an inside source, anything that would give more substance to her story.'

'What substance did she have?'

'She was reporting conversations that had apparently taken place with Mayor Daley in Chicago. A rumor that Daley had held back Cook County votes until he knew exactly how many were needed to tip the balance in Kennedy's favor. It was controversial and contentious stuff, believe me, and there was little in the way of hard, cold evidence. And there was another issue that obsessed her. She honestly believed that Joe Kennedy had been complicit in John Patterson's election as governor of Alabama back in '58. Why the hell Kennedy Senior would be interested in gubernatorial campaigns only makes sense when you look at the 1960 presidential election. In truth, she was trying to tie things together without a great deal of string. She got obsessive. You know how driven she could sometimes be.'

'And her sources?'

Byron smiled wryly. 'A good investigative journalist—'

'Never reveals their sources,' Mitch interjected. 'So how did this unprinted story create a problem for you?'

'Well, somehow it wound up in the hands of someone at the *Post*. They called me. I suspected that Jean got it to them covertly in the hope they'd run with it, but the more I think about it, the less likely that seems. Jean was loyal. I don't believe she'd have gone behind my back.'

'So someone here leaked it?'

'You know, Mitch, I really don't know. I've had to reconcile myself to the fact that ending Jean's career at the *Tribune* might have been a contributory factor in her decision to take her own life. She was unhappy. She was angry. I could go so far as to say she was afraid. She was a career journalist, and a damned fine one at that, and coming back from this would have been tough for even someone like her.'

'So the *Post* ran the story?'

'No, they did not. However, word of it leaked to the White House press bureau, and I got a call. I was told in no uncertain terms that Jean Boyd's employment needed to be reviewed. That was the word they used. *Reviewed.* What they meant was unequivocal.'

'And the press bureau is the final arbiter on who gets into briefings, who gets the interviews, who's given a heads-up on new policy issuance, right?'

'Correct. A bar on White House press briefings would be the death knell for a DC paper, as you know.'

'So Jean was fired.'

'Effectively, yes. She argued. She disagreed. She told me to grow a backbone, the usual stuff, but she understood what had happened and why there was no leeway. She knew she was going, and she just wanted to voice her protest.'

'Which she never had a problem doing.'

'Right. She was never one to keep her opinion to herself.'

'And do you think this could have been a factor in what happened?'

Byron shrugged. 'Who the hell knows, Mitch? We think we know people, and so often we're wrong. I always took her for bulletproof, but she was fractured by this. It hit her hard. She knew I had no choice, but she took it personally anyway. Hell, she took everything personally. She was just one of those people. Do I think it could have precipitated the kind of depression that would result in suicide? I don't know. Do I think Jean was capable of getting depressed? Yes, I do. The thing I don't know is whether there was anything else going on that was the straw that broke the camel's back.'

Byron rose from his chair and walked to the window. 'So tell me, Mitch. If all she was was a long-lost girlfriend from high school and you hadn't seen her for more than ten years, why are you up here digging into this?'

Mitch did not challenge Byron's comment. Jean was a great deal more than a high school girlfriend, long-lost or otherwise. 'For her mother,' was the answer he gave. 'I don't think Jean told her that she'd been fired. I think she hid that fact. Her mother is devastated. Jean was an only child. There's no father. I think she turned to me out of desperation. I just want to do whatever I can to help her deal with this.'

'That's very noble of you, but this is a harsh business. You want my opinion, Jean Boyd was headstrong and single-minded. Perhaps too headstrong. She got her sights on something, she would not let go. That whole thing in Dallas last November—'

'Dallas?'

'She was hobby-horsing it, the vote-rigging thing. She was determined to get someone inside the Kennedy camp to let something slip. She went down there even when I told her not to. Paid for her own ticket. Like I said, she could be a real nightmare.'

Mitch thought of the Dallas Metro PD card he'd found amongst Jean's papers.

'I don't know what kind of person you have to be to consider suicide as an option,' Byron said, 'but maybe she just was that kind of person. Maybe she was too much personality for one mind to contain and she finally imploded. I don't know. I'm no psychologist. I do know that the vast majority of suicides we report on are routinely unexpected. The one thing those left behind always seem to say is, "I never would have thought them capable of that." That's what they say.'

An hour later, Mitch was once again standing in the street across from Jean's apartment. He did not go into the building. He didn't want to appear interested for the second time in forty-eight hours in what had happened there.

He looked at the windows, black and lightless, and wondered why Jean hadn't told her mother that she'd lost her job, or if she had, why Alice hadn't mentioned it. He wondered what had happened in the five weeks between her last day at the *Tribune* and the moment of her death.

Most of all, he wondered if Lester Byron was right; if Jean

really was the kind of person – headstrong and single-minded – who possessed the capability to make such a final and irreversible decision.

He felt sympathy and grief. More grief than he'd ever experienced for his father or mother.

Loneliness, hurt, sorrow: so many times we have visited, so many times yet to frequent.

The memory of something seismic. The memory of the greatest loss of all.

And memories of Jean suddenly became priceless and rare. The soda shop. The movie theater. The music they'd shared. The handful of stones they'd collected. The image of her face was distant and fragile, and he tried hard to hold onto it.

It felt like a part of his life had been torn from his hands and obliterated before his eyes.

He glanced once more at the windows of her empty apartment, and then he turned and walked away.

12

'Shaw.'

'Detective Nelson Shaw, Dallas Metro?' Mitch asked.

'Yes. How can I help you?'

'Detective Shaw, my name is Mitchell Newman. I'm a free-lance photographer and journalist up here in DC. I was calling to speak to you about Jean Boyd from the *Washington Tribune* ... You knew her, right?'

'Well I wouldn't say I knew her as such.' Mitch could hear a wry smile in Shaw's voice. 'Kind of professionally, you might say. She bugged the hell out of me for a few days at the end of last year.'

'She came to Dallas, right? She actually flew down to Dallas and you met with her?'

Shaw hesitated. 'Why are you asking me this, Mr Newman? You want to know the whereabouts of Miss Boyd, I suggest you ask her yourself.'

It was Mitch's turn to pause. He closed his eyes for a moment.

'Jean Boyd is dead, Detective Shaw. She killed herself five days ago.'

'Is this some kind of fool stunt? What the hell are you talking about?'

'Just as I say. She was found dead in her apartment last Friday. Overdose. Sleeping tablets.'

'Oh Christ.'

Mitch waited in silence. He wanted to hear what Shaw had to say.

'This is the very last thing in the world I expected to hear. That she was in trouble, yes. That maybe she wrote something she shouldn't have and wound up with a lawsuit, but this ... this is just ... Christ almighty, I don't know what to say.'

'She was fired. The *Tribune* let her go at the end of May. The assumption, predictably, is that she went into a serious depression, but there's no real evidence of that. From what I understand, she didn't even tell her mother that she'd lost her job.'

'You've spoken to her doctor? You know where she got the tablets from?'

'I'm not investigating her suicide, Detective. I'm just interested in what it was she contacted you for, and why she came to Dallas.'

'Did I say she came to Dallas?'

'You said she bugged the hell out of you at the end of last year.'

'Right.'

'So she didn't come and see you?'

'I don't think I want to have this conversation, Mr Newman. I have no idea why my very brief acquaintance with Miss Boyd is any of your business. I have to go.'

'Detective Shaw?'

Shaw had not hung up. There was silence at the other end of the line, but Mitch knew he was still listening.

'I went to her home, back to where she grew up in Virginia. It's a nothing place called West Haven. Her father died when she was eight. He was thirty-four years old, and his heart just stopped. Jean was raised by her mother, Alice. She was her only child. I was with Alice yesterday, and she is utterly devastated. I am just trying to get some kind of an idea why a woman like Jean Boyd, a woman I remember as brave and tough and fearless, would do something as drastic as taking her own life.'

Mitch paused. Shaw said nothing.

'If you knew Jean, if you knew even a little of how she was, then perhaps you'll understand why her suicide doesn't make a great deal of sense. Maybe that's just the way it is. Maybe no suicide ever really makes sense. But I know that I have some questions, and I think there are answers. What happened during the last weeks of her life? What was she involved in, where was her work taking her, who and what was she writing about? That's all I'm trying to find out. Do you understand? I'm just trying to help a grieving mother make sense of why her only child killed herself in an apartment in Washington DC last Friday night.'

Again, nothing. Mitch could hear Shaw breathing.

'Please, Detective, give me a break, would you? Did Jean come down to Dallas last November? Did you meet her? What was she chasing? What was she trying to find out?'

There was a further moment, and then Shaw said, 'I'm sorry for your loss, Mr Newman, and for Miss Boyd's mother, too. Please don't call me again.'

The line went dead.

Mitch sat there with the burring sound in his ear, and he knew, without a shadow of a doubt, that whatever had just happened was very wrong indeed.

That same afternoon, sometime after three, Mitch headed back across town to Jean's apartment. The police were not in evidence, and he knocked on a door on the floor below.

When it opened, an elderly gentleman stood there with an expectant expression on his face.

'Oh,' he said. 'I thought it would be the police again.'

'I'm sorry to disturb you,' Mitch said. 'I was a friend of Miss Boyd's.'

The gentleman nodded. 'Dreadful,' he said. 'So very, very sad. She was a wonderful young lady. My wife and I are just heartbroken.'

'You knew her?'

'Yes, of course. We used to look after her cat.' The man frowned. 'I don't know what's happened to it. I guess it's been taken away. I hope they don't put it to sleep. I would have taken it, but they won't let anyone into the apartment. You don't think they just left it in there, do you?'

'I wouldn't have thought so,' Mitch said. He recalled the precarious descent from the fire escape with the cat inside his coat.

'Jean was often away, just for a night, sometimes home to Virginia. She was always so busy. Tireless, she was. It was a terrible shock, and it just goes to show that whoever you think someone is, there's always some part of them that is completely unknown.'

'What was the cat's name?'

'Oh... Mitch. It was called Mitch. Little tortoiseshell thing. Very sweet-natured. Always running away, but always came back.'

Mitch took a step back, if not physically, then within. Later, he would understand that that was the moment he truly reconnected to Jean. The moment he really understood that she was dead, gone forever; that she was never coming back.

'And her apartment?' he asked, fighting the wave of grief that was battering at him like a storm.

'I guess the landlord will repaint and get rid of her furniture and let it to someone else. I don't know, Mr...?'

'Newman.'

'I don't know what will happen, Mr Newman.'

'What about her papers, all her work for the *Tribune*?'

'They came and took it. Boxes and boxes of the stuff.'

'Took it? Who took it?'

'People from the newspaper. That's what they said. There was a police officer here and he supervised everything, made sure they took nothing they shouldn't. I guess her mother might want to come up and see if there's any personal effects she wants to keep.' The man shook his head wearily. 'Just awful, you know. A parent should never have to bury a child. That's just not the way of things, is it?'

'No, sir, it's not.' Mitch paused. 'Might I ask your name?'

'Yes, of course. I'm Ernest Harper.'

'Thank you for your time, Mr Harper. It's really appreciated.'

'You're most welcome, Mr Newman, and please pass on my condolences to Jean's mother.'

Mitch went on downstairs to the lobby. He stood in the cool silence for a good two or three minutes before he could gather himself sufficiently to navigate the sidewalk and get to his car.

The cat was called Mitch.

He felt like the world had rolled right over him and broken every bone in his body.

The tears came then. They tore through him, pulling him apart in every direction. He could do nothing to stop it. He sobbed until he couldn't breathe, and then he sobbed some more.

13

The history of humanity was a history of inhumanity. It was a history of war. A history that would never end.

In Korea, Mitch Newman had seen things he'd believed he wanted to see; things he'd believed the world needed to see. Quickly, perhaps too quickly, he'd understood he was neither spectator nor observer. A war photographer was a vulture, picking over the remnants of death; he was an uninvited funeral guest, showing up solely to feign sympathy and take advantage of the open bar; he was a non-combatant in a combat zone. The camera only pretended separation. The bullets were just as real, the blood just as red, the odds on his dying even greater, for he possessed no training, no experience, no battle sense.

For the soldiers, he was a distraction and a liability. For his mother, he was a constant worry. For himself, he'd soon realized that the reality and the fantasy were a world apart.

From the first terrified, overwhelmed moments, he made some small improvement. After a week, he stopped jumping at every report and explosion. He wore mud-spattered battle fatigues, a helmet and heavy boots. After his second week, he looked like a soldier, even sounded like one. He took photographs, spoke to other press correspondents, allied himself with the UN Public Relations Unit, and began to get a grip on what was happening.

US and British carriers had made successful strikes against

Pyongyang. The Department of Defense requisitioned commercial aircraft to ferry in more troops. From Suwon the North Koreans came; they crossed the Kum River and took Taejon, and President Rhee fled. The Americans were low on ammunition and anti-tank guns. Their forces were in disarray; promised reinforcements from England and Australia seemed never to arrive. It wasn't until the Inchon landings that the tide started to turn. Mitch was there for the Battle of Seoul; he witnessed the Namyangju massacre. By the end of October, the South Koreans were only fifty miles from the Manchurian border. Pyongyang fell, and MacArthur – keen to hammer on through North Korea to China – was reined in by Truman.

And yet, for all the progress that seemed to have been made, everything turned once again in November. UN forces were driven back by a massive Chinese assault. US Marines were trapped at the frozen Changjin reservoir and had to fight for their lives all the way back to the Sea of Japan.

It was here, during these fateful days, that the Korean War came to an abrupt and dreadful end for Mitch Newman. Radioing pictures back to Lester Byron, he was receiving word that what was needed was on-the-ground photographs that really conveyed a true sense of the war.

'We need powerful images,' Byron had said over a static-distorted phone line. 'Images that put the man in the street right there in the line of fire.'

After arguing his case with the divisional commander, Henry Urquhart, Mitch was given a jeep and a driver: Private First Class Raymond Bancroft, or Ray-Ban to his fellow soldiers. Ray-Ban was all of twenty-two years old, a devil of a card player, with a wise sense of humor that belied his years and the same motivation as Mitch.

'Do something valuable with your life, or quit early,' he said.

'Once I've done my tour here, I'll opt out, go back to school. I have notions of being an architect or a designer or something.'

He was born in Broken Bow, Nebraska.

'It's in Custer County, right there in the middle of the state. Hell, we only got the railroad in 1884. You get born there, the first thing you realize is that you have to leave.'

His father was a dentist, traveling from farm to farm extracting impacted wisdom teeth and infected molars. His mother had had seven children, two of whom had died in infancy, and she'd reconciled herself to spending the rest of her years looking at predictable weather and an unchanging horizon. Love and respect his parents though he did, Ray-Ban was determined not to become anything like them. The army was his way out, the educational subsidies and grants available, the respect afforded for having served for his country. He had it all planned out, and it was working just fine until the late afternoon of Friday, November 24, 1950.

Mitch had followed instructions to take a known route out toward the heaviest fighting. It was a good two hours from where they'd been billeted. Ray-Ban talked about army life, how basic training was as much use as a lead parachute when it came to the real deal of combat.

'Well at least you got some basic training,' Mitch said. 'Only training I got was how to wire pictures back to the States.'

'You get no sympathy from me, my friend. You volunteered to come out here with a camera, for Christ's sake. That makes you a special kind of crazy, you know?'

Halfway, they took a break, checked the map to make sure they were still following the right route. Mitch took some pictures of Ray-Ban intently studying the map that was spread out on the hood of the jeep. The territory had become less passable, the road little more than a rutted track, the undergrowth cut back here and there but still capable of slowing the jeep. It was in moments such as these that Mitch grasped the enormity of what the Americans had undertaken. Whatever tactics and strategies might have worked in Europe were redundant and inapplicable in such a terrain. A Sherman might have been able to plough through the bocage of western France, but the jungle of Korea was an entirely different animal. The density was overbearing. It wasn't until the trees and vines began to spread at twenty feet that he could even see daylight. Everywhere seemed fetid and rank, deep shadows and sunken trails, places within which those familiar with such an environment could hide gun emplacements, reserves of food and ammunition and water, even entire platoons. The Americans didn't possess the logistical expertise to run supply lines through endless swampland. This was a world unlike any other, and to fight a war here against those who knew it so well was a challenging and brutally tough proposition.

Feeling sure they were still on track for their destination, Ray-Ban headed off to relieve himself in the bushes. Mitch waited, smoked a cigarette, ever alert for the sound of anyone on the road ahead or behind.

Ray-Ban came back. 'Hey,' he said. 'I got a joke for you.' He climbed into the jeep. 'So there's this guy, right? He goes into a bar and he's got a suitcase. He tells the barkeep that he's got something in the case that no one has ever seen before, something that will knock him speechless. The barkeep says okay, and what happens if it does? The guy says that the barkeep has to give him free drinks for the rest of the night—'

Where the shooter was, there was no way of knowing.

The sound came after the impact, rocketing through the jungle, echoing in triplicate.

The bullet entered Ray-Ban's face just above his right eye, and the back of his head lifted clean away. Back and to the left. Even as it happened, he was smiling, finishing the joke, ready to laugh with Mitch. But his words stopped dead, then there was a sound like air trapped in his throat, and he just slumped forward.

Mitch held what was left of Ray-Ban's head in his hands, and the head was so heavy, and his body deadweight, and he understood what that word really implied. The weight of the dead.

Blind panic set in. Mitch rolled sideways and out of the jeep. Ray-Ban's body fell also. It rolled once and then came to rest. He was face down, his left eye just visible through the under-growth. He was watching Mitch, seeing what he would do, that single eye seeing everything inside him, testing his courage, his fortitude, his sanity.

Mitch lay there on the ground, and waited with his heart in his mouth for the sound of voices, more gunshots, the feeling of a bullet as it tore into his body. This was it now. Four months living on a razor's edge, and Fate had found him. This was where it would end, right here in the middle of some stinking, fetid jungle in a war that he should never have come to.

How long he lay there breathing dirt as Ray-Ban watched he did not know. He felt as if his mind had slipped its moor-ings. He wanted to scream. He wanted to run headlong into the wilderness and leave everything behind. He wanted to vanish and find himself in West Haven, back before all this happened, Jean right there in front of him as he told her that yes, she was right, and he wasn't going to Korea after all.

He knew he had to move, but he did not dare. Not yet. Not until he felt certain that he would not meet the same fate if he got up off the ground.

An hour passed. Perhaps two. He looked at his watch but he had no point of reference. Every single minute was the longest that had ever elapsed. Every breath, every heartbeat was earned, all the more valuable knowing that it could be his last.

Finally, summoning all the will he possessed, he started to

inch back toward the road. He had to lift Ray-Ban's body back into the jeep and get out of there.

He moved slowly, kept his body pressed as close to the ground as he could. His nose was full of dirt, but still there was the stench of gasoline, and beneath that the haunt of blood.

He knew that if the shot had come from ahead of them, over to the right perhaps, then he needed to stay behind the jeep.

There was not a sound out there. Nothing at all.

At one point he had to get to his knees to make it around to the other side of the vehicle. He expected the shot to come then, clean and fast and perfectly aimed, tearing his own head in half just as it had Ray-Ban's.

But no shot came.

He snatched his camera and tossed it into the footwell on the passenger side, then went back a yard and grabbed hold of Ray-Ban's right arm just above the elbow. He pulled as hard as he could, but the body didn't move at all. In death, Ray-Ban seemed to weigh twice, three times what he had in life. He pulled again, hauling with everything he possessed, and then he realized that Ray-Ban's body was up against the back wheel. To move him, Mitch would have to go back the way he'd come and roll him away from the jeep. It seemed a truly impossible task, but there was no choice in the matter.

He moved painfully slowly, ever alert for the slightest sound from the undergrowth around him. The jungle breathed with its own rhythm, and once you were aware of that rhythm, you could sometimes perceive a change. If something moved out there, it created a ripple of responses that circled ever outward.

At one point he looked up over the back of the jeep towards where the shot might have originated.

Again, waiting for the crack of a rifle, he was surprised to meet silence.

He rolled Ray-Ban away from the rear wheel and sat back, his feet against the side of the jeep, using it as leverage to haul the body further out so he could maneuver it back into the passenger seat. At some point he would have to kneel and get Ray-Ban over his shoulder. There was no other way it could be done.

After a good ten minutes, he was in a position where he could do what was needed. He knelt forward and lifted Ray-Ban beneath the arms, all the while trying not to look at the gaunt and dreadful expression on his face, conscious that the moisture he felt on his hands from the back of Ray-Ban's shirt was the contents of his head. Pulling Ray-Ban toward him, he got his shoulder down against his stomach. With a single swift effort he might just be able to haul the body forward sufficiently to lift it.

His first attempt failed, but on the second try he managed to use Ray-Ban's weight to his advantage. The upper body fell with gravity, and Mitch knew that if he leaned backward he could get the purchase required.

The sound of voices was unmistakable, and they were not American.

Terror, so far beyond anything he had ever experienced or witnessed, took over. He let go of Ray-Ban and leapt up into the driver's seat, gunning the engine into life.

Even as he reversed and turned the jeep, he knew what would happen. It was inevitable and unavoidable.

The feeling of driving over Ray-Ban's body was sickening. Above the sound of the engine he heard the sound of bones breaking. He could barely see for the tears in his eyes. He flattened the accelerator to the floor, and he tore that jeep back through the undergrowth and back along the route they'd taken, and he didn't stop until he'd made it back to base.

He was questioned by Urquhart. He lied. He said that he and Ray-Ban had rendezvoused with another unit, that Ray-Ban had gone on with them, told Mitch to head back to base. Which unit? Urquhart had asked. Mitch said he did not know.

Did Mitch know where the unit was heading? Again, he knew nothing, merely that Ray-Ban seemed intent on leaving with the others and insisted that Mitch return, alone.

After a while, Urquhart seemed satisfied. He had been resistant to the idea of using a soldier to chauffeur a journalist. Mitch was dismissed.

That night, sitting alone in his billet, tearing the film out of his camera and exposing it to the light, destroying forever the last images of Private First Class Raymond Bancroft, Mitch knew that his war was over.

What had really happened, he would never tell another soul. He knew it would haunt him, but he could not face the ignominy and shame of his own cowardice. He knew he would go on lying to himself for the rest of his life.

By January of 1951, the South Koreans and their allies were holding a defensive line along the 38th Parallel, the old north–south divide, but Mitch was already home. By the time a ceasefire was in place in November, the Korean War and all he'd experienced was nothing but nightmares.

Mitch Newman had lost his innocence and his naïveté. He'd lost his dream of being the dynamic frontline photojournalist, heralded not only for his spectacular work, but also his bravery.

A hero dies but once; a coward dies a thousand times.

14

As if to underline and exaggerate his very real sense of being alone, Mitch knew within just a few days of his return from Korea that Jean, too, was irretrievably lost.

There had been no reply to his letters, and it was only now that he knew they'd even arrived. They were right there amongst her papers in the room where they'd shared so much. In a way, that made it worse. Until that moment, he had been able to maintain the fragile pretense that perhaps she'd never seen them.

He and Jean had argued so fiercely. She'd given him an ultimatum. *Leave, and the engagement is over.* He'd tried to win her back, tried to get her to see his point of view, but she had laid down the law. He'd gone, and thus voided his promise to her.

Even as he'd sat in some mud-caked foxhole, bullets flying over his head, the twisted wreckage of broken men around him, he'd *known* she would take him back. He'd *known* she would forgive him. But he'd been wrong. So very wrong. Even as he held onto her, she had let him go. All the words he'd written between the start of December and the end of February had gone unacknowledged. Only now did he appreciate how much he'd hurt her. And when he'd driven up to the UVA campus in the spring of '51, he'd seen her but didn't dare speak to her. He could not bring himself to again derail her life. In Korea he'd

81

lost his nerve for war. It seemed also that he'd lost his nerve for living.

That evening, Wednesday, July 8, Mitch Newman sat a while in the cool silence of his own apartment. He put the radio on, but the music on every station aggravated his nerves. He tried to watch TV. It was hopeless. He hated himself. He hated his life. He did not know what he was doing. He was adrift, and the reasons to get up in the morning were becoming ever more scarce and insignificant.

He found himself talking to the cat that he had now adopted, a cat with the same name as himself.

'What was she like? Did she change? Were you there when she died?'

The cat just sat on the coffee table and looked at him unerringly.

'You wanna know what I thought of her?' Mitch said. 'I knew she was different. Really, I did. You know, one of those people that you meet and you think that whatever happens now, it's gonna be special. That's what it was like being around her. She didn't stop. Nothing ever stopped. She was always doing something or about to do something, or she had some great idea about how good it would be to hitchhike to the coast and live on the beach for a month just to see what kind of trouble we'd get into.'

He reached out and stroked the cat's neck.

'When I told her I was going, I was surprised at her reaction. You know what I wanted? You know what I hoped she'd say? I hoped she'd say that she was coming with me. She would be my sidekick. Crazy, I know.'

He paused and looked at the cat. The cat looked right back at him.

'She would be my everything ... just like she was for you.'

Mitch remembered his ideals, his aspirations. He would be as great as Capa. He would take pictures that would find their way into *Life*, *Collier's* and *Illustrated*. The real irony was that Robert Capa, already heralded as the greatest war photographer in the world, had arrived in North Africa just a month after the death of Mitch's father. Those pictures taken as Company E, 16th Infantry Regiment attacked German recon patrols on the northern flank of Hill 336 could so easily have been pictures of II Corps, his father right there in the ranks. Images of wooden crosses in the American cemeteries at Béja, the German Iron Cross markers and engraved propeller blades silhouetted alongside the twisted skeletons of downed planes and gutted tanks, everywhere the stench of smoke and diesel and death. All these things filled his mind when he thought of his father, when he thought of how he could honor his family name. He had gone out to Korea to prove to himself that he was as good a man as any; that he was strong, that he was brave, that his life could serve a purpose. He returned having proven that not only had he failed himself, but he'd lost the only person who'd given his life real meaning.

Finally, he knew he had to let her go. He'd convinced himself he had, but it was a pretense. Each time he'd thought of her, he'd forced himself to think of something else. Regardless, she would find him. She would look back at him – a reflection in a store window, a face in a crowd – and there would always be that same expression: an expression only he would understand.

Why, Mitch? Why?

He couldn't bear the silence any longer. He left the apartment and headed to the bar down the block.

Tom greeted him as he entered, had a bourbon on the rocks ready without being asked.

'You look like someone shot your dog... or maybe that cat you've inherited.'

Tom brought the drink to where Mitch had taken a seat at the counter.

'So things are looking up?'

'No matter how bad it gets, it can always get worse.'

'We're in for one of those nights?'

'Rough couple of days. The girl I nearly married committed suicide.'

Tom looked stunned. 'She committed suicide?'

'Apparently so.'

'Okay... well, apparently and definitely are two very different things.'

'Officially it's a suicide, though there's too many reasons it doesn't make sense.'

'When did this happen? When did you find out?'

'Saturday. After I left here, actually. Got home and her mother called me.'

'Jesus Christ, Mitch. What the hell do you do with something like that?'

'I don't know yet,' he replied. 'Look after her cat. That's about as far as I've got.'

Tom hesitated, and then said, 'You know I forgot, but there was someone here on Monday evening asking after you.'

'Who?'

'I guess it was official,' Tom said. 'A guy in a suit. Said it was personal business.'

'No message?'

'I asked if he wanted to leave one. He said he'd come by your apartment.'

'I haven't been there much. Must have missed him. What did he look like?'

'Hell, I don't know. A stiff in a suit. Dark hair, regular height, regular build.'

'A cop, maybe?'

Tom shrugged. 'I don't think so. He would've said, right?'

'You didn't ask?'

'He was in and out. Place was busy. Football game. Maybe it was nothing. Maybe you didn't pay your utilities.'

Mitch smiled. 'Wouldn't be the first time.'

'Another?' Tom said, holding up the bottle.

'Yeah,' Mitch said, 'and another two or three after that.'

Tom refilled the glass, fetched more ice. 'I'm really sorry,' he said. 'A friend's loss is your own, too.'

'Old relationship,' Mitch said. 'We were engaged. We were kids. I was all on fire to change the world and I took off for Korea.'

'Seriously? You never told me that.'

'What's to tell? Had my mind set on being the great photo-journalist. Didn't know what I was getting myself into, and didn't realize what I'd left behind until I'd lost it.'

'What was her name?'

'Jean.'

'From here?'

'Nope. We grew up in West Haven. Met her when she was sixteen. She followed me to UVA, but I dropped out and went to war. She got through her degree, was a good reporter by all accounts. Worked for the *Tribune*.'

'She was young.'

'Too young.'

'Hell of a shame, Mitch.' Tom set the bottle down. 'Help yourself. It's on me.'

'Appreciated, but no need.'

'Hell, man, I can't do anything but help you get drunk, so let me at least do that.'

Mitch raised his glass. 'No man so poor as the friendless.'

'Aye to that.'

Customers were growing impatient at the other end of the bar.

'Go,' Mitch said. 'I'll sit awhile and feel sorry for myself.'

'Let me know if you need a sympathetic ear.'

'Will do, Tom, will do.'

Mitch got home unaided, but did little more than kick off his shoes before collapsing on the bed. The cat came through and jumped up onto the mattress. He gave it some fuss. The cat purred, then lay down and started washing itself.

'Hey, Mitch,' he said.

The cat knew its name.

'How goes your life? You doing okay?'

The cat moved over and lay beside him, curling itself against him for warmth.

'I have to tell you that I'm drunk, buddy. I'm drunk and I'm gonna fall asleep, and I'm probably gonna snore like a train, okay? I just feel that it's good to forewarn you about this if we're going to be living together.'

The cat didn't move, didn't respond at all.

'Don't say I didn't warn you,' Mitch said, and laid his head back down on the pillow.

If things had not already been a mess, they sure as hell were a mess now.

His comment to Tom about feeling sorry for himself was half a confession. He did that too much, always had done, and he knew that no one but himself would ever reverse that dwindling spiral.

Tomorrow, he thought. *I will get things under control tomorrow. If not for me, then for Jean.*

Somewhere in the subdued haze of his drunkenness, he heard

the phone. It rankled and grated, but insufficiently for him to summon the will to answer it.

Whatever it is, it can wait, was the last thought he remembered.

15

'So he's where?'

'His apartment. I'm across the street right now.'

'News?'

'Nothing significant. He saw Byron at the *Tribune*, went back to the girl's building and spoke to a neighbor.'

'We have a line on his phone yet?'

'No, not yet.'

'What's the hold-up?'

'Generating sufficient semblance of legality to cover our tracks should there be a problem.'

'How long?'

'Shouldn't be more than a couple of days, three at the most.'

'So damned slow.'

'Always.'

'Okay. And the mother?'

'We're dealing with it.'

'I want everything, okay? Nothing gets left behind.'

'I do understand, sir.'

'Good. I don't want to hear that something got forgotten or overlooked.'

'You won't hear that.'

'Okay. Progress report as soon as that's done.'

'Yes, sir.'

The line went dead. The caller hung up the phone and stepped out of the booth. The light burned in the window of Mitchell Newman's kitchen. The guy had been drunk, no doubt about it, and odds were he'd stumbled in, collapsed, and was oblivious to anything.

Christ only knew what he'd done, what the girl had done, but that was not the point. Keep an eye on him, where he went, who he spoke to, and report back.

Best not to ask questions; they so often prompted answers you didn't want to hear.

16

The phone kept on ringing. It roused Mitch from sleep, almost as if it had continued uninterrupted throughout the night.

He had drunk too much. He had sworn off liquor so many times, and yet demonstrated so little willpower. The drunkenness was an escape; the consequences were a curse. He needed coffee and aspirin.

But the phone kept going, and it wouldn't stop.

He answered it.

'Mitchell.' It was Alice.

'Alice … hey. How are you doing?'

'Mitchell, some people came to the house yesterday and took everything. They took all her papers, every notebook. They said they were from the *Tribune*, and there was a policeman here too, and he said that it was part of the investigation into her death.'

'They took everything?'

'I hid the letters, Mitchell. The ones you wrote to her. I took those before they got into her room. I didn't think it was right for anyone to have something so personal.'

Mitch was not focusing. He was struggling to absorb what Alice was telling him.

'I'm sorry, Alice. I just woke up. When did this happen?'

'Yesterday. I called you. Kept on calling you. You didn't answer the telephone.'

'I'm sorry, yes. I got in late. I must have just missed you.'

'I'm so upset, Mitchell. It feels like they're taking my Jean away from me all over again.'

'Okay, Alice. Okay, okay.' Mitch's thoughts raced. For some reason, he felt a deep sense of unease. Something was very wrong about this. Police at Jean's apartment, and now all the way out in West Haven to take papers from her home. The newspaper, yes. He could see that they might want to retrieve sensitive research notes and archive records, but why such an interest from the authorities?

'I'm going to call someone,' he said. 'Leave it with me. As soon as I have anything to tell you, I'll call.'

'Yes, yes, please do that,' Alice said, and Mitch could hear she was crying again.

'It's going to be okay,' he assured her, but he felt very much the opposite.

'Please telephone me, Mitchell,' Alice iterated. 'This is just an awful business. I'm so sorry to burden you with it, but I really have no one else to turn to.'

'I'll call you back,' he said. 'I give you my word.'

Mitch went through old notebooks. Names, dates, places, snippets of conversation, references to photographs he'd long since forgotten taking. He was looking for one name, one number; whether that person would still be there, he had no idea, but he had to try.

It took him close to an hour, and by the time he was done, he'd emptied three boxes of paperwork across the table and floor of the kitchen. It was like looking at a history of his own past, a history of what might have been had he been less resolute in his determination to be a victim of all that had happened to him. Jean had moved on with her life. He'd hit a roadblock and stalled. To her failure to take him back he had ascribed all subsequent failures, both personal and professional. To the loss of Jean he had apportioned the weight of all subsequent losses. He had made that decision, and his current life was the result. It was a sad state of affairs, and there was no one to blame but himself. That was the painful truth, and though he knew it, he could not face it. Postponement of reality had become his specialty.

At last he found the name and number he was looking for.

'John Riley quit the department four, maybe five years ago,' was the reply he'd hoped he wouldn't hear.

'Retired?' Mitch asked.

'On medical grounds, as far as I recall.'

'Do you know if he's still in the city?'

'I'm sorry, sir. Even if I knew, it's not the kind of information we give out.'

'Yes, I understand. People with grudges and long memories.'

'Exactly.'

'Thanks for your help.'

Mitch went through the phone book. There were six *J. Riley* entries. He found him on the fourth try, but he wasn't home.

'Long time ago, we worked on a few cases,' Mitch explained to Riley's wife, Kathy. 'You and I even met one time, but I doubt you'd remember me. I just needed help with something, and thought John might be the man.'

Kathy Riley asked for Mitch's number, said she'd get her husband to call him when he returned home.

Mitch hung up, started to pack away his history, found a binder of negatives, amongst them pictures of Jean, pictures from some other life now almost forgotten. It was so hard to think of her. The memories were clear and succinct and unavoidable. They came at him one after another – birthdays, Thanksgiving,

Christmas, the fights they'd had, the reconciliations, the nights they'd spent together at UVA, late for class, making excuses, close and getting closer to one another every day. And then out of nowhere – a bolt from the blue – this obsessive drive to do something so different, so *necessary*, the idea that he could be so much more than he already was. She had fought it; he had fought back, not against Jean, but against the idea of being restrained from fulfilling what felt like destiny. Crazy thinking. Crazy behavior. And what good had come of it? Really, honestly, had *anything* good come of it?

He tidied everything away, sat quietly for a little while, trying to forget, to push away the regret, the dismay, the self-doubt. So many times it all began and ended with *what if?*

The phone rang.

'Mitchell Newman. *The* Mitchell Newman. Photographer, right?'

'John Riley,' Mitch said. 'Christ, man, it's been years. I tried tracking you down through Metro PD personnel. They told me you'd retired.'

Riley paused. 'Ah, well,' he said. 'There's a story.'

'They said medical grounds. Are you okay?'

'Okay, but took a bullet through the knee. Laid me up for weeks; walk with a stick now. Can't run, can't pass a medical. They offered me a desk, but I thought it best to make a clean break.'

'I'm sorry to hear that,' Mitch said.

'Life deals you a hand, right?'

'It does. It really does.'

'So, what's with you? How's life going? Must be – what? – five years?'

'More,' Mitch said. 'Seven.'

'Where the hell does the time go?'

'No idea.'

'So, why are you tracking me down?'

'I need your help, John. Got something that doesn't make sense, and I really need someone who knows the beat to help me out.'

'What's the trouble?'

Mitch gave him the backstory.

'Suicide. If it's a suicide, it's not a police matter. Well, once it's been established as a suicide, no foul play, no other possible influential factor, then no investigation would be warranted. As for the removal of personal papers and effects, that couldn't be done without a warrant. Did her mother say that a warrant had been produced?'

'She didn't say, and she wouldn't even have known to ask.'

'If there was no warrant, then it was both trespass and illegal search and seizure. You need to find out if there was one.'

'And how do I do that?'

'Without sticking your head above the trenches, you don't,' Riley said. 'I got to ask you, Mitch. You think this wasn't a suicide?'

'I really don't know, John. It may be exactly as it looks. But there's something about this that makes no sense to me, and it sticks in my craw.'

'I can make a couple of calls. Find out whether there was a warrant to take stuff from the mother's house.'

'Would you do that?'

'Sure I would. Give me the mother's name and address.'

Mitch did so.

'Give me a day or two. Let me turn over a few stones, see what crawls out. Might be nothing at all, but if there was no warrant, then that's a red flag, at least.'

'Appreciated, John.'

'You're welcome, Mitch. Good to hear from you. You take care.'

Riley hung up. Mitch replaced the receiver. He sat back in the chair, craved a drink, didn't succumb. He needed to make a decision. Was he going to get dragged into this – whatever this was – or was he going to leave it all alone?

He knew the easy answer, and that was his first and instinctive reaction. Just back away, don't say a thing. But he had done that so many times before, and there was something about this that would not let go of him.

Maybe it was time to do the right thing, the decent thing. Maybe it was time to finally stop being a victim of circumstance.

If not for Alice, then for Jean's memory; didn't she deserve the truth to be known?

He looked at the cat. 'What do you think, Mitch?'

Mitch stared at him for a good ten seconds, and then looked away.

17

July 10, 1964

Bobby Kennedy stood in the doorway of the office and surveyed the faces of the gathered group.

His brother's chief of staff, his press secretary, and then the Secretaries of State, Treasury and the Interior.

They wore serious expressions; the conversation that Friday morning was one more in a long sequence that none of them wanted to have.

What did they have to do – what did they *really* have to do – to ensure that Jack secured not only the party nomination, but another four years in the White House?

Jack was out of town, a speech for the Rotary, maybe awarding a President's Appreciation Award to some branch of the Lions. As far as Bobby knew, Jackie was at the O Street house with her mother and the kids. Since the spring, Jack and his wife had spent less and less time together. Bobby tried to stay out of their personal lives, but the gap between his brother and sister-in-law was growing so wide it was almost impossible not to fall in. It was an emotional whirlpool. When the President of the United States was using members of his own Secret Service detail to cover the tracks he left behind as he committed adultery... well, that was not only politically explosive, it was downright madness.

Bobby was genuinely concerned that Jack had crossed too many lines, broken too many promises, and left himself personally vulnerable. It was one thing to court impeachment by Congress for whatever he'd done to get into the White House back in 1960; it was quite another to risk it on moral grounds. The ignominy of lying to a congressional hearing about his brother's sordid personal life was more than Bobby could bear.

Those who worked closest to Jack knew about the girls. They did not know the number, nor the frequency, nor the risks Jack ran by involving himself with people who were anything but discreet. Even more people knew about the physical ailments – the migraines, the abscesses, the bad stomach, the colon and prostate issues. They did not know the quantity and range of drugs Jack was taking – Ritalin, procaine, the phenobarbitals and testosterone shots, not to mention the endless consumption of Tuinal to help him sleep. He took antihistamines for allergies, and on more than one occasion these had produced such violent mood swings that Jackie had had their personal physician administer anti-anxiety medication and antipsychotics. The president also suffered from Addison's disease, leading to low blood pressure, vomiting, back pain, and, when he was stressed, blackouts and fainting spells.

The Republicans had done their best to question Jack's capability to hold office. Internal support and public opinion had cried them down. Jack and Jackie were the King and Queen of Camelot, and that was the way they'd stay as long as the facade wasn't torn away by revelations of scandal, impropriety, immorality and abuse of power. For Jack was guilty of all these things, and more. And he, Bobby Kennedy, the president's brother, the most senior law enforcement officer in the country, had seen it all, heard even more, and let it all slide.

Every man in the room today was guilty of deception and divisiveness. They had engineered cover-ups, misrepresentation of fact, even perjury before congressional hearings and ethics committees. Of course, some of it had been perpetrated for the common good. Even heroes had lice. The public needed to know that the country was in strong and capable hands, that their jobs were secure, that the economy was thriving, that threats of organized crime, communism and war were as far from their stoops and porches as possible. How those feats were accomplished was of no concern as long as anything that was done was done for the greater good.

Douglas Dillon from the Treasury spoke first. A formidable man in his own right – ambassador to France, member of the executive committee of the National Security Council during the Cuban missile situation – Dillon had been rock-like in his dependability and level-headedness.

'And so here we are again,' he said, and there was a degree of resignation in his voice.

'Christ almighty, Douglas, anyone'd think it was a funeral,' Salinger said.

'It very well may be,' Dillon retorted.

'And where's that wonderfully bright and positive attitude we've all come to know and love so much?' Dean Rusk interjected, the sarcasm obvious.

'Guys, we need to face facts,' Bobby said. He came forward from the doorway and sat down. Like his brother, he commanded attention, but in a very different way. Whereas Jack possessed infinite charisma and charm, Bobby inspired confidence with his calm and measured certainty. There were some who believed Bobby might have been the better choice, but such a thing was never directly stated.

'Six weeks to the DNC,' he said, 'and where we might take it for granted that Jack will get the party nomination, the old guard may swerve toward Lyndon, or they may decide that a new face is what's needed. If Lyndon took the vote, I don't doubt that Hubert Humphrey would be his VP, but let's just suppose that Lyndon doesn't want the job. Would Hubert run against Jack for the nomination? I doubt it. So who would he be up against? California's got Pat Brown and Sam Yorty, Alabama has George Wallace; there's Reynolds out of Wisconsin—'

'Porter from Ohio, Welsh from Indiana,' Salinger said.

'I don't think that's what you're driving at, is it, Bobby?' Udall said. 'What we're all thinking and what no one is saying is that we might not get sufficient support for the president to run at all.'

Ken O'Donnell nodded in agreement. 'What we're afraid of is that the Republicans know what we know.'

'So let's not bullshit one another,' Salinger said. 'Let's all voice the things that everyone is so damned terrified to mention.'

'The girls,' Dillon said.

'Their sham of a marriage,' Udall added.

'The illnesses,' Dillon said, 'and the fact that he doesn't seem to be getting any better. Walk in that office and see him on the floor while two Secret Service men tie that corset around him. For God's sake, he's using a cherry picker to board Air Force One. How long can we keep on saying that it's nothing more than a bad back?'

'It's the election,' O'Donnell said. 'We all know what we did to put him in the White House. The lies, the cover-ups, what Daley did with the Chicago votes, what happened in Alabama. There's not a man in this room, if called before a Senate hearing, who would not have to lie in order to avoid prosecution.'

'So what's the deal with Warren and this investigation?' Udall asked.

'Earl Warren is a stubborn son-of-a-bitch, but he's not a revolutionary,' Bobby said. 'He doesn't want to cross the line. I'll talk to him, answer questions, keep him sweet. If he rocks the boat too much, he's going to drown with the rest of us.'

'So what do you want from us?' Dillon asked.

'Same thing I always want, Douglas. Jack is the president. We put him there, and it's our duty to do everything we can to keep him there. His personal life, as long as it doesn't affect the office of the president, is none of our concern. As soon as it does, then we will have to make decisions, and though those decisions may be very tough, we have to think of the good of the country. Service before self, right? Take away the fact that he's my brother, he is still our commander-in-chief. Our loyalty is to the office, not the personality. Whatever issues may exist, they are of no consequence unless they directly influence his ability as our head of state. We look at Cuba, we look at the Civil Rights Bill, the Peace Corps, the Khrushchev negotiations, the New Frontier program, the Equal Pay Act, ending the recession. On it goes. I don't know about you, but I am hard pressed to think of another president who has accomplished as much in so few years.'

There was a murmur of consent in the room.

'And we did those things too, because we are the delegates and ambassadors and generals. We are the executive branch of my brother's office, and we were just as influential and important in making those things happen. That makes me proud, and I hope you feel the same sense of pride, because what we have done is to lead the greatest nation in the world forward to even more greatness. As Hesburgh said, "The very essence of leadership is that you have to have vision." Jack has vision. Perhaps more vision than all of us combined. That's what we believed in, and that's what we have to go on believing in. If we falter in our faith, then the country will falter, and that we cannot allow to happen.'

'Agreed,' Salinger said, and it was accompanied by another murmur of consent from the others in the room.

'And so, what do I think? I think we view our own Democratic

National Convention not as a challenge, but as a continuation. Honestly, I do not believe there are any other serious contenders for the nomination. I think Jack will be president until 1968, and then we will all have to think about getting real jobs.'

Everyone laughed.

'Let me deal with personal issues. I hold the highest legal office in the country, and if I cannot competently and successfully counsel my brother, then I shouldn't have the job.'

'I couldn't agree more,' Dillon said. 'Enough about the reasons why it can't be done. Let's just focus on how it is going to be done, come what may.'

'That's the attitude we need,' Bobby said. 'Jack sold the nation a dream back in 1960, and he can do it again. We all know what happens when he really communicates. He needs to do that again, and do it better than he's ever done, and that will happen at the DNC in August. If he does that, I don't think there's any real challenge for the nomination. Everything hinges on those four days in August. We have to make it happen, because I, for one, do not want to work for anyone else.'

'Same here,' O'Donnell said.

'So let's get to work. Predict every possible avenue the Republicans may take on this thing. Look at every possible outcome of every revelation you can think of, and work out contingencies and rebuttals and counterattacks. We cannot be ill-prepared or naïve about how tough this might be.'

In that moment, there was not a man present who did not think that the younger brother would have been the better choice. Forget Humphrey and Brown, Yorty and Wallace; the only man of sufficient caliber to run against the president for the Democratic Party nomination was the president's own brother.

But no one said a word.

18

Even before he'd had a second cup of coffee, the phone rang.

'Mitch, it's John Riley.'

'Hey, thanks for coming back to me. Did you find out something?'

'Have you been in touch with anyone at the *Tribune*, Mitch?' John asked.

'I saw Lester Byron on Tuesday. He's the city editor over there. Why d'you ask?'

'I spoke to him too. Early this morning. He said that he was not aware of anyone taking anything from either Jean's apartment here in DC or the mother's house in West Haven.'

'Okay. Well, I guess it would have been handled by someone in security. Byron might not even have been informed by the PD.'

'Right,' John said, and then he paused.

'What?'

'That's the other thing. As far as I can see, and I've had a thorough look every place I can access, there is no extant warrant to remove anything from either location.'

Mitch did not believe what he was hearing. He could not help but feel a deep sense of suspicion. It was against the law to remove anything from a property without a duly signed and witnessed warrant. This was not a murder case. It was a suicide. Jean's documents, irrespective of whether they could be classed as property of the *Tribune*, could only be part of an investigation if there was reason to believe that whatever she was working on had contributed to her state of mind, and that her state of mind had driven her to suicide. Even if that was the case – and that was a big *if* – whoever was involved would still have had to follow due process of law.

Alice had said that people from the paper had come, and there had been a policeman present. Jean's neighbor, Ernest Harper, had also talked about people from the paper, again with a police officer present.

'What the hell is going on here, John?' Mitch asked.

'Your guess is as good as mine,' Riley said. 'I can only tell you what I've found out. The paper appears to know nothing, and there's no evidence of a warrant.'

'But wouldn't the warrant for the West Haven house be an Orange County PD matter? It's Virginia, not Maryland.'

'Sure. I checked that. Checked Rockbridge County, too, just in case there was a crossover jurisdiction. Nothing happening.'

'You spoke to someone?'

'I spoke to a bunch of people.'

'What the hell is going on? Really, who is posing as newspaper people and getting help from the police to take Jean's stuff away?'

Riley didn't say anything for a moment, almost as if he was working out the best way to express his thoughts.

'I'm a company man, Mitch. Being a cop was my whole life for more than twenty years. I've seen and heard a lot of stuff that bothered me, but generally speaking it turned out to be a whole parcel of nothing. I don't know what's happening here, and I'm loath to guess. I just know we're in the capital, we're dealing with the press, and there's a world of sensitive and confidential business that people like you and I are unaware of, and even if we were, I doubt we'd understand it. Decisions get made for the greater good—'

'Bullshit, John,' Mitch interrupted, feeling indignation rising even as he listened. 'Don't give me that. Jesus Christ, the woman killed herself. Now there are people taking her papers away without a warrant... people who are saying they're from the *Tribune* when they're not. You're still a cop, John. You might not wear a uniform anymore, but you still understand the law better than anyone, and your duty is to uphold it. At the very least, and no matter the justification, someone has perpetrated a robbery at Jean's apartment and at her mother's house—'

'Listen to me, Mitch,' John interjected. His voice was calm and measured.

Mitch was annoyed, as if he was being balked. He felt like Riley was doing his utmost to back him off without telling him why.

'Sometimes you have to acknowledge that there is a game in play and there are rules to that game, and even if you think you understand them, which you probably don't, you never just walk onto the field—'

'Be straight with me, John. We've known one another a long time, and I trust you to tell me the truth. Has someone told you to drop this? Has someone told you to tell me to drop this?'

'No one's told me anything, Mitch.'

'Then what the hell is this?'

'The voice of experience.'

Mitch's irritation tipped over into anger. 'Really? Is this the game we're playing? Drop it, don't ask why. Just trust me, I'm a cop. Is that the tune we're dancing to?'

'Mitch, if you're gonna get angry—'

'Angry? Angry? I'm upset, John. I'm really upset. Jean is dead. Her mother is heartbroken. They're saying it was a suicide, but I knew her. Granted, it was a long time ago, but I think I'm a pretty good judge of character, and I can't see her doing that. Okay, she screwed up and lost her job, but we all screw up, right? We don't go stepping off bridges or in front of cars or taking overdoses, do we? We pick ourselves up and get back on the horse, right?'

'Some do, Mitch. Others lie down and let themselves get trampled to death.'

'Not Jean,' Mitch said, and even as he said it, he knew he believed it. 'That was not how she was,' he went on, 'and that is not the person I believe she became. I just cannot accept that she intentionally killed herself.'

'I'm not going to try and convince you otherwise, Mitch. I'm just saying that you are a smart guy. You've been in this business long enough to know exactly where we all are on the food chain. My advice? The hyenas don't hunt the same territory as the lions.'

Mitch didn't know what else to say.

'I appreciate your help, John.'

'You take care, my friend,' Riley replied, and hung up.

Mitch didn't know what to feel, aside from the ironic realization that Jean's death had provoked in him emotions that he could barely recall experiencing. He was angry, somehow afraid, challenged, uncertain, above all resolute. Whatever had happened, however it had happened, it was not right. The event itself, and now the consequences.

There was only one person to whom he now wanted to speak, and he felt sure that that person would not want to speak to him.

He found the number in his notebook and dialed it.

Before Nelson Shaw could even utter a word, Mitch said, 'They emptied her house, Detective Shaw. People who said they were representatives of the *Washington Tribune* went to her apartment and her mother's house and took all her papers. They had a police officer with them. I have no idea who they were or what they were trying to find, but I believe that you know something about this and you're saying nothing, so you better start talking or I'm going to the *Post* and I am going to name names and make so much noise that you are going to have to say something.'

'I told you not to call me again, Mr Newman.'

'To hell with that, Shaw. Didn't you just hear what I said?'

'Every word.'

'So what do you have to say about it?'

'Mr Newman. I have nothing to say to you. I am in Dallas. You are in DC. You are looking into the suicide of someone you once knew. The fact that she and I knew one another professionally, and only very briefly, has absolutely no bearing on her death. I have work to do, and I am going to hang up now, and you are going to do as I asked last time we spoke and never call me again.'

Mitch remembered the business card he'd found in amongst Jean's papers. He remembered the scribbled notes she'd made from her Dallas trip.

'Who is JR, Detective? Who are Joseph Civello and Carlos Marcello? Do those names ring a bell? What is Carousel? Do you know someone called Holly? What about the initials HW? Why would Jean write these things on the back of your business card?'

'Goodbye, Mr Newman.'

'Detective Shaw, you need to—'

The line went dead.

19

Mitch packed a few things into an overnight bag. He called Tom at the bar, explained that he'd be away for a couple of days. Could he feed the cat?

'Sure thing.'

'It's really good of you to do this. I owe you.'

'Hey, one thing ... does it have a name?'

'Yes, it does. She called it Mitch.'

'You're kidding me.'

'Nope.'

'Okay. I can't call it that. As far as I'm concerned, it's just Cat.'

Mitch drove to the bank and emptied his checking account. He ate a sandwich at a diner, and then headed for West Haven. He was there by four.

'I came to get the letters,' he told Alice.

Alice looked dreadful. Mitch guessed she was barely sleeping.

She asked him in, insisted he stay and have a cup of coffee, at least.

'I'd take a sleeping tablet,' she told him when he asked if she was getting any rest at all, 'but, you know, considering every-thing ...'

Mitch closed his eyes for a moment and breathed deeply.

'These people,' he said. 'The ones who took Jean's papers. What were they like?'

'Very polite. Very careful. There was a policeman here too.'

Mitch took a notebook from his jacket pocket. 'Any names?'

'I only remember one. Mr Andrews. He was from the news-paper. There were three of them, but he did all the talking.'

'And the cop's name?'

Alice shook her head. 'He didn't say, and I didn't ask. I didn't think about it. I was flustered. I mean, the police were here and the people from the newspaper said they needed to take all her notes and everything. I should have called you. I should have—'

'It's okay, Alice,' Mitch said.

Alice got up and left the kitchen. She returned a moment later and handed him the neat bundle of letters. They repre-sented his most valiant efforts to win Jean back. Now they seemed utterly insubstantial.

'And something else.' It was a photograph of Jean. It was recent, and her hair was shorter than Mitch remembered it. But otherwise she was just the same. She was beautiful. She was the greatest and most profound regret of his life.

'And... and this too,' Alice said, and from the pocket of her housecoat she produced a ring box.

'No,' Mitch said.

'Please... please take it.' She held it out. Finally, inevitably, he had received Jean's final comment on their relationship.

It was as if the past had waited for him right here. Here were memories of the person he'd believed himself to be, the person he'd wanted to become. Those memories were numerous and unafraid, perhaps now relishing the chance to remind him of his failings. A person might change, but the past remained forever the same.

Mitch looked at the letters, at the picture. He opened the box and looked at the engagement ring. He fought back tears.

'I kept expecting to stop loving her,' he said, his voice crack-ing. 'But it never happened.'

He drove to Richmond and booked into a cheap motel. He left his bag behind and took a walk, stopping near the perimeter fencing of the Richard E. Byrd Airport and watching the military planes hauling out of there. He had taken one of those, one of the very same planes, when he left Arlington for Seoul back in July of 1950.

Most of him had returned. Not all, but most.

He headed back to the motel, had a steak and a beer in a bar, picked up a pint of bourbon at a Wawa. Back in his room, he poured a couple of inches into a tooth glass from the bathroom and sat on the bed. He could not help himself. He opened one of the letters he had written to Jean back on December 5, 1950. Less than a week after his return, finding her, reaching her, explaining everything to her had been his single most important purpose.

The man who had written this letter was a very different man from the one drinking bourbon in an airport motel.

Dear Jean,

How can I ever explain how sorry I am? You were right. I was wrong. All I want is for you to hear me out. I know we talked and talked before I went, but that was without the understanding I now possess. Things happened out there. Things that will haunt me for the rest of my life. Everything about me has changed as a result, and I want you to give me a chance to explain. Surely what we shared together is worth that much?

I have always loved you, and always will.

Mitch

And then, as if to punish himself further, he read the next, written less than a week later.

December 11, 1950
Dear Jean,

There have been too many days when I woke and believed that it would be my last. And then the day came to a close, and I understood that I'd made it through. I felt not only a sense of relief, but also a strange sense of disappointment. As I lay down again, the sound of gunfire still pounding in my ears, I knew that the only reason I was alive was so that I could return home and find you. And since I got back, the life I have been trying to live is no real life at all. I am not even clear as to what purpose I am trying to fulfill. The simple truth is that the things that made sense before I went no longer make any sense at all. I am trying to be the person I once was, and that is not possible without you.

He paused, took another drink. Footsteps passed outside his door.

What I did was unforgivable. It still is, but that does not stop me asking for your forgiveness. Please will you see me, if only to let me tell you how sorry I am for all that happened.
Mitch

He folded the letters carefully and put them back in their respective envelopes. He could not read another one. Not yet. He could not look at her photograph. He switched the TV on, heaped a couple of pillows against the wall, and lay on the bed with his bourbon and his memories.

Standing in the queue to board the flight to Dallas on Saturday morning, Mitch pictured Jean taking the same flight in November of the previous year. Jean was awkward and complex. She did not know what she was striving for because she did not know herself. She was unpredictable, and yet she was strong.

Emotional strength was no indicator of who might take their own life, for everyone had their limit. Had events conspired to drive Jean beyond her tolerance level? Was Mitch charging off on some wild goose chase based on nothing more than paranoid assumptions?

But *were* they paranoid assumptions? He had not called the *Tribune* and asked for a Mr Andrews, but he was pretty certain that no such name was registered anywhere with their employment records. Documents had been removed from Jean's apartment and the West Haven house without a warrant. Tom had said that there'd been someone in the bar asking after Mitch. Of course, it could be nothing. All of it could be nothing. But what if it wasn't?

'Sir?'

Mitch looked up. The queue ahead had vanished, and he was standing some distance from the booking counter. He took half a dozen steps forward.

'One way to Love Field,' he said.

20

July 11, 1964

Mitch waited for Detective Nelson Shaw in the reception area of the Dallas Metro PD building. Had he really thought it through, he would not have come out here on a Saturday. But clear-headedness had not played a part in his planning. He was driven by emotion, not pragmatism.

The desk sergeant had told him that Shaw was in and out of the place on an irregular basis.

'Detective Bureau does things the way it does them,' he explained. 'They don't run a routine like beat because the folks they investigate don't keep us informed of their whereabouts and itineraries.'

'How inconsiderate,' Mitch said.

The sergeant gave him a weary smile. 'How much easier would all our lives be if the deadbeats and murderers and arsonists let us know what they were doing in advance, eh?'

They talked for a little while about crime reporting. Mitch had done enough to sound knowledgeable, and he had an endless catalog of murder scene stories, some of them his own experiences, most of them picked up from the photographers he covered for back in DC.

By five in the afternoon, he was convinced that Shaw wouldn't show. He had a choice. Lie low in Dallas until Monday, or try to track Shaw down at his home. He might just get sent packing, he might even get arrested, but he had to try. Shaw knew something about why Jean had been here in Dallas, and Mitch needed to find out what it was.

He thanked the desk sergeant, said he'd drop by again.

The Dallas phone book gave up two numbers for *N. Shaw*. The first rang and rang but no one answered. The second was answered by someone who said, 'Hi, this is Nancy.'

'Nancy Shaw?' Mitch asked.

'Yes, this is Nancy. Who's this?'

'Is Nelson there, please?'

'Nelson? There's no one here called Nelson. Are you sure—'

Mitch hung up. Either Shaw had chosen not to be listed, or it had been the first number he'd called. There was only one way to find out. He took a note of the address. It was in Belmont, out on the east side of the city, just a few miles from the PD building.

The house was a substantial Prairie Foursquare with dormer windows on each side and a porch that spanned two thirds of the frontage. The yard was neat and trimmed. It did not look like the property of a police detective. This was a family house, or perhaps it had been. Maybe Shaw lived with his folks, or they'd passed and he'd inherited.

Mitch paid the cab driver and got out. He waited until the cab had vanished, then walked over.

There were lights on on both lower and upper floors.

Even before he reached the top of the steps, he knew he was out of his depth. This was tantamount to harassment. This wasn't just a regular Joe; this was a Metro PD detective who had asked him – twice – not to call again, and now he was showing up at his personal residence.

But he had come this far, all the way to Dallas, and he could not turn back. He'd been stepping away and turning back for most of his life. At some point it had to stop.

He raised his hand and knocked on the screen door. He waited for a small eternity. He was sure he heard someone laughing inside. A girl?

He knocked again.

The door within opened suddenly.

There was no one there.

Mitch was thrown. The sound of a girl laughing once more, louder, and then a little voice said, 'Hello!'

A woman's voice from inside the house. 'Kathleen! Kathleen!'

Mitch looked down. A small girl looked up at him, smiling like Christmas morning.

'Hello,' Mitch said. 'You must be Kathleen.'

A woman appeared behind her, walking on through from the rear of the house, drying her hands on a towel as she came.

'Kathleen, sweetheart. Back to the kitchen. Hurry now.'

Kathleen waved at Mitch, and then turned on her heel and ran back past the woman and down the hallway.

'Can I help you?' the woman asked.

'Mrs Shaw?'

'Yes.'

'I'm here to see Nelson. You are his wife, right?'

'I am. Nelson's not here currently. And you are?'

'Mitchell Newman. I'm a journalist. I've flown down from Virginia.'

'You have an appointment with him?'

Mitch hesitated.

'I'm sorry, Mr Newman. I don't think my husband is in the habit of receiving uninvited members of the press. This is our home, you understand.'

'I haven't come as a member of the press, Mrs Shaw. A friend of mine committed suicide, and your husband knew her. She came down here last November and I need to talk to him about her.'

There was a split second's hesitation. Was that a flash of anger in the woman's eyes?

'Well, your luck is in, Mr Newman,' she said. Her attention was focused over his shoulder and toward the street. 'You can take this matter up with him directly.'

Mitch's heart missed a beat. He had butterflies in his stomach.

Shaw's car turned off the street and came up the driveway. The engine killed, he opened the door and got out. He stood for a moment, regarding the stranger on the porch, then he closed the door, and started over. His expression was one of uncertainty, and then realization dawned.

'Newman,' he said, in his tone anything but surprise.

'Am I that predictable?' Mitch asked.

'All of you are that predictable. You guys are like fireweed. Only a reporter would deal with being told not to call any more by showing up at someone's home.'

Mitch didn't respond. He walked down the front steps and stood in the yard. Somehow it made him feel less like a trespasser.

'You know something?' Shaw said. 'The last person in the world you want to upset is a cop.'

'Nelson? Is everything okay?'

'Go inside, sweetheart,' Shaw told his wife. 'I can deal with this.'

Ellen Shaw went inside and closed the front door firmly behind her.

'So, what do you want, Newman?' Shaw asked, his tone aggressive now.

'The truth,' Mitch said. 'Someone I cared for killed herself, except I'm starting to believe that she didn't. Not only because she never seemed to me to be the kind of person that would do that, but because of what's been happening since.'

Shaw said nothing. Mitch took it as an invitation to remind him of their previous conversation.

'JR. Someone called Rubenstein. Someone else called Holly W. The initials HW over again, and what appear to be dates at the end of last year. Joseph Civello. Carlos Marcello. Carousel.'

'You don't need to remind me,' Shaw said.

'Who are these people, Detective Shaw?'

'I answer the questions I want to answer, and no more. Then you leave me and my family alone, okay?'

Mitch didn't reply. He didn't want to commit himself to such an agreement.

'Okay?' Shaw repeated.

'She was thirty-three years old, Detective. She had her troubles. Who doesn't? She caused some stir at the *Tribune* and they let her go. Big deal. The Jean I knew would have fought back in no time. I know there's something wrong, and I believe you know it too. I'm a photographer. I'm no journalist. Maybe I was, once upon a time, but not now. I just want to find out what happened to a very dear friend of mine, and as it stands, you seem to be the only person I can go to.'

Shaw didn't say anything for a good thirty seconds.

It was a very long thirty seconds.

'What assurances can you give me that I won't be dragged into whatever the hell it is you're digging up?' he asked eventually.

'I can't assure you of anything,' Mitch said. 'I don't know what I'm getting into, and if you're that concerned about becoming involved, then that tells me you already know a great deal more about this than I do.'

'I know that some people did some things that needed a warrant they didn't have.'

'The papers from her apartment. The things they took from her mother's house.'

Shaw nodded, then glanced over his shoulder as if suddenly aware that he was standing in the street, observable by anyone.

'Did you fly down here today?'

'I did, yes.'

'I heard you waited a good few hours at Metro.'

'That's right.'

Shaw puts his hands in his pockets and shook his head slowly.

'I liked her,' he said. 'I liked her a lot, you know?' He looked away and down the street, lost in a memory. Then he smiled. 'She was feisty, a real pain in the ass, but you couldn't not like her. I honestly think she cared about people, about telling the truth, about people finding out things they should know.'

'Then help me,' Mitch said. 'If for no other reason than that.'

Shaw nodded slowly. Something had changed. There was an air of inevitability, perhaps even reconciliation to the fact that he was connected to something that he could no longer avoid. Human nature, perhaps nothing more, but when he spoke again, it seemed to Mitch that he'd decided to stop wrestling with whatever was fuelling his conscience. Perhaps he knew that they were tied together in this sea of confusion, and if they didn't help one another then both of them would drown.

'I admire your persistence,' he said.

'I don't have a choice, Detective.'

Shaw nodded again, like he understood all too well. He looked back at the house, and then down the street once more. He seemed like a man taking stock of something before it became something else.

'Everything is out of school, you understand?'

'I understand.'

He hesitated a moment longer, and then said, 'You hungry?'

'Hungry?'

'Yes, hungry. You know, when you get that feeling in your stomach that maybe you should eat something?'

Mitch laughed. 'Er, yes, I guess so.'

'And you'd accept a dinner invitation from a cop?'

'Sure.'

'Then consider yourself invited, Newman.'

21

'Gone? You're telling me Newman is gone?'

'Yes, sir.'

'And you have no idea where?'

'No, sir.'

'What the hell happened?'

'Right now, I don't know, sir. Shift changeover, maybe. Somehow he gave us the slip.'

'Well you better damned well find him, hadn't you?'

'Yes, sir, of course we'll find him.'

'That means now, you understand?'

'Yes, sir.'

'Then please explain why you are still on the other end of this line.'

'Sorry, sir. Yes. We're onto it.'

'Hours. That's what you have. Not days. Hours. And it better be good news.'

The line went dead.

22

Kathleen was eight. Cynthia was six years, three months and two days. They sat beside one another at the dinner table in Shaw's house, and to Mitch, this seemed like the family of which every American dreamed.

Ellen Shaw, at first surprised at the unexpected guest, had quickly organized another setting, and Shaw himself had fetched beers from the fridge.

Before they sat down to eat, Shaw took him to the den, and there on the walls were his Police Academy graduation plaque, family pictures, both his daughters' birth certificates in a frame, a photo of his parents. The decor said everything and nothing about Shaw himself. It was plain, utilitarian, almost absent of feminine influence, and Mitch was struck by the idea that Shaw might actually be a very lonely man.

'I come here,' he said, 'when I need to hide.'

'You have a beautiful home, and a great family,' Mitch said.

Shaw indicated a chair. Mitch sat down.

On the desk beside him were manila files, an ashtray, half a bottle of Scotch and a glass.

'Sometimes you see things,' Shaw went on, 'and you can't talk to your wife about them. Hell, the only other people you can talk to are cops, and they don't want to hear. People killed, you know? Lives ruined. Rape victims. All that stuff.'

Something caught Mitch's eye. It was a Purple Heart in a small frame.

'Yours?' he asked.

Shaw nodded. 'Korea.'

'I was there,' Mitch said.

'You served?'

'Photographer. Four months. Damn near killed me. I was engaged to Jean. Did I tell you that?' He paused, took a swig of beer. 'We were engaged and I was all on fire to go out there, take the best war photographs anyone had ever seen. Be famous. Be a legend.' He smiled sardonically. 'She pleaded with me not to go. She thought I'd get killed. I kind of did. Died a little. There's been that little bit less of me ever since.'

Shaw looked at him, and there was something altogether unnerving in that moment, as if the cop was trying to see something inside of him, trying to read him, trying to understand something beyond the visible.

And then it broke, and he leaned forward and pulled up his right trouser leg. There was a hideous mass of scar tissue down his shin. 'That goes all the way up my thigh,' he said. 'Gets worse. Flamethrower. I was out there for less time than you. August to October of 1950. Didn't even know I was hurt until I woke up in a military hospital back here.' He sighed. 'I can't remember a goddam thing about it, but I have that to remind me every day.'

'We were there at the same time,' Mitch said.

Shaw didn't acknowledge the coincidence. 'Seems endless, doesn't it? The evil that human beings are capable of doing to one another.'

Neither of them spoke for a little while, each lost in the thoughts provoked by Shaw's comment.

'So, you said you left Jean behind?'

'I did,' Mitch said. 'Dumbest thing I ever did. Left her behind, went out there, nearly got my head blown off, came back a mess. Wrote to her at the paper, at her home. She never replied.'

'Maybe she never got your letters.'

'She did. I got them back from her mother yesterday. She'd read every one.'

'Hell,' Shaw said.

'Exactly.'

'So you're doing this out of what? Guilt? Shame?'

Mitch shook his head. 'I'm doing this to try and remember who I was before I went to Korea.' He paused in thought. 'Mostly for Jean. Because she doesn't deserve to be remembered as a lonely suicide.'

Dinner was good. Mitch couldn't remember the last time he'd sat down at a table and eaten a home-cooked meal. Ellen Shaw served up brisket and creamed potatoes, slaw, green beans and a bowl of black-eyed peas, corn and avocado that Shaw called Texas caviar. The girls had sweet tea, and Shaw brought more beers from the fridge for himself and Mitch.

'So how do you boys know each other?' Ellen asked.

'I phoned your husband about a case and he told me twice not to call him again, so I flew here from DC to see him.'

Ellen started laughing, had to hold a serviette over her mouth. Shaw laughed too. The girls looked puzzled.

'You're a reporter, I gather,' Ellen said.

'A has-been reporter who now calls himself a photographer.'

'Better than some of the things I've been called,' Shaw said.

'And you're from Washington?'

'Virginia originally,' Mitch said. 'But these days I live and work in Washington.'

'So what on earth are you doing following something up in Dallas?'

'Ellen,' Shaw said. It was an emphatic silencing.

Ellen looked awkward for a moment, and then she fussed with the younger of the girls, told her to please try and keep her food on her plate.

The conversation did turn, and to the everyday. No, Mitch did not follow any football teams. No, he didn't have a wife or a girlfriend. His parents? Sadly, they had both passed away, his father in the war in Europe, his mother back in 1961.

What Ellen said was, 'Well, you must have very inexpensive Christmases, unlike us!' but what Mitch heard was, *Is that even a life? You must be a terribly lonely human being.*

When they'd finished eating, he carried plates and cutlery through to the kitchen. He offered to help wash and dry. Ellen thanked him, but said that it was one of the girls' chores.

'We're going to go talk for a little while,' Nelson told her. It sounded like *Do not disturb.*

'The woman is a marvel,' Shaw said when they were once again seated in the den. He fetched another glass from a drawer and poured an inch of Scotch for both of them. Mitch didn't much care for it, but felt it inappropriate to refuse. 'She's done an amazing job with the girls. To think I never wanted kids. Free and unencumbered, that was my idea. Now they're my life. You can have the worst day ever, you know, and you come home, and one word, one kiss, one hug from those girls and none of it matters a damn. It's a release valve. If they weren't here, I'd lose my mind.'

Mitch smiled, but stayed silent. Shaw was opening up, and he didn't dare say or do anything that would dissuade him. Even cops needed a priest, and that priest could take any guise.

'We deal with the raw side of life any which way we can, right? Some guys drink, some gamble, some don't do anything but work...like they're afraid to stop because they'll see there's so many things going on that they don't have.' Shaw sipped his whisky. 'Sorry,' he said. 'You didn't fly all the way from DC to listen to me complaining about my life.'

'I came to ask you for your help,' Mitch said, 'but now I've seen your home and your family, I really don't want you to get involved in something that makes you uncomfortable. I have nothing to lose. But this? What you have here is good. It's important. This is a real life, Detective, and I wouldn't want to jeopardize your well-being or that of your family.'

'Nelson,' Shaw said. 'You just had dinner in my home. You can at least call me Nelson.'

'Nelson,' Mitch said.

'I'm not gonna say or do anything that would jeopardize anything, believe me.' Shaw paused, leaned forward a little. 'So, what do you want to know?'

'I want to know what Jean was doing down here.'

'As far as I knew, she was chasing Kennedy. At least, that was what she told me. She was interested in a whole bunch of things, but that was her primary reason for being in Dallas.'

'Jack or Robert?'

'The president.'

'For what? What was she after?'

'To be honest, she didn't tell me a great deal. It was obvious that she thought he was no good. She had opinions about the election. She said that Joe Kennedy's money had put his boy in the White House, and that the money was dirty, that it came from bootlegging and graft and protection rackets in Hollywood and all sorts of things. She didn't have an opinion about Nixon one way or the other, but she did have an opinion about what was right and what was wrong. She was relentless, you know? She had the bit between her teeth, and there was nothing I could say or do that would get her off it.'

'So why did she come to you?'

'Kennedy was down here in November. Back in '60, he swung

the Texas vote by an eyelash. He also had Governor Connally and Senator Yarborough feuding with one another. They had long-standing disagreements about all manner of things. White House PR said it was a goodwill trip, but I think Kennedy came down here to get the two of them to cool it off. That kind of thing could throw Texas to the Republicans, and if Kennedy wasn't in the White House, then they might wind up unemployed too. Anyway, Jean was down here a couple of days before the Kennedy circus was due to arrive, asking for press credentials. She wanted access to Kennedy's people, press officers, things like that. As you know, that kind of thing has to be authorized by the police.'

'Why you?'

'Why anyone? She showed up at Metro, asked to see a detective, and I just happened to be on duty and in the building.' Shaw smiled unashamedly. 'I gave her the time of day because she was pretty and had a bad attitude. She asked me for help, I told her no, and she called me six feet of stupid in a bad suit.'

Mitch laughed. He could hear her saying something like that.

'So that broke the ice, you could say, and I got her the credentials. She hung around until they all showed up. Kennedy and his entourage, Jackie included, arrived in Fort Worth on the twenty-first. Jean went over to the Hotel Texas that night. That's where the Kennedys stayed, and that's where they left from the following morning. Jean came back here ahead of them, was out at Love Field when the flight landed on the morning of the twenty-second. After the motorcade and the meet-and-greets, he had a fundraiser at the Municipal Auditorium in Austin, and then spent the weekend at the Johnson ranch. I didn't see her until the twenty-third. She left on the twenty-fourth, and as far as I know, she went straight back to DC. I think she was stonewalled by everyone she spoke to. No one wanted anything to do with her.'

'That doesn't surprise me, considering that she thought the election was rigged.'

'Hell, that thing has been dragged like a dead cat through the papers for months. The Republican hardheads wanted Nixon to put up a fight, but I think he's just biding his time. If he runs in November, I wouldn't be surprised if he winds up in the White House. Considering all these rumors about Kennedy's health and his affairs and Lord only knows what, it seems to me that it would have been a whole lot simpler if Nixon had won in the first place.'

'Your business card was among her papers. That's how I found you.'

'I know.'

'She'd written Rubenstein on the back, and the name Holly. Any idea who they might be?'

Shaw shook his head. 'Holly was a name she mentioned. I don't know who she was. Jean said she was looking for her, that she'd gone missing. That's all she said. She asked me if I could help find her, and I told her that she or someone else would need to file a missing persons report. She said she didn't want to do that.'

'And the girl's surname? She wrote "Holly W.". Any idea?'

'She must have told me, but I honestly can't remember.'

'And these other people. Joseph Civello and Carlos Marcello. You know who they are?'

'Civello has been a mob boss down here for forty years, even though he's originally from Baton Rouge. Dallas organized crime used to be run by a guy called Joseph Piranio. He died back in '56 and Civello took the reins. He's a hoodlum, a nasty piece of work. Related to Frank DeSimone out in LA and the Coletti brothers who run things in Colorado, and best buddies with a host of big shots in New York, San Francisco, Tampa, Chicago too, I'd bet. Carlos Marcello is New Orleans, and there's a close tie there because Civello is a Louisianan. Some say that Marcello manages Dallas through Civello, but I don't buy it. Civello is in long pants, you know? He runs his own show here in the city.'

'So why would Jean be interested in organized crime when the story's about the election?'

Shaw smiled. 'You need to catch up, my friend. The story was not about the election. The story was about the election being rigged. You want to rig an election, you go speak to the people who influence the working majority in the major cities across the country. Truck drivers, cabbies, garbage men, you know? You need to deal with the Teamsters. Thanks to a guy called Jimmy Hoffa, they're now the union for the airlines, the laundry industry, bakers, construction, freight, the movies, the railways, warehousing, you name it. You get Hoffa, you get the unions; you get the unions, that's a hell of a lot of votes.

'Anyway, now that Kennedy's in the White House, Bobby has been using the Department of Justice to hound Hoffa. Why he's gunning for him is anyone's guess. Now it looks like he might have him on a witness tampering thing. They'll do the appeals dance for a while, but I think Hoffa will do time.' Shaw smiled sardonically. 'Get this. The evidence against Hoffa came from a guy called Edward Partin, the Teamsters' business agent in Baton Rouge, Joe Civello's hometown.'

'So...'

'So everything and nothing. Hearsay, rumor, you sift through it as best you can, you find out who's willing to talk, and you wind up with a story worth printing. I couldn't tell you if the Kennedy administration bought its way into office. I couldn't tell you why Bobby Kennedy seems to want the president of the International Brotherhood of Teamsters in jail, especially if his unions helped put Kennedy in the White House, but Jean came down here with a conviction. You knew her a great deal better than me. If ever there was a woman on a mission, she was that woman.'

'Relentless,' Mitch said.

'And impatient and indiscreet and sometimes too self-assured for her own good.'

There was silence for a moment, and then Mitch said, 'When I told you she was dead, what was your first reaction?'

'Bullshit,' Shaw said. 'I thought it was a joke. Then when I got that she really was dead, I figured there was no way she'd kill herself. A day later, I wasn't so sure. I didn't know her well enough to say one way or the other. I've dealt with a lot of suicides, and they have all been suicides. I can't think of a single one that's turned out to be foul play.'

'So am I chasing a ghost? Is there no story here? Should I just pack my bags and head home, let Jean and the whole thing rest in peace?'

'I can't answer that for you,' Shaw said. His expression changed.

'What?'

'I'm a cop,' he said. 'It's in my blood. I can't let anything go until I'm sure.'

'So what did your intuition tell you?'

'That was what it was. Intuition. Nothing more or less than that. I thought she was onto something. There was something in the way she asked questions that made me feel she was not so much trying to find out something as get confirmation for something she already knew.'

'Such as?'

'Something big. Something that could get her and a whole bunch of other people in a great deal of trouble.'

'Something to do with Kennedy?'

'She was here because of Kennedy. That was why she came to Dallas in the first place.'

'So do you think she was onto something that might have put her in the line of fire?'

Shaw smiled wryly. 'All I can say to that is that Jean Boyd seemed the kind of person who would go after something even if it did mean taking that kind of risk.'

There was silence between them for a few moments.

Shaw looked up. 'So?'

'So what?' Mitch asked.

'Do you need to know what happened to her?'

Mitch hesitated. He knew that saying it out loud would commit him to an irreversible course of action. This was his weakness, his Achilles heel.

Finally he said, 'I want to let it go, but I don't think I can.'

'Then you have your answer,' Shaw said. 'It's not me or Jean or anyone else you have to satisfy. It's yourself.'

'So where do I begin?'

'I don't know. While she was here, I saw her a couple of times, for no more than an hour. She was here from the twentieth until the twenty-fourth. What was she doing? That's what I'd want to know.'

'And how do I find out where she stayed?'

'I'll find out and let you know. Where are you holed up?'

Mitch gave Shaw the name of the motel.

'Last of the big spenders, eh?'

'I'm paying my own ticket. No expense account.'

'I have to go in early tomorrow. Not usual for a Sunday, but I need to see someone. When we got Jean her press credentials, she would have given us her Dallas address, even if it was just a hotel. It'll be on file.'

Shaw got up. He walked Mitch out to the front door, and Mitch made a point of saying goodbye to the girls and thanking Ellen for her hospitality.

At the door, they shook hands.

'Walk up the street, take a left, a couple of blocks, turn right and there's a cab stand,' Shaw said. 'I'd say until next time, but I'm kinda hoping you won't have any more questions for me.'

'I really appreciate everything,' Mitch said.

'I'll call you in the morning,' Shaw said, then he stepped back inside the house and closed the door.

For a moment, Mitch stood there. He heard the girls laughing. He heard Ellen's voice, and then cartoons on the TV or music coming from somewhere.

He wondered if he and Jean might have found themselves in such a place had he made the right decision. He wondered a lot of things, and none of them offered anything but irresolution and doubt.

23

December 19, 1950

Dear Jean,

I do not know if my previous letters arrived with you. I am assuming they did.

I have been back home little more than three weeks, and there is a hole in my heart and my life that will never be filled without you. It seems now that I spent our last weeks together saying things that sounded like something but meant nothing at all. Seems I have spent my whole life saying things, explaining things, doing my best to convince people that I am more than I really am. I don't want to be that person. I want to tell the lesser story so people don't think I'm lying.

In truth, all of this is meaningless now. From here, any life I have will be a lesser version of the life I would have had with you.

How many times does a man have to say he's sorry before a girl believes him? How many letters does he have to write before she replies? I'm ready to find out.

I need to tell you what happened in Korea. I need to tell someone, but that someone can only be you. Things happened out there, and to think that I have to carry them alone for the rest of my life is a burden I do not feel equipped to bear. You were right in so many ways, and though I am writing this, I still feel that I have to tell you in person. I appreciate that it may sound selfish, but the mere fact that I can see it as selfish is evidence that I have changed. I am not who I was before I went.

I believe with all my heart that only now am I able to be the man you wanted me to be. I am asking you to give me one more chance to prove it.

Love you, always and forever.
Mitch

24

Jean's whereabouts during her days in Dallas, the things she believed, the things she suspected, occupied Mitch's mind after his meeting with Nelson Shaw. He wanted to know what she was chasing; he wanted to know the significance of the names she'd noted, what their connection was, where they were now. He also felt that for all that Shaw had told him, there was something more, and when he thought of such a possibility, it unsettled him.

He had the cab driver pull over near a liquor store en route back to the motel and bought a bottle of Jim Beam. The last thing he should do was get drunk, but he was ragged and weary. He fetched ice from the lobby, poured himself a couple of inches. Seated on the floor, his back against the bed, he smoked one cigarette after another. The TV played quietly in the background, perhaps so he didn't have to deal with complete silence, perhaps to drown at least some of the thoughts that came like a torrent.

The question was simple: was he really going to pursue this? Was he going to try to unearth whatever she believed was there to be unearthed? Now, with her papers gone, the only way to find out was to follow in her footsteps. He was halfway there, had flown all the way to Dallas, and the decision had to be made. Stay and keep digging, or head home and try to forget?

As Shaw had said, the question did not actually concern Jean. The question concerned Mitch himself.

He had bailed out of his relationship with Jean to go to Korea. He had bailed out of Korea when it became too fraught with danger. Even when he'd returned, he'd given his career as a photojournalist nothing more than a half-hearted commitment, and here he was – thirty-five years of age, no wife, no kids, a rental apartment, an empty checking account, no security to speak of – alone in a Dallas motel with a bottle of bourbon and a crisis of conscience.

He had betrayed Jean once before.

Was he now going to betray her a second time?

He had read the next letter – the one from December 19. He remembered that time as if it were no more than a week ago. He recalled the sense of being lost, without anchor, without any point of reference, as if whatever script he'd written for his life had been rewritten by someone he did not know.

Losing Jean had left a spider's-web crack through everything. One more impact and it would all have come apart.

He poured another drink. He closed his eyes and leaned his head back against the edge of the mattress.

He asked himself what Jean would have done had the roles been reversed, and there was no doubt in his mind. Even now, even after all these years, despite all that had happened, if he had died and she was in this situation, he knew she would have pursued the truth to the ends of the earth. That realization shone a spotlight directly into all the corners of himself. What was he afraid of? What was it that he feared he might lose? That was the whole issue in a nutshell. There was nothing *to* lose, so why did he hesitate? Was he worried for his own safety, or about saving face? Perhaps, having made so many wrong decisions, he feared all decisions, even those that were obvious and inescapable.

When did he become so afraid? Or had he always been this way? Had the war merely been a way of testing himself, seeing if he had the courage to make a bold decision and carry it through? Or had it been an evasion of the inevitability of his relationship with Jean? Had he gone to Korea to escape commitment, or to prove his ability to commit?

He did not know. He could remember how he had felt at the time, but he could not remember his thoughts. The decisions and conclusions had faded over the years, but the emotions seemed as strong as ever. Perhaps, in reality, he had been doing nothing more than proving himself right. Had Jean persuaded him to stay, it would have been tantamount to admitting that his decision to go was unfounded and foolish. And he could never have done that. Not ever.

He turned toward the TV. The news was playing. Behind the anchor, they were showing the president's face. He reached over and upped the volume.

'...establishing cause for an inquiry that addresses the very nature of the electoral process. A representative of the White House press bureau declined to comment, stating that the attorney general's office would be working alongside the house subcommittee to establish the veracity of these claims. A Republican faction has consistently maintained that there were irregularities in the vote-counting procedure, but Mr Nixon has resolutely refused to challenge the 1960 result. Whether such claims of unethical practice will influence the ongoing campaign for re-election are unknown, but with the forthcoming Democratic National Convention in New Jersey, and challenges being leveled at the attorney general's impartiality in this matter, it certainly seems that the swing votes that gave the presidency to the Democrats will have to be a great deal more secure than they were four years ago. And now, with the latest sporting results...'

He turned the volume down again and busied himself with loading film into his camera – a Nikon F, bought six months ago for $285. It was a staggering amount of money, but somehow he'd justified it, convincing himself that it was a definitive statement of intent about making it as a photographer, a real journalist. Yet no sooner had he bought the camera than he regretted it. Owning such a thing was not a passport to success. The trappings were merely trappings. Nevertheless, he had it with him and he was determined to make use of it.

When he had finished up with the camera, he reached for the bottle.

He knew what he was risking in pursuing the truth of Jean's death, and he had made his decision.

25

'It's Finch,' Ken O'Donnell said. 'I know it. He's driving a train right through this, and he's loving every minute of it.'

'Okay, so it's Finch,' Bobby said. He reached for his glass and rested it on his knee. 'We've had to deal with Castro, with Hoover, Khrushchev, de Gaulle. I think it's safe to say that in the past three years this administration has had to overcome more prejudice, lack of faith, political upheaval, world crisis and internal strife than any other since Lincoln. I am goddam proud of what we have accomplished, and I am not having some second-rate Nixon hooligan like Don Finch drive us off the road just when we have our destination in sight. You know as well as I that what can be done in eight years is way more than double what can be accomplished in four.'

'I couldn't agree more, but we have to face facts. Earl Warren has been appointed to investigate, and he is a stubborn son-of-a-bitch who won't stop until he's gone through everything.'

Bobby closed his eyes for a moment and breathed.

It was late, past ten. The kids were asleep. Ethel was a miracle-worker. How she managed to get eight children into bed and settled with only two nannies to help never ceased to amaze him. And now she was pregnant with their ninth. Somewhere it had to stop, they kept telling one another. *What are we doing?* he'd ask her. *Raising a family or founding a dynasty?*

'The simple truth is that the deeper they dig, the more likely they are to bury us,' O'Donnell went on. 'Irrespective of whether they find evidence of election-rigging, vote-tampering or that the president buys Cuban cigars direct from Castro himself, the mere fact that it's getting press and air time is causing damage we can well do without. The last election was tight, tightest for a hundred years, and slurs on the Kennedy name or the administration itself could see us out. Not since Herbert Hoover has there been a one-term president, and that was before the war. And he was a Republican, for Christ's sake. Last Democrat to do a one-term was Cleveland in 1897!'

Bobby raised his hand. 'Cool down, Ken. Really, you're over-reacting. There is no way in the world that anyone is going to be proving anything before November. Who've they got down there, eh? If you can name one man in that outfit who can bring a case like that together in sixteen weeks, then I'll stand against Jack at the National Convention and then we'll see what happens.'

Ken smiled. Bobby possessed a great deal more self-assurance and perspective than he was credited with. If Jack was the captain of the ship, then Bobby was not only the master-at-arms, he was also navigator and helmsman.

'Look,' Bobby said, 'just get your people to run some interference. We can throw a few spanners in the Republican works too, you know. The worst thing to do in a crisis is panic, so let's not panic. Let me handle whatever happens with this committee they're convening, and let me deal with Jack as well.'

'Which is another issue entirely,' Ken said.

Bobby paused. 'And which issue are we referring to now, Ken?' His tone was slightly defensive. There was thin ice on this pond.

'The medical matters are for his doctor,' Ken said, 'but Pierre is—'

'Pierre Salinger,' Bobby interjected. 'I know Jack would never consider anyone else for that post, but sometimes our good friend Pierre hears things that were never said, and sees things that never happened.'

'And sometimes it's the opposite, Bobby. You know what's going on. You better than anyone. The hotels. The way he uses his Secret Service detail to organize liaisons. I mean, for Christ's sake, Walter carries not only a regulation sidearm, but five grand in cash. Why on earth would the president's security chief need to carry that kind of money?'

Bobby smiled. 'Incidentals.'

'Seriously, Bobby, you need to talk to him. Word gets out about these girls, and this ship will sink faster than the *Titanic*.'

'You really think so? Seems to me the red-blooded blue-collar working men of the good old U S of A would be even more committed to their president if they knew he was a hound dog.'

Ken smiled. Many a true word was spoken in jest.

'This administration is a crusade, Ken. Do you know what that word means? It means a vigorous campaign for political, social or religious change. It comes from the Spanish *cruzado*. Literally, it means that you have been marked with a cross.'

Ken sighed inside. *Here we go*, he thought. *A Kennedy monologue.*

'The presidency is bigger than the man. The presidency is a mission. Yes, it absolutely *is* a crusade. You look at everything we have accomplished, everything we have yet to accomplish—'

'I know, Bobby, I know all this. We've said it before, and we'll keep on saying it. I admire and respect your brother as much as any man you'd care to name, but my admiration and respect will not keep him in the Oval Office if he does not—'

'I will deal with Chief Justice Warren,' Bobby said. 'And I will deal with Jack.'

'Okay,' Ken said resignedly. This was a battle that had been fought and lost before. 'Just let me know if there's anything I can do to help.'

'Only help anyone can be is to do their own work the best they know how, or none of us might have a job come Christmas. All you need to focus on is August. Get Jack up on the podium at the DNC, let him say what I know he's more than capable of saying, and we're home and dry.'

'You really believe that?'

'I do, Ken, I really believe that.'

'Then that is what we'll do.'

Once Ken had left, Bobby rose from his chair and walked to the window. He knew what he was doing; he had done it before, and he would go right on doing it. He was selling himself and everyone else a bill of goods.

Jack had lashed himself to the wheel, and even now was steering this ship toward the rocks.

It was tearing Bobby apart, but there was no going back.

26

July 12, 1964

The phone roused Mitch from a deeper sleep than he'd had in weeks. The bourbon had drowned him good, but he was grateful. Since Jean's death, his mind had been like a radio between stations, nothing but grating interference and random noise.

'Mitch Newman,' he said.

'The Town Plaza, Elm Street,' Shaw said. 'That road runs all the way from Old East Dallas to the freeway. The hotel is up between North Olive and North Harwood.'

'Appreciated, Nelson,' Mitch said. 'I'll let you know—'

'Maybe better if you didn't,' Shaw said, and hung up.

Mitch sat there for a moment on the edge of the bed with the receiver in his hand. He had not expected that. He'd imagined Shaw would be eager to know of his progress.

He took a shower. He shaved, put on his least-wrinkled shirt. It was Sunday, but hotels were hotels. There would be someone there, and he could make a start. He took a notebook, his camera and a couple of rolls of film.

Whatever reservations he might have possessed the previous day had evaporated. This was about Jean, of course, but it was just as much about himself.

He had breakfast at something called the '59 Diner. They served brunch from nine. Politely declining shrimp and Cheddar

141

grits, cornmeal griddlecakes, fried chicken and buttermilk biscuits, he opted for some straight over-easy eggs and a sausage patty. He drank three cups of strong coffee and felt his head arrive from wherever he'd left it the night before.

The Town Plaza was a fifteen-minute cab ride. He thought about taking a bus, maybe hiring a car. Some slight paranoia about leaving tracks, letting others know where he was and who he was speaking haunted him. What was he afraid of? That Jean had in fact been murdered? Such a thought seemed ludicrous, too fantastic for words. So why the hesitancy? Why the urge to conceal his whereabouts? And had he been right with his intuitive feeling about Shaw? Did the man know something he hadn't said? Was that why he'd changed the topic of conversation so abruptly at dinner? Why he'd been so dismissive on the telephone?

Maybe better if you didn't.

Was Shaw afraid, or was his concern merely personal? Had his wife's question – so obviously unwanted – related to something concerning Jean that Shaw didn't want known?

Mitch ignored the noise. He had to keep his mind clear and focused. He could not afford to wander down a dozen different routes. He was here to find out what Jean had been doing, and that was all. He was here to find out if her four days in Dallas had any connection to the events of her death.

The Town Plaza was as he'd imagined it would be. He took a couple of pictures of the facade from across the street, and then walked over. Inside, it was wood paneling, cheap rugs, vinyl furniture. The man behind the reception desk could not have been younger than sixty-five. He had on a white shirt that had seen better days, a jacket with frayed cuffs, and a vest that did not match the suit. Mitch felt a degree of sympathy for him. Did anyone choose to be so employed at such an age?

'Help you, sir?' the man said.

'Hello,' Mitch replied. 'I hope so, but it's maybe a long shot.'

'Well, shoot and let's see, eh?'

'What's your name?' Mitch asked.

'Fred Harman,' the man replied.

'Well, Mr Harman, the thing is this. Last year, November, you remember when the president came to town?'

'I remember it very well indeed, sir,' Harman said. 'Place was packed. Had to take on some temporary staff.'

'Well, during those few days a woman stayed here. She was a journalist from Washington, DC.' Mitch reached into his jacket pocket for the photo Alice had given him.

'Miss Boyd, you mean?'

Mitch's surprise was evident. Harman smiled like he'd won a good poker hand.

'Right,' Mitch said. 'You remember her?'

'Sure I remember her. How could I forget her?'

'Okay ... well, that helps a great deal.'

'You're a friend of hers?'

'Mr Harman ... I'm sorry to say that she passed away.'

Harman frowned. 'What?'

'She's dead, Mr Harman. Jean ... Miss Boyd died just over a week ago in Washington.'

'Oh my Lord,' Harman said. 'That is just the most tragic thing I ever did hear. Such a bright young woman, so charming. She was so wonderfully funny, Mr—'

'Newman,' Mitch said.

'So wonderfully charming and funny, Mr Newman. Oh my Lord, that is just terrible.'

'Yes,' Mitch said. 'It really is terrible, and I'm sorry to have to bring you such news.'

'Might I ask how she died?'

'Well, they're not sure yet,' Mitch said. He just could not bring himself to tell the old man that Jean had committed suicide. 'They have to do the autopsy and all that. They really don't know what happened.'

'Oh my Lord,' Harman said again. He was visibly shaken. Evidently Jean had managed to leave quite an impression on the man.

'So I wondered if you might know what she was working on when she was here,' Mitch said. 'I'm trying to trace her last steps, trying to put together some kind of understanding of the last year of her life ... you know, for her family. Her mother.'

It sounded implausible, but Harman wasn't really listening. He was lost in his memories of Jean Boyd in November of the previous year.

Eventually he looked up. 'She spent a lot of time in bars,' he said.

'Bars?'

'Bars, clubs, you know? Not drinking. Nothing like that. She was working on some kind of story. At least that's what she told me, and I had no reason to disbelieve her.'

'Any particular bars?'

'Not that I remember. There's a lot of bars and clubs downtown, you know? She was looking for someone, I think.'

'Did she mention any names?'

Harman shook his head. 'I don't think so.'

'Civello? Marcello? Rubenstein? Did she mention a girl called Holly?'

Harman looked up. 'She went to the Carousel. I remember that.'

That name had been amongst Jean's notes.

'The Carousel. You're sure?'

'Yes. I remember telling her it wasn't the kind of place I felt she should go, even if she was writing a story.'

'Because?'

144

'Because it's that kind of club, Mr Newman. Girls, you know? I think they call it a burlesque club.'

'Oh. Right. Yes.'

'Anyway, it's downtown. The thirteen-hundred block of Commerce Street. I think it's across the street from the Adolphus Theater, but I couldn't be sure.'

'And she was going there to meet someone?'

'I don't know what she was doing down there, Mr Newman. I didn't really ask her any questions. She was always smiling, always took a moment to ask me how I was. She was a very thoughtful young lady. At least that's how it seemed to me.'

'She was thoughtful, yes,' Mitch said. 'Always very thoughtful.'

'Such a dreadful thing to find out. Such a terrible, terrible shame.'

Mitch could not console the man; he could not even console himself.

'And that was the only name she mentioned, the only place she referred to as far as you can recall?'

Harman smiled weakly. 'My memory is not what it was, Mr Newman. She may have said something else, but nothing that I can remember.'

Mitch took a pen and wrote down the telephone number of his hotel. 'I'll be here for another day or two,' he said. 'If anything comes to mind, please give me a call, would you?'

'Yes. Yes, of course,' Harman said. 'I'm sorry I couldn't be of more help.'

'You've been a great help, and I appreciate it.'

'Well, you take care of yourself, son, and my sympathies for the loss of your friend.'

'Thank you,' Mitch said, and he meant it.

27

The Carousel was as unsubtle and cheap as such places got. Advertising not only *ALL-GIRL • ALL-STAR REVUE • DANCING • BEER • SETUPS*, it also had a *Real Pit Bar-B-Q*. It was right where Fred Harman had said it was, and though the sign read *CLOSED*, Mitch could see there were people inside.

It was past noon. He crossed the street and photographed the club as discreetly as he could. Down the street fifty yards was a diner. He ordered a corned beef sandwich and a cup of coffee. He wanted a little time to gather his thoughts.

Seated in a booth at the back, he made notes regarding the Town Plaza, Fred Harman, the Carousel. He needed to know why a downmarket strip joint had been of interest to Jean. Had she met someone there? Was it Mafia-run, and thus a connection to Joseph Civello, this reputed Dallas mob boss? Was she tracking him down because she believed he could give her something on Kennedy?

There was no way to know unless he started asking questions, and this place was the only solid lead he had.

He finished up his lunch and smoked a cigarette. He walked back up the street to the Carousel and looked for an alleyway or side entrance. As he was doing so, a cab pulled up to the sidewalk and a girl got out. Blonde, five seven or eight, she wore a calf-length fur coat, sunglasses, dark blue high-heeled shoes.

Once she'd paid the driver, she headed for the front door.

'Excuse me, miss,' Mitch said.

The girl stopped, turned, took off her glasses. At first she seemed strikingly pretty, but there was something blunt about her features. Cigarettes and alcohol, a lot of late nights, a lot of parties. The lifestyle would age you five years for every two.

'Miss,' she said. 'Well how's about that?' Her accent was New York, unmistakably. 'Long time since anyone's called me miss, you know?'

Mitch smiled. He liked her right away.

'You work here?' he asked.

She looked put out. 'It's that obvious?'

Mitch felt awkward. 'I'm sorry, I didn't mean...'

The girl started laughing. 'Hell, yes, of course I work here. I'm just kidding with you. Who the hell else is going to show up at a place like this on a Sunday wearing a fur coat and sunglasses?'

She dropped her cigarette on the sidewalk and ground it out beneath her shoe, then took another from the pack in her purse and lit it.

'So, who you after? What's your explanation for hanging out in front of this dive?'

'I was looking for someone who might be able to help me.'

The girl winked salaciously. 'That might be me, sugar... depending on the kinda help you're after.'

'You've been here a long time?' Mitch asked.

'Coupla years, maybe. Why?'

'Were you here last November?'

'Sure was.'

'I had a friend, a journalist from Washington, DC. She was down here last November, stayed at the Town Plaza. She was following up on a story, and I wanted to find out if anyone remembered her.'

The girl seemed puzzled. 'I have no idea, sweetheart. Come on inside and ask the other girls. Maybe they can help you.'

'Thank you,' Mitch said. 'That's really kind of you.'

She smiled. 'A gentleman,' she said. 'Way to a girl's heart is paved with good manners. That's what my mom used to say.'

The girl's stage name was Terri Truelove. Her real name was Sandra Baxter. She hailed from upstate New York, but had spent much of her adult years in Manhattan. She took Mitch through the front of the club, past the stage, out through the side corridor to the dressing rooms in the back. Already there were four other girls there, all carrying that same worn-out and weathered look. Their names were Marion, Patricia, Shirley and Carole. Once they'd been beautiful, and perhaps, if they left the life, they could be beautiful again, but it was doubtful. Where else would they earn this kind of money for so few hours? It was a trap, and they knew it. It was merely a matter of reconciling themselves to the nature of that trap and learning to survive the best they could.

'So,' Sandra said. 'This here is Mitch. Tell your story, Mitch.'

Mitch did so. With Harman, he could not tell the truth. But these girls had seen the rough edges and sharp corners of life. There was nothing that needed to be tempered. He told them that Jean had committed suicide; that they'd once been engaged and now he'd set himself on a mission to find out what had happened to her.

'Well if that isn't the damnedest thing I ever heard,' Patricia said. A brunette, her hair piled high in a beehive, she possessed an air of sadness even when she smiled. She reached out and closed her hand over Mitch's, squeezing it tight, and looked at him with a consolatory expression.

Mitch produced the photograph and they passed it around.

'I remember her,' Marion said. Marion was blonde, her hair in bangs, and she wore the largest gold earrings Mitch had ever seen. 'November. When the president was here.' She laughed suddenly. 'Not *here* here. He didn't actually frequent the Carousel.'

The other girls laughed.

'I remember because it was right around the time Holly left, and your friend was trying to find her.'

'Holly?' Mitch said. It was the name that had been written on the back of Shaw's card.

'She used to work here. Real sweetheart. Too young for this game. Anyway, she upped and left after a month or so.'

'Do you happen to know her surname?'

'Walsh,' Marion said. 'Holly Walsh.'

That was it, right there. *HW at C.* Holly Walsh at Carousel. October and November of 1963.

'Do you know where she was from?'

'Originally?' Marion said. 'Some place out east, I think. She looked like she'd stepped right off the farm.'

'And she was here for a month?'

'A month, maybe six weeks,' Marion said. 'Showed up late September. Stayed through to the third week of November, as far as I can remember. You know pretty much right away if you can do it, but it took a little longer for Holly to see that she didn't belong here, and I think she knew she never would. She was here one day, next day no show, and we haven't seen her since.'

'Did anyone make inquiries?'

Marion shook her head. 'About what? People come and go. That's the nature of this life.'

'So did Jean tell you why she was interested in this girl?'

'She came to see Mr Ruby,' Sandra said. 'Jack Ruby,' she added. 'He's the owner. That's who she wanted to talk to.'

Jack Ruby – the *JR* on the card.

'She wanted to ask him about Holly?'

'I have no idea, sweetheart. You're gonna have to ask him about that yourself, I guess.'

'And where could I find him?'

Marion shrugged. 'He was here on Friday night. He should have been here last night, but he didn't show. Really unusual for him not to be here on a Saturday.'

'You know where he lives?'

'Well, he used to have a place on—' Carole started, but Sandra interrupted her.

'Okay,' she said. 'Let's just take a moment here.' She pinned Mitch with an unerring gaze. 'You seem like a really nice guy an' all, but we don't know the first thing about you. You say you're a friend of this Joan—'

'Jean. Jean Boyd.'

'Sure, Jean. You say you're a friend of this girl, this reporter from Washington, but we don't know that, and we don't know what she was doing down here. Before we start giving out the address of our boss, we'd like a little more certainty. Know what I mean?'

Mitch produced his press card.

Sandra looked it over. 'Sorry,' she said. 'That's not going to do it. I've seen 'em all, sweetheart. Police badges, FBI IDs, you name it.'

Mitch smiled. 'You know, I understand. I really do. It's no big deal. I can track him down some other way. I have a couple of contacts back in Washington, and there's a police detective here who's helping me find out what happened to Jean. I'm not here to cause any trouble for Mr Ruby, and certainly not for you ladies.' He started to get up. 'You've been really helpful, and I'm really grateful.'

He left quickly. He walked left for close on a block and crossed the street. There was something about the place, something about the way Sandra had silenced the other girl. The whole thing had unnerved him. Jack Ruby. This Holly Walsh. The Carousel. The Dallas Mafia and Joseph Civello, perhaps connections into New Orleans, Los Angeles, San Francisco and New York.

What was he getting into, and how many people already knew his name and the reason for his presence in Dallas?

He looked back down the street. It was deserted and quiet.

He needed to get away from here, and he really needed a drink.

28

Monday morning. Just as Mitch was phoning the *Tribune* to ask for someone called Andrews, and discovering – disconcertingly, but somehow not altogether unsurprisingly – that there was no employee of that name, Nelson Shaw was receiving a call at home.

It was the station chief, Victor Webb.

'Nelson, we got a bad one for you.'

'Is there such a thing as a good one?'

'Compared to this, I think that'd be a yes.'

'So what is it?'

'Three weeks, maybe. Some guy in an apartment. Took that long for the neighbors to figure out it wasn't his crappy cooking that was stinking the place up.'

'Just what I need on a Monday morning.'

'Shot in the head. Couple in the torso as well. Looks like a mob hit. I'd send someone else, but I know you've been pining for a good murder for weeks.'

Shaw smiled sardonically. 'Give me the address.'

The building was on Browder, off Commerce. Shaw knew the kind of place it would be – low rent, poor amenities, a fire hazard. The city council and tourist board were busy pitching Dallas as a modern metropolis, but the civic scheme to tear those places down was long overdue. Dallas, whichever way it was upended and shaken out, was still Texas. Texans loved to be hated, and they wouldn't change that for the world. They knew what they had, and they were more than happy to keep it for themselves.

As Shaw was leaving the house, his wife called to him. He'd already said his goodbyes to her and the girls.

He paused in the hallway, hat in hand, and waited for her.

'I just wanted to check you were okay,' Ellen said.

'Okay? How okay?'

'You know, with that newspaper feller here, and everything that happened with the girl who was down here last year.'

'He was just a newspaper guy. She was just a newspaper girl. I deal with people like that all the time.'

'Sure you do. I know that. But one o' them done killed herself, and one o' them followed you home.'

Shaw nodded. It had not been good, and there was no pretending.

'Don't get me wrong,' Ellen said. 'I know being married to a homicide detective isn't always going to be a million kinds of wonderful, but when it turns up on your porch...'

'I know,' Shaw said. He reached out and pulled her close, burying his face in her hair. It smelled of cilantro. How lucky was he? Only once had he forgotten, and he'd regretted it every day since.

'I'll deal with it,' he said.

'I know you will,' Ellen replied. 'Not for me, but for the girls, okay?'

'For all of you.'

She stood in the doorway and waved as he pulled out and headed down the street.

He caught sight of her in the rearview and wondered if he would make it through to retirement. He didn't think of such things often, but every once in a while the idea haunted him. He was a detective. Times were changing. It was a tough city, and the mob had designs on controlling more and more territory. He saw the proliferation of drugs, the increase in stick-ups and bank robberies. It was Texas, after all, and rarely was a man unarmed. If not in the street, then there was always a gun in his car, another in his home. That was the way of things. Maybe one day one of those guns would be pointed at him, and there would be nothing he could do about it. Following close on the heels of having to bury one of your own children, the thought of never seeing them grow up was the very worst of all.

Shaw lit a cigarette and put the radio on. Such ideas belonged nowhere but the dark place from which they'd surfaced.

There were three uniforms and the coroner's wagon at the scene. It was, as he'd expected, a run-down tenement, three floors, an apartment on each. The dead guy was on the third. Had he been on the second, his upstairs neighbor might have complained earlier, but there was a window open in there and the stench of rot and decay had somehow been minimized. However, three weeks in and it had become perceivable from the street.

The smell of a corpse was like nothing else. Fermented, sickly sweet, like shit and rotten meat doused in cheap perfume. Apparently the bacteria clung to nostril hairs and you could find that smell for weeks. It penetrated everything – clothes, skin, your mouth and throat. No matter the number of times you'd smelled it, it was almost impossible to proof yourself against the reflexive need to gag and run.

Shaw stood in the doorway with a handkerchief to his face. The coroner and a couple of his boys were in there. They were not going to move anything until Metro had been down, and they had been waiting a good hour.

Shaw knew the coroner. His name was Harold Russell and he

listened to jazz. Oftentimes he wore a bow tie, and someone at the office said he dated a colored girl. However, Shaw liked the man's sense of humor, and he was as professional as they came.

'We heard about this one a week or so ago, but figured we'd let him ripen for you,' was Russell's opening gambit. He extended his hand. Shaw took it. 'Good to see you, Nelson.'

'Good to see you too, Harold.'

The dead man was seated in an armchair. There appeared to be no primary murder scene, no other scattering or pooling of blood in the vicinity. That alone suggested that the victim had either known his killer, or been taken completely by surprise.

'One entry wound in the face, two in the chest,' Russell said.

'Execution?'

'Perhaps. You're going to have to figure out why someone would want to execute a man like this.'

'You found ID?'

'Over there.' Russell nodded toward the bed.

Shaw took a moment to look at the distended gray-blue features of the dead man. He was maybe five six or seven, a hundred and fifty pounds, and even taking into account the fact that flesh shrank and thus gave the illusion of longer facial hair, this man was still unshaven and unkempt. His clothes were cheap, his apartment untidy and unhygienic, and from the abundance of empty bottles it seemed that he was also a drinker. It appeared to be an undignified end to an ignominious life.

On the bed were laid out a driver's license, a social security card and a wallet. The dead man was one Leland Webster, born in Plano, forty-one years of age as of February 9. The wallet held all of three bucks, a pawnshop stub, an expired union card and a photograph of a brunette with heavy-rimmed glasses and a forced smile.

Shaw set the items down and surveyed the room. It was filthy. What purpose would be served by fingerprinting he did not know, but he had to follow protocol. As if by preordination, a crime scene officer showed up as he was looking over the scene.

'What's your name?' Shaw asked.

'Lansdale.'

'Take the routine shots. Do the glasses in the sink, the edge of the window frame, the door handles, all the usual.'

Lansdale's expression said *Really?*

Shaw smiled understandingly. 'I know, I know, I know,' he said. 'Follow procedure. What are we going to do? Say we didn't much feel like it this time?'

Lansdale, reconciled to his thankless and somewhat futile task, got to work.

Shaw supervised the photographs, asked for close-ups of each bullet wound; also the back of the head where the exit path had left a hole the size of a baseball.

'Close,' he commented to Russell.

'From the burn marks, I'd say no more than six to nine inches. Your slug from there is in the wall. Flat as a dime. No exit wounds from the torso, though. I'll get the slugs out and over to Ballistics as soon as I can.'

'Oh, I can't wait,' Shaw said.

Russell smiled. 'Then I shall take as long as possible just to heighten the anticipation.'

Shaw watched as they went through the laborious process of getting the body onto a stretcher without it bursting open. The smell worsened considerably, and the sight of escaped fluids that had soaked into the armchair was about as much as he could take. It really was not a good way to start a Monday. Not a good way to start a week.

After the body was gone, Shaw saw Lansdale out. He called for another officer and waited until he arrived. Together they taped the door, put up a *POLICE – NO UNAUTHORIZED ENTRY* sign, and closed the place up.

'I hope you're not here for the rest of the day,' Shaw said. 'If only for the smell.'

The officer shrugged. 'No sense of smell. Boxed a good deal when I was younger and it wrecked my nose.'

'Silver lining,' Shaw said, and headed on down to canvass the neighbors.

29

Mitch Newman's inquiries as to the whereabouts of Holly Walsh and Jack Ruby were tinged with a sense of anxiety. That moment at the Carousel had been uncomfortable. Why, he could not say. For the first time, the questions he was asking – what had really happened to Jean Boyd, and what was she looking into before her death – seemed so much greater than a need to satisfy his own curiosity. Nelson Shaw had distanced himself with a simple request not to be kept up to speed on developments, and the girls at the club had been defensive. There was no other word to employ. They had been defensive about their boss, this Jack Ruby, and that smacked of secrets.

Information did not have a listing for Holly Walsh. That did not surprise Mitch. She had come from out of town and stayed only a matter of weeks. The prospect of finding someone that no one really knew anything about in a city like Dallas seemed daunting. Mitch figured that his energies would be better directed toward finding Ruby, and then Ruby could help him find Holly.

He *was* surprised to find no listing for Ruby, however. Dallas Public Library had a newspaper archive, but it was accessible only on Wednesdays and Fridays. Funding cutbacks had limited available staff. Next stop was Dallas City Courts. He arrived there a little after eleven, showed his press credentials and explained that he was researching backstory on Dallas mob connections. The girl was very interested and very helpful. Her name was Caroline Lassiter, and she wore red barrettes that matched her shoes. She walked Mitch back into the records section.

'Arrest cards,' she said, when Mitch asked if there was a means by which he could look over someone's criminal record without actually getting their police file. 'They're all filed here. Of course, the arrest card won't tell you if the person was charged, arraigned or tried. Just when they were arrested, the arresting officer, and what they were arrested for.'

'That'll be enough,' Mitch said.

'And it's alphabetical. A to E down there, F to J over there, and then it goes all the way back to the far wall.'

'And I can just go look myself?'

'Knock yourself out,' Caroline replied, and smiled a winning smile.

Mitch found Ruby without any difficulty. He'd been busy, but it was all small-time stuff. The first recorded arrest was for disturbing the peace in February of 1949. His address was listed as 1717 South Ervay. It was the same address for a July '53 arrest for carrying a concealed weapon, but he gave 1719½ South Ervay when he was arrested for the same charge in May of 1954. The fourth arrest was in December of the same year, this time for violation of the statute liquor laws, again at 1719½. By June of '59, he was giving his home address as 4727 Homer, and was arrested for permitting dancing after hours. A $25 bail bond was issued in August of 1960 when he violated Dance Hall Ordinance #1156.

The seventh and eighth arrests, for simple assault, and then for an alias ticket when he didn't show up to court on a parking violation, had Ruby living at 3929 Rawlins. His dates of birth were variously March 25, 1912, March 25, 1921, and March 19, 1911. He owned a strip joint. He carried a gun. He didn't close up his place on time and he parked too close to the crosswalk. From his arrests, there seemed to be nothing that would justify the degree of defensiveness that Sandra had evidenced at the Carousel. Had he misread her reaction completely? Was she being nothing other than discreet about her boss, and it had merely fed into his own paranoia?

He made notes of all the arrests. 3929 Rawlins was the last known address. That would be his next port of call. He thanked Caroline and headed back toward the library. En route he bought a map of the city. Rawlins was out in Oak Lawn, not far from Love Field. He took a bus this time, and when he arrived, he had some lunch at Whataburger.

The address was easy enough to find. The house was similar to Nelson Shaw's, smaller, less well maintained, nothing out of the ordinary. Mitch took a photograph, and then hesitated before crossing the street.

Why was he there? Very simply, to find out why these people had been of such interest to Jean during her trip the previous November. And if that came to nothing, then what?

There was no point trying to resolve a problem until the problem arose. He would deal with that when it came.

The elderly woman who opened the door at 3929 Rawlins was more than helpful. Mitch got the impression she didn't see a visitor from one week to the next.

'Ruby?' she asked. 'No, no one called Ruby. There was a man called Rubenstein, though.'

'Rubenstein?' Mitch asked, realization dawning.

'Yes. The man who rented the house before me was called Jacob Rubenstein. His mail still comes here. I do have a forwarding address for him, but I just haven't managed to get it arranged.'

'I have to meet with him,' Mitch said, 'and I'd be very happy to take it for you.'

The woman seemed hesitant. 'Well, I'm not so sure,' she said. 'Tampering with the mail is a federal offense.'

Mitch backed off. He didn't want to give the impression that it was of any real significance.

'Well, when I see him, I'll tell him that you have mail for him, and maybe he'll come over and collect it.'

'Yes, yes,' she said. 'I think that would be best.'

'So could you give me his new address, please?'

'I think that would be fine,' she said, and closed the screen door.

She returned within a few moments, and Mitch had his notebook ready.

'Two two three South Ewing,' the woman said. 'It's in Cedar Crest,' she explained. 'Only six or seven miles from here.'

'I could take a bus from near the Tollway, maybe?'

'Oh yes,' she said, and explained where to wait.

Mitch thanked her and set off. He consulted his map before he reached the end of the street, finding South Ewing relatively quickly. The distance was considerably less than six miles, and he decided to walk. He figured he could make it in about forty-five minutes, and it seemed like a good idea to get some fresh air and daylight. He'd spent the last couple of days cooped up in planes, cabs and his motel room.

He tried not to think of his own situation. He tried not to focus on the things he regretted, the things he hadn't said. How many times more could he have said he loved her? How many more letters could he have written? That time at Virginia campus, he could so easily have waited until her friend left and then gone to speak with her. A letter could never take the place of an actual confrontation. He could have convinced her to listen to him, to hear all he had to say, and then – even if she had finally rejected his efforts – he could have walked away knowing that he'd done all he could. That was the crux of it. He struggled to think of any situation in his life to which he'd given everything he was capable of giving. Would that be his epitaph? *Gave half he could; lived half a life.*

He had to resist the temptation of self-pity. It was strong, and it pulled relentlessly. He had been the architect of the situation, and yet he had convinced himself that he was somehow not wholly responsible. Such a viewpoint was idiocy.

Jean used to say: *If you can't trust yourself, then who can you trust?*

Finally, so many years later, he understood what she meant.

He tried to focus on Jean, and what exactly she'd been doing in Dallas. Why had she taken an interest in Jack Ruby and the Carousel? Why had she noted the name of Holly Walsh, and where was this girl right now? Why was this particular girl of greater interest than any of the others who had worked there? Had she just gone home, or did she actually go missing? Did she know something that would help explain Jean's interest, or would Ruby himself be able to shed some light on it?

As he neared his destination, he realized that the need to know what Jean was really doing now ran parallel to the need to know about Jean herself. As if discovering the truth of what she was investigating would explain something about her that he – as yet – had failed to comprehend. He was chasing ghosts, and the ghosts were saying nothing.

223 South Ewing was as ordinary and nondescript as the house on Rawlins. What had he expected? From across the street – once more compelled to take a photograph – the building exuded emptiness and silence.

Even before he knocked on the door, he knew there would be no answer. He was struck with the sudden and inexplicable fear that he might never find Ruby, that his search for the truth of Jean's presence in Dallas would end right here on the porch of an empty house. The idea possessed the same sense of dismay and loss as his memories of Jean.

He headed back to the motel. He was tired, hungry, somewhat disappointed. However, there were rules to this game, and the first one was 'Never quit'.

As he passed through the lobby, the receptionist called him over. He wore a badge that said *Peter*.

'You're Mitchell Newman, right? Number seven.'

'Yes. Yes, I am.'

'Couple of calls for you. One from some guy at ...' Peter reached for a bundle of notes beneath the desk and leafed through them. 'A guy called Byron at the *Washington Tribute*? Is that right?'

'*Tribune*.'

'Sure, yes. Newspaper guy, right?'

'Yes, a newspaper guy,' Mitch replied. Why on earth would Jean's editor be trying to reach him on a Sunday, and how the hell did he know where to call? Mitch had told no one where he was staying.

'There was another call?' he asked.

'Yes, someone called Ellen Shaw. She didn't leave a message. Didn't leave a number. Just said she'd try and call again.'

'Ellen Shaw.' He said it matter-of-factly, registering no surprise. In truth, he was unsettled.

''S what she said,' Peter replied.

'And Lester Byron didn't leave a number either?'

Peter shook his head. He handed Mitch the two messages.

Back in his room, Mitch poured a couple of inches of bourbon and downed it.

The feeling was akin to something crawling beneath his skin.

He didn't like it. Not at all. He poured another drink and put the TV on, but the feeling didn't go away.

30

December 27, 1950
Jean,

Christmas has been and gone. Remember last year, when we walked across the frozen lake, and by the time we got back you couldn't feel your toes? I think of such things, and I feel very little but anger. I am not angry with you. Just myself. I hate how I have made you feel, and I hate the way I feel as a consequence. Nevertheless, whatever is happening, I have brought it upon myself. That much I know.

I do not know what to do with myself. I am working as much as I can, but my drive and motivation has gone. Ironic, but the very passion that compelled me to go to Korea now seems completely absent, as if it was nothing more than a figment of my imagination. I am filling my hours and days with work, but it is work that has no real meaning.

I wish I could tell you what happened, and why I came home. Before I went, I know that I behaved as if you had no right to challenge my decision. To now ask you to challenge your own is not only deeply ironic, but deeply self-serving. I was gone for four months, and yet the hurt I caused you during that time is something I truly believe I can repair. The hurt that I believe both of us might experience if we do not deal with this face to face is something that we will carry for the rest of our lives. Remember how you used to say that 'What if?' was the question with which *to begin your life, not end it? I truly feel that this is one of those moments.*

It is hard for me to admit my pride, my selfishness, my stupidity, but there we are. Those were the things that caused the rift between us, and I would give anything in the world to turn back time and make it good. I say 'anything', knowing that there is one thing I would not sacrifice, and that is you. The irony, once more, is self-evident. Can I ever reconcile myself to the fact that this is how it will always be? Time will tell.

I think of you all the time, and I miss you terribly. I knew that things would not be easy. But I never guessed they would be this hard.

    Mitch

31

Pierre Salinger glanced at Ken O'Donnell. O'Donnell looked at Bobby. They were seated at the table in Salinger's secondary office. Situated close to the Kennedys' personal living quarters, it had once been a laundry and maintenance room, but Salinger was so often needed to deal with out-of-hours situations that it had been refitted.

Walter Lambert stood with his back to the door, as implacable as a cigar store Indian.

'The life of the president is my responsibility,' he said. 'I am the head of the president's security detail, and thus responsible for determining whether the arrangements made for the president and the first family are adequate. No one overrides that, Mr Salinger.'

Lambert was thirty-seven years old. He knew the White House far better than anyone who'd ever lived there. He'd served on Eisenhower's detail for two years, and – by personal request – had headed up Kennedy's detail since inauguration.

'Walter, no one is saying that you have to change anything, but we have the convention in Atlantic City in less than six weeks, and the president and first lady will have to be available on a twenty-four-hour-a-day basis, at least for the last two days. It's the same as the election—'

'I understand that, sir, but during the election the president was not the president.'

Bobby caught Kenny O'Donnell smiling that oh-so-familiar smile. Lambert was a hard-headed, ball-breaking son-of-a-bitch; he was a company man, a by-the-numbers autocrat, but it was doubtful there was a man more suited to the task at hand.

'Walter,' Bobby said, his tone one of accommodation. 'As soon as we have the tour itinerary, you will be the very first person to get a full rundown. As always, you will have complete authority over your own people. Standard protocol does not change. The only thing you will not be able to do is tell us that the president cannot go somewhere where we need him to go.'

'I understand that perfectly well, sir, but I have to say—'

A commotion distracted everyone's attention – voices in the corridor, a sound like a crying child.

Lambert stepped back from the door as someone knocked. Ethel came in, ushering ahead of her a tearful Caroline.

'I'm sorry, Bobby,' she said. She acknowledged Lambert, Salinger and O'Donnell.

'That'll be all for now, Walter,' Bobby said, and got up from his chair.

Lambert left the room and closed the door behind him.

'She won't talk to anyone but her Uncle Bobby,' Ethel said.

Caroline ran across the room to Bobby. He swept her up into his arms and held her.

'Hey, hey, hey, sweetheart,' he said, his voice gentle and comforting. 'What's all this about?'

Salinger got up. Bobby waved his hand for him to stay right where he was, then looked at Ethel, raising his eyebrows.

They're fighting again, Ethel mouthed, and Bobby shook his head resignedly.

He sat down, held Caroline on his lap, and after a minute or so she started to settle.

Ethel stood silently by the door. She was neither embarrassed nor self-conscious. Always poised, always elegant, she was an indomitable island amidst the rough seas that sometimes characterized the Kennedy family's political voyage.

'D-Daddy shouted at me,' Caroline said, her voice hitching. 'He shouted at Mommy and then he shouted at me.'

'There, there,' Bobby said. 'It's okay, sugar. Really, everything is just fine. Your daddy is just tired, okay? He loves you very much indeed. He loves you more than anything in the world. He's just cranky sometimes, that's all. He doesn't mean it.'

Bobby's jacket hung from the back of his chair. He reached back, took a handkerchief from the pocket, and wiped Caroline's eyes.

Ethel stepped forward, held out her hand.

'Come on, Caroline, it's late. Let's get you to bed, okay?'

'But I want to stay with Uncle Bobby.'

Bobby hugged her. 'Uncle Bobby has a little more work to do, darling. I won't be long, okay? You go on with Auntie Ethel and I'll come check on you in a little while. If you're still awake, I promise I'll read you a story, okay?'

Caroline peered up at him with her doe eyes, then slid off his lap. Bobby kissed her forehead, then she took Ethel's hand and they headed out of the room.

There was silence for just a moment.

'We have Walt Lambert protecting the president, but who do we have to protect everyone else from the president?' Salinger said.

Bobby cut him dead with a cold stare. 'Enough,' he said. 'We'll wrap this up another time.'

Neither Salinger nor O'Donnell moved.

'That means we're done, boys,' Bobby said, irritation evident in his voice.

The pair of them stood and headed for the door. As Salinger left the room he said, 'Bobby, I didn't mean—'

Bobby raised his hand. Salinger fell silent.

Alone, Bobby sat for quite some time. Salinger was right. Jack was losing it. Whatever *it* was, he wasn't sure, but things were getting frayed around the edges on so many fronts.

Deciding that there was no time like the present, he went back to the main residence and found his brother in his den.

'Caroline came up to the briefing room in tears,' he said. 'She told me that you yelled at your wife and then you yelled at her.'

Jack looked up from the book he was perusing. There was something both defensive and aggressive in his expression, a cornered animal.

'Are you drunk?' Bobby asked.

'Don't start, Bobby,' Jack said.

'Jack, seriously, we need to figure out what's going on with you. Six weeks until the DNC and we have our own people looking at you sideways.'

'What people? What the hell does that even mean?'

'What it means, dear brother, is that there is a growing sense of doubt that we are still going to be here come Christmas.'

'You think we're going to lose the election?'

'I have actually wondered whether you're even going to get the party's nomination.'

Jack laughed suddenly, and the sound was superior and ugly. The suggestion was beyond preposterous.

'Take a look for a moment, Jack. Really. You think people don't see through the charade sometimes? Okay, so you have your buddy Joe Alsop, and his place over on Dumbarton. You think I don't know how many times you've returned to DC a day earlier than scheduled? And yes, I know exactly what goes on over there.'

'You can't talk to me like this.'

'Jack, I am the *only* person who can talk to you like this. I've got the Secretary of the Treasury allocating petty cash to pay off messengers, doctors, journalists, even these damned women.

You ever ask yourself how long this can go on? Your wife knows, your staff knows, and it's only a matter of time before it's headline news around the world. John F. Kennedy, President of the United States, is fucking anything he likes the look of.'

Jack smiled. He was drunk, for sure. 'Bobby, Bobby, Bobby—'

'No, Jack. Listen to what I'm telling you for one goddam minute, would you?'

Jack leaned back in his chair. He exhaled, and then waved his hand as if granting indulgence to his younger brother.

Bobby looked at him. The photographs did not convey the truth. Jack had aged years in just a few months. Behind the facade of Camelot was a lonely, embittered queen and her arrogant, unfeeling husband. The charm and grace of the first lady, the strong and resilient head-of-state charisma of Jack that so epitomized the world's impression of them was a sham. Jack's skin was tired and jaundiced, his hair prematurely graying. That bright and unrelenting gaze that had commanded attention and admiration from senators, congressmen, foreign ministers and ambassadors, even kings and queens of other nations, now seemed like the dull eyes of a trapped animal. Once upon a time Jack had been Bobby's role model, the standard to which he aspired. Now his older brother was the very last person in the world he wished to be.

'Since Dad's stroke, you've spiraled out of control,' he said. 'You know what he would say if he knew what was going on, right? We're both a goddam disappointment. He wanted Joe Junior, the all-American fighter pilot hero, to be president. You know that, I know that, and ever since Joe died we've been trying to catch his coat tails. You don't think I feel it? I have it right here,' he placed his hand over his heart, 'but I don't look for compensation with sluts and whores.'

'Enough, Bobby, really—'

'No, Jack. We're having this conversation, and we're having it right now.'

Jack shook his head and closed his eyes. He leaned his head back and slowly exhaled.

'Nixon's people are still challenging the election result. We know exactly what they're after and where it's buried. This administration has an army of skeletons. If they can't get you on the election, they'll get you on finance, and if they can't get you on that, they'll figure out some way they can impeach you on moral grounds. The DNC is happening in Atlantic City in six weeks, and it's gonna take a great deal more than a few comforting words to get this party reinvigorated. If ever you needed internal support, it's now and right through until November. The way you're behaving, the way you're treating Jackie and the kids—'

'My family is my business—'

'No, goddammit! No, it's not! How can you be so blind? Your family is America's family, for God's sake. This isn't some God-given privilege, Jack. You earn it, and you keep on fighting for it every single goddam day. And the longer you're in office, the harder you have to fight, because you inevitably stack up failures and opposed bills and public relations situations, and if there's one thing the press love to get their hands on, it's a public officer derelict in his duty.'

'You think I'm derelict? What about everything we've achieved?'

'Sure, like the conquering commander who returns to Rome in glory. He wears the laurels, Jack, but he better not rest on them. You know, they would have a parade through the streets, and right there, behind the commander's shoulder, was a public slave. He was there to remind the commander that despite all the adulation and celebration, he was still a mortal.'

'The *memento mori* . . . I know my Roman history, Bobby.'

'Well you're not the conquering hero right now, Jack, and you haven't been for quite some time.'

Jack hoisted himself up in his chair and gripped the arms to steady himself.

'You want me to apologize for shouting at Caroline? You want me to treat my wife with more respect? Fine. I can do that.'

'Jack, you're being an asshole. Deal with your family whichever way you see fit, but I am here to talk about your presidency, the election, and most important of all, the DNC in six weeks' time.'

'I have it under control.'

'What the hell does that even mean?'

'You think I don't know what people want? I have a pledge for them that will give me another four years, I guarantee you.'

'What pledge?'

'I will get us out of Vietnam, Bobby. I am going to promise the American people that by the time my second term is done, we will not only have completely withdrawn from Vietnam, but that war will have been won hands-down, no contest, by this great United States of America.'

Bobby looked at his brother as if he'd lost his mind completely.

'You're crazy,' he said. 'You can't make a promise like that. Have you even the faintest clue what's going on over there?'

'What's going on over there and what people think is going on over there are not the same thing, Bobby. You tell the voting public what the voting public want to hear and you will get their vote. It's not complicated.'

'There is no way in the world you could ever effectively challenge a rebuttal on that. You still have to do the public debates. You still have to fight an election. You promise something like that and you might as well just write your own resignation state-ment for CBS to air.'

Jack laughed. 'Oh ye of little faith.'

'Faith has absolutely nothing to do with it! This is polit-ical suicide. You're selling us out. You're selling out the whole goddam country! Have you forgotten Vienna? The Berlin Wall? You're juggling sticks of dynamite and telling yourself it's candy cane. You make a promise like that and fail to deliver, what do you think is going to happen in Europe? You think the Russians haven't got their eyes on a great deal more than East Germany? What the hell are you thinking?'

'What am I thinking? I am thinking about this country, the millions of lives we are responsible for! You don't sit in the Oval Office and make the decisions. You don't deal with the Bay of Pigs and Khrushchev and de Gaulle and Christ only knows who else. You don't have to explain Berlin and the communist infiltration of Southeast Asia. You don't have to do any of that. I do! This is my presidency, and it would be most appreciated if you would understand that for just one goddam minute and let me take care of it!'

Bobby could not believe what he was hearing. Jack had lost control of his senses. He was talking crazy. Four years to get out of Vietnam, and with the war won? It was utter insanity.

'You're drunk,' he said.

'Leave me alone. Go make some more babies, why don't you? If you keep going at this rate, you can fill the Senate with your offspring.'

'You are a son-of-a-bitch—'

'And you are my kid brother, so go to hell.'

Bobby walked to the door. He stood there for a moment looking back.

'If you have something to say, just say it,' Jack said. 'If not, leave.'

Bobby gritted his teeth. He knew that nothing he could say would even be heard.

Closing the door behind him, he walked down the hallway. His mind was reeling. He felt the world closing in around him. He knew that something drastic had to be done before that world collapsed and buried them all.

32

July 14, 1964

Before leaving the motel, Mitch called Lester Byron at the *Tribune*.

'Lester, it's Mitch. You called me yesterday.'

'I did, yes.'

There was silence for a few moments, and then they both spoke at once.

'I wanted to—'

'How did you know where—'

'Go ahead, Mitch … please.'

'I just wanted to know how you found me,' Mitch said.

'The police told me.'

'The police?'

'Yes. They came to see me, asked me some questions about Jean, asked if I had spoken with you, what questions you had. Just general matters. I guess it's all part of the routine investigation after … well, a suicide, you know?'

'And they told you I was here?'

'They gave me the name of your motel, yes.'

'Why would they do that? More importantly, how did they know?'

'I have no idea how they knew. Why they told me where you were is very simple. They've tried to reach you and haven't succeeded. They wondered whether you were perhaps unwilling to talk to them. They merely suggested that I call you, that you might speak to me.'

'But they haven't tried to contact me,' Mitch said. 'No one from the police has called me here.'

He could hear the bemusement in Lester's voice as he said, 'Well I don't know anything about that. I shouldn't imagine the police would be in the business of lying about such a matter. Anyway, more to the point, they wanted you to know that the investigation into Jean's death is coming to a conclusion, and there will be a statement issued by the city coroner. After that, arrangements can be made for her funeral.'

'And the police contacted you to ask you to tell me that?'

'Er, yes.'

'And they want me to call them?

'They didn't say that, no.'

'Who was it that came to see you? What were their names?'

'I don't know that I remember their names, Mitch. There were two of them. Franks, I believe ... I think one of them might have been called Detective Franks.'

'And did they say where they were from? Which precinct? Which division?'

'I don't really understand why you're so surprised by this. All that happened is that the police asked me to forward a message as they believed you might be more responsive to a call from me, and the fact that you called me back justifies their assumption.'

'Okay, Lester. Thanks for passing on the message.'

'You're welcome, Mitch. Is everything okay?'

'As can be, considering the circumstances.'

'Of course, of course. Well, you take care, okay?'

'Sure thing,' Mitch replied, and hung up.

He sat there on the edge of the bed. How the hell had they found him? There was only one possible way. Nelson Shaw had called DC and told his colleagues there that he was down in Dallas asking questions.

He gathered up his notebook and his camera. He had intended to call Ellen Shaw, but he wanted to speak to her husband before anything else. Jack Ruby could wait a little longer. There was enough to warrant his paranoia now, and he needed answers.

On the way out, he spoke to Peter.

'Aside from the two messages yesterday, has anyone else tried to contact me here?'

'Not that I know of,' Peter replied. 'Of course, I'm not here all the time, but any messages are written down and left here.' He held up a bundle of handwritten notes.

'Is there any possibility someone left a message and it wasn't written down?'

Peter shook his head. 'I wouldn't think so. The manager's really strict on that. Every message gets written down.'

'Okay. Thanks, Peter.'

'Mr Newman?'

Mitch turned back.

'Is everything okay?'

He paused, frowned. 'Why do you ask that?'

'It's just you seem really agitated.'

'Something bad happened to a friend of mine,' Mitch replied.

'I'm sorry to hear that. Are you in some kind of trouble?'

'I don't know, Peter. I really don't know if I'm in trouble or not.' He laughed, suddenly, spontaneously. It was a ridiculous situation. Things were happening that he couldn't explain, and he was alone in a strange city chasing people he couldn't find, while being followed by people who had no business following him.

He wanted to know why Ellen Shaw had called him. And he really wanted to know why Nelson Shaw had told the cops in DC where he was.

He took a cab to the Dallas Metro PD building. He was spending a small fortune on cab fares. If he was going to stay much longer, it would make sense to rent a car.

Shaw was on duty and in the building, but Mitch was told he was not available to see anyone.

'I'll wait,' he told the desk sergeant.

'Guess you'll be waiting a long time,' the sergeant replied.

There was a phone booth on the street. Mitch headed out there and looked up Shaw's home number. Ellen answered almost immediately.

'Mrs Shaw, it's Mitch Newman. You called me at the motel.'

She was silent for a moment. There was a palpable tension.

'Mr Newman,' she said. 'I just wanted to tell you ... to tell you that I don't want you to come to the house again. My family is my business. My personal life should not be disturbed as a result of my husband's work.'

'Yes,' Mitch replied. 'I really am sorry about—'

'I'm not upset with you, Mr Newman. I appreciate that you're trying to understand what happened to your friend, but I don't want you to come here again.'

'Mrs Shaw, I—'

'That's all I wanted to say, Mr Newman. Goodbye now.'

The line went dead.

The woman had sounded afraid. What had happened after he'd left? And why had Shaw cut his wife off so abruptly when she'd mentioned Jean's presence in Dallas the previous November?

A further sense of unease invaded Mitch's thoughts. Had something happened back in November that Ellen Shaw didn't want known?

He went back into the precinct house.

'I need to speak with Detective Shaw,' he told the sergeant.

'I do understand that, Mr Newman, but like I said, Detective Shaw is otherwise engaged.'

'This is urgent. It's about Detective Shaw's wife.'

The sergeant frowned. Mitch glanced at his name badge and said, 'Sergeant Ryan, please put a call through to wherever Detective Shaw is and tell him that I just got off the phone to his wife, Ellen.'

Ryan pointed to a bank of seats against the wall. 'You go sit there.'

Mitch watched as Ryan made a call. It was brief. Within a minute, Shaw appeared on the stairwell at the far left side of the lobby. He indicated for Mitch to follow him. It wasn't until they were in an interview room on the first floor that he spoke.

'You are beginning to annoy me,' he said. 'Actually, that's an understatement. You are making me very angry.'

Mitch didn't respond.

'Did you call my wife?'

Mitch nodded. 'Yes, I did.'

Shaw closed his eyes, tilted his head to one side and took a deep breath. Mitch could see his knuckles whitening as he clenched his fists. 'And why, might I ask, did you call my wife, Mr Newman?'

'Because she called me.'

Shaw opened his eyes. 'She called you,' he said, his tone one of disbelief.

'Yesterday. At my motel. She called but I wasn't there. I just returned her call.'

'And you spoke to her?'

'Yes.'

Shaw sat down, motioned for Mitch to follow suit. 'What did she want?'

'She told me not to come to the house again. She told me that my business with you should not interrupt her personal life.'

'She's right.'

Mitch took a gamble. 'She may very well be right, but that wasn't what she meant.'

There was silence between them.

'So?' he prompted.

'So what?'

'So what happened after I left? Why, all of a sudden, after her generous hospitality, did she call me and tell me not to come to the house again?'

'I can't be held responsible for what my wife might think and do, Mr Newman. You came to the house. What was she going to do? Throw you out? She was hospitable because that's her nature. Now she's asked you not to come again, and I would very strongly recommend that you abide by that request.'

Shaw was defensive. Mitch was more convinced than ever that he was hiding something.

'What really happened last November, Detective Shaw?' he asked. 'What happened with Jean that your wife knows about or suspects?'

'What the hell—'

'I know something happened. You cut her short when she mentioned Jean. Now she's asked me to not to come to the house again. She was afraid, Detective. She sounded anxious, like she was really worried... or maybe you said something to her?'

Shaw's split-second hesitation gave up his hand as clearly as laying it on the table.

'You and Jean...' Mitch said.

'No,' Shaw said emphatically. 'It was not what you think it was.' He looked unerringly at Mitch. It was disconcerting. He looked at him and just kept on looking, like he was trying to see right through him and out the other side.

'Did you and Jean have an affair, Detective Shaw? Is that what happened? Is that what you don't want your wife to know?'

'I have nothing to say to you,' Shaw said. 'I don't have to answer any questions or explain anything or justify anything to you.'

'Sure you don't, but if I go to your section chief or the captain of this precinct and tell him that you were inappropriately involved with a journalist from Washington who has subsequently taken her own life...'

Shaw raised his hand. 'Enough,' he said. 'Don't say another goddam word, Newman. Really, I am not kidding around.'

'Nor am I, Detective,' Mitch said. He felt angry. He believed he'd been misled and lied to. He was convinced that Shaw knew a great deal more about Jean than he'd revealed. What he felt about the possibility that Jean might have been romantically involved with the cop was something he would have to consider in his own time.

There was another tense and uncomfortable silence between them. Mitch knew that, just as in most stand-offs, he who spoke first would lose.

'Are you a man of your word, Mr Newman?'

It was a telling question. Had he been asked the same thing two weeks earlier, he might very well have given a different answer.

'Absolutely,' he replied, without a moment's hesitation.

'And so am I,' Shaw replied. He paused. 'At least I am now...'

Again Mitch said nothing.

'You are not to speak to anyone,' Shaw said. 'No one must know what you have just implied. You are not to contact my wife, nor anyone else in this or any other building that may be connected to my work and career.'

'What did you do, Detective Shaw?'

Once again, that same resolute gaze that pinned Mitch to his chair. Shaw possessed a forbidding presence.

'You give me your word that whatever you find out concerning Jean does not get back to my wife.'

It was like being hit in the face, right out of left field. Mitch had suspected, but Shaw had just given him a confession. In that moment, he could not respond, he could not think, and he had no idea what to feel. What could he possibly say? He had let Jean go all those years before, and thus he was the very last person to make judgments about her personal life.

For now, until he had time to process this revelation, he forced himself to think about the real reason for allying himself with Shaw.

'And what do I get for keeping my mouth shut?' he asked.

'My help,' Shaw said.

'To find out what happened to her?'

Shaw nodded.

'Okay.' Mitch took a deep breath. 'Did the two of you have an affair?'

'I am answering no questions about my personal involvement with Jean Boyd, Mr Newman. Her death, yes, but nothing else.'

'But—'

Shaw shook his head. 'But nothing. A deal is a deal. You said you were a man of your word; I expect you to uphold it.'

'I will. And in return, you're going to tell me what you know.'

'You're a journalist. I am going to tell you what I'm willing to tell you.'

'I haven't come here as a journalist. I came here as her friend.'

Neither man spoke for a moment, as if each was evaluating his approach to this new relationship.

'I need to talk to people and I can't find them,' Mitch finally said.

'And who are these people?'

'A girl named Holly Walsh, and a local businessman called Jack Ruby. His real name, as far as I can tell, is Jacob Rubenstein.'

Shaw's shock was evident.

'What?' Mitch asked.

'Ask me who I was interviewing when you had me called down to the lobby.'

Realization dawned.

'That's not possible,' Mitch said.

'Anything is possible, Mr Newman.'

'You have Ruby here in the precinct house?'

Shaw nodded. 'A gun that is registered to him was used in a killing.'

'Has he been charged?'

'Not yet.'

'I was out at his club,' Mitch said.

'The Carousel?' Shaw said the name with familiarity, and Mitch jumped on it.

'You knew who he was all along. You knew who he was when I asked about him at your house. What the hell is this, Shaw? Jean was looking for him, and you didn't tell me.'

Shaw responded with measured calmness. 'I'm a detective here in Dallas, Mr Newman. This is what I do. I am aware of a great many things about this city and its people that I would not share with you. Mr Ruby is now part of an ongoing investigation into a first-degree murder—'

'I want to speak to him.'

'That won't be possible.'

'You agreed to help me find out what happened to Jean. She was after Ruby when she was here. She was also trying to find a girl called Holly who worked at Ruby's club around the time that Jean was in Dallas. If Jean was after Ruby, then maybe he knows something that might help me find out what happened to the girl, and also why Jean killed herself; and that, whether you like it or not, is part of the deal.'

'Not now.'

'When?'

'Maybe when we're done with him.'

'I need more than a maybe, Shaw.'

'Okay, okay,' Shaw said. He looked away. He was evidently under considerable stress. 'How the hell I'm going to explain this, I really do not know. Hell, you shouldn't even be here. You certainly shouldn't know that we have Ruby.'

'Well, I do,' Mitch said matter-of-factly. 'We're not going backwards on this.'

'If I can see that it won't materially influence our investigation or jeopardize the successful resolution of the murder case, then yes, I will let you speak to him. However, anything he tells you will be off the record. You are trying to find out what happened to Jean, not write a newspaper article. Agreed?'

'Agreed,' Mitch replied.

'Go back to your motel,' Shaw said. 'Stop digging, stop asking questions.'

'I have one more question for you,' Mitch said. 'I got a call from Jean's editor at the *Tribune*. He said that the police had been to see him about her. He said they gave him my where-abouts. That could only have come from you.'

'It did, yes.'

'Why would you give my whereabouts to the police in DC?'

'Because they asked.'

'The DC cops called you and asked if I was down here?'

'Yes, Mr Newman, they did.'

'And you didn't find that strange?'

Shaw didn't reply. He glanced away for just a moment, as if he didn't wish to acknowledge the question.

'You're walking along a very fine tightrope,' he said. 'Don't even think about looking down. You've made your decision, and you're going to have to deal with the consequences of that, just like Jean had to.'

'You're telling me that—'

'I'm telling you nothing except to go back to your motel and wait for me to call you. I don't know when that will be. Hopefully not too long. Be patient. I know that's hard for you. You're like a short-fuse grenade. You need to slow down on this. You need to bide your time. I will call you. Until then, do nothing.'

With that, Shaw opened the door and left the room.

Mitch Newman sat there feeling like some vast abyss had opened up before him, and he was teetering on the very edge.

33

January 4, 1951
Jean,

There is no country as shadowed as that of a man's heart. *I read that today in a book of poetry. Another line came home to me: it is the simple acts of kindness that keep the darkness at bay. I can see now – only now – how unkind I was to you. More than that, I was unkind to what we had created together. Our relationship was important – far more important than I ever understood. Why is it that so often you only realize what you had when it is no longer there?*

When I was a child, my father used to tell me that people never reach the end of their lives and regret the things they did. They only regret the things they did not do. I did not love you enough. I did not trust you enough. I did not keep the promises I'd made about the future we'd planned together. And now that my words don't seem to be reaching you, I regret not saying whatever needs to be said to get you to hear me.

Reply, I beg you. Tell me what you think and feel, and if those are the last words I ever hear from you, then so be it.

Even though I deserted you, I am asking that you don't desert me.

Mitch

34

Mitch did not hear from Shaw for two days.

He did not dare upset the arrangement by harassing the cop with calls. He knew that he had merely scratched the surface of what Shaw knew, and Shaw was the only person in Dallas who was likely to help him.

The question foremost in his mind was: *Why?* Shaw had withheld information about Jean, and Mitch did not doubt there were further revelations. His first instinct was now more than a suspicion. Shaw and Jean had had an affair, even if only briefly. Did Ellen know? Shaw did not think so, but that did not necessarily mean she didn't. Mitch doubted it, however. Had she known, her question regarding Jean at the dinner table would have been tinged with far more anger and bitterness. Having said that, Mitch knew nothing of these people. It was all assumption and supposition. A day alone in a motel room, the boredom interspersed with nothing but restaurant visits and trips to the liquor store, gave him more than enough time to feed his own uncertainties and paranoia.

What he did know as a result of this discovery was that his feelings for Jean were different. Having thought of her forever as the girl he knew, he now appreciated that she had changed just as much as himself, if not more. She had gone on to lead her own life, deal with her own emotions, meet new people, form new relationships. He could now see that the notion that she had held onto her past with him as ardently and regretfully as he himself had done was pure fiction. Sure, Alice said that she'd never really gotten over him, but that was Alice's perception, perhaps even what Jean wanted her mother to think.

No. Life had gone on, and Jean had gone with it. Of that he felt sure. Such a thought would once have upset him – the idea that she could walk away, however slowly – but now it was different. In a strange way it served to resolve some of the loss, for he could see that she had in fact recovered more of herself than he'd imagined. Though her life had been cut drastically short, she had lived far more fully than he himself had done.

Her presence had always inspired him to greater accomplishments. Even now, no longer part of his life, no longer part of any life at all, she still managed to generate the same impetus and motivation.

As for Shaw, the question was: *Why had he turned?* Why was he now willing to cooperate with Mitch, if indeed that was the case? After twenty-four hours and no word from the detective, Mitch was beginning to suspect that Shaw had fobbed him off with a hollow promise, and that he would never contact him again. Meanwhile, he would resolve whatever situation might have existed between himself and Jean Boyd – with his superiors, with his wife – so that Mitch no longer had any leverage over him.

There was another possibility, and this unsettled Mitch even more. Shaw, knowing a great deal more than Mitch even imagined, understood that Jean's death could not have been suicide. Wanting to know the truth, and yet not wishing to be in the firing line, he saw Mitch as a means by which further investigation could be undertaken that would compromise him neither professionally nor personally. Mitch Newman was nothing but a scapegoat. He could be manipulated and maneuvered from a distance, used to find things out, and Shaw himself could deny any and all involvement. There was nothing in writing. Phone calls had not been recorded. If Ellen sided with her husband, which he had no doubt she would, Mitch could not even prove that he'd been to Shaw's house.

By Thursday morning, Mitch had had enough of silence and oppressive thoughts. Any way he looked at it, he could not see how to make progress in finding Holly Walsh without registering an official missing persons report. But on what basis could he do that? He did not know her. She was a name on a business card. The girls at the Carousel had not been able to tell him where she came from, and none of them had heard a word from her since her departure. Perhaps Jack Ruby knew what had happened to her – if anything had in fact happened to her – but he was in custody, and Mitch could not reach him save by going through Shaw. He did not know where Holly had lived, nor in which hotel she might have stayed, and there was no one else he could think of that could help.

Notwithstanding the fact that Shaw might call him, he had to get out. If motel management policy was as Peter had said, then any message would be received and relayed.

He left just after ten and went to the city library. He wanted to understand more about Jean's pursuit of Kennedy. Ahead of anything else she might have been investigating, Kennedy had been the primary reason for her trip to Dallas. Mitch needed to better appreciate why the man had become a subject of such interest. He was certainly in the news, that was for sure. The questions that Jean had been asking about the legitimacy of the electoral count in 1960 were now being asked on television. Nixon was evident in his absence, despite the vocal nature of the Republicans on the subject.

In the newspaper archives, there was little coverage beyond

the usual concerning the election itself, the inauguration and the beginning of Kennedy's presidency. What Mitch did find, however, was a raft of articles about the president's handling of the Vietnam crisis, the Bay of Pigs and the civil rights movement. For an administration only three years in the White House, it had certainly not been short of drama and challenges.

The situation regarding 'military advisors' in South Vietnam seemed to be garnering attention, if only from the perspective of cost to the taxpayer. From what Mitch could see, the Kennedy administration was inextricably embroiled in a war that could not be won, but – more importantly – in a political and cultural backlash that appeared to be growing ever more tense and difficult.

After two or three hours of reading and taking notes, his perspective had widened. Of course, he understood that both Democratic- and Republican-slanted opinions were represented in the press reports, and there were those who very much wanted to shatter the illusion of the 'House of Camelot' idealism that the Kennedys had created. John Kennedy as captain of an unsinkable ship, the elegance and poise of the first lady, the seeming perfection of the first family – all was under considerable scrutiny. There were rumors of ill-health and extramarital affairs, none of which were substantiated, but – as was so often the case – a rumor could often do great damage. An outright allegation could be challenged, defended, attacked, disproved. Hearsay could spread like wildfire and there was little that could be done to stop it. Kennedy was a man under the microscope, and he would have to work very hard indeed to convince voters that he was capable of winning another election.

From what Mitch could surmise, Jean had been following the allegations that Joe Kennedy had funded a rigged election. Certainly the Kennedy patriarch, with money from interests in the movie industry and all that he'd made after the repeal of

Prohibition, would have had no difficulty funding anything, but paying for his son to be president? Was that even possible?

And now, with that very son perhaps proving himself inadequate to the task, there seemed to be some doubt in the Democratic camp that John Kennedy would survive another election. Would he stand down at the Democratic National Convention in August? And if he did, who would stand in his place as the party's presidential nominee? Lyndon Johnson? Hubert Humphrey?

Leaving the library in the late afternoon, Mitch took a long walk around downtown Dallas. He had been in the city for six days. He was tired – mentally, more than physically – and he was short of money. With what he had, he could perhaps last another week, and then he would have to go back to ... to what?

He stopped right there on the sidewalk. For a moment he struggled to think of any real reason to return to Washington aside from Jean's cat. With his line of work, he could work anywhere. He did not own an apartment, he had a car worth little more than scrap. The most valuable thing he possessed was his camera, and that was with him.

The moment was akin to an unwanted epiphany.

He stood for nothing, he fought for nothing, he was challenged by nothing.

There was an old adage: the man who lives forever is he who has planned his tomorrow.

If that was true, then his life expectancy was perhaps a week.

Whether he wished to believe it or not, Jean's death had given him purpose and resolve, the very purpose and resolve that had taken him out to Korea. She had somehow, yet again, managed to propel him out of his self-imposed complacency.

With her death, he had discovered more about how much she meant to him than he'd ever understood while she was alive.

Mitch wanted a drink. He *needed* a drink.

He took the bus halfway, then walked to his motel.

A message awaited him. Shaw had called and said that he could meet with Jack Ruby on Friday morning. How he had swung that, Mitch almost did not wish to know. Jean had wanted to speak with Ruby, had perhaps met him, found out what she was after, and now he had a chance to find out as well.

Regardless of the consequences, nothing would stop him from making that appointment.

35

'This never happened,' Shaw said. It was his greeting on Friday morning. He and Mitch were sitting in the same interview room as their first meeting at Metro.

'Then why are you letting it?'

'Because, like you, I have to know,' Shaw said, 'and I can't ask questions.'

'Because you've been told not to ask?'

'I'm saying nothing. All I'll say is that I've used up any leverage I might have had around here.'

'So what's happening with Ruby? Has he been charged yet?'

'Yes. We charged him last night, but only so we could keep him. He's said nothing. He doesn't deny the gun is his. He also isn't denying that he knew the victim, though he says it was only socially.'

'And the victim was ...?'

'Leland Webster. Forty-one years old. Coroner said he died around the beginning of the third week of June. Unmarried. Blue-collar guy. No criminal record. Took jobs here and there. Last place of employment was the Texas School Book Depository. It's a warehouse on Elm Street.'

'And does there seem to be any motive for Ruby to kill this guy?'

'Not that we know of, no.'

'Any prior connection?'

'Tenuous. According to unsubstantiated reports, Webster was a member of a communist splinter group. All that pro-Castro, anti-government stuff. Small-time. We found boxes of handouts in his apartment. Looks like he wasn't very active. Anyway, there was a meeting, perhaps several meetings, of this crowd in one of the upper floors of the Carousel a while ago. That's unsubstantiated, and Ruby won't confirm or deny it. He's saying nothing, like I said. And if we don't get something better than the circumstantial evidence of his gun being the weapon of choice, then the DA will throw it out. We need something, and we're getting nothing.'

'Jean was at the Carousel. I went there, spoke to some of the girls. They remembered her. She was after Ruby, and she was also trying to find out about this girl Holly.'

Shaw said nothing.

'What does Ruby's lawyer say?'

'He doesn't have one.'

Mitch frowned. 'How can he not have a lawyer?'

'Refused one, even a public defender. He put it in writing. He doesn't want a lawyer.'

'That makes no sense.'

Shaw shrugged his shoulders. 'Don't ask me why. I have no answers for you.'

'Is that another reason for letting me see him? That he might talk to me because I'm not a cop?'

'Maybe,' Shaw said. 'Ruby's been around a while. He's been arrested a few times. Nothing serious, though. How much he knows about due process is anyone's guess. We're not telling him a thing beyond the fact that he's booked on a Murder One. He's scared, but defensive. He's backed into a corner. I think he knows a great deal more than he's saying. What he's waiting for, I don't know.'

'Are you going to sit in?'

'No, but I'll hear you. We have an interview room with a listening system.'

Mitch got up from his chair. 'So let's find out if he knew Jean.'

At five-eleven, Mitch was a good couple of inches taller than Ruby. Ruby was dressed in charcoal pants and a creased white shirt. He had no belt, no tie, and he hadn't shaved for a couple of days. He looked tired and agitated, but somehow reconciled to whatever fate had befallen him.

Mitch had been in the room for a good ten seconds before Ruby said, 'Who the hell are you?'

'Mitchell Newman.'

'That's your name, not who you are.'

'I'm a photographer. I cover crime scenes, general reporting.'

'You took the pictures... this guy they're saying I killed?'

'No, I didn't.'

Ruby walked forward and sat down at the table. 'So what's the deal? They're gonna kill me in here, call it a suicide, and you're gonna take the snaps? You're like that Fellig guy, right? The one who took pictures of all those dead people and no one could ever figure out how he got there just at the right time.'

Mitch smiled. 'No, I'm not like that guy, Mr Ruby.' He sat down facing the man, took out a pack of cigarettes and offered them.

Ruby hesitated. He was on edge.

Mitch took a cigarette, lit it, left the pack and his lighter on the table. 'I'm here to ask you some questions, but they're not to do with this present situation.'

Ruby frowned. Suspicion was etched into every angle of his expression.

'I have an idea that you and I might have something in common.'

'Is that so? And what might that be?'

'Before I tell you, I'm curious as to why you have no lawyer.'

'Why do I need a lawyer?'

'You've been charged with first-degree murder.'

Ruby's expression didn't change.

'You do understand that, right?'

Ruby nodded.

'So why no lawyer?'

'You think I whacked this Leland Webster guy?'

'I don't think anything. I'm not interested in Leland Webster.'

'Man gets a lawyer if he needs the law to protect him. That man's already sayin' he's broken the law.'

'You're saying you didn't kill Webster.'

'You know I am.'

'They have your gun.'

'I'm not denying it's my gun.'

'Ballistics says it was the murder weapon.'

'Ballistics can say whatever they want about the gun. They can't say who pulled the trigger.'

'Are you concerned they'll railroad you?'

Ruby took one of Mitch's cigarettes. He lit it, leaned back, and sighed. 'I'm sayin' nothin'.'

'Are you protecting someone else?'

Ruby smiled. 'You are a goddam cop. What is this bullshit?'

'I'm not,' Mitch said. 'Do I look like a cop? I am who I said I am. I went to your club to speak to you. I went to your old house on Rawlins. A woman there told me you'd moved to Cedar Crest, so I went there as well. I've been looking for you since Monday.'

Ruby didn't reply. He just looked at Mitch as if trying to read between the lines.

'I'm here on a personal matter, and the fact that they're letting me talk to you has nothing to do with whether or not you killed Leland Webster.'

'Everything is about whether or not I killed Leland Webster.'

'Meaning what?'

'Meaning nothing. Meaning everything. You don't know me, and I don't know you. You have no idea why I'm here, and you have no idea why Webster is dead.'

'So tell me.'

Ruby laughed dismissively. 'I ain't got nothin' to hide.'

'Everyone has something to hide, Mr Ruby.'

Again Ruby's expression did not change.

'I want to ask you about something that happened last November,' Mitch said.

Had he not been watching Ruby intently, he would not have noticed the flicker in the other man's eyes. He'd reacted, there was no doubt about it, and for just the briefest of moments there was a flash of anxiety there. Mitch stayed quiet and waited.

'What about last November?' Ruby asked, and there was a feigned nonchalance in his voice.

'Someone came looking for you.'

'What can I say? I'm a popular guy.'

'This was one very specific person,' Mitch said. 'Someone I knew. Her name was Jean Boyd.'

Ruby ground his cigarette into the ashtray. Mitch felt sure it was a way of avoiding eye contact.

'You remember her, Mr Ruby?'

'Maybe.'

'Your name is in her notes. She wanted to talk to you about something to do with the Kennedys.'

There was that same flash of fear in Ruby's eye, this time unmistakable. Mitch saw it, and Ruby knew he had.

'Tell me about Jean Boyd, Mr Ruby.'

'I'm tellin' you nothin'.'

'You met her, didn't you?'

Ruby stayed silent.

'You met her and she asked you questions about the election. Why would she ask you about that? Why would someone like you, a strip-joint owner, be of interest to a Washington DC journalist?'

'You are jumping to a lot of conclusions.'

'Am I?'

Ruby leaned forward, placed his hands flat on the table as if to emphasize his immovability. 'Ain't nothin' in this life comes for free, buddy.'

'I'm not asking for anything for free.'

'Okay.' Ruby leaned back, crossed his arms. 'Say if I answered some of these questions, what you gonna put on the table for me?'

'I have nothing to offer, but right now, you're charged with first-degree and you have no lawyer. It seems to me that a heavy-handed police report, an inadequate defense and an overzealous judge might see you on Death Row.'

Ruby laughed. 'You're good,' he said. 'You ain't a cop, but you sure as hell sound like a journalist. You guys just make this garbage up as you go along, right?'

'I'm just interested in Jean Boyd, Mr Ruby. There are certain other people who would like to know about her as well.'

'Hey, if you're so goddam interested in whether or not this Jean Boyd came down here last November and spoke to me, why the hell don't you ask her?'

'Because she's dead, Mr Ruby.'

The expression on Ruby's face changed. It was not disbelief

exactly; more like shock. He could not hide his reaction, and he knew it.

Mitch paused for effect, and then took a gamble. 'I have a very clear idea that her death might have had something to do with what she thought you knew.'

Ruby looked away, then down at his hands. He got up and stood with his back against the wall. It was clear to Mitch that he knew exactly who Jean Boyd was, and more than likely had a very good idea of what she was chasing in Dallas.

'Get me a lawyer,' Ruby said.

'You have one in mind?'

'Someone who doesn't know me. Public defender. Anyone. I don't care. I just want a goddam lawyer here.'

36

By the time a public defender was arranged, it was nearly two in the afternoon.

Ruby hadn't said a further word. Shaw returned him to a cell, had some lunch taken down, but Ruby left it uneaten. The man was a cat on hot coals, pacing back and forth in the cell, chain-smoking, pausing as if considering options, cursing to himself.

Shaw was also wound tight. He had opened up a can of worms. Mitch Newman was a wild card. He wasn't supposed to be in the precinct, let alone in an interview room with a man like Jack Ruby. But Shaw was caught between a rock and a hard place. The only person to have gotten something out of Ruby was Newman. How long Shaw could conceal what had happened, he did not know.

Regardless, there was no way Mitch Newman could be in the same room as Ruby and a public defender. He would have to sit on the other side of a two-way mirror in the adjoining interrogation room. He could watch, he could listen in, but he could no longer be present.

The PD was a cut above the usual. His name was Art Hallam, and Shaw had seen him at work before. He was a self-proclaimed bloodhound, seemingly far more interested in the truth and seeing justice done than writing his own paycheck in the private sector. How long it would take to dull that ardent sheen, no one knew, but for now he seemed driven and purposeful in his desire to help his fellow man. He was young, but he was serious and methodical, and it gave him an air of seniority. Shaw gave him some backstory, as much as was required, and then Ruby was brought from lockup.

Hallam and Ruby spoke together for a good thirty minutes. Hallam came away looking uneasy.

'Who are Jean Boyd and Mitchell Newman, Detective Shaw?'

'He talked about Jean Boyd?'

'He did. He also said that he'd spoken to this Mitchell Newman. You didn't mention either of those names to me.'

'I didn't feel it was necessary.'

'Well I think it's necessary now.'

Shaw explained as best he could. He answered Hallam's questions as succinctly as possible.

Hallam was pensive for a moment, and then he said, 'Mr Ruby says he won't say anything unless Newman is present.'

Shaw was incredulous. 'You have to be joking.'

'My client is insisting.'

'Did he give you a reason?'

'He wants someone else present. He says that he will only divulge what he intends to divulge if someone who is neither law nor justice is also in the room. He says it is a non-negotiable condition.'

'Jesus Christ.' Shaw turned and took a few steps down the corridor.

'I don't see there's any choice,' Hallam said. 'You want information from him, then your Mr Newman is going to have to be included.'

'I get it, I get it,' Shaw said. 'Okay, but Newman says nothing.'

'I agree. I'll speak to him.'

Shaw fetched Mitch from the other interrogation room and introduced him to Art Hallam.

'This is a very unusual situation, Mr Newman,' Hallam

said. 'Detective Shaw has explained to me the current state of play, and I have to say that it's something I've not come across before. I will ask questions of Mr Ruby, and both yourself and Detective Shaw will be present. Regardless of how he might respond, I entreat you to keep calm and not allow your emotions to influence your reactions. I appreciate that this relates to a very sensitive matter in respect of the death of Miss Boyd, but nevertheless ...' He left the statement unfinished. The message was received loud and clear.

A different room was selected, one that would comfortably accommodate all four of them.

Ruby was nervy, unable to sit still, and when Hallam went through the formalities and indicated that the meeting would be recorded, he protested vehemently.

'For your own welfare and legal protection—' Hallam started.

'I don't give a damn about that. No recordings. Seriously. I want your word that everything here is off the record, or I say nothing.'

Hallam looked at Shaw. Shaw nodded.

'Detective Shaw has indicated that there will be no recording. I am present. If any recording does take place, then it would be utterly useless to him or any other authority.'

'That's what you think?' Ruby asked.

'That's what I *know*, Mr Ruby,' Hallam said.

'Then you've got no goddam idea who you're dealing with,' Ruby replied. He looked at Mitch. 'And this guy really isn't a cop, right?'

'No, Mr Newman here is not a police officer,' Hallam said.

Ruby asked for a cigarette. Shaw slid a packet of Pall Malls across the table.

'So Mr Ruby has indicated to me that he is willing to answer some questions concerning Jean Boyd and potential – and I must stress *unsubstantiated* – factors that may or may not have contributed to her death. He is not agreeing to answer all questions, only those that he wishes to. Are we understood?'

Shaw nodded, Mitch too.

'In addition, he wishes to make an affidavit to the effect that he is in no way responsible, directly or indirectly, for the death of Leland Webster. Is this also agreed and understood?'

'Mr Ruby can make whatever statements or affidavits he wishes, Mr Hallam. In fact, we have asked him numerous times if he wishes—'

'That's not all I want,' Ruby interjected. 'I want immunity from anything you find out as a result of what I am going to tell you.'

'How can I offer immunity if I don't know what you're going to tell me or what you've done?' Shaw asked.

Ruby looked at Hallam.

Hallam nodded.

'So what if I told you that maybe Jean Boyd didn't commit suicide, and that her death is connected to another dead girl?'

'Okay, okay... hang fire a minute. You're saying that Jean Boyd was murdered?'

'I'm making a jump, sure, but she was digging for something, and I think there were those who didn't want her to do any more digging.'

'Digging into what?' Shaw asked.

'Whatever it was, it brought her here to Dallas and my club, right?'

'The communist meetings?' Shaw said. 'The meetings that Leland Webster attended?'

'I'm saying nothing else until I get an agreement to immunity.'

'Give us a name, at least. Who was this other girl?'

Ruby shook his head.

Mitch took a pen and a scrap of paper from his pocket and wrote on it. He passed it to Shaw.

'Holly Walsh?' Shaw ventured.

Ruby looked like the ground had disappeared beneath his feet. He glared at Mitch, his eyes fierce. 'Who the fuck are you?' he said. 'How the hell do you know about Holly?'

'Mr Newman is saying nothing, Mr Ruby,' Hallam said.

'No, I'm serious now ... how do you people know about Holly?'

Shaw shook his head. 'How does any of this relate to Jean?'

Ruby was flustered. He took another cigarette and lit it with the first still burning in the ashtray. He looked at Hallam, back at Shaw, and then he said, 'She asked questions, okay? She asked a lot of damn questions of a lot of people, and she got herself a lot of attention, that's how.'

'Are you saying that she upset someone and her death was not a suicide?'

'I told you, I'm not saying anything until I get an assurance from the cop here.'

'Okay,' Shaw said, 'we're getting ahead of ourselves. Let's backtrack. Give me some kind of an understanding as to why anyone would want to kill Jean Boyd.'

'She was looking for Holly Walsh, and I guess that someone didn't want Holly to be found, okay?'

'Who didn't want her to be found? What happened to her?'

Ruby laughed coarsely. 'Hey, maybe I'm talkin' garbage. I'm just some two-bit hoodlum runnin' a strip joint. What the hell would I know? Who do I listen to? Hoods and gangsters who hang out in titty bars, right? I can only tell you what I hear.'

'So tell us what you heard, Mr Ruby. Give us something that makes sense, because right now you haven't said a great deal of anything. You're asking for immunity for some unknown crime, and you're putting nothing on the table.'

'I gave you a name.'

'Holly Walsh.'

'Right.'

'We already had that name,' Shaw said.

'Well maybe you had the name, but you don't know anything about her. Where she came from, who she was connected to, what happened to her.'

'And now she's dead?'

'Let's just say that you could be looking for her from here to kingdom come and I don't think you'd find her.'

'And Jean Boyd didn't commit suicide? You're saying she was murdered?'

'I'm doing my best not to gamble any more, Detective Shaw. *I* wouldn't put money on it, but there might be some who'd think the odds were pretty good on that one.'

'Okay, say this … this … hell, I don't even know what to call it … this *theory* is true, how does any of it relate to the death of Leland Webster?'

'You got plenty out of me,' Ruby said. 'Put a deal on the table or we're done.'

'The only way any kind of deal is gonna happen is if you have something solid on Leland Webster's murder,' Shaw said. 'And I wanna know what you know about Jean Boyd and this other dead girl. That's what I want.'

Ruby shrugged. 'I'm not sayin' another word until I get a deal. Complete immunity or nothin'. And afterwards, I want out of here, away from Dallas, away from all of this. Take it or leave it.'

Shaw looked at Hallam, then at Mitch. He rose from his chair.

'You'll be processed and remanded to the county jail up on Dealey Plaza Park,' he said. 'I can't hold you here indefinitely, and this may take a day or two.'

'Ironic,' Ruby said, 'considering everything that happened last November.'

'Meaning what?' Shaw asked.

'Meaning nothing at all, Detective.'

'November … when Kennedy was here?' Shaw asked.

Ruby smiled knowingly. 'You want me up in the county jail, then so be it. You do whatever you gotta do. Right now, a six-by-eight cell is the safest place for me to be.'

Hallam reached for his briefcase and closed it. He stood up. 'I want your assurance that Mr Ruby will be placed in solitary confinement, Detective Shaw. I don't want him in general population.'

'That can be arranged, Mr Hallam.'

'And you're taking him there now?'

'Soon enough. I have to make a couple of phone calls.'

'Then I'll wait with him, and I'll accompany him to the jail. There were riots there in April, and it's already more over-crowded now than it was back then.'

'Very well,' Shaw replied. He opened the door, indicated that Mitch should leave with him.

At the door, Mitch turned back. He looked at Hallam, then at Ruby. 'Mr Ruby … I need to know if Jean Boyd was murdered—'

'Mr Newman, please. You really shouldn't say anything at all.'

'Let him ask his question,' Ruby said.

'I was once engaged to Jean,' Mitch continued. 'I have to see her mother when I get back to Washington. She's an old woman and Jean was her only child. Personally, I cannot believe that Jean would take her own life.'

Ruby looked back at Mitch without the slightest change in his expression.

'Did she kill herself, Mr Ruby, or, as you seem to be implying, was she murdered because of what she was trying to find out?'

'I don't know why you're even here, Newman,' Ruby said. His voice was calmer, and the earlier tension and agitation seemed to have subsided a little. 'I lost someone too. I know how you feel.

But I ain't here to sympathize with you or the girl's mother. I'm here for me, and that's all there is to it.'

Mitch opened his mouth to ask another question, but Ruby cut him short.

'I'll give you this much, okay? If I had done some of the things that have been done, then I would do whatever it took to keep it hidden, no matter who got in the way. There is a great deal more at stake here than the lives of your friend and a girl whose only crime was being both too beautiful and too naïve for her own good.' He paused. 'Do you understand what I'm sayin'?'

'Yes,' Mitch replied. 'I think I do.'

He felt a rush of nausea and dizziness. It took everything he possessed to hold back the grief and anger. He had to get out of the room, and he had to get out now.

Shaw went with him, walked him to the front of the building and out into the street. Sitting on the steps in front of Dallas Metro, Mitch held his head in his hands and cried.

37

'I think we can assume that whoever this Holly Walsh is ... whoever she was, she's dead.'

'He seemed very clear about that,' Mitch said.

'And she was just some girl who showed up in Dallas and worked at the Carousel for a while. That's all you know?'

'That's all I know.'

'And her name was on the back of my business card, the one I gave Jean.'

'Right.'

'So now it seems that Jean was investigating a murder as well as the election.'

Mitch didn't reply.

'You want to believe that she didn't kill herself. That's what you want.'

'I believe it,' Mitch said. 'Doesn't matter if I want to or not. And as for what else Ruby knows, I think we've only scratched the surface.'

Shaw was reticent. 'Ruby's a hood, a thug, a small-time nobody who runs a strip joint and cheats on his taxes. He is not the fount of wisdom you might think he is.'

'I thought Jean came here to investigate Kennedy. Now we're talking about the possibility that she was murdered because she was looking into the death of Holly Walsh. I'm finding it very hard to understand how these two things might be related.'

'Maybe they're not.'

'And what about Leland Webster?'

'I don't know what to think,' Shaw said, 'aside from the fact that I have a man in custody who may or may not have murdered him. We have a ballistics match, that's all, and I don't even have an explanation for why he's telling us this stuff. He could've just kept his mouth shut and the DA would have thrown the thing out on the basis of lack of evidence.'

'Unless he really does want protection. He's become a person of interest. Maybe some of what he's saying is true; hell, maybe all of it is true, and he knows that now the police are speaking to him he's actually in very considerable danger ... like Jean.'

'Or maybe he really did kill Webster and this thing with the Walsh girl is an unexpected opportunity for him. Jean was looking into her death. Maybe she found out who killed her and told Ruby, and now Ruby is using it to barter for immunity on Webster.'

Mitch looked out across the street.

'I need to go make some calls,' Shaw said. 'And you?'

'I'm going to take a walk, try not to think where this could be going.'

To Mitch, pursuing the whereabouts of Holly Walsh now seemed futile. Had he even possessed a means by which he could do it, how far would he get? Needing something to focus on, he chose to direct his attention to the initial reason Jean had come to Dallas. Byron had said she was chasing Kennedy, and Mitch felt the best thing to do was follow in her footsteps, at least from a research point of view.

One of Ruby's final comments had concerned 'everything that happened last November', and it was then that Kennedy had been in Dallas. Jean had been here too, as had Holly. Shaw had given Jean the necessary credentials, and whatever she may or may not have discovered had somehow led her to the Carousel, to Jack Ruby, and also to Holly. Now Ruby was telling them that Holly was dead; not only that, but that her death possessed some relevance to Jean. He'd also said that there was a great deal more at stake than just the lives of Jean Boyd and Holly Walsh. That smacked of a cover-up, something hidden that someone wanted to remain hidden.

Finding Kennedy's November '63 itinerary was straight-forward enough. The Dallas papers had printed it several days in advance, and they were all archived at the library. Kennedy's motorcade had started at the south end of Love Field, taking a route along Cedar Springs, North Harwood, Main, Houston and Elm. There would have been thousands of people along that route, but Ruby had reacted when he'd been told he would be remanded to Dealey Plaza. He'd said it was ironic. Mitch wanted to go take a look, to find out if there was anything about the location that would give him a further line of investigation.

The Plaza was a triangle of land bordered by Elm to the north, Houston to the east and Main to the south. The presidential motorcade had crossed Record Street and joined Main between the County Criminal Courts Building and the Old Court House. Taking a right, with Dealey Plaza on the left, the cars had passed the Plaza's reflecting pool and then turned to join Elm, coming out beneath a triple underpass to meet North Stemmons Freeway in the direction of the Dallas Trade Mart.

Mitch walked the route, consulting the notes he'd made from the newspaper articles, noting that the Courts Building also housed County Records, and that Elm ran between that and the Dal-Tex Building. At the corner of Houston and Elm he saw the imposing facade of the Texas School Book Depository. Seven floors in height, and of no real architectural merit, it was a functional government-owned facility. Nevertheless, he took a couple of photos.

And then he remembered Shaw saying that Leland Webster – the man apparently murdered with Ruby's gun – had worked in that very building. Mitch crossed Elm on the very corner where Kennedy's parade had turned, and walked up the front steps and into the lobby.

The receptionist, a pretty young woman in her mid twenties, asked if he needed help.

'I was just looking for a man called Leland Webster,' he said. 'From what I understand, he works here.'

The girl smiled, said, 'Let me see now,' and proceeded to check some sort of employee register. Puzzled, she appeared to go through it again, and then said, 'Are you sure it's this building? We have another warehouse at 1917 Houston.'

'No, I'm sure it's this one,' Mitch said.

'Well there's no record of a Leland Webster here presently. Of course, he could be temporary or seasonal. We often have additional people here during the semesters. Perhaps you'd like to speak to someone from Personnel?'

'It's okay,' Mitch said. 'Thank you for your help.'

The girl smiled and told him he was welcome. Mitch left the building.

He needed County Records, and it was right there on the facing corner.

'Yes, of course we have what you're asking for.' The middle-aged woman behind the counter had a too-pale complexion, batwing glasses and hair drawn back so tightly it couldn't have been anything but uncomfortable. 'If a private company is contracted by the Education Board to deliver a service, then it's a legal requirement for them to maintain current and accurate employee listings with us.' She said it as if such a thing was common knowledge. 'But you'll need to complete an internal requisition form, and I will have to approve it.'

'Of course,' Mitch said.

'Your credentials?'

Mitch produced his press card.

The woman took it from him and inspected it as if it were something fished from a blocked sink.

She returned it with, 'I am Miss Danforth. I am responsible for all such matters. Please follow me.'

Mitch gave his reason for requesting a list of employees of the Book Depository Company as 'pursuing research avenues for an in-depth article into the changing needs of our modern educational system', which seemed to satisfy Miss Danforth.

He waited a good fifteen minutes on a hard chair in a narrow hallway. He'd skipped lunch and his stomach growled.

At last Miss Danforth returned, in her hand half a dozen sheets of paper. 'You can make notes,' she said, 'but these lists must not be removed from the building. Please return them to the receptionist as you exit.'

'Yes, of course,' Mitch said, and waited for Miss Danforth to leave him alone before he took photographs of each page.

Heading back toward the Metro building, he found the offices of a local newspaper, the *Dallas Monitor*. Once inside, he got talking to one of the staff reporters and asked if they had their own photo lab facilities.

'We use a place two blocks down,' the man said. 'Go down there and ask for Louie. He'll take care of you for a couple of bucks. Tell him Ron Cartwright sent you.'

Louie was a tiny guy with an unlit stogie that never seemed to leave his mouth. It moved as he talked.

'I'll do it now,' he said. 'What do you want... eight-by-tens of everything?'

'There's only half a dozen or so. That would be great.'

'Come back in an hour.'

A sandwich and a cup of coffee later, Mitch collected the photographs and went back to find Shaw.

He had to wait a while. Shaw was out or unavailable. Mitch went down the block and had another cup of coffee.

Shortly after he'd sat down at the counter, another man came in. Dark suit, hat, nondescript, but there was something about him that caught Mitch's attention. The man took a seat in a booth to the rear of the diner. He ordered coffee, smoked a cigarette, read a newspaper. Once or twice Mitch glanced up at the mirror behind the counter and felt sure that the man was watching him. He couldn't explain the feeling, tried to pass it off, but it nagged at him, even to the point of not looking through the photographs until he had returned to the police building.

Once there, seated in the lobby, he studied the pictures of the Town Plaza Hotel where Jean had stayed the previous November, the Ruby houses on Rawlins and South Ewing, the Carousel, the Texas School Book Depository building and finally the list of employees. Leland Webster's name was there. He was listed as a 'storage and dispatch clerk'. Perhaps his death was too recent for the information to have filtered through the system.

By the time Shaw appeared, it was mid afternoon.

'Where did you go?' he asked Mitch.

'Up to Dealey Plaza.'

'And?'

'Nothing much. That's where the Book Depository is, the place Leland Webster worked.'

'Yes, of course.'

'So what are you thinking?'

'I don't know what to think,' Shaw said. 'All we know for a

fact is that Jean came here last November. Did she talk to Ruby? I reckon she did. I think she did exactly what you've done and chased him down, and got the interview she was after. Ruby has tenuous connections to Marcello and Civello. Maybe she thought he was a way into the Dallas underworld. Maybe she had some idea that the organized crime syndicates had used their influence in the unions to bolster Kennedy's vote. Maybe Ruby's just making it up as he goes along. You appear out of nowhere, he's facing the chair on Leland Webster, you express an interest in a girl who worked at his club who may or may not be dead; also someone he spoke to last November who actually is dead and thus can't refute anything he's saying, and off he goes. He's grasping at anything that might be a lifeline.'

Mitch didn't question Shaw's reservations, but he did not share them.

'So what happens now?'

'Nothing.'

'What do you mean, nothing? You told Ruby you were going to find out if there was some kind of deal on the table.'

'A deal for what?' Shaw asked. 'What he knows? He doesn't know anything. Really, I guarantee he knows nothing that could be of any interest to you or me or anyone else. I just said that to see if he would venture anything else, and he didn't.'

'So you just leave him?'

'Sure we do. We let him sweat on it for a few days. The longer he hears nothing from me, the more desperate he becomes and the more likely he is to come forward with something that we can bargain with . . . or, as I suspect, he shows his true hand and he's got nothing.'

'And are you going to pursue an investigation into the possible murder of the Walsh girl?'

'Based on what? Ruby's hearsay? I have no body, Mitch. How

the hell do I pursue an investigation when there is absolutely no evidence that a murder has been committed?'

'Treat it as a missing persons case, then.'

'No one has reported her missing. I'm employed by the city. I have real murders and real missing persons reports, and I don't get to pick and choose what I investigate. Until there is something specific and substantive that tells me that Holly Walsh is dead, then there really isn't a great deal I can do.'

Mitch was quiet for a moment, then he looked at Shaw. 'You said you didn't think that Jean killed herself. Do you still believe that?'

Shaw looked away, then back at Mitch. He opened his mouth as if to speak, but said nothing.

'You have to take a stand on this,' Mitch said. 'One way or another, you have to let me know what you think.'

'Why?' Shaw asked. 'Why do I have to tell you anything?'

'Because you and she were involved,' Mitch said. 'I know you were, and I know your wife either knows or suspects that something happened.'

'What my wife—'

'Nelson, stop kidding yourself. I'm not stupid. Something happened last November. I don't know what it was, and I am not asking you to tell me. Hell, even if I did ask you, you wouldn't tell me. What do we know? We know Jean is dead. We also know she came down here and chased Ruby for information she believed he had. Maybe it was the election, maybe it was this other girl, Holly. All I know is that he's scared. Yes, it could very well be that he killed Leland Webster and he's doing anything he can to stay off Death Row. Or it could be because of something else. Webster worked at the Book Depository. That building overlooks the route that Kennedy's motorcade took. Were he and his communist friends planning a protest because of Cuba? Did Ruby's gangland buddies tell him to kill Webster, and if so, why so long after Kennedy was here?'

'Needle in a haystack,' Shaw interjected. 'This is all hearsay and rumor and supposition. And it's coming from a man who runs a strip joint and doesn't pay his parking fines.'

'And what if some part of it is true? Does someone else have to die for you to consider the possibility that a rigged election and Jean's supposed suicide and the murder of this Holly Walsh might be connected?'

'So what do you actually want from me?' Shaw asked.

'I want you to answer the question, Detective. Do you honestly believe that Jean sat alone in her apartment and swallowed enough pills to kill herself?'

Shaw paused, then turned to look at Mitch.

'No,' he said. His words were slow and certain. 'No, I do not.'

38

After the oppressive heat of Dallas, Washington was a cool relief.

Mitch flew back into Richard E. Byrd and collected his car from Richmond. He thought about driving to West Haven to see Jean's mother – it was en route to DC and barely a diversion – but he didn't think he could face her. He would call her. That was what he would do. Monday, Tuesday perhaps. He would tell her that he was still working on things, still trying to figure it all out, and as soon as he had some real information he would let her know.

That was the crux of it. The need for *real* information. He was a journalist, and there was nothing that would support even a single paragraph of reportage. Rumor, hearsay, assumption, guesswork, the possibility of slim coincidence. Nothing substantive, nothing provable, nothing sound.

The cat greeted him enthusiastically, and before he'd even managed to set down his bag and take his jacket off, it was winding its way back and forth around his legs and purring.

He picked it up. 'Mitch,' he said. 'You do understand that having the same name makes conversation kind of awkward.'

The cat looked back at him with an expression that could only be translated as bemusement.

'We both need to eat,' Mitch said, and set the cat down.

The apartment was musty and airless. He opened windows

and emptied the garbage. He was hungry, but there was nothing in the refrigerator. Even as he left for the grocery store, he realized something had changed. A week ago he would have thought, *To hell with it*, and opened a bottle of bourbon. Two or three shots and a handful of saltine crackers would have sufficed. But not now. He wanted food – a steak, eggs, some fresh coffee – and he was going to make it himself.

As he returned from the store carrying a bag laden with provisions, he saw Tom.

'The prodigal returns,' the barkeep said. 'And man, are you popular these days. Seems half the world has been looking for you.'

Mitch stopped walking.

'Seems I'm becoming your social secretary. Had a couple of cops asking after you. Someone from a newspaper. Another couple of suits showed up the day before yesterday and I really didn't understand who they were.' Tom smiled knowingly. 'You got yourself in a fix, I guess.'

'I got myself into something I don't even understand.'

Tom's expression changed from nonchalance to concern. 'You okay? You in some sort of trouble?'

'No, no trouble,' Mitch said.

'Sure? Anything I can help with, aside from feeding the cat?'

'No, I'm good,' Mitch said, 'but thanks for asking, and thanks for looking after the cat. Did any of these people leave names or numbers?'

Tom shook his head. 'No, none of them, which seemed odd to me. They all said not to worry about it, that they'd track you down elsewhere.'

'Well it makes a change, right? All of a sudden I'm big man on campus.'

'Certainly seems that way. Come down later. Catch me up on what's happening, okay?'

'Sure thing, Tom.'

Mitch went on his way. He hoped that the sudden sense of anxiety he'd experienced had not been obvious to Tom. Police, newspaper people, unidentified men in suits, all haunting his local bar and asking after him but leaving no names and no messages. It was unsettling, to say the least.

He made food, and ate with a somewhat lessened appetite. The cat did not. Once it was done with its own food, it jumped up on the table to see what else was available.

Mitch cut off a small piece of hamburger and offered it. The cat seemed unimpressed. He set it down on the table and the cat pawed it around a little.

'Beggars can't be choosers,' Mitch said. 'Anyway, we should probably catch up, you and I, right?'

The cat glanced up, didn't look away, and Mitch had the definite impression it understood what he'd said.

He smiled, stroked its head.

'So, I'm in some kind of trouble, but if you ask me what kind of trouble, I couldn't even begin to tell you. I wouldn't expect you to understand—'

The cat moved its head, looked at him askance. Mitch laughed.

'Okay, sorry... maybe you would understand perfectly. Here's the deal. Jean went down to Texas and kicked over a few stones, and now I'm thinking that it might take us all the way to the White House.' Mitch paused. 'What do you think about that, my friend? You think that's the kind of trouble we need around here?'

The cat blinked.

Mitch leaned forward, smiling. 'For this relationship to work, especially if you're gonna be my confidante and counsellor, I'm gonna need you to be a little less vague in your responses, okay?'

The cat lay down on the kitchen table and waited to be

stroked. Mitch complied. It was an invitation that couldn't be refused.

Once he'd cleared away the plates, he called Lester Byron, asked if it was possible to come over and speak with him.

'I understand it's Saturday, but it's important,' he explained.

'I work every day with a *y* in it,' Lester said. 'The news doesn't stop for the weekend, as you well know.'

They met at noon in Byron's office at the *Tribune*. Mitch would have preferred somewhere else, somewhere neutral and un-connected to the paper, but for now he was in no mind to grant further importance to recent unexplained incidents.

He was reminded of their previous conversation about the events leading up to Jean's resignation – the article about Ken O'Donnell's alcoholism, and whether or not the Chicago mayor's office had been complicit in withholding a vote count until other areas had filed. That discussion had taken place only ten days earlier, and yet the time elapsed seemed like months, even years.

'So…' Lester began.

'So I went to Dallas.'

'I'm well aware of that, Mitch. You called me last Tuesday.'

Mitch sensed a reticence in Lester's demeanor. The mere fact that the police had spoken to him about Jean, had implied that Mitch was unwilling to talk to them, had perhaps put him on edge.

'I just wanted to let you know how things were going, that's all,' Mitch went on. 'And I wanted to allay any concerns you might've had about… well, about having to let Jean go from the paper.'

'You found out something?' Lester asked. He leaned forward.

'A number of things, yes.'

'Such as?'

'Well, until I have something more substantial, I don't really want to say anything. I don't listen to rumors, and I don't like to pass them on. However, just between you and me, I feel sure that Jean losing her job was not a factor in her suicide. I really am certain about that.'

There was an immediate and visible relief in Lester's body language. It was as if a tightened cord somewhere within him had been released. He sat back. He inhaled, exhaled slowly. He closed his eyes for a moment, and then he cleared his throat.

'Thank you for telling me that, Mitch,' he said. 'That really has been troubling me.'

'We're in the same boat, Lester,' Mitch said. 'I betrayed her far worse than you ever did. Okay, it was nearly fifteen years ago, but the fact that she committed suicide... well, I think it takes a great deal more than one situation to prompt something like that.'

He didn't want to say anything about what he really believed. For now, he preferred to keep what he suspected to himself.

'Anyway, as far as Dallas is concerned, I think she might have turned over a few rocks. What was underneath, I really couldn't tell you.'

'And the fact that she didn't write the story means that she didn't find what she was looking for?'

'I don't think she did, no.'

'And now?'

'I'm pursuing it, but for my own interests. I'm not a hound like Jean, but there are some unanswered questions. Just for my own peace of mind, I'd like to get to the bottom of them.'

'Yes, yes, of course.'

'What I wanted to know was whether you had anyone down in Dallas last November.'

'Sure we did. We always send someone to cover the road trips. That's part and parcel of being a DC paper. It's all about the president.'

'Who did you send?'

'You know Bill Sandford?'

'Sure, yes. He's still working?'

Lester smiled. 'Bill Sandford will keel over at his desk at eighty-five years of age while trying to finish an article. He knows more people and has seen more presidents in office than any working reporter in DC.'

'Do you think he'd be willing to talk to me about the Dallas trip?'

'I have no doubt,' Lester said. 'I don't think there's anything Bill enjoys more than listening to the sound of his own voice.'

'Well if he can spare me a little time, it would be really appreciated.'

Lester got up. Mitch followed suit. As they reached the door, Mitch said, 'Oh, one more thing, before I forget. You didn't happen to remember the name of the other detective who came to see you, did you? There was Detective Franks and...'

Lester looked pensive, and then shook his head. 'I'm sorry,' he said. 'To be honest, he might not even have said his name. I wasn't paying a great deal of attention. I was in the middle of a hundred and one things.'

'Okay, appreciated. I should get in touch with Franks, then. Let him know I'm back and find out if there are any questions. Did they say what precinct they were from?'

Lester looked apologetic. 'I'm sorry,' he said. 'Cops turn up, they flash IDs, you answer their questions, they disappear. Like I said, I had a lot of things on the go, and they were after you, not me.'

'I'm sure I'll find him without any difficulty,' Mitch said, knowing with sufficient surety to put money on it that there was no such person as Detective Franks.

39

'I liked her a lot,' Bill Sandford said. 'But as far as being a reporter was concerned, she was a two-dollar pistol. Just as likely to blow her own hand off as she was to hit the target.'

He leaned back in his chair. His eyes were old and wise and tired. 'Sad business. Truly, a very sad business.'

The office within which they sat was a testament to an extraordinary life. Sandford was a DC legend. His career went back to the last few months of Woodrow Wilson's presidency in early 1921. Back then he had been a cub reporter for the *Times*. In '39, Cissy Patterson – part of the family group that owned the *Chicago Tribune* and the *New York Daily News* – bought both the *Times* and the *Herald* from William Randolph Hearst. The *Times-Herald* was born, and aside from a brief spell with the *Post* in the late forties, Sandford had stayed with them until the paper wound up in '54. Since then, he'd been political editor at the *Tribune*, and even though his post duties were supposedly editorial, he rarely missed a White House briefing session. His byline accompanied the vast majority of any reportage from the Hill. He had seen Warren Harding, Calvin Coolidge, Hoover, Roosevelt, Truman and Eisenhower in and out of office. Rumor had it that many of the West Wing staffers and spokespersons looked to Sandford's columns to find out what was really going on in their own camp.

'You went down to Dallas to cover the presidential trip,' Mitch said.

'I went to talk to Yarborough and Connally,' Sandford replied. 'When you have the governor and the senator of a state in a seemingly perpetual dogfight, especially when you're talking about a state that was won by a two percent margin... well, I guess the president's advisors suggested he go down there, shake some hands, say some nice things about the rednecks.'

Mitch smiled. He liked Sandford. He was a no-nonsense press man who'd seen and heard enough to be afraid of nothing, least of all his own reputation.

'Why were they fighting?'

'Many reasons. Different politics, clash of personality, who knows? It was enough that they were feuding. Kennedy's people evidently thought that the only way to straighten it out was for him to get down there personally and knock their heads together. The thing you have to understand is that east and west Texas are almost two different states. Texas has an anti-Catholic demographic. They have an anti-civil-rights and integration demographic. Nixon did well in the Panhandle, Hill Country, Harris County and the Dallas–Fort Worth areas, but your average Texan farmer doesn't trust anyone out of boots and checkered shirts, let alone someone who isn't Texan. Notwithstanding the fact that Kennedy had Johnson on his ticket, and Johnson was born in a farmhouse in Stonewall, a lot of Texans are still of the view that politicians are all so much hogwash and horseshit. Primary attitude, certainly in the west, is that a politician says he's there to serve the people, but really he's there to serve himself. What Texas does have is Mexicans, and they went with the Catholic minority. That wasn't the case for Hoover in '28, but it was good enough for Kennedy.'

'What do you think about Kennedy?'

Sandford smiled ruefully. 'What do I *think* about Kennedy?

I try to think about Kennedy as little as possible.' He paused. 'I think he is a politician.'

Mitch smiled understandingly.

'Politics is a sales pitch. You see the propaganda. Hell, we even push it in the paper. You get the civil rights stuff and the American University speech about peace and all that, but we're not told about all the screw-ups. Kennedy lied back in 1960. Right there on TV in the presidential nominee debate. Him and Nixon talking about rocket development and the Soviets. Kennedy said we needed rocket production to match theirs. Hell, we already outnumbered them a hundred to one. If Ike had come forward and told the voters that Kennedy was talking out of his hat, then it might have been a very different election – one that Joe Kennedy couldn't buy off. Then there was the invasion of Cuba. Kennedy told the CIA to pull that stunt, and what a fiasco it was! He was shamed in front of the whole world. Then he goes to see Khrushchev in Vienna. He makes matters even worse and the wall goes up across Berlin. You know, it's ironic, but the only thing that actually saved Kennedy was the fact that that wall went up. That wall meant the Soviets wouldn't cross their own boundary. Had they done so the Cold War would've gotten very hot very fast.'

Sandford sat back in his chair. It creaked beneath him. 'Jack Kennedy defies the status quo. He defies the military top brass. He's the only one who says we shouldn't bomb the living hell out of Cuba. It goes on and on. He's a wild card. Right now his popularity is off the bottom of the scale, and there are some very significant people who are concerned that he might just get the Democrats kicked out of the White House at the end of the year.'

Mitch felt a sense of disquiet. Bill Sandford, one of the most respected and knowledgeable political journalists in Washington, was echoing some of his own thoughts about the President of the United States.

'You think the election was rigged?'

'I think the entire game is rigged.'

'Meaning?'

'Meaning that for a man to even arrive on the threshold of the Oval Office, he must already have sold his soul a dozen times over to a succession of highest bidders. The presidency is a piece of theater; the president is a character that is cast. There are numerous directors, numerous producers, and it's rare to find any of them agreeing on the plot. The world is the audience, and instead of everyone sticking to the script, they ad lib depending upon audience reaction. That, in my experience, makes for a very confusing and very unsatisfying type of entertainment.'

Mitch laughed.

'You can laugh all you like, young man, but I speak sooth. I have been around a good while, and there's nothing any of these folks can say that I haven't already heard.'

'So you do think it was rigged?'

'Is that what Miss Boyd was looking into?'

'Yes.'

'And now you're following in her uncertain, yet dogged footsteps?'

'Uncertain?'

'I don't think she knew what she was looking for. I remember talking to her. She wanted to get to O'Donnell, Salinger maybe. She wasn't even sure who she should approach, and had she had an opportunity to speak to them, I don't know that she'd have had the right questions. She was out at the hotel, back at the press office, was gone for a day, then down in the bar looking like she hadn't slept the whole time she'd been there. She was on edge, that you could see.'

'I think she wanted to get comments from those in the inner sanctum about the election controversy.'

'Well, I can tell you that there's no way in the world she would have gotten within a mile of those people if that was her intent. They don't like surprises, and they sure as hell don't like people with searchlights looking in their closets. They keep everything buttoned up nice and tight and they manage it very carefully and very closely. Of course, I can understand that. They're responsible for keeping the ship afloat, and they don't want random journalists and other lowlifes kicking holes in the stern, do they?'

'Do you think he'll stay in office?'

Sandford leaned forward. 'Give-and-take, young man. Tell me what you've got.'

'Ethics committee hearings about the election, rumors about his medical conditions, rumors of numerous affairs, a perceived weakness in dealing with Khrushchev, the Bay of Pigs fiasco—'

'You think he's alone in this kind of thing? Hell, every damned president I have seen has had situations like this.'

'But we have TV and far greater press coverage now than has ever been the case before. People know about this stuff. They talk about it. Even ten years ago it was far easier to keep it under wraps.'

'You're a bright fellow,' Sandford said. 'However, you are also quite naïve ... interestingly enough, naïve in the same way as Jean Boyd.'

'Naïve how?'

Sandford was quiet for a moment, and then he said, 'There's a trap here. It's rare that you see you're in it until you're stuck. You get an idea, you pursue it. You think you're onto something. You become too fixed on that one idea, and you start to read connections into things. You see links where they don't exist, almost as if you so want your original theory to be true that you manipulate everything to agree with it whether it agrees or not.'

'You think that's what happened to Jean?'

'I don't know what happened to Jean, Mr Newman, but I know the situation I have just described.' Sandford sighed quietly. 'She and I spoke in Dallas.'

'When?'

'The day Kennedy came in at Love Field. She was there, I was there. Hell, there were a thousand people there. I knew who she was, and I knew what she was after. I told her straight. I said that she better be damn sure of what she doing because it was a fierce animal with big teeth and you could stick pins in it for only so long. One day it would wake up and fight back.'

'You think she upset some people?'

'I *know* she upset some people. Ken O'Donnell showed me a list of people and organizations and Lord knows what else that were in the Democrats' black book. Our Miss Boyd was right there alongside the communist sympathizers and the KKK and every other crazy that had it in for Kennedy and his left-wing, liberal, equal-rights circus parade, so intent on sending the good God-fearing people of this great nation down the Suwannee.'

'I find it hard to believe that a journalist...' Mitch stopped mid flight. He knew he was demonstrating the exact kind of naïveté of which Sandford had spoken.

'Journalists have toppled governments,' Sandford said, 'as I am sure they will do again.'

Thoughts filled Mitch's mind, so many of them contradictory, so many of them unanswered.

Eventually he looked up. 'So if you were me, what would you do?'

'I would ask myself a very specific and searching question.'

'Which is?'

'What am I really trying to accomplish here? Resolve the

questions that surround the nature and circumstances of Jean's death, or pull that same thread she thought she'd gotten hold of in the belief that it would unravel a sitting administration?'

'Is that what she was trying to do?'

'Seems to me that everyone, no matter who they are, is trying to do the same thing.'

'And what is that … aside from find some happiness?'

'Find some happiness?' Sandford laughed dryly. 'That's not what people are trying to do, Mr Newman. They want to be heard. They want people to know that they are there, and that they have something to say. That, and nothing more. They just want to know that they matter.'

40

Back at his apartment, Mitch started calling police precincts in the hope that he'd find Detective Franks. He began with those closest to the *Tribune*, and then went further out. After an hour, there was nothing. He'd expected as much. Of course, Lester could have misheard, but Mitch didn't believe so. He knew that Detective Franks was as much a myth as Andrews from the *Tribune* who had taken Jean's paperwork from the West Haven house.

There was now no doubt in his mind. People were looking for him. Who they were and why they wanted to talk to him could only relate to what he was doing. He did not believe this issue stopped with Jean's death, or the deaths of Leland Webster and Holly Walsh. There was something beyond even that, and that was what had obsessed Jean.

His thoughts went back to the man in the diner in Dallas, the people who'd asked after him at Tom's bar. Paranoia was a dangerous thing. Perhaps that was what Sandford was actually trying to tell him. Yes, it had gotten hold of Jean, but it had also gotten hold of Mitch himself.

If those who were looking for him were not the police, then who were they, and what were they trying to prevent? Sandford's question had been the only relevant one. Was he trying to find out what happened to Jean, or was he trying to complete what she had begun? Had the Dallas trip started out as a hopeful venture to uncover more about the election, and then become a personal obsession to find this Holly Walsh? And had that been connected to Kennedy, or someone within the Kennedy camp? If Holly had been killed, was it because of something she knew? Had she perhaps seen something, overheard something, maybe at one of the communist meetings that Webster had attended? Had she mentioned something to Ruby, and Ruby had killed not only Webster but Holly too? Webster was a loner, it seemed. Unmarried, working in a low-paid job that just happened to put him in a position overlooking the route that Kennedy's November '63 motorcade had taken.

Mitch's thoughts stopped right there. Ruby. Civello. Marcello. Dallas organized crime. Meetings of communists at the Carousel. Holly had been right there, then she had vanished, believed to be dead. Webster had been killed by a weapon registered in Ruby's name. That in itself was entirely circumstantial, but the mere fact that Ruby's arrest had opened up this whole can of worms suggested connections that could not yet be identified. Ruby had turned as soon as he'd learned of Jean's death. That had either been entirely opportunistic on his part, or it was very important.

Did this thing go far beyond an investigation into election-rigging? Did it go into something that would more than adequately justify the killing of three people?

What had Jean discovered? Had she even been aware of it?

Mitch did not like the direction his train of thoughts was taking, but it was a destination that seemed somehow inevitable. It took a little while to summarize everything on paper, to list the questions he felt needed answering. He had not the faintest inkling regarding Jean's state of mind in the days and weeks leading up to her death. His experiences between when they'd known one another and the present had changed him irrevocably, so much so that perhaps Jean would not have recognized the man he'd once been. Perhaps the same had happened with her. Had he met her two, three months ago, what would he have found? Lester had fired her, irrespective of whether it was termed a resignation or not, and such a thing would have been devastating to her. If nothing else, she was proud and self-reliant. Had this all been part of some personal crusade to get her job back? Had she been trying to find some scoop, some exclusive, that would garner so much attention there was no way the *Tribune* – or some other paper – could ignore her? Had it been the last act of a desperate woman, afraid – as Sandford had said – that her voice would no longer be heard, that she would no longer matter?

And in her desperation to find something, *anything*, had she strung threads together that would never tie up, given substance to rumors, extrapolated a reality from hearsay that was neither factual nor accurate? What, in truth, did Mitch even know about her, her method of working, her intentions, her purposes? Nothing. That was what he knew.

It was a cold, hard moment for him, and there was no sidestepping it. The question needed to be asked and answered, and he could not pretend to himself that this was anything but very real, and potentially very dangerous.

Did Jean Boyd die by her own hand, her self-belief destroyed, her career finished, her future so bleak that she could not face it? Or did she die because she was looking far too closely at something that desperately needed to remain hidden?

Did she jump, or was she pushed?

And if she was pushed, who had pushed her, and why? Was Holly pushed too, Webster also? Had Ruby pushed them, or did Ruby know who was responsible? Was he even now planning to use this information to secure his own survival?

What had really happened in Dallas in November 1963?

Mitch knew that the answer to that question would determine what he was going to do, and thus the obstacles that would face him.

41

Judith Wagner rose late on Saturday morning. For the past week she'd been suffering from a head cold, and she was exhausted. That sense of bone-deep fatigue did not only seem physical. There was an abiding feeling of mental and emotional weariness that accompanied each day. She'd thought it would pass, but it hadn't. She was twenty-eight years old, and yet she felt sixty. The prospect of parties and dinners and the interminable need to be upbeat now seemed anathema. After all, she was a farm girl. That was the truth of it. A Midwest cattleman's daughter, raised amongst Black Angus, Holstein and Shorthorns. Washington was the center of a loud and busy world, yet her nature had always been to haunt the quieter corners. How she had arrived here was a story all its own, but she'd been here long enough to realize that what she'd sought was superficial, and ultimately meaningless.

The apartment she occupied was not her own. It was not registered in her name, and aside from her clothes, all of them bought for her, there was very little to say that she even lived there. In the beginning she'd spent very few nights there, but as the novelty she provided wore thin, she'd been there more frequently, careful not to miss the phone, leaving the bathroom door open when she showered, ever ready for the inevitable summons. Predictably, those summonses grew ever more infrequent, and she knew that soon it would be time to pack the few possessions she could call her own and head back to Kansas. Just like Dorothy.

She spoke to her mother at least once a week. Her father, a cattleman through and through – tough, laconic, businesslike, pragmatic – thought it reprehensible that she lived alone in Washington, unmarried, no discernible source of income, and yet arrived home unannounced and inappropriately dressed, expensive city-folk gifts for all and sundry, at Thanksgiving, Christmas, even days that possessed no significance whatsoever. He considered she was buying acceptance for some unvoiced apology, and he was not willing to forgive. He had spoken to her coldly last time, more than six months earlier.

'I don't know what you're doing, and I don't want to know,' he'd said. 'I see what I see. You look like a Jezebel, and I didn't raise my girl to be no Jezebel. You think you can come back here any time that pleases you? You left us, my girl. You left me and your mother and your siblings and went off to find whatever you thought you were looking for, and I can see you're not happy. You think I can't, but I can. When you come back for good, and I know you will, then you can cry on my shoulder and tell me whatever you want to tell me, but until that happens, I'd rather you left me out of it.'

Her mother had consoled her, but had not contradicted her husband.

She did look like a Jezebel, and that was the life she'd been living ever since she'd left Nemaha County in the vain belief that the meaning of life would never be found in Topeka or Great Bend. The conclusion she'd arrived at was that there was no such thing as the meaning of life, and that was all there was to it. She also knew, as her father had surmised long before, that she would eventually return home. She would find a husband, she would have children, and she would die somewhere within a ten-mile radius of where she'd been raised.

Such a thought was both strange and strangely comforting. The promise of homecoming was a potent force, and it pulled at her like a proverbial Kansas twister.

She dragged herself out of bed a little before noon. She made coffee, and stood for a while at the kitchen counter. From there she could see out into the street. Kids played. People talked to neighbors. A woman went down the sidewalk carrying a pie covered with a square of brightly patterned linen. The woman was smiling; she looked genuinely happy.

Judith lit a cigarette and let her mind drift. Maybe she would go out later. Not to dinner, not to a party, just for a walk somewhere. She would dress in forgettable, inconspicuous clothes, tie a scarf over her hair, forget the make-up and jewelry, and just walk somewhere for no other reason than to walk. Maybe she would go to a department store, have a cup of coffee and a sandwich in a diner, do the kinds of things that ordinary people with ordinary lives did without even thinking about it. To be normal. What did that even mean? She smiled to herself.

Finishing her cigarette, she went through to run a bath. Just as she reached for the faucet, the phone rang.

She hesitated. What if she just ignored it? She wondered what would happen. They would send someone to get her, to find out why she was being troublesome, to give her a good talking-to.

It wasn't worth it. It really wasn't.

She picked up the phone.

'One hour,' a voice said.

'Okay,' she replied.

The line went dead.

Judith took her bath. She fixed her hair, her make-up, got dressed. She wore the things she was supposed to wear. She brushed her teeth twice so he wouldn't smell cigarettes.

Two blocks east, she waited in the entranceway of the bus

station. She read a magazine. The car pulled up across the street; she folded her magazine, dropped it in the trash as she left.

'Where's—'

The Secret Service agent shook his head. 'Just get in.'

Judith got into the car. Where she was going, she didn't know. It could be any number of places. When he wanted her, he sent for her. No discussion.

The driver took a route with which she was unfamiliar. That in itself was no surprise. She'd lived in DC for two years, but knew very little of the city itself. Security and complete discretion were paramount. One time she'd been driven around and around for close to an hour before she wound up somewhere a stone's throw from her own place.

She sat back. She didn't try to make conversation. There was no point.

The drive was all of twenty minutes, perhaps less. It was a new destination. She'd been paying little attention, but as far as she could tell, they were down near the Southwest Waterfront. There was no hotel, no apartment building, just a plain office block. The car turned right and headed down a narrow alleyway to the rear. Beyond that was an underground parking garage. They drew to a halt; the agent got out, opened the door for her.

'You have to go up in the elevator,' he said, and indicated to the left.

The agent called the elevator, waiting with her, and when it came, he ushered her in. He reached for the button panel and pressed for the fourth floor. As the door closed, he turned back toward the car.

On the fourth floor, she was met by a man she'd not seen before. He was too old to be an agent, heavy-set, with steel-rimmed glasses. Around his neck he wore a stethoscope.

He smiled. It was both welcoming and authoritative.

'Miss Wagner,' he said. 'I'm Dr Portman. I know this is all a little cloak-and-dagger, but there have been a couple of cases of influenza amongst the staff and we need to ensure that you're all fit and well before ... well, before you ...'

Judith was surprised. Did they know she'd had a cold? There was something altogether avuncular and reassuring about the man, and she sensed his awkwardness. 'I think we both understand one another perfectly well,' she said.

'Yes,' Portman replied, and his relief was evident. 'If you'd like to come through.'

Judith followed him. The room into which she was taken was clearly a medical facility, but evidently more suited to dentistry than general practice.

'We use what is available,' Portman said in a somewhat apologetic tone. 'I hope you're not phobic.'

'About dentists? No, no phobia about dentists.' She relaxed. 'I have good strong Kansas teeth.'

'Could you remove your overcoat and roll up the sleeve of your blouse. I need to take your blood pressure.'

Judith did as she was asked.

'Please,' Portman said, indicating the examination chair. 'Sit. Be comfortable.'

He proceeded with his examination. He took her blood pressure, her temperature, asked her routine questions about her general well-being, her diet, whether she exercised at all.

'You seem to be in excellent health,' he concluded. 'So let's just give you an influenza inoculation and then we're all done.'

'If I don't have influenza—'

'I'm sorry,' Portman said. 'I don't much care for injections myself, and I have to administer them all the time. However, prevention is better than cure.'

'Okay,' Judith said. Resignation. That was the overriding emotion in everything she was doing. She resigned herself to it and accepted it. It was just the way it had to be. At least for now.

She sat back and relaxed. Dr Portman prepared the inoculation. He hummed some ditty to himself as if he'd forgotten she was there. With an alcohol-moistened cotton swab he wiped a small patch of her inner forearm, then he flicked the hypodermic needle and said, 'Look away if you need to.'

She didn't. The needle punctured her skin. She watched the doctor depress the plunger and the glass barrel empty out.

'Best just relax for a moment,' he said. 'You might feel a little woozy for a few moments.'

He smiled with such kindness. He reminded her of a friend of her father's, the county insurance agent. He used to show up quarterly, make his inspection, jot down his notes, always asked her about school and her horse-riding and how many boys' hearts she'd broken since last he saw her.

She felt a little dizzy, but she knew it would pass.

Dr Portman reached out and took her hand in the most comforting way.

For a moment, and for no explicable reason, she thought she heard her mother calling her in for supper.

Her sister said she'd race her to the porch. She shouted, 'Slowpoke!' and hurtled away with no warning.

'Cheater, cheater, cheater!' Judith hollered, but her voice was strained.

'It's quite usual to feel a little tired,' Dr Portman said.

Judith smiled. He really did have such a kind face.

'I'll sit with you if you want to rest for a while,' he said.

Judith breathed deeply and closed her eyes. She'd been so very weary, and it was so comfortable here.

'Thank you,' she said. 'Thank you, Doctor.'

42

The news was dominated by riots in Harlem. Police lieutenant Thomas Gilligan had killed a fifteen-year-old student, James Powell, in front of a dozen or more witnesses. An estimated four thousand people took to the streets of Harlem and Bedford-Stuyvesant. The Congress of Racial Equality and the Black Citizens' Council were front-and-center, and Malcolm X commented that 'there were probably more armed Negroes in Harlem than in any other spot on earth'.

Mitch's first instinct was to get on a plane for New York. He'd not experienced anything like that since his decision to go to Korea. The need to be present; the need to know what was happening; the need to see what was taking place and express an opinion.

He remembered feeling this exact emotion before. He went to the letters he'd written to Jean, those of January 10 and 16, 1951.

Sometimes you are drawn to something. I was drawn to you. It was a force of inescapable power. Going to Korea was the same, but it possessed a different rationale and motivation. My desire to be with you was physical, emotional, perhaps spiritual. Whatever drove me to walk into a war with a camera and a notebook was entirely different. It had everything to do with who I am, why I am here, whether I make an impression on the world.

Now I feel alone, not only without you, but almost without myself. I am trying to find something new each day, something that will reorient me to the person I believed I was as opposed to the person I think I have now become. I talk to people, I visit crime scenes, I take photographs, and yet it all seems disconnected. I share a conversation, and it is as if I am watching myself from a distance. Only yesterday I went to the grocery store and stood looking at a display of cans on a shelf. I had not only forgotten what I was planning to buy, it was almost as if I had forgotten how to buy it. Perhaps it makes no sense. It is difficult to make sense of something you yourself cannot understand.

And the subsequent letter carried a line that read:

Like you once asked me, if I am not true to myself, then how can I be true to anyone else? But if you do not know who you are anymore, then where do you begin?

The letters were thirteen years old, and yet he could remember the day, the hour, the moment he wrote each and every one of them. He had known even then that the likelihood of Jean's return was close to non-existent.

He put the letters away. He had read seven of them. There were a further five. He did not know why he read them, aside from motivating himself further to pursue the truth, so he could tell Jean's mother that she need not torture herself with the idea of her daughter reaching such a low point in her life that suicide was the only escape route.

And for himself, of course. For here he had found a reserve of will and determination that he believed he'd lost. He had not lost it; it had merely been sleeping somewhere. He had used

Korea and the subsequent failure to win Jean back as a means to abdicate responsibility for his life. He had been sadly noble, hoping to engender sympathy in others, and for what? Every day since had merely been a postponement of the inevitable.

The call came as Mitch was readying himself to leave the apartment. He intended to scour the national newspaper archives to see if there was any connection between Ruby and Webster. Then he would return to Dallas, go back to the girls at the Carousel and find out if there was anything else they could tell him about Holly Walsh, no matter how insignificant it might have seemed to them. Perhaps he could get Shaw to help in some unofficial way. If they could at least find out where she'd come from, then they could determine with certainty that she had not gone home to her folks. And if that hadn't happened, then perhaps finding her family could prompt an official missing persons report and an actual investigation. Perhaps it would come to nothing, but with Ruby unwilling to talk and Webster dead, there was no other route. It was a job of work, whichever way he looked at it, and it had to be done if he was to make any progress.

He was out in the hallway and closing the door behind him when he heard the phone. He went back in, expecting – understandably – that it would be Alice Boyd.

'Newman,' Shaw said.

'Detective Shaw, what's—'

'I'm off the case. They got to Ruby. He might not make it. He was beaten within an inch of his life. He's in a coma at Parkland Hospital.'

'What the—'

'Do whatever you have to do. I'm out of it.'

'But—'

'I have a family. They got to my family. Don't call me again, and don't come to the house, okay?'

Mitch was unable to speak.

'Do you understand me? Don't come to the house, don't contact me in any way.'

The line went dead.

43

Lester Byron refused him money, albeit apologetically.

'I cannot authorize it alone, Mitch,' he said, 'and there's nothing here I can pitch. I want to help, but my hands are tied on this one.'

Mitch approached another two editors who had previously bought his work. The promise of an exclusive about 'something very significant concerning the Kennedy administration' failed to generate any excitement. Mitch possessed a reputation for unreliability. Too many times he had failed to deliver. It was troubling, but for this he had no one to blame but himself.

And so, finally, he stood in a pawnshop a block and a half from his apartment and haggled on the price of the engagement ring.

A hundred and ten dollars. That would get him to Dallas, cover a motel, a rental car, food and whatever else he might need for a week or so.

He took the money.

It was heartbreaking, but there was no other option. He did it because he believed that Jean would have done the same.

From there he went to the national newspaper archives. The news about Ruby had heightened his need to understand what part he and his club had played in Jean's investigation. Ruby was bargaining for his protection with something he knew. Had he told Jean, and had that led to her death? Had Holly Walsh also known, and been murdered as a result? Ruby had become the lynchpin that held it all together. Find out why it had been so important to silence Ruby, and he would find out why Holly and Jean had had to die.

Beginning in January of 1964, he backtracked through editions of the *Dallas Morning News*. He was looking for any reference to Webster or Ruby that might open the door to a further lead in Dallas itself. There was nothing to clearly suggest any actual connection between them. Nevertheless, Mitch persisted. If he didn't do this and his efforts in Dallas came to nothing, he would only regret his own lack of patience. He had sufficient regrets already, and life had a keen way of constantly reminding him of them.

He finally located something in July of 1961. It was a Friday edition, the 21st of the month, and it had been penned by a journalist named Don Carlton. The headline was *COMMUNIST GROUP FACES CHARGES*. It detailed events earlier in the week, when a pro-communist group had been broken up by police following a tip-off. The location of the meeting had been an upper room at the Carousel. The article named the owner as local entrepreneur, Jacob Rubenstein. Rubenstein, according to the report, had been cautioned to the effect that his license would be revoked if any further meetings took place. Such activities were in violation of the 1951 Communist Control Act. That confirmed Shaw's unsubstantiated report of the Carousel meeting he'd spoken of when Ruby was being questioned.

Additional members of this group – the Texas Communist League – were named as Joseph Hunter, Leonard Fox, Myriam Turnbull, Isaac Greaves, Marshall Jeavons and Leland Webster.

The Texas Communist League. Was Ruby himself a communist, or did he merely accept money from anyone for the use of his place, irrespective of their political persuasion?

Mitch copied out the names. It was another thread, if nothing else, and demonstrated that there had possibly been a prior connection between Webster and Ruby. Again, though, it was supposition. Webster might never have met Ruby, might have been utterly unaware of the club's ownership. Ruby himself might not have been present when the meeting took place. The room may have been rented under false pretenses. The mere fact that Ruby was the legal proprietor had nevertheless been sufficient to threaten him with revocation of his license.

In the absence of anything else, Mitch would take it and pursue it. Dallas was where he needed to be.

Ruby had been afraid for a reason. He wanted protection. He believed his life was in danger. He'd been unwilling to say anything further until Shaw provided a guarantee of immunity and safety. That this was somehow unrelated to Jean, to Holly Walsh, to the murder of Leland Webster seemed impossible. Mitch did not believe that Ruby had implied a knowledge of Jean as an opportunist get-out-of-jail card.

Whatever Ruby knew, it was big enough for someone to get to him, even in the county jail system. The details of the attack were unknown. Again, that information would be in Dallas, for it seemed unlikely that an event of such insignificance would find its way into the national news system. Ruby was a nobody, a lowlife club owner in Dallas. If *they* could get to him in jail, then *they* certainly had the power and authority to keep his name out of the newspapers. Who had that power? The police? The federal authorities? The government, for sure. People were not killed or beaten half to death because they heard rumors. Such things happened to people who needed to be silenced.

Back at his apartment, Mitch put some clothes, his camera, additional rolls of film and notebooks in an overnight bag. He wondered if he should approach the Secret Service. He decided against it. Questions had been asked about him. People had been questioned about his activities and whereabouts. He was a known quantity. Nevertheless, he currently possessed a degree of freedom of movement that he was determined to maintain for as long as possible. To approach the Secret Service would necessitate some sort of official application, perhaps paperwork, time spent waiting for an appointment, and to say what? He thought this, he guessed the other, he had a number of suspicions. Was there any evidence? No, there was not. Was there anyone else who might be prepared to come forward and make a statement that would substantiate any of these suspicions? Well yes, there was one man, but he was in a coma in Parkland, and – even if he came through it – Mitch guessed that the last people in the world Jack Ruby would be wanting to share information with were the Secret Service. Give them what he knew, and any bargaining chips he might have had to get out of Dallas would be spent.

Mitch was on his own. He understood this completely.

Tomorrow he would head back to Texas. Meantime, he would try not to think. If Jean had given her life for what she believed in, he had to be prepared to do the same.

44

Jackie stood quietly in the White House's East Room, her hand on the lid of the open piano. Eric Gugler had designed it for Franklin D. Roosevelt, and Jackie had shared it with the nation in a TV broadcast back in February of 1962, telling viewers about the portable stage for the Shakespeare Players, and the time Pablo Casals enthralled the governor of Puerto Rico, Luis Muñoz Marin, and the many guests present for his honorary dinner. That had been little more than two years ago, and yet it seemed an age. She had worked so hard, so diligently, doing all she could to restore the building and make it the people's house. She had been proud of what she'd done, yet now she viewed it as if through a fine mist, a curtain of organdy. It seemed so shallow and meaningless. Every room in the building served as a reminder of things unspoken, emotions left unexpressed, secrets and lies and so many broken promises.

As she thought of it, she felt a weariness through every inch of her body, her mind, her soul.

Jack was away again. She knew where he was. She didn't know the address, nor with whom he was sharing his crass jokes, his temperamental comments, his sudden shifts of mood. Perhaps, though, he saved those solely for his wife, while the others saw the side with which she had fallen in love – the sophisticated humor, the charm, the masculine elegance, the very things with which he'd seduced a nation.

There had been no doubt in her mind that she was marrying a driven man. That had been such a large part of the natural, powerful attraction that had drawn her to him. But a man of passion was a man of passion, and rarely could that passion be applied with judicious selectivity. Jack wanted the whole world or nothing, and people were pulled into that vortex of charisma. It was hard not to crave his attention. It was addictive, even more so now she knew that other nameless, faceless women were suffering from that selfsame addiction.

She loved him, but he hurt her. She longed for him, but he pushed her away. She wanted to hear soft and considerate words, but too often she received harsh rebukes or straightforward dismissals.

Lord knows, she should have married Bobby.

She laughed at her own girlish naïveté. The Kennedys were the Kennedys, and once you took their name, you lived by their rules. She remembered when she and Jack had met, back in May of '52, at a dinner party. Charles Bartlett had introduced them. She was bowled over. Jack had been running for the Senate then. She'd had no doubt he would succeed. He was a man who would prosper irrespective of the direction he'd taken in life. She believed that that would have held true even without his father's money and influence. If Jack had been a plumber, he would have been the most successful plumber on the Eastern Seaboard. He would have tightened faucets and fixed leaks until he was a millionaire.

He'd proposed in November of that same year. She didn't say no. She didn't say yes. She was working for the *Washington Times-Herald*; she'd already agreed to go to England to cover the coronation of the new queen. Away for a month, she had struggled, not because she didn't love Jack, but because she knew she would have to make a complete sacrifice. Her job, her home, her ties with her own family would all suffer. It would be a trade-off.

Bobby told her Jack would be president, and she would be first lady. The thrill of such a crazy idea! But marrying Jack meant marrying his family, and with that family came dark secrets.

She remembered Rosemary. By the time she met Jack, Rosemary was already thirty-three years old. No one spoke of her. No one except Bobby.

'My sister was beautiful,' he confided in Jackie one night. He'd drunk too much champagne and was maudlin over some fight he'd had with Ethel. 'She was bright and funny and she didn't give a damn about her grades or whether she was liked by anyone. You know, she was going to be a kindergarten teacher. She studied all that Montessori stuff.' He had seemed on the verge of tears. 'I loved her, Jackie. We all loved her, and then Dad had those bastards stick a knife in her brain and now someone has to carry her to the bathroom.' Bobby called his father a heartless and selfish man. 'All he cared about was how she appeared to others. He thought she would embarrass us. He thought she would do something foolish or stupid and bring shame on the Kennedy name. And you know where she is now? I'll tell you where. Jefferson, Wisconsin. The St Coletta Institute for Backward Youth.' He spat the words out as if each was more bitter than the last.

For a while, he was quiet. It seemed a long time, but it couldn't have been more than a minute. Jackie had felt awkward, as if he knew he'd spoken out of turn. But that was not the case, for when he spoke again, it was with a clear and precise tone, and the words sounded both definite and prophetic.

'Be careful,' he said. 'This family is cursed. My father … my father has done things that no one knows about. The money came from bad things. Rosie got out. I know she lives alone and she doesn't even know who we are, but she's not part of this crazy family any more. If ever there was a silver lining …'

He changed the subject then, made a joke. He never spoke

of Rosemary again, nor of his father, nor of the kind of family Jackie was marrying into. It was the only honest glimpse she'd ever had into what really lay behind the superficial theater of the Kennedy empire.

She'd accepted Jack's proposal. Seven years after their marriage, she was indeed the First Lady of the United States of America, just as Bobby had predicted.

And yet here she was, alone in the East Room with Roosevelt's piano and its damned American Eagle legs, the Gilbert Stuart portrait of Washington, the Monroe candelabra, the three twelve-hundred-pound chandeliers that came all the way from Bohemia – all so beautiful and opulent and empty.

'Mrs Kennedy?'

Jackie looked up. 'Walter.'

'I'm sorry to disturb you, but Caroline is asking for you. She said you'd promised to read her a story.'

'Is she feeling a little better?'

'If I might speak honestly?'

Jackie laughed, and waved her hand for him to go on.

'I think Miss Caroline is of a mind to milk her head cold for all it's worth.'

Jackie walked toward the door. She touched Walter's sleeve as she passed.

'Oh, you know this family's little secrets too well,' she whispered in her gentle East Hampton accent. 'You should be careful, Walter, or we might have to do away with you.'

45

July 21, 1964

Mitch stayed in a different motel. He used a different name. He hired a car, and even though he paid in cash, he was conscious of the fact that the rental would make finding him all the easier.

The simple truth was that if he was even close to right in his suspicions, then whoever might be involved would have no issue in locating him, regardless of where he went or how he tried to cover his tracks.

The car was a '59 Nash Metropolitan, the cheapest he could get. It was small and inconspicuous, and that was all that mattered. He spent much of Tuesday at Parkland, hoping against all odds that there might be some change in Ruby's condition. According to one other reporter, who appeared briefly and then vanished, there was a good chance that Ruby would never regain consciousness.

Due to the nature of the assault, right there in Dallas County Jail, Ruby had been assigned a guard. Mitch headed back to the hospital on the Wednesday morning and found the same beat cop standing sentinel. He bought him a cup of coffee and got him talking.

'I know Nelson Shaw up at Metro,' he said. 'You know him?'

'Can't say I do, no.'

'The guy in there, Ruby . . . hell, I was having a conversation with him only last Friday. He owns the Carousel downtown, you know?'

The cop shook his head. 'Don't know it. Not my beat.'

'So what the hell happened?'

'Nothin' to tell you, save he got himself a real good kicking from some other inmate. It happens. Not the first time, won't be the last.'

'Guess whoever it was wanted him dead, or you wouldn't be here.'

'He's still in custody, technically speaking, even though he ain't going nowhere in a hurry, so I stand here and keep him company until he goes back or … well, until …'

'Until he dies,' Mitch said. 'Reporter that was here yesterday told me it was real bad, that he might not make it.'

'Couldn't tell you.'

'Terrible business.'

'Well, he sure as hell upset someone.'

'I guess he did,' Mitch replied.

'Anyway, I shouldn't really be talking to you. The coffee's appreciated, but you understand, right?'

'I do, and I'm not here to cause any trouble. I'll head out then. I guess I can find out from the switchboard if he's doing any better.'

'I'm sure you can.'

Mitch checked back in again on Thursday, once more on Friday. There was no change in Ruby's condition. If anything, the mere fact that there had been no improvement confirmed the severity of his injuries. Having scoured the papers each day, Mitch had found no reference to the incident, and thus was none the wiser about what had occurred.

In between times, notwithstanding numerous visits to County Records, newspaper archives and the city library, he was also no clearer on what the Texas Communist League actually was, and who else might have been a member.

He went back through local newspapers to November of the previous year, looking for Holly Walsh. It was mind-numbing, and there was every possibility that even had there been some three-line squib about her, he would have missed it. Nevertheless, he could not let it go. Finding nothing in the newspapers, he headed out to the Carousel, but found the club locked up, a sign on the door that read: *CLOSED UNTIL FURTHER NOTICE*.

He wanted to call Shaw, even considered returning to his house, but the man had told him in no uncertain terms that he would not be welcome. Shaw had been taken off the case. Someone else was investigating the murder of Leland Webster, and the only suspect, as far as Mitch knew, was now more than likely going to die himself.

He'd hit an impasse yet again. He felt a profound sense of frustration and impotence. He spent his time going back through the many and varied notes he'd made on his previous trip, looking at different possibilities, even asking at bars and diners in the vicinity of the Carousel to see if anyone remembered a girl called Holly who might have worked at the Carousel. He didn't have a picture of her, not even a definite description. Those who'd worked with her had known her for little more than a month. They had not known where she'd come from, nor where she'd gone. And had Jack Ruby not said that it was Holly that Jean was looking for, had he not made it clear that he believed Holly was dead, then she would have warranted no attention.

The irony of the situation did not pass Mitch by: in death, he was giving Jean a far greater amount of his time and attention than he ever had when she was alive. That, in and of itself, was perhaps the saddest comment of all. Had he afforded her this much consideration when they were together, he would never have gone to war, and she would perhaps still be alive.

By the middle of Saturday, Mitch was climbing the walls. He steeled himself to call Alice, doing so from a booth in the street. His paranoia and caution even entertained the possibility that *they* already knew where he was and had tapped his motel phone.

'It's Mitch,' he said. 'I'm sorry it's been so long.'

'Mitch. Oh, it's so good to hear your voice. I've been worried sick.'

'Yes, I understand, Alice, and I really am sorry. I've been so busy trying to find anything that might help us.'

'You're still trying to find out what happened?'

Mitch was surprised. 'Yes. Yes, of course I am.'

'But the coroner's report came, and they concluded that she really did take her own life.' Alice's voice broke, and Mitch could hear her trying to stop herself from crying.

He was torn then – whether to say nothing and let Alice slowly reconcile herself to the fact that her only child had committed suicide, or to tell her that he really didn't believe it, that he was sure, absolutely sure, that Jean would never have done something like that and that there were people who were trying to cover up the truth.

He remembered a missing child case. The parents were distraught, terrified, inconsolable. He had seen them after the girl's body was found, and they were calm – grief-stricken and desolate, yes, but calm nonetheless. He'd realized that it was the not-knowing that had been the worst thing of all. Once they knew she was gone, they could come to terms with it. While she remained unfound, it was just further torture.

This was the same, in effect. Alice had an anchor. Okay, he believed it to be wrong, and he believed there were many lies behind it, but in the absence of anything else, it was something.

To give her hope, to present her with the possibility that it was not suicide, not only took away her one point of stability, it also raised so many other questions that he could not answer. Who would do such a thing? Why was it being covered up? Why would the coroner file a false report concerning cause of death?

He listened to Alice gather herself together, and then he said, 'I'm still trying to understand how this could have happened.'

'Yes, yes, of course,' Alice said. 'Thank you for doing this, and for calling me.'

Mitch sensed that she wanted to get off the phone. For all her apparent gratitude, she perhaps would have been better without any contact. He couldn't give her anything to ease the distress. His voice and words had merely served to reinforce the anguish she already felt.

'As soon as I have anything to tell you, I'll call again,' he said.

'But you'll come to her funeral, of course, won't you?'

It was as if he'd been hit in the head with a baseball. Her funeral. Her *funeral*. How could he have not realized that as soon as the coroner's report was filed, her body would be released for burial?

'Yes,' he said. 'Yes, her funeral.'

'Friday,' Alice said. 'It will be here at the First Congregational Church on Friday. You remember where that is, Mitchell? On Sumner Street?'

'Yes, of course,' he said, his mind reeling at the prospect of having to return yet again to West Haven.

It seemed that with her photograph, her bylines in the newspaper archives, her engagement ring, the letters read but never replied to, the universe was conspiring to remind him time and again that she was as much a part of his life now as she had ever been.

He was experiencing emotions that belonged to a different time and place, emotions he should have found the words to express. Those words were the very ones he should have shared with Jean, and perhaps – if he had listened, if he'd been patient, conscientious, methodical, the very attitudes he was now demonstrating – this entire chapter of their lives could have been something imagined, not something real.

Mitch hated himself. That was the simple truth. He hated the young man he'd been, the person he'd then become as a result of his own self-centeredness and lack of consideration. And now? Now he was just beginning to appreciate who he truly was, and in doing so, to understand what it was about himself that Jean might have loved.

But it was too late. Too damn late. He could not shed tears, but he cried inside.

'You take care now, Mitchell,' Alice said. 'I'll see you in a week. Three o'clock. First Congregational. You can say something if you want to. I don't think there'll be many people there, so it would be nice if you'd say something for her.'

'Yes,' he mumbled. 'Yes.'

He hung up the phone. He stood there on the street and looked out toward the horizon. It was as if everything he believed himself to be had been shown to him in one single, clear moment, and he did not like what he saw.

46

July 27, 1964

The Carousel remained closed, and thus he had no opportunity to ask further questions of Marion or the other girls. There had been no change in Ruby's condition, and though he had made several attempts to get through to Shaw, he had not succeeded. Nothing was moving in any direction.

He went back to chasing the connection between Ruby and Leland Webster, and that was where he got a break. The DMV records department gave up traffic citations on both Marshall Jeavons and Leonard Fox, two of those who had been named as members of the Texas Communist League alongside Webster.

Jeavons' ticket was recent – just six weeks prior – and Mitch took his address.

The man he expected and the man he found were very different indeed. What had he imagined? Some hard-faced, angry Marx-spouting subversive with a hammer and sickle sewn onto his cap and a repertoire of anti-capitalist rhetoric? Jeavons was not only well beyond sixty years of age, he was frail, softly spoken and rheumy-eyed. His house was a worn-out plankboard affair with peeling paint and broken window boxes. If anything, he seemed very pleased that Mitch had tracked him down.

'Yes, I know Leland,' he said. They were seated together in

the living room. Jeavons had offered him a drink, but Mitch had declined.

'Though I haven't seen him for some time, of course.'

'Of course?'

'Well, you know how these things go. Groups like that start with great enthusiasm, and then the enthusiasm sort of dies down and you realize you're not actually accomplishing a great deal.'

'We're talking about the Texas Communist League?'

'Yes, yes, the communist group.'

'You aren't concerned to know how I found you?'

'Because of my communist sympathies? Because I'm concerned what other people might think?' Jeavons laughed wryly. 'You get to my age and what other people think is the least of your concerns. Besides, if you know Leland, then I don't think you're going to be from the authorities, Mr Newman.'

'I came to ask you about him. I actually tracked you down from an old newspaper article and a traffic citation.'

'Even at my age I'm more than capable of being a subversive.' Jeavons smiled. 'So, how is Leland these days?'

Mitch paused. He looked squarely at Jeavons. 'I'm afraid Mr Webster is dead.'

Jeavons was visibly shocked. 'Dead? What? How can that be possible?'

'He was murdered.'

Jeavons looked like he'd been slapped. 'Murdered?'

'Apparently so. Shot by someone called Jack Ruby.'

'Ruby? The club owner? That Ruby?'

'Yes, the man who owns the Carousel, the place where the League met.'

'That's ridiculous! Why on earth would Jack Ruby want to kill Leland?'

'I don't know, Mr Jeavons, but it's part of a whole mess of things I am trying to unravel.'

Jeavons was quiet for a while. He was evidently distressed and agitated. A couple of times he gripped the arms of his chair, and his knuckles whitened. 'Poor Leland,' he eventually said. 'Poor, poor Leland.'

'You were close?'

Jeavons shook his head. 'No more than any of us were. Myriam and Leonard and the others. We were just interested in politics. We weren't serious. We talked about Marx and Engels and whatever else, you know? It was just good to have a group of friends with similar interests, and I imagine it would have stayed that way, had Ruby's friend not showed up.'

'Who was that?' Mitch took out his notebook.

'Lee Oswald. That was his name. Young man, couldn't have been more than twenty-two or three. Married to a Russian girl. Can't remember her name. He used to be in the Marine Corps. His father was a cousin of Robert E. Lee, believe it or not. So full of himself. Angry, arrogant, a most unpleasant individual. I didn't like him at all.'

'And he was a friend of Jack Ruby's?'

'Friend, acquaintance, I don't know. We rented the room above the Carousel club for our meetings. We met there perhaps a dozen, fifteen times. After a while, Oswald always seemed to be there before we arrived. I really didn't have time for him, to be frank, even though he perhaps had more reason to be there than any of us.'

'How so?'

'Well, he actually defected to the Soviets. After he came out of the Marine Corps, he went to Russia. They gave him a visa for a week but he pretended a suicide attempt and they put him in a psychiatric hospital for observation. Then he lived in Minsk for a while, and I guess that's where he met his wife. Eventually they got tired of him, or he got tired of them, and he came back here to Dallas with his Russian wife, but not before trying to renounce his American citizenship at the US embassy in Moscow. Remarkable story, really, but absolutely true.'

'So did the group stop meeting after Oswald arrived?'

'We met right up until August or September of last year, and then it all sort of fell apart and we stopped organizing things. If you want my opinion, it really was down to Oswald. He was so opinionated, so passionate... I say passionate, but it was obsessive, driven, and behind it was a real anger and resentment. I just felt he was a very unpleasant person, and he tried so hard to dominate things. He always had an opinion, and sometimes it seemed that he stated that opinion just to be contrary. The atmosphere was tense and hostile. That was not why the group was founded, and when the meetings all seemed to end in friction and dispute, it seemed pointless to continue.'

Mitch took the photo of Jean from his jacket pocket and handed it to Jeavons.

'This is a friend of mine,' he said. 'A journalist. She was down here in November of last year and I know she was trying to speak with Jack Ruby. Did you ever see her?'

Jeavons reached for his glasses and put them on. He looked closely at the picture, and then handed it back.

'No,' he said. 'I have never seen her before.'

'Were you aware of a girl called Holly at the Carousel? Holly Walsh.'

'Holly?' Jeavons said. 'Yes, I think so. Was it Holly, or maybe Sally? There were a lot of girls there, Mr Newman, and I'm of an age where such temptations are part of history.' He laughed at himself. 'And even if they weren't, I'd probably forget within an hour.'

'Is there anything else you can tell me about Jack Ruby?'

'Well, Jack was a crook. That was obvious. I mean, he owned and ran a strip joint. I didn't particularly want to meet there, but it cost us next to nothing and we were never there during official opening hours. We saw some of the girls who worked there every once in a while, but they were arriving or leaving.' Jeavons smiled. 'They had their clothes on. That's what I'm getting at.'

'Have you ever heard of either Joseph Civello or Carlos Marcello?'

Jeavons shook his head. 'No, those names don't mean anything to me.'

'And can you tell me anything more about this Lee Oswald?'

'There's always the assassination attempt.'

Mitch's surprise was evident.

Jeavons laughed. 'Lord, you look like you got hit by a bolt of lightning!'

'You're saying he tried to assassinate someone?'

'Well, he said he did. Whether or not it was true is an entirely different matter, but he said he defected to Russia and that proved to be true, so who knows?'

Mitch immediately thought of Dallas. The president's visit the previous November. He thought of Leland Webster and the Texas School Book Depository, right there on the motorcade route.

'Who did he try to assassinate?'

'A United States Army major general called Edwin Walker.'

'Not the president?'

Jeavons looked puzzled. 'No, not the president. Why, did someone say that he had tried to assassinate the president?'

'No. Sorry. I'm just jumping to conclusions.'

'The only thing I know relates to this General Walker. I don't know all the facts, of course ...'

'Just tell me what you can, Mr Jeavons. Everything is helpful.'

'Well, from what I understand, Walker was a very outspoken anti-communist. Back in '61 he was relieved of command of his unit in Germany after he started spouting right-wing propaganda to his men. He was hauled back here, and started raising a storm about integration and what-have-you. Eventually he was arrested, and the attorney general had him thrown into a mental institution. The grand jury didn't indict him, however, and he resigned from the army. Only US general ever to have done that, as far as I know. Anyway, he went on to run for governor of Texas, but Connally got in instead.

'I don't know if Oswald actually did fire a shot at Walker like he claimed, but he used to say that Walker was a fascist and that it was our duty as good communists to stand up against fascists, just as Stalin had against the Nazis. The boy was a hothead, full of crazy opinions. Not uneducated, and certainly no stranger to texts and materials on the subject, but he tended to rant on about those things he agreed with, and those things he agreed with were only half the story.'

'Do you have any idea where he is now?'

'None at all.'

'Did Oswald and Leland Webster argue, perhaps?'

Jeavons raised his eyebrows in surprise. 'You think Oswald killed Leland?'

'I have to consider any and all possibilities, Mr Jeavons. The ballistics report states that Jack Ruby's gun was used to kill him, but that doesn't mean that Ruby was the one who fired it.'

Jeavons was quiet for a time, pensive and focused. 'You know, I don't think I ever saw them anything other than friendly. Leland and Oswald. Leland wasn't the brightest light in the harbor, and I got the impression he admired Oswald, if only because Oswald didn't just talk about doing things, he actually did them. The fact that he'd been in the army, that he'd gone to Russia, that he brought home a Russian wife. He didn't just read pamphlets and complain about the government, you know?'

'Was there anyone else who knew Leland? Anyone else who might be able to shed light on why he was murdered.'

'There was a girl he knew. Ruth something or other. He brought her along to a couple of meetings. I remember she'd just been through a divorce. She and Oswald's wife were friends, I think.' Jeavons smiled and shook his head. 'I get confused. Dates escape me. Maybe Leland met this woman through Lee and his wife – Marina, that was the wife's name. Marina Oswald. Yes, I think that's what happened.'

'Can you remember Ruth's surname?'

Jeavons closed his eyes. 'I can see her now. Dark hair, long face ... pretty.' He suddenly looked up and smiled. 'Paine,' he said. 'Ruth Paine.'

'So Ruth Paine was friends with Marina Oswald, and Leland met her through Lee?'

'Yes, I'm sure that's how it was. I think Ruth helped the Oswalds when they came back to Dallas. You'll have to ask her, of course, but I think that's right.'

'Do you have any idea where I might find her?'

'I'm sorry, no. I pretty much keep myself to myself these days, and she and I were nothing more than acquaintances.'

'This has been immensely valuable,' Mitch said, 'and I really appreciate your time.' He closed his notebook. 'And I'm sorry to have to bring you the news about Leland.'

'Indeed,' Jeavons said. 'Have they arrested Jack Ruby? Is he in custody?'

'He is, yes,' Mitch replied. He couldn't bring himself to comment further on what had since happened to Ruby. He'd delivered enough upsetting news already.

'Such a tragic situation. Hard to imagine. I mean, people get murdered, of course, but you never think it's going to be someone you actually know.'

'No, you never do,' Mitch said, thinking that such a sentiment applied also to supposed suicides and near-fatal physical assaults.

Jeavons got up. He walked with Mitch to the front door.

'You're most welcome to come back if there's anything else I can help you with.'

'Thank you,' Mitch said, and headed down the path to his car.

47

July 28, 1964

Mitch located Ruth Paine without difficulty. She was listed as Mrs R. Hyde Paine in the telephone directory, an address out in Irving, and when Mitch called the number, it was she who answered.

'Mrs Paine?'

'Yes.'

'Hello. My name is Mitchell Newman. I got your name from a man called Marshall Jeavons.'

There was a hesitation at the other end of the line. 'Marshall Jeavons?'

'He was part of the Texas Communist League—'

'Oh yes, I remember him. I wasn't any part of that, to be honest. At least not directly.'

'I appreciate that, yes. I understand that you were friends with Marina Oswald, however.'

Again a hesitation, and then, 'Might I ask what this is about?'

'Yes, I'm sorry. I'm following up on something. A friend of mine, a journalist from Washington DC, came down to Dallas last November and was working on a story that related to a man called Jack Ruby.'

'Oh yes,' Ruth said, an inflection suggesting distaste in her tone. 'He owned that dreadful club.'

'Yes, the Carousel. Anyway, my friend was trying to speak with Mr Ruby, but things didn't work out exactly, so now I'm trying to make sense of a few things.'

'And how does this have anything to do with me, Mr Newman?'

'It's my understanding that Marina's husband, Lee, was an acquaintance of Mr Ruby, and I wondered if you might explain to me how you knew Marina, and whether I might be able to find Lee.'

'Well, there's no real mystery there, Mr Newman. My ex-husband, Michael, and I moved here to Irving some years ago when Michael got a job with Bell Helicopters. I have always maintained a great interest in all things Russian. I am also a Quaker, and I was involved in pen-pal programs and hosting Russians who came over to visit in the United States. It kept me occupied while my husband was working.'

Mitch was maneuvering the phone between his shoulder and his ear while fishing out a notebook and a pen. For some reason the woman was talking, and he didn't want to miss anything important.

'Anyway, I met Marina at a party. We became close friends. I wasn't really involved with her husband. To be completely honest, I didn't care for him very much, though Marina was quite devoted. Both Michael and I tried hard to be friendly, but Lee was just not a very friendly sort of person. When Lee decided to move to New Orleans in April or May of 1963, I drove Marina down there to join him. There was all that trouble he got into for handing out pro-Castro leaflets; he even got himself arrested in August for disturbing the peace. I guess you could say that things didn't go as planned for him.'

Ruth laughed. She was a gossip, and though Mitch didn't much care for it, it was actually exactly what he needed.

'I brought Marina back here to Irving in September,' she went

267

on. 'She stayed with me, and Lee went to Mexico. From what I understood, he was trying to go to Cuba, but the Cubans didn't want him and he came back with his tail between his legs in October. That's when I heard about the job at the book place.'

'The book place?' Mitch asked, scarcely able to believe the coincidence.

'Yes, that big warehouse up on Elm Street.'

'The Texas School Book Depository?'

'That's the one. My neighbor's brother worked there, and my neighbor told me there was an opening. Lee went on up there and they hired him on a full-time seasonal contract. He stayed in a rooming house in Oak Cliff, and he would come over weekends and visit with Marina and their daughter, June. Marina was pregnant with Audrey, and she was born toward the end of October, just after Lee got the job downtown.'

'And they are still separated?' Mitch asked.

'I think so, yes. Last I saw Marina, she hadn't seen him for a good while. He didn't seem interested in the girls either, but I have to say that all three of them seem to do an awful lot better when he's not around. Marina and I aren't really in touch these days. We sort of drifted apart, I guess.'

'Do you know where she lives? Or, even better, do you know where I could find Lee?'

'Well, I guess he might still work at the depository. You could try there. Otherwise, I don't know what to tell you. Like I said, Marina and I are just not in touch anymore and I don't know where she moved to.'

'Okay. It's really kind of you to take the time to speak to me.'

'Well, I hope I haven't said anything out of turn, Mr Newman. You just got me talking, and off I went like a chatterbox.'

Ruth Paine laughed again, and to Mitch she sounded a little nervous. She had volunteered a great deal of personal information, without any real prompting.

He thanked her again, told her that everything she'd said would be treated in confidence, and hung up.

He went to his notes and photographs and found the list of Texas School Book Depository employees he'd photographed at County Records. There it was: OSWALD, LEE H. The name had been right there all along, but until now, it had carried no greater significance than any other on the list.

He glanced at his watch. It was close to four. If he went directly there, he might make it before the place closed up for the day.

Arriving even as the nightwatchman was checking in, Mitch found the same girl at reception. This time she seemed distracted, almost determined to be unhelpful. Perhaps it was merely that he was preventing her from leaving as planned.

'I'm really sorry,' he said. 'I don't want to trouble you, but I'm trying to find a man called Lee Oswald.'

The girl looked at the employee register. She scanned the names, shaking her head as she went. She paused, hesitated. Mitch leaned forward in anticipation, but she said, 'Osborne,' and went on down the names.

Finally she looked up. 'No,' she said. 'Not here. Like I said before, we have another warehouse at 1917 Houston.'

'You're sure?' Mitch asked, knowing that the question would do nothing but further irritate her.

'I am sure,' the young woman said, 'and I am also sure that we are now closing and you have to leave.'

'I appreciate your time,' Mitch said, 'and I understand that you need to close up, but is there any way to find out when Mr Oswald stopped working here?'

'That would be Personnel.'

He looked at the girl with his most forlorn and desperate expression.

She smiled. 'You are a real pain-in-the-you-know-what,' she said. She lifted the receiver, dialed a number.

'Mr Thomasson? Hi, this is Janice downstairs. I have someone here who's trying to find a Lee Oswald. Apparently he used to work here. Do you have any record of that name?'

She was silent.

'Yes,' she said. 'That's it. O-S-W-A-L-D.'

Again, silence.

Mitch's heart raced.

'Yes, exactly. Okay. Yes. The twenty-first.' She paused, and then said, 'Thank you, Mr Thomasson. You've been really helpful.'

She replaced the receiver. 'Well, he used to work here,' she said. 'Sixth floor. Storage and dispatch clerk. Until the twenty-first of November last year. Didn't show up on the twenty-second, and there's been no contact with him since that time.' She shrugged her shoulders. 'Maybe he got a better offer someplace else.'

'Twenty-first of November, 1963,' Mitch said, and wrote it down. He smiled. He was truly grateful. 'Janice,' he said, 'you are an absolute star.'

He left the Depository and went back to his car. He sat for a while and smoked a cigarette. Then he smoked a second. He looked through his ever-increasing sheaf of notes. There were so many facts, and yet so little substance. Things had happened, and he was certain they were connected, but how?

Both Leland Webster and Lee Oswald had worked in this building. Oswald was a no-show the day before Kennedy's trip along this exact route, and had not been heard of since.

He got out of the car. He looked up at the windows of the depository, counted up to the sixth floor. He took some photographs of the building, and then turned and looked down along Elm.

Ruby had connections to Civello and Marcello. Jean was down

in Dallas asking questions. She found her way to Ruby. She was interested in a girl called Holly Walsh, who just vanished into thin air. Leland Webster and Lee Oswald worked at the Book Depository. They were known communists. Oswald had even defected to the Soviet Union and returned with a Russian wife. Oswald had military training. There was a good chance he was responsible for an assassination attempt on an army general. He was a no-show the day before Kennedy's arrival.

Mitch looked up at the windows on the sixth floor, and then back down to the street.

Leland Webster was dead.

Jean Boyd was dead.

More than likely, Holly Walsh was dead.

And now Jack Ruby was clinging on after being beaten within an inch of his life in Dallas County Jail.

Everyone connected to whatever it was that had happened the previous November was unwilling or unable to talk. November 1963. The presidential visit. The motorcade. Elm Street.

A moment came back to Mitch. Ruby was being questioned. Shaw told him he'd be detained in Dealey Plaza. Ruby said it was ironic 'considering everything that happened last November'. Were those the words he'd used?

His thoughts went to some of the things Bill Sandford had said. Doubts in the Democratic camp about whether Kennedy would secure the nomination, and if he did, whether he would get a second term. The illnesses. The alleged affairs. The political near-catastrophes that had dogged his presidency. The rumors of a rigged election, the possibility that Nixon would run again and expose anomalies about the 1960 count.

What was he really considering here? That there might have been a plan to assassinate Kennedy? That Oswald had something to do with it? That Webster knew something, that Holly overheard something, that Jean had overturned some stones and found things that made her a liability.

And what possible connection could there be between Lee Oswald and what was beginning to formulate in his mind? The attempt on Walker's life. The fact that Oswald was an outspoken communist, that he was pro-Castro, anti-US government sufficient to have attempted to revoke his citizenship, that he was army-trained.

Everyone connected to this – whatever *this* was – had wound up dead, beaten or disappeared.

A feeling of quiet coolness took his thoughts, beneath that a real sense of fear.

What had Jean walked into here? What had she *really* walked into?

And considering that he was now following very closely in her footsteps, would the very same fate be waiting for him at the end?

48

'I know it's late,' Bobby said. 'And I know we've all had a long day, but the sooner we get on with this, the sooner we'll get out of here.

'My secretary, Catherine,' he went on. 'She's going to take notes and prepare whatever minutes we might need. So, just to keep some sense of formality here, I want you all to give names and posts.'

'Pierre Salinger, press secretary.'

'Stuart Udall, Interior.'

'Ken O'Donnell, chief of staff.'

'Ted Sorensen, special counsel.'

'Mac Bundy, national security advisor.'

'Mike Feldman, deputy special counsel.'

'Walter Lambert, chief of presidential Secret Service detail.'

'Frank Mankiewicz, press secretary to the attorney general.'

'Okay, so the National Convention is in twenty-six days. It will take place August twenty-fourth through twenty-seventh at Boardwalk Hall in Atlantic City.'

'Someone wants to hit the beach,' Bundy quipped.

There was a murmur of laughter around the table.

'Walter . . . why don't you tell us what you know.'

'Security-wise, it's really no better or worse than anywhere

273

else. The main hall is approximately four hundred and fifty by three hundred and ten feet. At a stretch, it'll take about twelve or thirteen thousand people. It has a barrel ceiling, no supporting columns. The roof is carried by steel trusses that span three hundred and fifty feet. It's home to the Miss America Pageant—'

'Oh, so it's not the surfing we're going for,' Salinger interjected.

Bobby glanced at Catherine. She smiled knowingly. She was used to this kind of banter.

'And,' Lambert went on, 'the week after we're done, The Beatles will be playing there.'

'The who?' Sorensen asked.

'The Beatles,' Udall said. 'It's an English pop group.'

Sorensen shrugged, none the wiser.

'Okay, so as far as security is concerned, what are we looking at?' Bobby asked.

'I'll have eight teams of twelve, local police for perimeter control. Feds want to run screening on all staffers, all invitees and their guests, but as far as the general public is concerned, we're limited to at-the-door searches, routine vigilance, the usual.'

'Known liabilities?'

'The Mississippi Freedom Democratic Party. There's a lot of noise about black MFDP delegates being overlooked. As we speak, all delegates are white. Their lawyer, Joseph Rauh, wants a meeting. He's suggesting that Hubert Humphrey and Walter Reuther, the labor union leader, meet with civil rights leaders, more than likely Roy Wilkins and Bayard Rustin. If that happens, which looks very possible, I'm sure a compromise will be worked out. If it's resolved, then I don't think we'll have a racial demonstration to deal with.'

Bobby turned to the special counsel, Ted Sorensen. 'The

president needs to know about this issue. All the work we've done on civil rights, the bill just passed…'

Sorenson made a note on his desk pad. 'I'm working on the speech now,' he said. 'We're going strong on law enforcement, equal rights, all the good stuff. Obviously we have to deal with Castro, Cuba, Bay of Pigs, Vietnam, but it's going to be along the lines of holding strong against communism as a threat to the American way of life. We're not going to ignore the mistakes, we're just going to put them in a wider context and minimize them as best we can.'

Mac Bundy leaned forward. 'I've had long and complex conversations on the whole Vietnam issue with Defense Secretary McNamara,' he said. 'To be blunt, it's a clusterfuck.' He looked sideways at Catherine.

'Don't mind me,' she said. 'I'm married to a navy man.'

'We're on eggshells out there. This is not Europe, this is jungle warfare. It's like Korea, but a hundred times worse. These people are merciless and unstoppable, and they just keep coming and coming. Ike had less than a thousand people out there before we got in. As of November of last year, we had sixteen thousand, and those were the ones we admitted to. Now… hell, I don't know, I'd say we have in excess of twenty-two, twenty-three thousand, and if you want my take on it, I can see that jumping way beyond any earlier estimates very quickly. Bob McNamara reckons that we'll have to send another hundred thousand out there in the next year alone.'

'I've spoken to the president,' Bobby said.

The room fell quiet.

'I have spoken to the president, and he has expressed…' Bobby paused. He looked awkward.

'The president is intending to make Vietnam the very crux of his speech—'

'Yes, and I think he should,' Bundy interjected. 'The American people need to understand that we will do whatever it takes to hold that line.'

Bobby raised his hand.

'The president intends to have the Vietnam War concluded in our favor and all US personnel out of there by the end of his second term.'

There was the expected explosion of indignant expletives and disbelief from the gathering.

'What the hell, Bobby,' Bundy said. 'There's not a chance in hell that we could do that.'

'Mac, I know,' Bobby said. 'Don't you think I know?'

'This is crazy,' Sorenson interjected. 'I wrote the inauguration speech, for Christ's sake. We said what we said. Any price, any burden ... oppose any foe to assure the survival and success of liberty ... all that wonderfully jingoistic stuff.'

There was an awkward silence around the table.

'I'm sorry, Bobby,' Mankiewicz said, 'but has the president actually lost his mind?'

'There's no way in the world we can conclude this in four years,' Bundy added. 'I doubt we can conclude it in ten.'

'This meeting is about the Democratic National Convention itself,' Bobby said. He looked at Sorensen. 'You're gonna have to speak with the president, Ted. Whatever he might say at the DNC will be challenged and taken apart and challenged again in every newspaper, every debate, every interview. If he makes a promise like that, there is not a hope in hell of us making it through to the election without being torn to pieces by the media and the GOP.'

'I'll speak to him,' Bundy said. 'I'll get with McNamara. We'll see the president together, try to make him understand that this is impossible.'

'Okay, good,' Bobby said. 'So, to other issues.'

'Well,' O'Donnell said, 'if we're here to talk about everything else, then let's talk about it. We have Castro, the Bay of Pigs, the missile crisis. We have Khrushchev, the Vienna talks, the division of Berlin.'

'Earl Warren and his ethics committee on the election,' Salinger said. 'I hear that Warren is already starting to take depositions from state electoral representatives. Word has it he's going to subpoena Mayor Daley out of Chicago and ask him point-blank whether they rigged the ballot box in Cook County.'

'And we can say the very same thing about Nixon in southern Illinois,' Mike Feldman said.

'Stay on point, guys,' Bobby said. 'We can dissect all of this later, one issue at a time.'

'Okay … so on the plus side,' Salinger said, 'we have civil rights, the progress on ending segregation, the nuclear test-ban treaty, the fact that the South Vietnamese coup that took out Diem was a success.'

'The space race, Glenn's orbit of the earth, the promise to put a man on the moon before the end of the decade,' Sorensen added. 'It's the old maxims. Firstly, we present more of whatever we think makes the country great in the eyes of the voters. Secondly, if we can't measure what's important, then we take whatever we can measure and convince people that it's important.'

'The rhetoric we'll leave to you, Ted,' Bobby said. 'Okay, apart from the Mississippi thing, any other realistic security concerns, Walter?'

Lambert shook his head. 'It's not like Dallas last November, for example, or one of the meet-and-greets. We'll have the president in Atlantic City on the afternoon of the twenty-third, and bring him home on the last day. That's the best part of five days. It's a lot of men on full alert for a long time. I'll be down there to meet the local authorities and the people at the hall itself, and we'll vet the caterers and the staff at the hotel in liaison with the Feds. I'm up to speed on what needs to be done, and my teams have already done a good deal of preparatory work.'

'Okay,' Bobby said. 'So, I need Ken, Pierre, Ted, Mike and Frank to stay behind. The rest of you are out of here.' Bobby glanced back over his shoulder at his secretary. 'You too, Catherine. You're off the hook.'

Within a few minutes, those not required had departed.

Bobby poured himself a cup of coffee from a pot on the trolley near the door, then sat down again.

'Okay, so now the suits are gone, we need to talk turkey,' he said. 'The man we're up against is Barry Goldwater, as we know.'

'We need one of those files you got together on Nixon,' O'Donnell said. 'A history of dirt. What did you call it?'

'The Nixopedia.'

'That's it. That's what we need.'

'Goldwater is no Nixon,' Bobby said. 'He's conservative, a staunch libertarian, son of the American Revolution, a Freemason, a World War Two pilot who flew more than a hundred and fifty types of aircraft and wound up with the rank of major general. He collects kachina dolls, is a firm believer in aliens and UFOs, and even applied for access to the Wright-Patterson Air Force Base to see what they were storing in their hangars. Access was denied, of course. He's been married since 1934, has never smoked a cigarette, doesn't drink coffee, but enjoys a sip of Old Crow after five.'

He paused. 'More importantly, however, he believes that the current President of the United States is too young and inexperienced for office, a foreign policy wildcard and a diplomatic hand grenade. According to an unsubstantiated source...' he leafed through some pages and found the memo he was seeking, 'Goldwater thinks that "Jack Kennedy is a drug-addled lothario, concerned far more with the conquest of the female species than the conquest of outer space, and if he continues to run this country as he has done since 1960, then the only place we will find ourselves is somewhere in the hinterland of moral turpitude and the laughing stock of the world." That sounds to me like a man who is angling for a fight.'

'Sounds like a man who could offer me some speechwriting tips,' Sorensen said.

The laughter around the table did little to ease the tension generated by Bobby's words. The gathered men knew what they were dealing with, and they were fully aware of the challenge the president had created by his own behavior.

'Take away the Vietnam issue,' Bobby said. 'Just set that aside for the moment. In truth, the greatest fight we have on our hands is against the damaged credibility of a sitting president, not only politically, but personally.'

He closed his eyes for a moment, as if deciding whether he would express a further thought. 'As it stands, I would not vote for my brother. If somehow, together, we can change my mind, then I believe we can change the minds of this nation.'

49

July 30, 1964

It was mid afternoon on Thursday before Mitch got some sketchy details about the assault on Jack Ruby. He had gone down to the county jail himself, only to be told that no one was available. He'd shown them his press card, said that a scathing critique of their facility was heading for the printing press if they didn't cooperate. Finally they realized he was going nowhere until someone answered some questions.

In a small interview room on the right-hand side of the induction wing, he got an audience with the prison chaplain.

'You are a persistent man,' the chaplain said. His name was Grant, and he seemed both aloof and unforgiving. Perhaps that was what was required for such a congregation.

'I want to know what happened to Jack Ruby,' Mitch said.

'My understanding is that you are well aware of what happened to Jack Ruby, otherwise you would not be here.'

Mitch paused and counted to three. He was angry, tired, fed up. They had strung him along with their bullshit for close to three hours, and now he was not only given the prison chaplain, he was being challenged by semantics.

'I shall rephrase my question,' he said. 'I understand that Jack Ruby was seriously injured, and I want to know how it happened.'

'This is a prison,' Grant said. 'A lot of men with too little space, not enough food, all of them innocent, all of them claustrophobic, and every once in a while the tension becomes too much for a minority, and that affects the majority.'

'Meaning?'

'Meaning that there was a fight in the yard. Not the first, certainly not the last. Ordinarily it's one man with a personal vendetta, but a single act of violence is akin to lighting the touchpaper on a string of firecrackers. They all go off. Everything explodes in turn.'

'The attack was not aimed at Ruby specifically.'

'As far as I understand, no.'

'He just happened to be in the wrong place.'

'It seems that way.'

'Wasn't he meant to be in solitary confinement?'

'I couldn't answer that, Mr Newman.'

'Was anyone else injured?'

'Yes.'

'Anyone else hospitalized?'

'I don't believe so, no.'

'So Ruby, who wasn't even the target of whatever personal vendetta this was, happened to be the only one seriously injured, and he is now in a coma at Parkland, and there's a good chance he might not make it.'

'Yes.'

'Do they know who was responsible?'

'Not exactly.'

'Which means?'

'Which means that a dozen or more individuals have been placed in solitary confinement, but it is not clear who was responsible for the direct assault on Mr Ruby.'

'That seems both ironic and very convenient.'

'Convenient?'

'Well, doesn't it seem odd to you that only one man would be injured so severely?'

'Mr Ruby is not a man of great stature, Mr Newman. This is a tough environment full of very violent people.'

'Do you think Mr Ruby might actually have been the target, and this supposed prison fight was merely a means by which he could be assaulted?'

Grant smiled sardonically. 'I think you are perhaps reading far more into this than is warranted. As I said, these things happen, and not infrequently. We also have instances of attempted escape, riots, hunger strikes, assaults on prison officers, even on chaplains. We have just about everything you might expect in a prison.'

'And what are you going to do about what happened here?'

'I am going to pray for Mr Ruby.'

'That's not what I meant, and you know it.'

Grant paused before speaking. He leaned forward. He was calm, but there was a definite undercurrent of hostility in his tone. 'I sense a degree of anger, Mr Newman. What, may I ask, are you so angry about?'

'That something like this could happen.'

'In general, or specifically to Mr Ruby?'

'To Mr Ruby.'

'Because?'

'Because he was an individual of significant interest to me in relation to something I am investigating.'

'I see.' Grant leaned back. The expression on his face was nothing but disdainful. Perhaps he was intending to be obvious about it; if not, he was a man seemingly incapable of masking his feelings.

'I do not believe that I am being told the truth,' Mitch said, 'and I don't think you have been told the truth either.'

'You are perfectly entitled to your opinion, Mr Newman.'

'Yes,' Mitch said. 'I am.' He rose from the chair and looked down. Grant might be a man of God, but Mitch wanted to hit him in the face, and hard.

Grant rose too. 'So, if there's nothing else I can help you with…' He left the statement open-ended.

'You haven't helped me at all,' Mitch said. 'This is a cover-up. I know it, you know it, and this won't be the last you hear of it.'

'I am sorry that you feel that way,' Grant said.

'Oh, I doubt it.'

'Let me show you out.'

'Yes, that would be best, otherwise we might have another prison fight to quell.'

Grant did not rise to the bait. He was a company man, minister or not, and he was quite prepared to say or do whatever was necessary to defend the institution's reputation. Mitch had met such people in the army, in the newspaper business, and they were legion throughout every stratum of officialdom in DC.

He left the county jail with the certainty that Ruby had been the specific target of whatever fight had taken place. It was too coincidental, too unlikely to be explained any other way. Ruby had opened his mouth to Shaw, Shaw had gone through channels to get a deal so Ruby would say more, and while Ruby was in custody he was beaten within an inch of life. They hadn't even put him in solitary as Art Hallam had instructed. Shaw was now off the case, the people at county jail were covering their backs, and Ruby had been silenced, perhaps forever.

Mitch wondered how long it would be before they got to him. And who were *they*? There was no way to find out without continuing to dig, to ask questions, to make himself a thorn in someone's side. Did that mean he'd wind up like Ruby, like Jean, even the unknown Holly?

Only time would tell.

50

Mitch did not possess a black suit, nor a clean white shirt. He had a tie and shoes that would serve, but that was that; having to rent a suit for Jean's funeral seemed to be the most telling comment on how ill-prepared he was for anything of significance.

Flying back to DC early in the morning and then driving down to West Haven through the Friday traffic brought him perilously close to missing the service altogether.

Alice had been right in her prediction. The First Congregational Church on Sumner Street was no cathedral, but even in such modest surroundings the number of mourners seemed ill-deserved. Jean had been worth so much more than this, and it hurt Mitch to the core to see Alice, now so much older and frailer than just two weeks before, glancing back toward the door as the service began in the hope that more people would arrive.

Mitch recognized very few of her colleagues from the *Tribune*. Lester Byron was there, another two or three whose faces seemed familiar, but their general air of awkwardness communicated all too clearly that they were there out of duty, not personal choice.

Alice was supposed to say something, but she could not. Mitch, standing beside her, knew what would happen, and was empty inside.

After the brief and seemingly perfunctory service, the minister offered an invitation for anyone who would care to express a few words. Alice tugged Mitch's sleeve, pleaded with him in a hushed and grief-stricken voice.

'Please, Mitchell ... please ... don't let her go without saying something.'

His heart in his mouth, Mitch made his way slowly to the front of the church. It was only as he reached the small podium and turned that he realized how many people had arrived after him. Three or four rows of pews were filled, and at the back, a half-dozen or so men and women sat or stood. It was not speaking in public that unnerved him, but the fact that he was finally confronting the reality of Jean's death. Her body was right there, no more than six feet from where he stood, and that simple fact alone tore a hole right through his heart.

'I ... I am here to say goodbye to Jean,' he said, 'and not for the first time.'

He looked at Alice. Her eyes were red-rimmed, her make-up already a disaster. She looked defeated and desperate. She smiled weakly, a fragile expression of thanks for his presence.

'I have to be honest and say that I had not spoken to Jean for more than ten years. Closer now to fifteen, in fact. I saw her once in December of 1950, but I didn't possess the courage to speak to her. Before that, I saw her in July of the same year. We were engaged to be married, and I broke off that engagement for a vain and selfish reason.'

He paused to take a breath. He was making a confession.

'Jean was ... Jean was ...'

He felt the grief rising through every vein, every artery, channeling through every nerve and sinew, tightening every muscle in his body. His knees gave for just a moment, and he gripped the edge of the podium as if to let go would be to tumble headlong into some dreadful emotional abyss. He closed his eyes and breathed deeply, and when he opened them again it seemed that the church was filled with twice as many people as before, and they were all looking at him, their eyes wide in expectation of what he was going to confess.

'Jean was a passionate human being, and that passion was contagious. It invaded you and overtook you, and no matter who you were and how you knew her, you just couldn't stop yourself from being caught up in whatever whirlwind it was that carried her.' He smiled as a memory returned. 'She used to make me read poetry to her. It now seems like a thousand years ago, but I can remember it so clearly. There was one line she had me say time and again. From Mordaunt. "One crowded hour of glorious life is worth an age without a name." She believed in that, believed in it completely. I used that sentiment to justify why I had to leave her, but now, in hindsight, I understand that the life I've since lived is just a fraction of the life I would've had if I'd stayed.'

Alice started to sob audibly. Lester moved across the pew and put his arm around her shoulder.

'And so I'm sorry. Sorry that I let her go. Sorry that I missed these past fifteen years with her. Sorry for the choice I made and how I convinced myself that it was right. It wasn't, and I see that now. Most of all I am sorry that she's gone, simply because her death has made me face myself, and if she can do that for me now, then I can only imagine what she would have done with her life had she lived...'

Tears filled his eyes. His knuckles whitened.

'I loved her right from the start. I still love her. I will always love her. I made a bad decision, and I am the one who is paying for it, and I will be paying for it for the rest of my life.'

He looked down for a moment. His heart was racing. He could feel the rush of blood in his chest, hear it in his ears.

He looked toward her coffin.

'Goodbye, Jean …' he said, and his voice broke with emotion.

He stepped away from the podium and walked back to his pew, aware then of how utterly silent the church had become.

They came for him later. There were two of them. A man and a woman. The man was taller than Mitch by a couple of inches, his features strong and resolute. While he was talking, he never looked away, not even for a second, and Mitch knew that such a thing was designed to unsettle and disturb him. It worked.

The woman had a kindlier face. There was something maternal about her, despite the fact that she could only have been five or six years older than Mitch. She said they were from one of the agencies to which Jean used to send her work, but they were no more newspaper people than Mitch was the governor of Maryland.

He didn't challenge them; he listened to what they said, and he knew exactly what they meant.

'Hello, Mr Newman. I'm Forrest Young. This is my colleague, Sarah Trent. We work over at Barton and Garrison. You know, the news agency?'

Mitch had never heard of it, but he feigned familiarity.

'We are very sorry for your loss,' Trent said. 'And what you said was very moving, very poignant.'

'You knew Jean?' Mitch asked.

'Yes, of course,' Young replied. 'Not well. Just professionally, you know? She used to send over her work sometimes, some of the investigative pieces that didn't run in the *Tribune*.'

'Is that so?'

Trent smiled. Young smiled too.

'Well, thank you for coming,' Mitch said. 'It's a shame there weren't more of her friends here, but you know how these things are. So many pay their respects privately. Funerals can be upsetting, especially when …'

He left the statement hanging. He didn't want to say *suicide*. He didn't believe it, and to utter the word gave it credence.

'I absolutely understand,' Trent said. She smiled that same ingratiating smile.

'Such a tragic thing to happen to someone so ... so full of life,' Young said. 'You just never know what's going on, do you? I mean, who would have known that there were things causing her so much stress and pain that taking her own life was the only apparent solution?'

'I didn't know,' Mitch said. He wanted to add, *And I don't think Jean knew either*. He was already sure who these people were. Were they the same ones who had followed him to DC? Had they listened to his phone conversations, followed up on every line of questioning he'd made? This was a gentle caution, a warning to back away, to keep his distance. He didn't want to goad them further.

'We all have to be so careful,' Trent said. 'Until something like this happens, you never fully appreciate how fragile life is, do you?'

'No,' Mitch said. 'You don't. Well, thank you again for coming. I have to go and spend some time with Jean's mother now.'

Young reached out his hand. Mitch responded, and they shook. Still holding Mitch's hand, Young looked at him with the same unerring gaze and said, 'You take care of yourself now, Mr Newman. Tragedies like this have a way of affecting us in the most unexpected ways, and I am quite sure that Jean's mother is very much reliant on your help.'

Mitch let go of Young. Young kept on staring.

'Yes, I'm sure she's very grateful for your support at this terrible time,' Trent added as a coda, and then they both turned and walked away.

Mitch watched them go. They did not look back. They did not

appear to share any words. They just left the church and headed down Sumner Street.

Was this how it was?

Was this how they came for Jean? They were polite and patient, but so very menacing. Did they warn her too, and she just didn't back off?

Mitch looked back toward the coffin, even now being removed from the trestle, and then at Alice.

The world slowed down. Everything was quiet. He could hear his own heartbeat. He could hear himself breathing.

To hell with all of them, he thought.

51

It would have been easy to get drunk and stay drunk, but Mitch willed himself to keep it together.

Once the burial was done, there was a small gathering of people hosted by Alice at a local bar. The back room had been cleaned up. Food had been laid on. It was all very awkward. People who had barely known Jean stood around with glasses of wine in their hands. They didn't know where to look. They didn't know what to say to one another. Mitch circulated; he talked to Alice, he urged Byron to say a few words about working with Jean. Byron spoke of her stubbornness, her resolute determination, her dogged attitude toward all things, her indefatigable sense of humor.

His final words were somehow more astute than anything that had previously been uttered.

'Seems to me that Jean was one in a million. I believed she would just go on forever. I didn't believe there was anything that could stop her from doing what she wanted to do. It just goes to show that none of us are invincible. There's always something bigger and stronger than we are, and most often it's something that comes out of left field with no warning. This was a shock to me, and it still is. I guess it reminds me, perhaps reminds all of us, that there are so many things we take for granted, and we don't realize how important they are until they're gone.'

And with that, he raised his glass and they drank a toast to the too-short life of Jean Boyd.

Mitch offered to stay with Alice, but she declined.

'I think I want to be alone,' she said. 'Just for now, for tonight. I need some quiet time, Mitchell. But thank you for offering.'

'If you need me, just call, okay?'

'I will.'

Mitch drove back to DC. It was late, and once he'd parked the car, he walked to the bar. Tom was there, as were a few of the regulars, and it was good to see familiar faces.

Mitch still had on his suit, but he took off his tie and stuffed it in his pocket.

'Funeral,' he said when Tom raised his eyebrows.

'Your friend?'

Mitch nodded, asked for a double.

'On me,' Tom said. He slid the glass down the bar, then let Mitch be.

Mitch's thoughts were not for Jean, but for Forrest Young and Sarah Trent. They were for Nelson Shaw, Jack Ruby and Holly Walsh. They were for Leland Webster and Marshall Jeavons, the members of the Texas Communist League, for Ruth Paine and all the others who were involved in whatever it was that had happened back in November of 1963. But what had actually happened? Was he really beginning to consider that there had been an attempt on Kennedy's life, or was he grasping at straws, merely jumping to some wild conclusion that would explain the reason for Jean's death, the hospitalization of Jack Ruby, the disappearance of Holly Walsh? And if it was the case, had this Lee Oswald been responsible? It seemed obvious that he was not well liked. He had earned himself a reputation as arrogant, opinionated, aggressive. He had – by behavior alone – somehow managed to disband the communist discussion group. He has carried out an assassination attempt on General Edwin Walker. Those who knew him did not want him around, and he had certainly made himself scarce. He'd left work on November 21, and vanished. Another coincidence?

Was there anything to substantiate Mitch's intuitive certainty that Oswald needed to be found? No, there was not. It had been a collection of small things, minor events, things that people had said and done. It was a belief that Jean would not have gone to Dallas and pursued Ruby unless she had been utterly convinced that he had known something of importance. Now Jean, along with Ruby, Leland Webster and Nelson Shaw, could not help him. But he needed help, and the only people he believed might give him the time of day were the Secret Service. They were duty-bound to preserve the life of the president and the first family. What other option did he have? He could not go back to the police. What evidence did he have that any crime had been committed? He could not write an exposé. What would he be exposing save unfounded suspicions and odd coincidences?

He had to speak with someone, and that someone had to possess sufficient authority to look into this matter. The crux of it was his own survival. He was caught between the devil and the deep blue sea. If the Youngs and Trents of this world were warning him off, then his life was already in danger if he continued. Who were they? In whose interest would it be to get him to give up on this? If he let it go to save his own skin, then what had been the point of any of it? Jean had not done that, and it had cost her her life.

It seemed now that his only option was to go to the authorities, and yet – and this was something he had to face – perhaps the authorities were the very people who did not want it known. It was do or be damned, and there was no other way to see it.

*

Later, alone in his apartment, Mitch fetched down the bottle of bourbon from the kitchen cupboard. There was ice in the icebox. He poured a good two inches and stood by the window. The cat came up and sat on the ledge. They both looked down into the street.

He raised his glass.

'Jean,' he said. 'Miss you more than ever.'

He reached down and stroked the cat. 'And this guy misses you too,' he added. 'Both us Mitches miss you like hell.'

The cat looked up at him as if it understood.

'You know, buddy, I wasn't even aware of how much I really loved her until now. She got herself into something bad, and I think she lost her life because of it.'

Mitch paused, took a drink.

'Least I can do is see it through, right? Whatever it takes.'

52

August 3, 1964

It was late on Monday afternoon before Mitch's request to meet with a Secret Service representative at the DC L Street field office received a response. He had not given a specific reason for the request, and this, he later discovered, was the reason for the delay. Had he stated that it was connected to a potential attempt on the president's life, then it would have been attended to with far greater efficiency.

Elsewhere, the Service might have occupied their time with money-laundering, counterfeiting and bank fraud, but in DC the agents and officers were primarily charged with the protection of the president and the first family, visiting diplomats and ambassadors, and all aspects of security relating to the Capitol.

By the time Mitch sat in front of someone who was prepared to listen, it was Tuesday morning. The agent's name was George Everett, and despite presidential security being his foremost duty, and though he worked hard to appear interested in what Mitch had to say, he gave the definite impression that he'd not only heard such things many times before, but he was not of a mind to give Mitch's information a great deal of credence.

Mitch appreciated, even as he was talking, that had the roles been reversed, he too would have doubted the credibility of what he was saying.

'So,' Everett asked at one point, 'you don't know this Lee Oswald?'

'No, I don't.'

'And you have never seen him?'

'No.'

'Do you know what he looks like?'

'I don't, no.'

'So he worked in the Texas School Book Depository until November the twenty-first last year, but according to their records didn't show up on the twenty-second, and has since made no contact with an explanation for his absence?'

'That is my understanding, yes.'

'And you have been following up on a fellow journalist's apparent efforts to find a girl called Holly Walsh. However, there is no evidence to suggest that Walsh has disappeared, nor that she has been a victim of anything untoward.'

'Right.'

'And there is no actual evidence to suggest that Lee Oswald might be responsible for the death of Leland Webster.'

'It sounds crazy, right?'

Everett didn't acknowledge Mitch's question.

'How did Oswald know this...' Everett glanced at the notes he'd made, 'this Jack Ruby?'

'I don't know. I mean, Ruby owned the club where the Texas Communist League used to meet, but how he knew Oswald I don't know.'

Everett made another note. 'And you say that Oswald defected to the Soviet Union.'

'Yes, he did. From what I've been able to piece together, he came back after living in Minsk for a while with a Russian wife. As far as I know, she still lives in Dallas, but she and Oswald are estranged.'

Everett nodded. He made a further note.

'So now. How do we string all of this together and arrive at the possibility that there might have been a plan to assassinate the president back in November?'

'I know it sounds far-fetched, and I appreciate that it's all supposition and guesswork, but there just seem to be too many odd coincidences. The fact that this Oswald may have been responsible for the assassination attempt on General Walker, that he worked in a building overlooking the motorcade route...' Mitch paused. He could hear an echo of Bill Sandford's voice in his head. *Sometimes we want to believe something so much that we force everything we see to agree with our theory.* 'I went there, Agent Everett. I went and stood outside that building in Dealey Plaza, and I could see how it might have been possible. And Jack Ruby knew something, you know? He was afraid for his life, and Jean went down there and now she's dead—'

'Okay, Mr Newman,' Everett said, cutting him short. 'You seem to have done a lot of legwork.'

'Yes, I have.'

'In the honest belief that your friend Miss Boyd was pursuing a real threat against the life of the president.'

'I don't know that she was pursuing that. All I know is that she was very interested in Jack Ruby and this girl who worked at his club, this Holly Walsh.'

'But none of what you're saying is substantiated by anything.'

'I know that,' Mitch said. 'And I also understand how it sounds to you.'

Mitch had not mentioned the fact that the Carousel was not where the story started; that Jean actually had gone down to Dallas to investigate vote-rigging and corruption in the 1960 election. A DC Secret Service man was there for the president, and the president alone. If he hoped to stay in his job, he wouldn't criticize and investigate his employer.

'Okay, I think I'm beginning to see how this appears to fit together.'

Everett stressed the word *appears* in such a way as to highlight the improbability of what Mitch was saying.

'Is there anything else you think we should know, Mr Newman?'

'I don't think so, Agent Everett. I believe that this Lee Oswald may have been responsible for the murder of Leland Webster, and he used Jack Ruby's gun. Oswald perhaps killed Webster because they worked together at the Book Depository, and it was from this vantage point that an attempt was made on the president's life last November.'

Everett raised his eyebrows. 'You're telling me that this Oswald character actually discharged a weapon from this building with the intent to kill President Kennedy?'

Mitch looked at Everett with surprise. 'No, I'm not saying that. Not exactly. To be honest, I'm not sure precisely what I am trying to say, save that there's a lot that doesn't make sense, and I don't believe I'm going to make any further sense of it without some help. More to the point, without some official help.'

Everett shook his head. 'I have to tell you that this really is nothing more than a very vague and unsubstantiated suspicion.'

'Yes, it is, but I think it's a suspicion that warrants further investigation. I'm neither a police officer nor a federal official nor a Secret Service agent. I'm a freelance journalist. I'm asking you to go and find Oswald and see how he fits into this, whether he might have been the one to kill Webster, if he knows who Holly Walsh is and what happened to her—'

'I have the information now,' Everett cut in, 'but you have to appreciate my position. A full-blown investigation involving the assignment of agents in the field is usually based on something a great deal more substantive than a few apparently unrelated suspicions and incomplete facts. What you have told me does not seem to conclusively indicate that a lone gunman might have intended to kill the president in Dallas.'

'And what if it did happen? What if Oswald did intend that? What if the attack on General Walker was just a dummy run? He left work the day before the president came to Dallas. He just didn't show. What if Oswald is also dead? Or what if he is planning another assassination attempt even as we speak?'

Everett seemed to relax a little. He unbuttoned his jacket and leaned back in the chair. 'We have the Democratic National Convention in less than three weeks, Mr Newman. I can assure you that the focus of our attention is the president's safety and security for this event. I am in no doubt of your good intent here. I also appreciate that you have lost your friend, and you have taken it upon yourself to continue her line of investigation. I can see how this will have brought to bear a great deal of pressure and stress.'

'Is that what you think is happening here? You think I am somehow compensating for the loss of my friend by getting involved in a fantasy about what she might have been doing in Dallas last November?'

'I'm saying nothing of the sort, Mr Newman.'

'From what I can hear, you're not saying a great deal of anything, Agent Everett. I have come here with a legitimate and not altogether implausible report concerning something that may have been a very real and very specific threat to the life of President Kennedy. From your tone and attitude it seems that you are not taking me at all seriously.'

'Mr Newman, please—'

'Is there someone more senior I can speak to? Who else is here? Who is the special agent in charge for this field office?'

Everett smiled, albeit a little sarcastically. 'That would be me.'

'So maybe I should go right on up to the White House and see if they'll buzz me in.'

'Mr Newman, listen to me.' Everett leaned forward and put his hands flat on the surface of the desk. He spoke with clarity and decisiveness. 'I need you to understand that every single report we receive concerning security issues relating to the president, the vice president, their respective families, visiting dignitaries and anyone else who happens to be in the Capitol by invitation of the White House is taken with the utmost seriousness. I apologize if I gave you the impression that your information was neither credible nor of value. It most definitely is, and it will be addressed with the same vigor and due diligence as are all such reports we receive. As I am sure you can imagine, we receive a great many, and they all take time. There are, of course, those that require greater urgency and attention. It is our task to prioritize, and then to act. I give you my word that this matter will be looked into as rapidly as possible, and with all appropriate resources. And as a final word, I thank you on behalf of the Secret Service and the office of the president, not only for your thoroughness but also your patriotism.'

'I understand,' Mitch said. He got up.

Everett got up too and they shook hands.

As Mitch left the office, he saw Everett watching him from the window. Everett raised his hand and nodded in acknowledgment.

Mitch drove down L Street with a real sense of concern and anxiety. He had told Everett everything he knew. He had relayed every fact, substantiated or otherwise, every suspicion, every assumption, every connection he'd made, however tenuous it might have been, save Jean's original motivation for coming to Dallas. Already people had been asking after him. He did not know who they were. Perhaps police, federal officials, even people Ruby knew in the ranks of the Dallas organized crime network. His mind had found a chasm, and he had leaped.

Where he'd landed had seemed at least as solid as anywhere else. He could not find Holly Walsh. He could not question Jack Ruby. Shaw would not help him, and now the Secret Service seemed to be doing nothing but humoring him. The only place left to go was to find this Lee Oswald. Perhaps it would be another hiding to nowhere, but he had to try. A young man, army-trained, a defector, a traitor perhaps, a man who had previously used a rifle in an attempt to kill someone, not only in Dallas at the same time as Jean and the president, but subsequently had also quit his job with no apparent reason.

Oswald – if he was not party to whatever chip Ruby was trying to bargain with – was sure to know something, and it was Oswald who now had to be found.

53

August 4, 1964

Later, much later, seated in the kitchen of his apartment, Mitch wondered if he should just let it go. If his supposition was right, if this Lee Oswald had really been of a mind not only to kill Walker, but also to kill Kennedy – and beyond even that, if he still possessed such a purpose – then to hell with it. Let him do it.

Everett had been wrong. None of Mitch's work had been motivated by patriotism. Personally, Mitch was of the viewpoint that irrespective of who might be in the Oval Office, the country was always run by the same people. Faceless suits. People with money. Ancient families that had been here since America was settled. Politics was a game for such people, and they never lost. Jean had started with an investigation of corruption. Mitch had followed that thread, and now here he was trying his damnedest to get people who thought he was crazy to do something about a situation that could not be proven, nor that appeared to make a great deal of sense. The one person who seemed sufficiently interested to help him, Nelson Shaw, had now fallen by the wayside. Mitch understood that if anything further was to be done, then he really would have to do it alone. Such a prospect troubled him greatly.

He poured a drink. He took out his letters to Jean once more.

He looked at the envelopes, his own handwriting, and he cast his mind back to the emotions he'd felt as he wrote them. Loss, dismay, hurt, even disbelief. Perhaps there had been a balance, and she had ultimately wound up hurting him as much as he'd hurt her. No, that did not make sense. He truly believed he'd hurt her a great deal more. She'd never married, never had children. Granted, she was young, but Alice had given no indication of stability or settlement in her life. Jean had wanted those very things. Yes, she'd wanted a career, wanted to make an impression on the world, but family and children and home had been very real desires.

He had not been honest with her. He truly understood that now. The very thing that had driven him out to Korea had been there all along – a sense of frustration, a belief that he was destined for something greater and more significant than the banality and routine of an ordinary life. But what about now? Was he doing this because he wanted to prove that he'd been right all along? Or just because it needed doing? Because there really was a situation here that was greater than all of their lives combined? For vanity? For the attention? To try and convince the world – and thus himself – that he had indeed been destined for greater things?

It was all bullshit. It was all meaningless bullshit.

He opened the letter from January 24.

Do you want me to give up, Jean? Is that what you really want? Just tell me that you never want to hear from me again, and I will disappear.

And from February 1:

I have decided to write a dozen letters. The twelfth will be my last. If I receive no word after that, then I will fade into the background and disappear.

It was all so melodramatic and selfish. He had been interested only in what *he* wanted, what he felt, what he thought, and he hadn't even understood those things himself.

The last one he could face was from the ninth of the same month. He counted them. It was his tenth letter to her. He had closed it with another vapid plea.

I am running out of words, Jean. To be honest, I am running out of hope.

At least it could be said that he'd kept his word in one way. He'd written twelve letters, and no more. He remembered the last one, how he'd labored over each sentence, each word. Finally he had mailed it, knowing in his heart that there would be no response.

For a while, then, he'd hated her. Truly hated her. After that, he hated himself with renewed passion and violence. He'd started drinking, and just gone on and on until it seemed there was nothing left to drink. He'd been ill, and so very angry. It was all so futile and desperate and pointless.

The death of his mother in September 1961 had been the catalyst for change. Even then, still drowning in an ocean of self-pity, he'd tortured himself with the idea that his behavior had driven her to an early grave. It had not, he knew that, but it seemed he was still looking for anything that would fuel his selfishness. For that's what it was, perhaps what it had always been. He had lived for himself, and when others had given up on him he'd used their imagined betrayal as further evidence that he was somehow not responsible for what had happened to his life.

Finally he got straight. He stopped drinking, started eating and sleeping properly. He got some work, paid his bills, and he was more reliable and methodical than he'd ever been. But it had not lasted, for the inherent weakness that had undermined his efforts to succeed was still there. He masked it as best he could, but it was not until now – not until he had somehow forced himself to fight for Jean's memory – that he had become the person he'd always intended to be.

That was why he needed to keep on fighting, no matter the Nelson Shaws and George Everetts of this world, no matter Forrest Young and Sarah Trent, no matter the potential whirlwind of trouble he might cause for himself.

It would stop with him. They couldn't threaten his mother. They couldn't threaten Jean. Those he'd cared for the most were gone, and gone for good.

Somewhere there were those who knew the truth. Somewhere, people had made a decision to beat Jack Ruby within an inch of his life. Perhaps those same people knew of this Lee Oswald – where he was, why he seemed to have just disappeared, whether he really had made an attempt on the life of John Kennedy in Dallas in November 1963.

Lastly, there were those who knew the exact circumstances of Jean's death, and – more importantly – why she had needed to die.

There was just too much hurt to let it go.

54

It was money that stopped Mitch returning to Dallas, and it stopped him for a good while. He needed airfare, a motel, car rental, food. He was as good as destitute, and rent was due on his apartment. The only thing worth selling was his camera, but even that would have been insufficient.

The only person he could go to was Alice, and asking her for close to three hundred bucks was tantamount to admitting that his entire adult life had been a dead loss.

He called her, told her that he needed to get back to Texas, that he had nowhere else to turn.

'Of course I can give you the money,' she said.

'Lend,' he corrected.

Alice hesitated before she acknowledged him. *If you had some way to repay me, then you wouldn't need to ask me in the first place* was what he heard in the silence.

He knew she was doing it for Jean. If supporting Mitch in his endeavor resulted in an understanding of what had happened, perhaps even the possibility that her death had not been suicide after all, it would have been worth all she possessed. Mitch knew that, and that was why he'd been loath to ask.

It took a couple of days for her to arrange things but finally the money was wired. By the time he'd organized tickets, it was a week since his meeting at the field office in DC, and he was frustrated to the point of rage.

Arriving back in Dallas on the afternoon of August 11, he chose yet another motel. He gave yet another false name. Caution was not paranoia. He only had to think of the unsettling conversation with Forrest Young and Sarah Trent to appreciate that he was very definitely a thorn in someone's side.

He needed to find Oswald. There was no way of avoiding the reality. Perhaps Oswald was running scared; certainly it appeared that he was now making himself as scarce as possible. If he had killed Leland Webster with Ruby's gun, then what was the motive? Perhaps because of something that had happened at one of the communist group meetings, perhaps because of something at the Book Depository. Webster had been killed around the third week of June. It was now approaching the middle of August.

Mitch knew he could not go back to Shaw, at least not in any open or official manner, and he was wary of dragging the man back into the fray when he'd been taken off the case. The reason for that was unknown. It could be as insignificant as prioritized workload in an already burdened department. He thought about Young and Trent at Jean's funeral. What was the name they'd used? Barton and Garrison. That was it. Mitch knew without checking that there was no such news agency. Did that have any significance, or was it just an off-the-cuff invention? And was it worth pursuing the assault on Jack Ruby? Mitch did not believe so. If ever there was a means by which someone could be silenced, then putting him in a coma was as good as any other. Again, too coincidental to be anything but suspicious. No, there really was no alternative route to take apart from tracking down Lee Oswald and determining whether he had played any part in this surreal theater of events.

Mitch called Ruth Paine again.

'I'm sorry to bother you with this,' he said, 'but I really do need to find Marina Oswald.'

'I don't know what to say that I haven't already said, Mr Newman.'

'Do you have her last address, perhaps?'

'I don't, no,' Ruth Paine said.

'Do you have a telephone number?'

'I did have, but I called it quite some time ago and it was no longer in use.'

Mitch thanked her and called Information. There was no listing for Marina Oswald. He wondered if she'd reverted to using her maiden name.

He went back to County Records. Births, Marriages and Deaths were in a separate department, and he had to wait for more than an hour before there was someone available to assist him. His patience wore thin as he searched through file after file. He found no marriage license. That seemed to confirm that Oswald had married Marina in the Soviet Union.

He explained his dilemma to the assistant, a middle-aged man called Herb Travis.

'Then you'll need the State Department,' Travis said. 'If your Mr Oswald left the US as a single man and returned with a non-national wife, then she would have to have been cleared by State.'

Mitch looked hopeful.

Travis smiled. 'Can't help you with that here. Wrong records, wrong department, wrong everything.'

'So how do I get hold of those records?'

'Do you know an approximate date, and which airport they flew into when they came back?'

'No idea. I think it was '62, but that's from memory.'

'They had children?'

'Yes. Two girls.'

'Born in the USA?'

'I think so, yes.'

'Then we look in Births. Any idea of ages?'

'I know one of them was born sometime around the end of October 1963 here in Dallas.'

'Then you have just saved us a great deal of work.'

Travis found the record of Audrey Oswald's birth. October 20, 1963. Father's name, Lee Harvey Oswald; mother's name, Marina Nikolayevna Oswald, née Prusakova.

'There you have it,' he said.

'This is really appreciated,' Mitch said. 'Couldn't have found it without you.'

He called Information from a phone booth in the street. There was no listing for a Prusakova anywhere in Texas, let alone Dallas. He was back where he'd started.

He had to become an astute and dogged investigative journalist – the very thing he'd intended to be in the first place. What did he have as a resource? Traffic citations and arrest records, the very things he'd used to track down Ruby.

Thus, on the morning of August 12, Mitch was right there on the steps of the Dallas City Court. He asked for Caroline Lassiter, was relieved to know she was due in that day, but not until ten. He waited across the street in a diner, drank two cups of coffee, and prayed that Lee Oswald had been arrested in Dallas for something.

When he saw Caroline go up the front steps, he left money on the diner counter and crossed the street.

If she was surprised to see him, she didn't show it. Again her barrettes matched her shoes, this time in blue.

'More arrest cards,' he said, and gave her the name he was after.

He was there for three hours. He was meticulous, careful not to miss anything, but he came away empty-handed. He thanked Caroline for her time, and she seemed genuinely sorry that he'd not found what he was looking for.

'I can only suggest employment records, but you'd need the individual's Social Security number,' she said, 'and to get that you'll need the Post Office.'

'Can I just go to the Post Office and ask for the number?'

Caroline shook her head. 'Not that simple. The Post Office is the issuer, but the number comes from the Social Security Administration itself. The other people who would have it would be the Internal Revenue, perhaps the armed forces if the person ever served in the military—'

'He did. He was in the Marine Corps.'

'Do you know when he was discharged?'

Mitch shrugged.

'If it was more than three years ago, his service record will no longer be classified as confidential.'

'And I find this where?'

'Armed Forces Administration Bureau,' Caroline said. 'Out of here, left, across the street diagonally, first right, and it's three blocks.'

Mitch smiled. 'You are a walking encyclopedia,' he said.

'I am a single woman with too few friends and an unhealthy interest in cats and books,' Caroline replied.

Mitch laughed and thanked her again.

Oswald had been discharged from the Marines on September 11, 1959. With Oswald's Social Security number in hand, Mitch called the Department of Labor, claiming to be the personnel manager of Dallas Commercial Construction. He gave the number and asked for Oswald's prior employment record. In July of '62, Lee Oswald had been hired by the Leslie Welding Company. He'd quit after three months. He was then employed as a photoprint trainee for a company called Jaggars-Chiles-Stovall. He'd lasted six months.

'The address I have for him is Rawlins Street,' Mitch lied.

'The last one we have is McArthur.'

'Oh yes,' Mitch said, 'I have that one here too. Over the page.'

'Eleven-eleven McArthur, as of June 1963. After that, no further record.'

'That's really appreciated,' Mitch said, and hung up.

Back at the motel, he looked up McArthur. It was across town, but not so far. He would drive over there, see if there was anyone home.

55

August 13, 1964

Mitch Newman sat in his car all night. At various points he dozed off, waking to the sound of a police siren somewhere, another time as a car roared past, its engine gunning aggressively. Oswald's building was in darkness, and even as the sun rose, there was still no sign of life. By ten a.m., he figured that if anyone was home, they would have given some sign of their presence. Against his better judgment, but needing to know whether the property was even inhabited, he walked over as if he had every right to be there. He went on up to the porch and pretended to knock. He waited, scratched his head, backed up and looked at the upper windows. To an observer, he might have seemed like a familiar visitor, knocking the door and then checking around the back of the building in case whoever lived there was in the yard.

The rear of the house evidenced very recent habitation. A fire had been lit in a trash can. There was a single shirt on a drying line inside the back porch, and through a small side window Mitch could see part of the kitchen, pots and pans and a box of Kellogg's OKs on the counter.

He went back to his car. Someone lived there, but was it Oswald? Out of cigarettes, hungry, aching from the cramped quarters, he nevertheless did not question what he was doing, nor his motivation. Something had changed, that was for sure.

By mid morning, he needed to get out of the car, if only for a short while. He drove to the first convenience store he could find, used their restroom, bought three packs of cigarettes and several bottles of Dr Pepper. Two stores down was a Texburger. He ordered three beef patty sandwiches to go. He made it back to McArthur before thirty minutes had elapsed. The house had not changed. There was nothing to indicate anyone had departed or arrived.

By three in the afternoon, he had begun to feel that sitting there any longer was a waste of time. Out of desperation, he went to the house across the street and knocked on the door. A middle-aged man opened it. He had a pipe clamped between his teeth, a newspaper in his hand.

'Hi,' Mitch said. 'I was looking for Lee Oswald over at eleven-eleven. Do you know him?'

'Lee? Sure I know him.'

'Would you happen to know where he is?'

'Who are you?'

'I'm a friend of a friend. A man called Ruby. He and Mr Oswald go a long way back, and Mr Ruby is over at Parkland. He's been injured quite seriously, and I figured Mr Oswald should know.'

'Is that so? Why didn't you leave a note through the door or some such? I saw you go on up there. I also seen you sitting in that car all night. I did have a mind to call the cops, but you didn't seem to be causin' anyone any trouble.'

Mitch didn't have an answer.

The man took the pipe from his mouth. 'Tell me what you're really doing and I might answer your question.'

'I don't think you'd believe me if I told you.'

'Try me. Worst case is I call the cops, and I may even do that anyway. I got your number plate, and now I know what you look like.'

'I'm a journalist,' Mitch said. 'I'm investigating the death of a colleague, and I've been all over Dallas. I've been with the Metro PD, up at County Records, the courts. I've tried to track down Mr Oswald's ex-wife, but I really am making a bust of it.'

'And what does Lee Oswald have to do with the death of your colleague?'

'I don't know that he does. I'm just following up on every possible lead. It may come to nothing, but my only other choice is to give up, and that's not really an option for me.'

'Well, I have to say I'm impressed with your persistence. You wouldn't get me staying out all night in a car for someone who may or may not show up.'

'Depends how much you needed to talk to them.'

'Yes, I guess it does. So, what's your name?'

'Mitchell Newman.'

'You got any credentials?'

Mitch took out his wallet and showed the man his press card.

'Okay, so I guess you are who you say you are. Lee's been gone two or three days. I have no idea where. He and I don't see eye to eye, you could say. He has some opinions that he seems intent on sharing with folks, and he doesn't much care whether they're interested in them or not.'

'The communist stuff?'

The man paused for a moment. 'You want to come in, Mr Newman? You want a cup of coffee, maybe?'

'That would be great.'

'Dan Wilson,' the man said, and extended his hand.

The house was plain, unadorned, comfortable. It was the house of a bachelor or a widower. Mitch guessed the former. There were no personal photos, no evidence of any feminine touch at all. Wilson had been home all day, so Mitch guessed he was retired. He asked him.

'Yes, retired.'

'What was it you did?'

'Oil rig firefighter. Close to forty years.'

'That's one hell of a tough job.'

'There's tougher.'

'Sure, but not many.'

'You could be right there.'

Wilson made fresh coffee. As of that moment, it was the best Mitch had ever tasted.

'So, your man Oswald. He's been causing trouble?'

'If he had, would it surprise you?'

'You want my opinion, he's a nasty little punk. All that commie stuff is whatever it is, but he's about as unpatriotic a man as I've ever had the misfortune to meet.'

'You said he likes to share his opinions.'

'He does indeed. He was in the Marine Corps, as far as I understand.'

'Yes, he was.'

'Okay. I never knew if that was one of his fantasies.'

'Fantasies?'

'Oh, you know. He's a little man. Little man with big ideas. He's done this, he's done that, he's gonna do great things and everyone will know how important he is. Big mouth, little dick, that's what we say where I'm from.'

Mitch laughed.

'Anyway, he seems incapable of holding down a job. Says he was married, has a couple of girls. I've never seen a wife nor any daughters, and he's been over there for the best part of a year now.'

'So you have no idea where he might be?'

'Not a clue.'

'And is there anything else he's ever said to you that seemed odd? Anything else that sounded like a fantasy?'

Wilson smiled. 'Like killing Edwin Walker?'

'You're the second person to know about that,' Mitch said.

'Well, he told me about it, even showed me the gun he says he used. Says it happened back in April last year.'

'You didn't report it to the police?'

'And say what? This is Texas. Everyone has a gun. It's a birthright. And if you start telling the cops about every crackpot story you hear, then you'd be taking on a full-time job.'

'Do you know what kind of gun it was?'

'Carcano, 6.5 millimeter. Said he bought it by mail. Used an alias so it wouldn't be traced back to him. Says he has a .38, as well. You know, from what I've seen, he really is a nutcase.'

'Do you know if the incident was reported?'

'No idea. Why, you think he was serious?'

Mitch shook his head. 'I don't know, but it's something to follow up on.'

'Well if you're going to follow up on that, you might as well see if there was any substance to what he said about becoming the most famous man in the world.'

'Meaning what?'

'Meaning the comments he made about how the best way to become really famous was to kill some really important.'

'Seriously?'

'Well, he said it, sure. How serious he was, I have no idea.'

'When did he say that? Was it recently?'

'Maybe a month, two months ago.'

'You think he's the kind of person who'd be capable of backing up such a statement? I mean, from your experience of him, you think it amounts to anything more than words?'

'Mr Newman, you have to understand that I didn't take any of the things he said very seriously. He was intense, angry, sometimes drunk, sometimes ranting about some imagined prejudice. He had gripes about everything, and he had no difficulty expressing those gripes.'

'And now?'

'Well, I don't know if an attempt was made on Walker's life, and I don't know of any really important people that have been killed. All I know is that Lee Oswald is singularly unpatriotic and has a thoroughly unjustified opinion of his own importance, and now you show up and tell me that he might be connected to someone's death.'

'Do you know where he worked?'

Wilson shook his head.

'At the Texas School Book Depository. It overlooks the route that the presidential motorcade took last year.'

'Last I heard, the president was alive and well and living in Washington.'

'I'm stringing things together, Mr Wilson. I might be stringing them together all wrong, but the whole thing is starting to look like a great deal more than one crazy little man with an inflated ego.'

'Okay, well I wish you the very best of luck with your investigation, Mr Newman, but I've told you as much as I know. I'm sorry I can't be of any more help.'

'Could I leave a phone number with you for the motel where I'm staying? I have some other things to follow up on, but if Oswald comes back, could you call and leave me a message?'

'Sure I can,' Wilson said. 'Be my pleasure.'

Mitch finished his coffee. He thanked Wilson for his time and assistance, and headed back downtown to the city library. As he drove, he ate his last beef patty sandwich. It was cold, and not so good.

The *Dallas Morning News* had carried the story on April 12, 1963. A shot had been fired through a window at the home of retired US Major General Edwin Walker. The bullet had struck the window frame, and fragments of wood had had to be removed from Walker's forearm. The article made no comment about Walker's resignation, but it did make mention of the fact that he was an outspoken anti-communist and a member of the John Birch Society. From what little Mitch knew of the Birch Society, they were considered pretty far right in their political views, even radical. As a vocal anti-communist, Walker's ideology would have been diametrically opposed to Oswald's.

Dan Wilson had seen a 6.5 millimeter rifle, and said that Oswald also owned a .38. Along with Marshall Jeavons of the Texas Communist League, that made two people who supported Mitch's belief – if only circumstantially – that Oswald was capable of doing what he said he'd do. Hadn't Leland Webster admired Oswald as a man of action, not just words? That was what Jeavons had said, and that viewpoint seemed to be holding water.

Had the attempt on Walker's life in April of '63 possessed some other significance? What was it that Ruby knew that he'd been so unwilling to divulge? What had he meant when he'd talked about 'everything that happened' in November? What could be so big that it would justify three deaths and a man in a coma?

Mitch needed to go back to the Secret Service. He needed to find someone who would take this thing seriously and follow it up.

There would be a field office in Dallas, and they could relay communications to someone higher up the totem pole in DC. Without help, and help from someone authoritative, he was adrift. To have gotten thus far was perhaps admirable, but it would all be meaningless if nothing was done as a result. Someone besides Jean Boyd and himself needed to appreciate that whatever was going on here, there were far too many things that made no sense at all.

56

'I am so very tired of it all,' Jackie said.

She was seated in his private study, not at the desk, but in one of the armchairs near the fireplace. She looked as if she needed a respite from the intensity of her day.

'I appreciate that. I really do,' Bobby said. His tone was compassionate, and he truly felt it. He understood her dilemma, and it troubled him. 'However, you are in a prison of your own making, Jackie. You don't have a choice, and you were the one who took away that choice.'

'How so?' she asked, knowing precisely what he would say.

'The White House tour, the interviews, the magazine articles. You're the most recognized and identifiable first lady that has ever graced the pages of a newspaper, and the first one to ever get yourself your own show on primetime television.'

Jackie didn't respond. Bobby had asked her to come and see him, and she had done so. He always asked, and he always asked politely. He treated her with respect and affection, and in his manner she recognized the same attitude that had so drawn her to Jack. In his own way, Bobby was the stronger of the two. Back when Jack had nominated his brother as attorney general, there was an outcry. The papers didn't use the word *nepotism*, but it was right there between the lines. The *New York Times* said that at just thirty-five years old, Bobby was inexperienced and unqualified.

Of course, they didn't know that Jack had never actually wanted Bobby as his attorney general; their father had strong-armed him, and he had conceded. And then Bobby had proved his father right and everyone else wrong. He'd surrounded himself with good people and gone after the Mafia and the Teamsters; even had the nerve to disagree with Hoover, that pig of a man down at the FBI. He backed Jack on civil rights, in the Berlin crisis, in Cuba. He had been a rock from day one, and Jackie loved him for that as much as she loved him as her brother-in-law.

'There's no way around it,' he said now. 'A re-election is sometimes even more demanding than an election. We have a term's worth of mistakes to explain and reconcile with our supporters, and we need more than just our supporters if you are going to be first lady for another four years.'

'And if I don't want to?'

Bobby looked at her in the way that only Bobby could.

Jackie glanced down. She didn't pursue an answer.

'Atlantic City will be fun,' he said.

'Bobby . . . honestly, I can think of a million places I would rather be than Atlantic City.'

'It's the Democratic National Convention. You have to be there. You have no choice. *We* have no choice. Half the influence of this presidency comes from the fact that you have the women's vote. Without that, we are undone.'

Jackie laughed. 'You're being far too melodramatic.'

'No, Jackie, I am being honest. There are a lot of critics. They are saying some dreadful things. We have a fight on our hands as it is, and to not have your support on this would be more of a blow than Jack could bear.'

Jackie was quiet for some time. Somewhere there was a life unlived. She wondered how different it would have been.

'Do you want another four years, Bobby?'

'Yes, I do.'

'And Ethel, and the children, what do they want?'

'They want what we all want.'

'And what is that?'

'The enormously positive effects we can create together for this country as a whole. Four years isn't enough time to get the engine running, let alone take us anywhere. Another four years and we can make civil rights a real and tangible reality, not just a bill, not just signatures and handshakes, but a national movement and an attitude that changes lives and changes the future for millions of people. We can deal with organized crime and communism and—'

'You really believe in yourself, don't you?'

Bobby smiled. 'I believe in Jack. I believe in you. I believe in the Kennedys. I think we're here for a reason, Jackie, and to give up now would be the biggest mistake and the very worst regret of our lives.'

Jackie leaned forward and took his hand.

'I believe because you believe,' she said. 'I will come to Atlantic City. I will be there on the first day, at least, and we'll see what happens. I will wear my best and brightest first lady smile, and I will show the world that we are all working together for your new American Dream.'

Bobby looked at her. She felt he could see right through her.

'I am sorry,' he said. 'I truly am.'

'For what?'

'That what you believed would happen and what has happened are not the same thing.'

Jackie shrugged and shook her head. In that simple physical expression he saw suppressed anger, grief, reconciliation, disappointment.

'It's called life, Bobby. It's the same for everyone, not just the Kennedys.'

He reached out and touched her shoulder. She closed her eyes, and then – for just a moment – she leaned sideways so her cheek touched his hand.

It was a moment of great tenderness and affection, and he felt his heart swell with a strange sense of loss and nostalgia.

It could all have been so good, so perfect. They could have made wonders here, but somehow things had become so very tainted.

Of course, they could rescue it. Anything could be rescued, but what would it take, and at what cost?

Someone knocked at the door.

Jackie stood up and straightened her skirt.

'You have my agreement,' she said.

'Thank you.'

She opened the door. Walter Lambert was outside.

'I'm sorry, Mrs Kennedy.' He glanced at Bobby. 'Sir. If this is an inconvenient time—'

'No, no, Walter. Mrs Kennedy and I are done.'

Lambert stepped aside and Jackie left the room.

'Come in, Walter,' Bobby said. 'I felt we should take a moment to clarify the issues we were addressing at the meeting on Wednesday.'

'Yes, sir, of course.'

Bobby took a seat at his desk, invited Lambert to sit too.

'Now, Walter, I fully appreciate your commitment and dedication, but I need you to understand what we are going to be dealing with at the National Convention.'

'Of course, sir.'

Lambert was implacable at the best of times, but now he seemed even harder to fathom. He was intense, perhaps as intense as any man Bobby had ever met, but such a job necessitated such an attitude.

'As the chief of the president's personal protection detail, the security and safety of the president and the first family are your paramount concerns. In fact, they are your only concerns.'

'Yes, sir. Absolutely, sir.'

Bobby paused. 'I know there have been issues with which you have had to contend that you perhaps did not...' He smiled. 'Aspects of security that do not necessarily fall into the standard remits and protocols for which you were trained.'

'Might I say something, sir?'

'Yes, yes, of course. Please go ahead.'

'This job is my life, Mr Kennedy, both as a vocation and a duty. I have sworn to uphold the office of the president, even to the point of giving my own life. You may not necessarily understand how and why a man would be willing to sacrifice his life for another, but that is what we do. That is what all of us do when we apply for this position. I can safely say that every single individual in my team would willingly and without reservation give his life if it meant saving that of the president.'

'Yes, Walter... it is a very noble commitment. I do understand.'

Lambert continued. 'Politics is of no concern to me. We defend and protect the president as the embodiment of democracy and freedom, the Constitution and the United States of America.'

'Yes. Yes indeed,' Bobby said. 'So this is what I want to say, and I want you to interpret it in whichever way you see fit for the challenges ahead. We are skating on thin ice. As a political force for good, we are being tested. In the days and weeks ahead, we will be subject to attack, to criticism, to a veritable trial by fire. Some of the issues with which you have had to contend may be brought to light, given an unhealthy degree of focus, even reported in the media...'

'I am sorry, sir, but—'

'Let me finish, Walter.'

'Yes, sir.'

'The most important issues here are political and social. Our international policies, the threats we are facing from communism, both foreign and domestic. Civil rights, the economy, employment, the very nature of what it is to be the greatest nation on earth. This is where my attention lies, Walter, not in vitriolic criticism and hearsay. People need to have their attention redirected toward the positive, toward the many things we have already achieved, and that is what will be accomplished at the DNC. It is my duty, and I know it is your duty too, to keep our eyes on that mountain, and to do whatever it takes – *whatever* it takes – to ensure that this presidency is not lost. We need to continue the work we're doing, and nothing can be permitted to derail it.'

Bobby paused for a moment, and then he stood up.

Lambert also rose to his feet.

'Your duty is to protect the office of the president, Walter. We can leave behind a legacy of truly extraordinary achievements that will continue to generate peace and stability for decades to come, or we can sink into a mire of obscurity, our memory shrouded in sleaze and sordid rumors.'

Neither man spoke for a moment.

'Do we understand one another, Walter?'

'Yes, Mr Kennedy. We understand one another perfectly.'

57

Special Agent in Charge Allan Dempster of the Dallas Secret Service field office was a man of similar years to George Everett but of far greater seriousness. That being said, he possessed a dry Texan humor, with which he peppered his conversation. When Mitch detailed all he knew, right down to the possibility that Lee Oswald – proud communist, one-time defector, married to a Russian girl, ex-Marine Corps, apparently in possession of a 6.5 millimeter Carcano rifle and a .38 revolver – might have been responsible for the April 1963 shooting at the home of Major General Edwin Walker, Dempster was on fire to know everything down to the last detail.

Mitch started talking. He went right back to the call from Jean's mother that fateful night of Independence Day. When he explained his search of Jean's paperwork, he also spoke of her initial motivation for coming to Dallas. For some reason he felt that Dempster would not allow it to influence his viewpoint.

'I think she suspected that vote-rigging and election corruption might have played a part in Kennedy's success.'

Dempster smiled wryly. 'I am a Nixon man,' he said. 'But the Secret Service is the Secret Service. We don't serve individuals. We serve the office, irrespective of the politics. Please go on.'

Mitch continued, detailing his communication with Detective Nelson Shaw at Metro PD and his discovery of Jack Ruby, by that time already arrested for the murder of Leland Webster.

Then there was the Carousel club, a woman called Holly Walsh who seemed to be nothing but a ghost, the Texas Communist League, and the possibility – albeit entirely suppositional – that Oswald might have used Ruby's gun to murder Webster. He told Dempster about the Texas School Book Depository, about Ruth Paine and Marshall Jeavons, and wound up with the conversation he'd had with Dan Wilson, Oswald's neighbor, and the fact that Wilson was the second person to mention that Oswald might have been responsible for the attempt on Edwin Walker's life.

With every further point he made, he could see that the whole was so much greater than the sum of its parts. Individually, each event could be easily explained away. Together, they presented a different perspective altogether.

He did not talk about the newspaper people taking Jean's paperwork from the West Haven house. He did not mention the fact that Lester Byron had been visited by police officers who seemed not to exist, or that those same people had known where he was staying in Dallas. He also said nothing of people looking for him at his local bar in Washington, nor Young and Trent at the funeral. If he gave the impression of being paranoid, that might well diminish the credibility of what he was saying. He needed someone to listen and understand – to *really* understand – and he believed that here in the Dallas field office, he'd finally found the right person.

Throughout, Agent Dempster took extensive notes, often asking Mitch for verification of exact dates, the precise spelling of names, or to backtrack and clarify the sequence of events as they happened.

'And you've been investigating this for the better part of six weeks, completely alone,' he said.

'I don't know if investigating is the right word...'

Dempster smiled. 'I'd hope that my own agents would have

the kind of determination and perseverance you've demonstrated here, Mr Newman.'

'I'm relieved to know that you're taking it seriously.'

'Seriously enough to invest some time and resources in finding this Lee Oswald. Seems to me he's something of a loose cannon. If nothing else, we can pursue further details about the shooting at the Walker house. I remember reading about it in the paper. As far as I know, no one was ever arrested or charged with that. Of course, it wouldn't have been our jurisdiction, but I think it would have warranted some news attention had the person responsible been caught.'

'I went back through a lot of copies of the *Morning News*. I didn't find any further reports on the case.'

'Well, we can engage the FBI, the local police, whatever resources we need. It won't be long before he's found, and then we can get to the bottom of all this.'

'So what do you want me to do?'

'To be honest, I don't think there's a great deal you can do that hasn't already been done. Whether the things you have detailed constitute a tangible and feasible threat to the life and well-being of the president, I do not know. Obviously, even if Oswald had intended to do something last November, that did not happen. And we have no evidence to suggest that he might intend to do something now. But these events are linked. Of that I have no doubt. I have to take into account Oswald's place of work, his political and ideological sympathies, his attempted defection, the shooting of General Walker, the deaths of his work colleague, your colleague too, the missing girl, and now the attack on Ruby. Whatever may or may not have happened, he certainly seems to be in the middle of a hurricane of trouble. That alone justifies some time and manpower. If we investigated only when something was right there in front of us, we would forever be too late to act. I'll get a warrant to search the

McArthur property. That Oswald appears to have obtained a gun under an alias is sufficient for that. After that, his bank account, his contacts, acquaintances, the usual. We'll find him for sure.'

Mitch said nothing.

'What I'm saying, Mr Newman, is that you can go home to Washington and get on with your life.'

Mitch laughed spontaneously.

'Something is funny?'

'No, not at all. I'm sorry. It's just that this thing has consumed me, obsessed me, you could say, for the past month and a half, and I've sort of forgotten what I was doing beforehand. It all started with the death of a very dear and important friend, and I am not sure that I can just walk away without knowing what really happened to her.'

'I think you should be impressed with what you have already done, Mr Newman. I certainly am. Without your commitment, these things would never have been known. I really feel you should now let us progress with this investigation.'

'Then could I ask something of you?'

'Of course, yes.'

'Would you let me know if you succeed in finding Oswald? The mere fact that you've tracked him down and he's not vanished into thin air would be … well, it would put my mind at rest to know that some crazy with a rifle wasn't plotting to kill the president.'

'That I can do. Unusual, against regulations, but I will do it. Of course, I will deny that I told you anything, but I think we have an understanding and it won't come to that.'

Mitch gave Dempster his DC number. They shook hands. Then he left the building and headed back to the motel to pack his things.

58

August 19, 1964

Mitch did not arrive home until late on Saturday. The remainder of the weekend disappeared in a blur of sleep and food and TV. He did not talk to anyone but the cat. His exhaustion caught up with him to the point that Monday saw him still fatigued and unwilling to do anything but wander from room to room, a drink in his hand, somehow trying to let go of all that had happened since Jean's death.

Some of the hurt seemed to ease, only to find him again as he woke. He could see her, hear her voice, remember so vividly the way she would laugh at his jokes and call him dumb. A birthday gift, a film they saw together, the time they smoked pot and laughed until they hurt. Memories found him, and he did not hide from them. It was painful but somehow cathartic, and by Tuesday evening he knew he had survived the worst of it. Perhaps now it would be possible to be nostalgic without grieving, to remember without regret.

On Wednesday morning, he went out. He just walked, and kept on walking until he didn't really know where he was. He stopped to have a cup of coffee in a diner, and there on the countertop was a copy of that day's *Tribune*.

DALLAS CLUB OWNER DEAD.

That was the headline, and before Mitch even read the report, he knew it was Ruby. The article went on to say that Jacob Rubenstein, local businessman and entrepreneur, had died at Parkland Hospital as a result of injuries sustained in an incident at Dallas County Jail. That word – *incident* – said everything and nothing.

He didn't read the rest of it. He just went quiet inside and drank his coffee. He didn't feel surprise; merely a sense of dismay and wonder that such a thing could happen. He knew that this brief squib in the *Tribune* would be all that was ever reported on the matter.

As he leafed absent-mindedly through the newspaper, his attention was caught by another article. Strangely, it was even more disconcerting than the report of Ruby's death, despite the fact that it had nothing to do with Mitch's investigation. A young woman called Judith Wagner had been found dead in her apartment; a suspected overdose. She was twenty-nine, and according to the report had been pursuing a successful career in cosmetics and fashion. She had been an assistant with the team producing the White House tour television presentation, and was believed to have styled Mrs John F. Kennedy's hair. Her father had expressed his disbelief and shock, saying, 'It is beyond us ... utterly beyond us why our beautiful, talented daughter would take her own life.'

Both Mitch and Alice had felt precisely the same way about Jean. A tragic and inexplicable waste of life.

He put the newspaper aside. He didn't want any more bad news.

His first impulse was to call Shaw. Ruby's death was now a murder, and Mitch wanted to know what he thought. He held himself back, but only for a while. He'd reached a point where he really didn't give a damn. Ruby was dead, and now the Secret Service was involved.

There was a phone booth down the block.

'Annual leave,' he was told.

'Since when?'

There was a pause at the other end of the line. 'I'm sorry, but that's not the kind of information we are willing to divulge.'

'So you can't tell me when he's back?'

'I'm sorry, sir. No.'

'Can I leave a message?'

'Yes, of course.'

'Just tell him to call Newman. Mitchell Newman.'

'I have that, sir. You have a good day now.' The line went dead.

Mitch next telephoned the Shaws' home. It rang out. Frustrated, he called Dempster at the Dallas field office.

'I am sorry, sir. Agent Dempster is actually away for the entire day. He'll be back in the office tomorrow.'

'Is there any other way to reach him?'

'I'm sorry, sir, there isn't. The agent in question is occupied with a field investigation.'

'Do you happen to know if he has made any progress in determining the whereabouts of a Mr Lee Oswald?'

'I wouldn't know anything about that, sir. I am sorry, but you're going to have to wait until the morning and speak to Agent Dempster in person.'

'Okay. Can I leave my number just in case he returns?'

'Absolutely, though I am quite certain he will not be here until tomorrow.'

Mitch gave the agent his number. 'If he comes back, please ask him to call me. It's quite urgent.'

'Yes, sir. Of course.'

He set down the receiver and stared at it. An elderly woman

knocked on the door of the booth. Mitch near jumped out of his skin.

'Are you finished, young man?'

He stepped out and went back to the diner. He ordered another cup of coffee. The newspaper was gone.

59

That evening, Mitch finally discovered the painful truth of Jean's refusal to even acknowledge his letters.

The last two he had sent – February 16 and 24, 1951 – were his last-ditch attempt to win her back. In them, he poured his heart out all over again. He told her how much she meant to him, how stupid he'd been, how sorry he was, and even though he was echoing things that had already been said, he expressed them with such clarity that it hurt to read his own words and remember how he'd felt. He knew the life he'd imagined for himself was gone, and gone for good. It was there, and then it had vanished. All through his letters, he understood that he'd made her responsible for what had happened. Now he saw it very differently. With the oh-so-clear rearview mirror of hindsight, he recognized that he had been the architect of his own loss.

What he did not expect, and what he found – tucked right there in the same envelope as his final letter – was a reply. It was pages long, and each and every word was a searing and indescribable pain through his heart, his mind, the very core of himself. He read it in disbelief. He read it in shock. He read it and could not understand what he was reading. When the truth finally arrived, he broke down and sobbed. The very center of his world collapsed, and he fell headlong into the abyss, out of control, unstoppable. He'd believed she had somehow returned the hurt by her lack of response, but the truth was far worse, far greater, even more profound and heartbreaking than he could have imagined.

Angry, stunned, unable to stand, to sit, to even think clearly, he stared at the words she'd written and finally understood what he had done.

March 10, 1951
Dear Mitch,

It's more than seven months since we last saw one another. Yes, I received your letters, but even as I am writing this, I know I'll never post it. I don't want you to read it, because I know how you'll use it to torture yourself. I loved you. You must understand that. I always loved you. Perhaps I loved you too much, for now I can see how I forgave you for things that should not have been forgiven.

You are your own world, Mitch. It's not selfish or ignorant. You can't be ignorant of things you are unaware of. You lived for yourself, and yourself alone. At first I believed that it was me. That, perhaps, is human nature, but now, away from you, I know it's not. You are who you are, and that strength of purpose and single-mindedness was perhaps the very thing that drew me to you. I don't doubt what you are capable of, and yet you doubt yourself so very much. To have watched you tear apart everything you have done and make nothing of it has hurt me too. I don't profess to understand what makes a human being do that to themselves, but I do understand how difficult it is to see it happening before your eyes and be able to do nothing. The thing you need to see, which you do not, is that to be so unforgiving of yourself is to be unforgiving of others. The closer they are, the more you push them away. The more you mean to them, the more they feel the hurt you inflict on yourself.

Perhaps in time you'll see yourself in a different light and appreciate how you are your own worst enemy. I don't know. Do I care? Yes, of course I do, but by the time that happens, I believe we'll have led separate lives for so long that you won't remember how it was between us. It was tough. Really tough. I didn't appreciate how tough until afterwards, until I had walked away and discovered who I really was. I was suffocated, Mitch. That's how I felt. Drowned and smothered and suffocated. My life became an extension of yours. I ceased to be myself, to even understand what I wanted, how I felt, where I was going, or why.

And then, when you told me you were going to Korea, I knew I had to leave for somewhere just as distant. I had to cut the ties and walk away and rediscover the person I believed I would have become had I not met you. I am nineteen years old. I know so very little, and yet I knew that I had to escape. That's what it felt like, Mitch. I begged you to stay, I pleaded with you, but I have to tell you that secretly, in my heart, I hoped you would go. I think I needed you to go. One time, I even wished you dead. I wished that you would die out there in the jungle, so that I had no choice but to start my life over again and do it differently. I didn't mean it, of course, but the mere fact that I thought it told me something about how I truly felt.

And now, my confession.

Do you remember when you told me that you were going? Do you remember that night? You said you had some news. I said I had news, too. I said you should speak first, and we went back and forth and finally you told me about quitting college and going to Korea, and then we sat up the whole night and talked about it? Do you remember that?

Well, I never told you my news.

I was pregnant, Mitch. I was pregnant with our baby, and I never told you. I didn't tell you that night, and I didn't tell you the next day, and after all the shouting and fighting, I decided never to tell you. And I knew then that it wouldn't be possible for me to have that child. A child would have tied us together forever, and that was something I couldn't allow. You might think that had you stayed it would have been different. Looking back and understanding how impossible it would have been, I think it would've been a mistake. Sad though I am, guilty, at a loss to even describe how it made me feel, I knew that I couldn't carry that child. I was little more than a child myself. I was alone. That's what I felt, and that's what I believed.

The world so often seems a dark and cruel place. For a child to grow, for a child to be safe and secure, they need to be raised with love and care and devotion. I guess I knew that even then. A while back, someone said to me that a child makes a great relationship even stronger, but also has the capacity to find weaknesses and drive people apart. You have a child because you want to. It should not be a mistake, something to regret, something to use to blackmail someone else into living a life they do not want. You were not ready to be a father. To be honest, I don't know that you will ever be ready; only time will tell. Our child would have been a burden, an unwanted obligation, and there was no way I could use that to stop you doing what you believed you needed to do.

Three weeks after you left, I had an abortion. It felt like the worst crime to commit, but I did it nevertheless. My mother didn't know. I told no one. Perhaps that secret will stay with me to my dying day.

To reply to your letters would only lead to more upset. You would try to see me, and I would find it so hard to refuse you. If I saw you, I don't know that I'd be able to keep my secret. And so I haven't replied, and I never will.

And even though it may seem that I have written this for you, I have really written it for myself. If I ever waver, if I ever doubt my decision, I will read this and remember how it really was. Our relationship was a possession. An obsession. You used to call me a firework in a bottle, and I think you were right. I smoldered in there, and one day, who knows when, I would have exploded. I think that explosion would have been sufficient to kill us both.

There we have it. That is my confession. My sin. My crime.

This is what I did, and even though you will never know, I hope that if you ever did discover the truth you would be able to forgive me. I doubt it, for to forgive another it is necessary to be able to forgive yourself, and that is something I believe you'll never be able to do.

I see now that I loved you more than I loved myself, and that was why it would never have worked. One of us would have quit. I don't believe I had the strength to do it, so you got to quit first.

I wish you happiness, though I believe you'll never truly find it.

I hope you find someone who will love you unconditionally, though I don't know that such a person exists.

Goodbye, Mitch. I said it when you left, but now it means something very different.

Jean

60

After reading the letter five, six times, he got drunk. He got so drunk he could not remember falling down in the kitchen.

At one point he slurred into semi-consciousness and realized that he was shouting at Jean, asking her where the child was … what had she done with the child, goddammit …

And then he passed out again, and did not surface for hours.

When he came to, he was still on the kitchen floor. He felt ill, blind with pain, and beneath that he felt the immense burden of what he had discovered in Jean's letter. He could not pretend it was not real. He wanted it to be some hideous nightmare, but it was not. The letter was right there on the table.

He needed to get up, to find aspirin and make coffee. He needed to shower, to get dressed, to get out of the apartment and face the daylight. He just went on lying there, seemingly unable to move, and at least an hour passed, his mind drifting in and out of focus, before the sound of the telephone drilled through the hangover and roused him from where he'd collapsed.

'Hello?'

'Mr Newman?'

'Yes.'

'This is Agent McCarry. We spoke yesterday on the telephone. You were hoping to reach Agent Dempster.'

337

'Yes, yes, that's right. Is he available?'

'I'm sorry, sir, no. Unfortunately, an assignment has taken him out of state.'

'For how long?'

'I really have no idea.'

'And even if you did, you wouldn't tell me, right?'

'Well, actually ... Agent Dempster did want me to pass on a message. He said that he had been assigned to an investigation in New Jersey. He said that it would make sense to you.'

Mitch thought hard. It was tough to even string a sentence together, let alone understand the significance of New Jersey.

'Did he say anything else?'

'No, sir, he did not. He just instructed me to tell you that he had gone to New Jersey and that you would understand.'

After McCarry had hung up, Mitch stood there with the phone in his hand and wondered what the hell New Jersey had to do with anything.

He showered, put on some clean clothes, drank two cups of coffee and stood by the window until the fresh air cleared his head a little.

He did not call Alice. What purpose would it serve? He could not tell her what Jean had done. Jean had not wanted her to know, and Mitch could not violate that decision. Instead, he called Lester Byron at the *Tribune*.

'It's Mitch.'

'Mitch ... how are you?

'Surviving.'

'That was very moving at the funeral. What you said was very heartfelt.'

Mitch did not want to talk about the funeral. He did not want to talk about Jean. He did not even want to remember her.

'Lester ... tell me what you know about New Jersey.'

'New Jersey? What has New Jersey got to do with anything?'

'Exactly my question ... what do you know about it?'

'I think it's the most densely populated state in the US, has a lot of forests, a lot of blueberries. I think Count Basie was born there—'

'Not that kind of stuff. Is it newsworthy? Has anything happened there recently that wound up in the nationals?'

'The Democratic National Convention is happening in New Jersey,' Byron said.

Mitch stopped breathing for a second. He'd known this but it had gotten lost somewhere.

'Atlantic City ... Hang on, I have something here ...'

He heard Byron shuffling through papers on his desk, then calling out, 'Kathy ... where's that press release on the DNC?'

Mitch waited. He could feel his heart racing.

'Here we are,' Byron said. 'Monday the twenty-fourth to Thursday the twenty-seventh, Historic Atlantic City Convention Hall.'

'Next week,' Mitch said.

'Yes, it starts on Monday.'

'Oh my God,' Mitch said.

'What?'

'Lester ... thank you. Thank you very much.'

'But—'

He hung up the phone.

Dempster had gone to New Jersey. Kennedy would be there in four days' time.

And Lee Oswald – a communist, a subversive, a man who'd tried to kill an army officer, a man who wanted the world to know just how important he was – had seemingly vanished into thin air.

61

August 21, 1964

Mitch decided to drive. He left late on Friday. It was a couple of hundred miles, up through Baltimore, on past Wilmington, skirting the south of Philadelphia, and down to Atlantic City on the coast. He'd never been there before, had never considered the need to go. But now there was no question. Why else would Dempster have wanted him to receive that specific message?

Maybe the agent had forwarded Mitch's story through command channels, and Oswald was perceived as a real threat, certainly real enough to warrant Dempster's assignment. Dempster was Dallas; that was where Oswald lived and from where he would be traveling. Dempster also had all the information that Mitch had relayed, so it would make sense for him to be there to communicate it first-hand to anyone who needed to know.

Mitch had to be there. The only other option was to stay home and think about Jean's letter, to think about the past, about what might have been; about the future they would have had together had he possessed sense enough to look at what he was leaving behind.

The ghost that haunted him was the child.

Jean had been right. There was no question. Her own astute perception, combined with the objectivity that must have come from several months of separation, had given her a clear and

340

untrammeled view of things. Mitch had lived life for himself. That was plain. He had absorbed her individuality, restricted her, imprisoned her by expectation, and then he had deserted her. That had been his crime, but to have done what she did? To have made such a decision without telling him, without explaining her thoughts, her feelings, her reasoning?

Yet hadn't he done the same? He had made a decision that caused her to lose him; she had made a decision that lost them a child. An eye for an eye. She had finally balanced the scales for the hurt he'd caused.

Mitch pushed the thoughts away. He couldn't sit alone in his apartment, talking to no one but the cat, punishing himself into an alcoholic stupor. He had to be away from DC, and this was a better reason than any he could imagine. Perhaps he could do something to help. Perhaps his weeks of investigation might bring something that no one else possessed. If Dempster was there, Mitch needed to find him, find out to whom he'd relayed what was known, and see if there was some further assistance he could provide.

Mitch found a cheap, nondescript hotel on North Bellevue, just a few blocks over from the Convention Hall. He was not required to present ID. He paid in cash, said his name was Jim Denton. It was the third time he'd used an alias, and yet he did not believe for a minute that he could successfully conceal what he was doing or where he was.

'And how long do you plan on staying here in Atlantic City, Mr Denton?' the receptionist asked him.

'Through the weekend,' Mitch said. 'Maybe into the middle of next week. I have business down here, some meetings and the like. Not really sure how long they'll go on.'

'Well, I trust you'll have a good stay. Anything you need, just let me know. My name is Stanley.'

'Appreciated,' Mitch said, and went on up to his room.

It was clean but spartan. A single bed, one straight-backed chair, a small writing desk, a narrow closet. The bathroom was down the hall. Mitch put his few articles of clothing into the closet, and then sat on the bed and thought about what he was going to do.

Dempster, he guessed, would be at the Convention Hall as part of whatever security preparations Secret Service protocol demanded. There would be a very significant presence, as was always the case when the president made a public appearance, though for the DNC it would go beyond that many times. The president would be here if not for all four days, then certainly for the majority of it. He might even come in on the Sunday night. His travel and accommodation arrangements would be known in advance to only a very select few. The number of agents and local law enforcement officials would perhaps exceed a thousand, all requiring the most strenuous and detailed organization. Add into the mix a tangible security threat, and everything would be doubled up. Perhaps Dempster had not been drafted in because of what Mitch had told him. Perhaps every Secret Service agent for a two-hundred-mile radius had been called on to bolster the ranks and meet the requirements of such a huge event.

For now, Mitch felt it best to just go down there. He wanted to walk the Atlantic Boardwalk and see the Convention Hall itself.

Already there was evidence of preparations. Trucks were lined up at the rear of the building along Pacific Avenue; gangs of men carried rolled-up banners and lighting rigs through the service doors. A line of police cars and wagons faced the trucks on the other side of the street, and a cordon of barriers had been erected to divert traffic away from the area. Here and there men in dark suits kept a watchful eye on the proceedings. They could be Secret Service, they could be Feds, perhaps plainclothes

342

PD. It was a scene of organized industry as vehicles disgorged their contents and pulled away, only to be replaced by a further caravan, more men, more equipment. The radio and TV station vehicles were further back along South Georgia and South Florida, and every person he saw wore an ID lanyard of one form or another.

Mitch headed back to the boardwalk. He was hungry. He needed to eat. It was getting late and he didn't imagine he'd easily track down Allan Dempster. There would be a field office here, or perhaps – considering the scope of the event and the number of people required – a hotel would have been requisitioned, not only to accommodate all the agents, but also to operate as a strategic headquarters for the security operation. Finding it would have to wait until tomorrow.

62

Walter Lambert stood in the window of his hotel room and looked down South Mississippi toward the Convention Hall.

It was August 21, three days until the commencement of the Democratic National Convention, the largest security operation he had supervised since the president's inauguration. Thus far – at an average of six a day – the Secret Service had received over one and a half thousand written death threats against John F. Kennedy. Second to Kennedy was Lyndon Baines Johnson, with a handful shy of thirteen hundred; close on his heels was the attorney general with a meager eleven hundred and forty-three. A total somewhere close to four thousand for three men, and those three men were all flying into Philadelphia International Airport on Sunday evening.

Robert Kennedy and the vice president would be driven to Atlantic City in separate motorcades; they would be accommodated at two separate locations. Johnson would be staying with a long-term friend and Democratic Party supporter, the banker Randall Hitchkiss. The Hitchkiss estate possessed walled grounds, a dozen attack dogs and its own security team. With a supplementary Secret Service detail it was perhaps the easiest location to manage. The attorney general would be housed on the fifth floor of the Atlantic City Regency Hotel. The hotel possessed six floors, and both the fourth and sixth would host no one but Secret Service.

The president himself was the real issue, just as he had been the previous November. In Dallas, he'd insisted that the presidential limousine should be open-top. When the car had been delivered back in June of 1961, Lambert had challenged the lack of bulletproof plating and glass. It was nothing more than a modified Lincoln Continental four-door convertible, but Ford had stretched it by forty-one inches, strengthened the frame, and fitted a hand-built 350 hp engine. The car's weight had increased by one and a half thousand pounds, and yet the windscreen was still the standard two-ply safety glass. To Lambert it had not made sense, but then a great deal of the tried-and-tested security protocols had been thrown out of the proverbial window when the Kennedys entered the White House.

John F. Kennedy, the first lady too, insisted on being *available*. That was all well and good, and politically it may have endeared them to the public in a way that no previous administration had done, but it was a security nightmare. Lambert had to be seen to have taken all necessary and possible precautions. For a Secret Service man, there was no greater fear than losing a president on their watch, irrespective of whatever personal opinions they might hold about the man, his actions, his policies and his politics. Democrat or Republican, it mattered not.

The Democratic National Convention had been months in the planning. Lambert's preparations had spanned more than a year. John F. Kennedy would be helicoptered in to the roof of the Crowne Excelsior Hotel, and from there taken to the penthouse suite. A team of thirty agents was assigned to that one floor, a further ten marksmen on the roof itself, the helicopter remaining there throughout the president's stay in the event that a rapid evacuation was required.

Not since September 1901 in Buffalo, New York had a president been assassinated. The murder of William McKinley was the very act itself that prompted Congress to assign protection of the President to the Secret Service.

Born in Annapolis, Maryland in May of 1925 to US Navy Ensign Eugene Lambert and Marion, née Carter, herself a Navy child, Walter was raised in his father's image. He attended the Naval Academy Preparatory School in Newport, Rhode Island, went on to the US Naval Academy right there in the city of his birth, and when he graduated he went into service as Chief Warrant Officer.

Younger than the President by eight years, Lambert had not served during the Second World War, but saw some action as part of the Pacific Fleet in Korea.

In 1957, now a Lieutenant Commander, Walter Lambert, USN, resigned his commission, much to the dismay of his father. Walter was thirty-two years old and single. He told his father that he did not see a long-term future for himself in the Navy.

'So what is it that you intend to do?' Lambert asked his son.

'Law enforcement,' was the younger Lambert's reply.

'The Police?'

'No, not the Police. Perhaps the FBI, maybe the Secret Service.'

Walter chose the latter. Whatever he may have lacked in passion and imagination, he more than amply made up for in commitment and loyalty. He had risen through the ranks of the Secret Service in an exemplary fashion, one of the youngest Special Agents-in-Charge ever posted in the capitol, and certainly the youngest Presidential Detail Chief in the history of the Service. Of this he was rightfully proud. Anything that could potentially undermine, diminish, damage or destroy the office of President of the United States was his business, and he took his business very seriously indeed.

The events of the twenty-third to the twenty-seventh of August, 1964, there in Atlantic City, New Jersey, had been planned with the most meticulous attention to detail. All possibilities had been considered, all contingencies covered, all scenarios rehearsed and rehearsed again. Under Lambert's direct command were two hundred and twenty-five Secret Service agents, sixty Federal Bureau agents, the entirety of the Atlantic City Police Department, even the US Coastguard running patrol boats offshore in the event of an assault by aggressors from the sea. He was not merely dealing with the safety of one man. He was dealing with an entire administrative staff, all the way from the vice president and the attorney general down through the chief of staff to the assistant deputy legal counsels and the girls who ran errands for the secretary of state's wife. And then, on top of all that, there was the first lady and the president's children, and the many family members of other administrative officials. It was a rolling circus that put P. T. Barnum to shame, and yet required the secrecy and logistical support of a military invasion.

But that was why Lambert was here, and that was why he was the only man for the job. He believed that no one else appreciated the sanctity and inviolable nature of what it was to be the most powerful man in the Western hemisphere, if not the world. Even as he watched the endless stream of traffic and the hordes of people thronging Atlantic Boardwalk, he knew that his own life was meaningless in the face of all that was at stake.

It was a life for a life. That was the oath, and he intended to keep it.

63

August 22, 1964

Lee Harvey Oswald was one of numerous named individuals discussed at the first of several scheduled Secret Service briefings on Saturday.

'Tell me about the source of this information,' Lambert said to Allan Dempster

'His name is Mitchell Newman,' Dempster replied. 'DC-based, originally from Virginia, thirty-five years of age, single, no known association to any group or organization on the current watch list. He's a freelance journalist, covers for crime scene photographers, has submitted work to numerous publications, human interest stuff predominantly. Doesn't appear to have an active political standpoint, has always voted Democrat. Father was military, killed in the Second World War, mother died in '61. He was out in Korea, July to November 1950. Medical records suggest he returned with stress, short-term trauma, the usual. No history of mental illness, no treatment. Never been arrested, clean tax records, never been under investigation by any federal body.'

'Earlier marriages ... children?'

'Neither.'

Lambert looked around the gathering of agents before him.

'Oswald,' he said, 'has been on our radar before. He was at

Love Field when the president arrived last November for the Dallas trip. Beyond that, he was not seen again, nor were there any substantiated reports of activity within the area that could be construed as potentially threatening. Ex-Marine Corps, active communist affiliations, one-time member of the currently defunct Texas Communist League, married to a Russian girl, but per latest reports they are separated and estranged. Concurring with Agent Dempster's report, Oswald's current residence is vacant. We have people working on tracking him through bus stations, train stations, airports.'

He paused in thought for a moment.

'The wrong thing to do is nothing. However, having said that, it's also wrong to do too much. Focusing our attention on one possible threat loses us our objectivity. We need to maintain peripheral vision at all times. Concentrating on one potential threat to the exclusion of all others just opens us up to failure.'

'Are we using open-tops?' Dempster asked.

'No, not this time. Dallas was a one-off, and that is something I have urged we never repeat. Hardtops, agents on running boards, the full standard protocol for urban motorized passage. The president's car will take him from the Crowne Excelsior to the Convention Hall on Monday morning, and a clear route will be facilitated between the Convention Hall and the hotel in the event that a rapid return is needed. The president's personal physician, Rear Admiral George Burkley, will be present at all times, and both the vice president and the attorney general will also have their respective physicians in attendance. The first lady and the children will arrive late on Monday. The specific route and hour of their arrival has not yet been disclosed, but a separate security team will be managing that under my direct supervision. For now, there is no plan to bring the attorney general's wife or children to New Jersey, but that may change.'

Lambert looked at the men around the table. 'Any immediate questions?'

There were none.

'Okay, good. So, as far as this Lee Harvey Oswald is concerned, Agent Dempster will run this, and Franklin will be his second.'

They all glanced at Agent Carl Franklin, a recent arrival from the San Francisco field office. Franklin nodded an acknowledgment.

'Oswald's photograph is being reproduced as we speak. Agent Dempster will ensure that you're all given a copy to add to the photographs that have already been distributed. In my opinion, this man is not a real and tangible threat. Nevertheless, this is the most public we have been since November last year, the Convention will host a capacity attendance, and the issues currently facing this administration will require an above-and-beyond level of vigilance and attention to every detail, no matter how insignificant it might seem.'

Lambert paused once more. He looked around the room. The men looking back at him were attentive, determined, professional.

'I have to say that I am nothing other than assured of your commitment to what you are doing. I do not believe that any head of state anywhere in the world is as invulnerable as the man we are charged to protect. I don't need to tell you this, but anything that threatens the office of the president is also a direct threat to the very foundation of liberty in the Western world. It is that important, gentlemen, and as we carry out our duties and fulfill our responsibilities over the forthcoming days, I want you to remember that we are the last line of defense between democracy and anarchy. If our man falls, we all fall. Am I understood?'

There was a brisk and emphatic response from the gathering.

'Good. So, Agent Dempster, I leave this new concern to you and Franklin. From my understanding, the information you currently hold is predominantly circumstantial, but you have whatever authority and resources you need to investigate it thoroughly. Keep me informed, and I will be your point of coordination and liaison.'

'Yes, sir.'

'Excellent.' Lambert rose to his feet. Everyone else followed suit. 'Our motto, gentlemen: Worthy of Trust and Confidence.'

The words echoed back from the agents present.

'Worthy of Trust and Confidence!'

'Aside from Dempster and Franklin, you are all dismissed.'

The agents filed out, and the last one closed the door behind him.

Dempster and Franklin took the seats closest to Lambert.

'So tell me, Allan,' Lambert said. 'This Oswald situation ... what, if anything, are we really dealing with here?'

64

Mitch was shunted from one Secret Service agent to the next for much of Saturday morning and into the early afternoon. He was even briefly questioned by two detectives from Atlantic City PD. By the time he finally sat in front of Allan Dempster, he'd lost count of the number of people who'd told him that everything was under control, that a multitude of agents were ensuring that no threat to the life of the president would ever be realized. These people were certain and self-assured, but once Mitch had ascertained that Dempster had in fact been flown in from Dallas, he would not quit until he spoke to him.

Thus, mid afternoon, he found himself in a small administrative office behind the lobby of the Crowne Excelsior Hotel. Another agent was present, introduced as Carl Franklin, though he said nothing during the entire exchange. As he stood by the door, arms folded like a cigar store Indian, Mitch perceived nothing but disapproval.

'I am struggling to understand why you're here, Mr Newman,' Dempster said.

'I am too,' Mitch said. 'At least a little.'

'Do you think there's something you can do that we can't, perhaps?'

It was a good question, and one for which he had no answer. 'No,' he said. 'It's just that I have managed to convince myself that this is a very real and present danger, and... Well, I just felt I had to be here. I called you at your office and...'

He left the statement incomplete. He was certain that Dempster's tip-off about going to New Jersey was a violation of procedure, and he did not know whether mentioning it would generate problems for him.

'I asked you if you knew what Oswald looked like. You remember that?'

The question was simple, and made Mitch feel very stupid. He'd been chasing someone for days and yet – had he seen him – he would not have recognised him.

Dempster opened a manila file in front of him. From it he took a single photograph and slid it across the table.

Mitch picked it up. The man in the photograph appeared clean-cut, unremarkable, even nondescript. Nothing about him seemed out of the ordinary, but then how was a potential presidential assassin supposed to look?

'That, Mr Newman, is Lee Harvey Oswald, and I am going to explain a few things about Secret Service protocol. In November of 1950, just around the time you came back from your four-month stint in Korea—'

Mitch looked up, surprised.

'You thought we wouldn't check you out? You think we don't know everything about you?'

Mitch said nothing.

'So, as I was saying, back in November of 1950, there was an attempt on the life of President Truman. The White House was being renovated, and the president was staying at Blair House across the street. Two Puerto Rican nationalists approached the house and opened fire on the duty White House police officers. One officer, a Private Leslie Coffelt, was shot three times with a Luger, but even though he was mortally wounded, he still killed one of the assassins with a single bullet to the head. The other assassin was caught and sentenced to death. Private Coffelt is the only man to have been killed in the line of duty while protecting a president.

'Only three presidents have ever been assassinated: Abraham Lincoln, James A. Garfield and William McKinley. There have been innumerable plots, several attempts, but no one has succeeded. The Secret Service has been responsible for the protection of the president since 1901. Congress assigned that duty to us after the murder of President McKinley. Since then, there have been nine presidents, all the way from Theodore Roosevelt to Eisenhower, and we have never failed in our duty.'

Mitch smiled. 'I am impressed.'

'You don't sound impressed, Mr Newman. You sound facetious. This is a deadly serious activity. Errors, mishaps, elements of unpredictability have no place in the business of the Secret Service. To accept responsibility for the life of the leader of the free world is not something that a man does lightly, and he does it on the understanding – just as Private Leslie Coffelt did – that if it is a question of his own life or that of the president, then there is no question.'

'I did not mean to sound facetious.'

Dempster said nothing for a moment, then he leaned forward and tapped the picture of Oswald with his index finger. 'You think this is the only anti-establishment screwball commie who poses a danger to President Kennedy? This guy hasn't even vocalized a threat. He hasn't even sent a letter. We receive letters from people like Oswald by the dozen every single day. We go through every one. We pore over them. We track down the people who sent them. We investigate everything. That is what we do. That is what we are trained for, and I really need you to let us get on with that. If you don't, and if you insist on being involved, then you become one of those unpredictable elements.'

Mitch looked once more at the face of the man he'd been trying to find.

'I can assure you, Mr Newman, that President Kennedy will attend the Democratic National Convention, and then he will return to the White House with the first lady and his family, and Atlantic City will not be remembered for anything but its enthusiastic welcome and abundant hospitality.'

'The Convention is open to the public?' Mitch said.

Dempster smiled. 'Are you asking if you should leave Atlantic City?'

'I'm asking if I am free to stay.'

'Mr Newman, let's get several things straight right here and now. This is America. This is a democratic, peace-loving nation that prides itself on the right to individual freedom. Everything we do in every branch of federal and government services is dedicated to the preservation of that freedom. To tell you to leave, to even ask you to leave, would be a contradiction of the very things we stand for, and made even more ironic by the nature of why we all happen to be in this city. That some crazy person might consider his only means of getting attention is to perpetrate a heinous act of violence against a public personality is merely a reflection of the state of mind of that person. There are no other ramifications, and the fact that you worked so hard to highlight this is – as I said before – not only commendable, but decidedly patriotic. Our Secret Service detail chief was nothing but complimentary about your efforts, but I am sure I speak for him when I say that we are now in control. Everything that needs to be done has been done, and will continue to be done during the president's brief stay in the city.'

Mitch listened. He was being lectured to, and he did not much care for it. The words were practiced and formal, and Dempster's attitude was quite different from when they had spoken in Dallas.

355

'Okay,' he said. 'I appreciate your time.' He looked once more at the photo of Oswald, intent on burning that image into his memory.

'If you intend to stay, I trust you will enjoy the Convention, and please just relax. We know exactly what we're doing.'

Mitch got up. He shook hands with Dempster, with Franklin also, and then Franklin showed him out through the lobby to the street.

He glanced back at the hotel. The number of Secret Service agents was considerable, seemingly more than at any other location near the Boardwalk, and from that observation alone, he suspected that the Crowne Excelsior was where Kennedy would be staying while in the city.

It was as he walked away that he was struck with an inexplicable sense of foreboding.

It was seeing Oswald's face. There was something so utterly forgettable and banal about it. Here was a man you would never look at twice. Here was a man who would go unnoticed in a crowd. That was the simple, frightening truth. Mitch himself had stared and stared at that picture, and now – only minutes later – he was struggling to retain a clear image of it.

He was convinced that Oswald was in Atlantic City, his every thought focused on finding a way to get to the president.

He hoped it would not be the case, but he felt that Dempster's words – that Atlantic City would be remembered for nothing more than its enthusiastic welcome and abundant hospitality – were somehow the very opposite of what would take place.

Elm Street, Dallas. November 1963. The Texas School Book Depository. Ten months later, a different city, a different building, and yet Mitch believed – with little more than unsubstantiated facts and intuition to support it – that the unrealized past would somehow become the terrifying present.

65

As Saturday segued seamlessly into Sunday, Mitch lay awake and thought again of the child that never was.

He asked himself what he would have done had he known that Jean was pregnant.

He asked himself what he would have said to her had she been right there in the hotel room.

He did not know the answers to those questions, and he did not try to find them.

His heart was broken. That much he knew. He wondered if he might somehow lose his mind.

He was anxious, stressed, on edge. He believed something bad would happen, and he knew there was little he could do to delay or prevent it. There was something here that smacked of Fate.

He recalled a story he'd read about a Persian merchant. The merchant had visited a fortune-teller and been told that Death would find him that very day. Terrified, he asked where it would happen, but the fortune-teller couldn't reveal this. The merchant was a man of routine. He was due to visit the market that day, as he did on the same day each week. Instead, he rushed home. He told his servant that he would not be going to the market, but was heading for Baghdad. He took his fastest horse and fled toward the city, hoping he would find someplace to hide in the great capital.

The servant, puzzled by his master's behavior, went to the

357

market alone. While he was there, he saw Death. He was stricken with horror. Surely it was not his day to die? Death smiled coldly, and said that he was surprised to see the servant here without the merchant. The servant asked why, and Death, leaning close, his breath cool against the servant's face, whispered that he had an appointment that very afternoon with the merchant in Baghdad.

Perhaps there was some inevitability in the course of events. Mitch remembered the men who had died in Korea, some of them falling right beside him as he took his photographs. He thought of Ray-Ban, the way his head had just exploded. Back and to the left. Back and to the left. That bullet could so easily have been the end of Mitch's own life. Why Ray-Ban? Why not him? Was it simply chance, or was there a meaning and structure to such things? It really was a matter of life and death, and when you saw enough of that, you also saw your own fragility, your own impermanence, your own insignificance.

Perhaps the child too had been inevitable, not only in its creation, but also in its destruction. The former had been unplanned, unintentional, the latter deliberate and final. Perhaps, had he stayed, there would have been no pregnancy. Perhaps, had he stayed, Jean would have died anyway. Why? Because everyone had a time to die, and there was nothing anyone could do to change it. When he was younger, he'd met men who'd known his father. They spoke of James Newman's bravery, the sacrifice he'd made for his country, the sadness they felt at his loss. It was all meaningless. At some moment the sword would fall, and your life would end.

Perhaps this was how it would be for Kennedy. If not Oswald, then someone else. Or some*thing* else. A heart attack, a stroke, a fatal illness, an accident. How many ways to kill a man? Endless ways.

Mitch would attend the Convention. He would stay and see

it through. All four days. He would walk the streets; he would scour the faces in the crowds on the Boardwalk; he would find a vantage point somewhere near the entranceway of the Convention Hall and look at people as they entered the building. He would not speak to the Secret Service. He would not speak to the Feds or the plainclothes police officers. He would keep himself to himself, and he would do everything he could with what he knew, maintaining his certainty that Lee Harvey Oswald had come to Atlantic City intent on doing something that would make him the most famous man in the world. Both Oswald and Kennedy would go down in the history books, tied together by a common event, but for very different reasons.

If something happened, it would not be because he had been derelict in his endeavors. If something happened, he would know that he'd done everything within his power to stop it.

Just like Jean.

66

Sunday began without event. Mitch chain-smoked and waited in his hotel. In the early afternoon he walked the streets around the Convention Hall, camera in hand, ever watchful for anyone who bore the slightest resemblance to Oswald.

There were dozens of men that on paper could have been described in precisely the same way. Similar age, of average height, hair dark and cut short, slacks and white shirts and sports jackets. After a while, Mitch believed that even if he saw him he would just be another blurred and immediately forgotten face. He willed himself to concentrate, but it was difficult. It was also futile, and in a way he understood that. The compulsion to do something was merely a means by which he could allay the feeling of impotence. He even asked himself whether he had pursued the matter so vigorously in an effort to reconcile himself to his betrayal of Jean. And now it was not just Jean; there was the child to remember, and he could not think of it without feeling the heaviest burden of shame and regret.

The security measures already in place around the venue seemed to grow steadily more formidable as the day progressed. More police, more plainclothes – perhaps PD, perhaps Feds – and then the unmistakable duos and trios of Secret Service agents. Despite whatever training they may have been given concerning concealment and inconspicuousness, to Mitch they seemed immediately identifiable. The way they stood, the way they spoke to one another, never taking their eyes off the street or the building, just made them ever more visible. Regardless, the effect – intended or otherwise – was impressive.

Somewhere after six in the evening, there was a wave of rapidly reorganized change, movement and commotion. It could only be that the president himself was arriving. The nature of Atlantic City's Boardwalk and the grid of streets meant that very little went unobserved from certain vantage points, and not only was Mitch aware of the sound of long motorcades with trooper escorts, but also a helicopter overhead. The motorcades would be carrying the vice president and members of the White House staff, but he guessed the president would be arriving by air.

He stood there on Pacific and South Florida and watched as Army One, the presidential chopper, hovered and then descended to the roof of the Crowne Excelsior, the very hotel in which he had met with Agents Dempster and Franklin. He assumed that the first lady and the Kennedy children would come in at some point during the weekend, if only to make their presence known and thus encourage the female vote. The press photographers and fashion columnists would be there for the requisite magazine spreads.

It was a circus, no doubt about it, and Mitch would have been lying had he said he felt nothing at all. He was American through and through, and even though he was no fan of the jingoistic, banner-waving nationalism that had been engineered and manipulated to support US involvement in Korea, and now in Vietnam, there was still a sense of inherent loyalty. He was a patriotic citizen, there was no doubt about it, even though his patriotism was to a kind of democracy and individual freedom that appeared to be growing more rare and constrained with each passing year.

Standing there as a small crowd gathered to look upward toward the sound of the helicopter, Mitch wondered about Kennedy himself. The man was an icon, a new type of leader – young, dynamic and liberal. Irrespective of his naval service, he was not of the old guard like his predecessors, Eisenhower and Truman. Instead he was a man for the future, for all the tomorrows that promised freedom from communism and war and divisive political controversies. That was the pitch, and it had worked. Had he rigged the election? Mitch believed he had. If so, did he even deserve to be in the White House? Perhaps not. Did that justify his death at the hands of a crazed loner with a thirty-dollar rifle? No, he did not believe it did.

Kennedy was in Atlantic City. He was here to fight for his political life in the face of criticism, censure, rumor and hearsay about the election, about marital infidelity, about the lack of experience of both himself and his brother, about the potential and also very real catastrophes of Cuba, Vienna, the Berlin Wall, the escalating war in Vietnam. The world was changing fast, and it was rapidly becoming a place that did not bode well for future generations. Stability was what was needed, and the death of a president would cause nothing but dismay, disbelief and confusion.

Mitch could not conceive of the ramifications and con-sequences of such a thing, and so he pushed it from his mind.

Tomorrow he would attend the DNC and see whether Fate would play a hand in the future of the free world.

67

August 24, 1964

News came into Secret Service command in the early hours of Monday morning that the first lady, Caroline and John Jr would not be arriving into Atlantic City until the evening of Tuesday 25. The intent had been to bring them in with the same motorcade that had been employed for the attorney general, but the first lady felt that the opening day of the Convention would be too stressful for the children.

Her prediction was right.

That afternoon, the capacity audience in the building rose to their feet during the first words of Kennedy's opening remarks – *Chairman McCormack, my fellow Democrats... I am here to secure your nomination... I am here to once again lead this party to victory* – and stayed there for a rousing ovation that lasted in excess of ten minutes.

If this was the reception for the opening comments, Mitch could only imagine how Kennedy's keynote speech would be received the following day. Whatever he said, it needed to be significant. He needed to show the country that he was still the man for the job, the man who deserved their unconditional confidence and trust. He needed to summon every ounce of charisma he possessed and present America with something so unequivocal and commanding that they could do nothing but follow him for another four years.

Mitch listened to proceedings from his place amongst the more than one thousand press representatives who crowded together, flash bulbs popping, hand-held recorders aloft, furiously scribbling in notebooks, relaying back and forth between the press section and the bank of telephones that had been installed on the right-hand side of the building for their use.

There was a sense of something happening, something to which he belonged, and he appreciated how significantly he had changed over the previous six weeks. It was not that he was a different man. Not at all. It was as if he had rediscovered the man he once was, the man he would have become had he not left for Korea.

At some point, having taken pictures of Kennedy and Johnson, of the attorney general and the secretary of state as they smiled and congratulated themselves, Mitch left his colleagues and walked through the endless sea of people. The atmosphere was one of jubilation and euphoria. Row after row of banners, people thrusting Kennedy buttons into his hand, waving flags and cheering, screaming at the tops of their voices despite knowing they could never be heard. Kennedy would captain the ship through these turbulent oceans of war and political dissent, and would bring them all into a safe harbor. That was what they believed, and they demonstrated it in their passion and enthusiasm.

KENN-E-DY! FOUR MORE YEARS! KENN-E-DY! FOUR MORE YEARS!

It became a chant, a litany, a tidal wave of noise, unified and biblical in its proportions, and Mitch just stood there and soaked it all in. He did not participate. He watched the faces, he took photographs – why, he did not know, but he took them anyway – and he asked himself time and again if Oswald was here. Perhaps right ahead of him, no more than a dozen feet away; perhaps somewhere amidst the light riggings and gantries that overhung the vast crowds, rifle in hand, his eye pressed against the lens of the telescopic sight, his finger on the trigger, his moment of infamy and recognition imminent.

Mitch looked up. The brilliant glare of the lights stunned him. There was no way to see beyond them and into the shadows. He looked for Secret Service people, but amongst the thousands of attendees they were lost and invisible. How could you ever control a mass like this? How could you identify a single individual with murderous intent? The idea was overwhelming, impossible, and he knew that his presence served no purpose.

By the time he managed to maneuver his way out of the Convention Hall, it was nearly four o'clock. He followed the Boardwalk and joined South Mississippi, heading toward the Crowne Excelsior, if for no other reason than to see the security procedure that the Secret Service would follow upon Kennedy's return.

He took his time. He stopped and had something to eat at a diner across the street, from where he observed the comings and goings of all manner of officials. It was from that vantage point, a direct line-of-sight to the side of the hotel, that he saw a sedan pull up. There was no doubt to whom the car belonged, for the number plates were clearly official, and the men who stood sentinel around the car as it drew to a halt were police and Secret Service.

Mitch raised his camera. He took a succession of shots as a young woman exited the vehicle, glanced back toward the street, and was then swiftly escorted into the building. There was something very telling in her coiffured hair, the calf-length tan-colored overcoat, the high-heeled shoes. This was no administrative secretary. Mitch could think of one reason and one reason alone for an attractive young woman to be shepherded into the Crowne Excelsior Hotel by the United States Secret Service.

He watched the detail of agents disperse as the sedan pulled away. The entire process had taken no more than thirty seconds, and had he not been there he would not have seen a thing.

He looked at his camera, and then he looked out at the street.

It was hard to believe he'd seen what he'd just seen. It was even harder to believe that he had the girl's arrival on film.

He wound the film and took it out of the camera. He put it in his pants pocket and loaded another roll. He stood up and went out onto the sidewalk. There was not an agent in sight, merely a squad car and a half-dozen uniformed Atlantic City PD officers on the facing junction. His heart was racing. He felt anger at first, as if he'd just witnessed some kind of personal betrayal. There had been rumors of Kennedy's infidelities. Of course, there would always be rumors concerning any man of power or influence, generated more often than not by opponents and detractors, but there was something about the covert nature in which the girl had been ferried to the side of the hotel, the manner of her dress, the very real sense of subterfuge that had accompanied the entire scenario that felt very wrong indeed. Worst of all, it had been perpetrated by the Secret Service and the police.

Mitch put his hand in his pocket and held the canister of film. Had he just captured evidence of an indiscretion on the part of John F. Kennedy, President of the United States? And what would happen if he went public with it, if he called up Lester Byron and told him he had an exclusive the like of which he couldn't even imagine?

It was a foolish idea. He was talking about the president. He was talking about the police and the FBI and the Secret Service being complicit in delivering a young woman to Kennedy's hotel suite. It was ludicrous.

Nevertheless, the film needed to be secure, and so Mitch went back to his own hotel and placed it inside a rolled-up pair of socks that he then buried beneath other clothes in his overnight bag.

He went back to the Crowne Excelsior and entered the lobby. The place was crowded with people – hotel staff, agents, police, onlookers. The buzz of conversation suggested that the president himself would be walking right through here. Mitch considered that unlikely, but no sooner had the thought crossed his mind than the hubbub of voices became almost deafening. Agents appeared from every corner of the lobby and reception area. One elevator was opened, the others blocked by armed police. An additional half-dozen uniformed police stood at the entrance to the stairwell.

As Kennedy came through, Mitch was right there, no more than a dozen feet away. The president was smiling, greeting people, waving, shaking hands, the detail of agents never less than a foot or two from him, their eyes every which way, their bodies blocking every line of sight save that from above. There was no balcony in the lobby, nor any raised mezzanine from which a vantage point could be secured. If someone wished to shoot the president, it would have to be a sudden assault from the crowd, a hand with a gun that somehow found its way through the melee and took advantage of a split second of opportunity.

Mitch raised his camera. Everything seemed to slow down. He saw Kennedy's face. People were shouting. The noise was deafening. Had there been a gunshot, it would not even have been heard until it was too late to do anything to prevent it.

He was suddenly filled with foreboding.

He knew something was going to happen. He could feel it. His heart was thundering in his chest. He felt light-headed, sick, a sudden need to be away from this place, to escape as fast as he could before the inevitable happened.

And then Kennedy was gone, shepherded into the elevator by three or four agents.

Mitch watched as the doors came together.

For a split second, it seemed as if Kennedy was looking right at him. The effect was profound. He felt invisible, everything about him utterly unimportant save what he had seen in the street. What *had* he seen in the street?

He stood there, his heart racing, and within another moment it was as if nothing had ever happened.

'Did you get a good shot of the president?'

Mitch turned. A woman beamed at him.

'Sorry? What?'

She nodded in the direction of his camera. 'The president? Did you get a good shot of him?'

'Yes,' Mitch said. 'Yes ... yes, I think so.'

He looked down at his camera. He looked up again. The woman was gone.

He stood there in the lobby of the Crowne Excelsior as the crowd dispersed, and he felt as if the whole world understood something of which he was ignorant.

68

Her name was Vivian Wheaton. She was twenty-six, and she hailed from Chapel Hill, North Carolina. Her mother had died when she was just seven, but her father – now a well-respected orthodontist with a chain of surgeries that covered three counties – had spared no expense in having her privately schooled. Hence, the small campus town girl was not only strikingly beautiful, she was also well-spoken, elegant and cultivated.

Vivian had first met the president at the inaugural White House Renovation Project fundraiser; her father, a staunch Democrat and an ardent antiquarian, had made a generous contribution to the first lady's building and contents restoration program. Subsequently, Vivian had been contacted by an unnamed member of the president's personal staff with an invitation to an exhibition of paintings. Believing that she was to be invited to assist in some further capacity with Mrs Kennedy's work, Vivian accepted the invitation. What she discovered – at first to her great surprise, subsequently to her even greater disbelief – was that there was no art exhibition. Instead, she was chauffeured to a hotel in downtown Washington and shown into a room where the president was waiting for her.

That rendezvous, defying all expectations, had led to a series of further meetings over the subsequent eight months. Her affair with the most important man in America was a secret she was instructed to withhold absolutely. The instruction came not only from Jack – as she now called him – but also from the chief of his personal security detail, Walter Lambert. Lambert was a good man, kind and considerate, but there was something altogether forbidding about him too. He was a man you very definitely wanted as an ally, not an enemy.

And so it was that on the evening of Monday, August 24, Vivian found herself in the penthouse suite of the Crowne Excelsior Hotel, Atlantic City, New Jersey, having been smuggled into the building by the Secret Service. Once through the side door, they had taken the service elevator, and then the final two floors via the stairwell. There were agents on each floor. None of them looked at her directly, something she found very disconcerting, almost as if they somehow hoped to convince themselves that what they were seeing wasn't real. By the time she reached the uppermost floor, she and Walter Lambert were alone. They waited twenty minutes or more. It seemed infinite. Neither she nor Walter spoke. And then, finally, as if following some predetermined arrangement, Walter turned and looked at her.

'Okay?' he asked.

She nodded. She was nervous. She had done this enough times before to know precisely what would happen, what was required of her, what she could and could not do, what she was and was not permitted to say, but it still unnerved her.

If her father found out ... If *anyone* found out ...

She composed herself. Walter opened the door, and in she went.

The President of the United States rose from where he'd been seated by the side of the bed. He smiled warmly, as if genuinely thrilled to see her.

'Vivian ... sweetheart ...'

69

Perhaps fate did indeed play a part in all things.

That was the thought at the forefront of Lee Harvey Oswald's mind as he crouched in the small pocket of shadow at the base of the stairwell just below the penthouse level of the Crowne Excelsior.

His uniform, delivered only that afternoon to the motel room, was a size too large. He looked like a kid play-acting in his father's clothes. He had turned the sleeves up inside themselves at the cuff, pulled the belt on his pants to the tightest hole, and still they were loose. It was a minor detail, but – as the old saw went – the devil was in the detail.

Here he was, second time around. That morning back in November had broken so clear and bright. The sky was cloudless, and there was nothing but a gentle breeze. He had felt such adrenaline, such unparalleled excitement at the prospect of what he was about to do. The schedule had been exact, everything calculated to the second, and all aspects of his escape route and departure from the country had been engineered with precision. Within twenty-four hours of Kennedy's death, he would be in Moscow. This time he wouldn't just be some ex-Marine Corps technician who spoke passable Russian and misquoted Engels. This time he would be, without question, the most important and recognizable man in the world, for he would have been responsible for something that no one could ignore or deny or refute.

Love Field. That was where it had all fallen apart. He should never have gone out there, but he had wanted to see them arrive. He had wanted to see the man close up, not just through the sights of a gun. He wanted to see him smile that smile and shake hands with strangers; perhaps even reach out and take the man's hand himself, and Kennedy would never know that he'd just been within arm's length of his killer.

Minutes, perhaps even seconds of delay because of that damn woman. He'd reached his car just as the police raised the barriers and cut off the freeway exit. As a result, he'd been held up by a further seven minutes, and even as he waited, sweat breaking out across his body, heart racing, anger rising in his chest like floodwater, he had prayed and prayed to a God in whom he did not believe that the motorcade would also be delayed.

It had been, but not by enough.

Even as he reached the Book Depository, he could hear the crowds cheering.

By the time he gained the sixth floor, he was already too late.

Frantic, desperate by then, he fumbled with the first bullet, felt it slip from his fingers. He heard it hit the floor and roll away, and he cursed himself, cursed the moment. He got a second bullet into the chamber, slammed home the bolt.

Raising the rifle, pressing his eye against the telescopic sight, he saw the rear of the follow-up car, the black four-door 1956 Cadillac Touring convertible, as it passed beyond his field of vision. Right behind it came the steel-gray Lincoln within which sat Johnson and his wife, then the yellow Mercury with police and Secret Service, and by the time he was settled and his heart and breathing were sufficiently stable to get a bead on the target line, he had the Dallas mayor's Mercury Comet Caliente in the crosshairs.

Because of that damn woman.

As the crowds at Love Field had clamored to see John F. Kennedy and the first lady, she had appeared out of nowhere. 'So you're after the president too?' she'd said, and he had turned. She had a press lanyard that was almost identical to his own, a notebook, a camera, an eager expression on her face, as if she wanted to share some revelation.

He'd not replied. He'd taken a step back.

'Don't worry,' she'd said. 'I'm not here to cover the visit. I'm after something a great deal more interesting.'

He remembered smiling at her as best he could. He needed to get away. He needed to be in his car and driving before the motorcade started on its route. He had to be ahead of it, or they would close off the road and he'd be behind schedule.

She'd grabbed his arm.

'Don't run,' she'd said. 'Are you here for the visit, or are you chasing his people for something else?'

'The visit,' he'd said. 'I have to go.'

'Which paper are you from?' she'd asked.

He said nothing.

'I've come down from DC,' she went on. 'Tell me, do you know anyone inside the Kennedy camp? Have you got any personal contacts?'

He was already walking away.

'I'm staying for a few days,' she said. 'You might be interested in what I'm investigating. I need to talk to someone who's close to all of this. Maybe we can help each other out, you know?'

He started to jog.

'The name's Jean Boyd,' she called after him. 'Jean Boyd from the *Washington Tribune*!'

And then he could no longer see her or hear her, and he was elbowing his way through the enthusiastic crowd to get to his car. But he knew, even before he gunned the engine into life, that he'd been dealt a bum hand and he was running out of time.

But that was then. Not now.

Now it was all under control. Now there were no cars, no reporters, nothing but a few stairs and a single door behind which he would find the president. He held the .38 in his hand. He wished it was a larger-caliber weapon, but Kennedy would be at close range, entirely unprotected, and he knew he could hit him twice, three times, maybe more.

No one would ever know that this had been anything other than the work of a single-minded, calculating, ice-cold killer. They would give him the Order of Lenin. They would bring him through the streets of Moscow to the Kremlin as a conquering hero.

It was as good as done.

Lee Harvey Oswald took a deep breath, and waited for the signal.

70

Vivian lay there for quite some time afterward. The sensation was one of disconnection, as if what was happening wasn't happening to her, but to her body alone; it was a purely physical thing – no emotion, no real feelings, no sense of reality. Like watching a movie with the sound turned down.

She knew it could not last. She knew it would end badly. But what had she expected?

How long can I keep doing this to myself?

Jack stirred. He eased himself up on one arm and looked at her. The smile was there, but it was vacant. It was his for-the-camera smile, and she knew what it meant.

She reached out to touch his face – a gesture of affection – but he withdrew suddenly, as if he'd perceived her action as a threat.

'You have to go,' he said.

'I know.'

She got up, felt suddenly vulnerable and defenseless, even ashamed, as she stood there naked. She grabbed the robe and put it on.

'It was good to see you,' he said.

How many other girls are there?

'You too, Mr President.'

He scowled at her. 'Please, Vivian...'

Does he treat them all the same?

She wanted to slap him then. Hard.

The thought struck her like a bullet – *Sometimes ... sometimes, Jack Kennedy, I wish you'd just die* – and even though she wished it back, it was too late. She'd thought it so very strongly, and for a moment she wondered whether she'd actually vocalized it.

And then he smiled, and it was almost real, and he said, 'I'm sorry we can't spend more time together, but you know how it is.'

She nodded. In a strange way, she almost felt sorry for him. He was as trapped as she. He was the bird in the gilded cage, and everyone wanted to look, to see, to hear what he had to say. Was it ever possible that such a man could be himself?

She turned at a sound behind her. A man stood in the doorway.

'Hello,' he said. 'I'm Dr Portman.'

Vivian frowned.

'Don't worry,' the man said. 'Everything is fine. I'm going to take care of you.'

'Let me get my clothes on,' she said.

Portman stepped forward. 'We'll just go into the next room. Walter will bring your clothes.'

'Ralph?' Kennedy said. 'Is that you? What's going on?'

'Nothing to concern yourself about, Mr President. We just need Miss Wheaton out of here a little sooner than planned.'

Kennedy nodded. He waved his hand as if dismissing children who'd needed a telling-off, and lay down again.

Portman took Vivian's arm. His manner was gentle, avuncular, and there was something so very kind in his eyes.

Vivian went with him.

She did as he was told. She knew better than to ask questions.

71

The door above him opened barely enough to see the light, but it was all the signal he required.

Oswald stood up. He gripped the .38. He ran up the last dozen steps and stopped.

The door opened further. The light flooded the top of the stairwell. He hesitated for just a second. He heard footsteps, and then a silhouette passed the doorway. His heart thundered.

He took one further step. The door opened wider. Walter Lambert stood there, resolute, impassable, gun in hand.

It had all come to this, this very moment. Every thought, every idea, every notion, every element of the plan. Everything he'd worked toward since things had gone so terribly wrong last November were now present in his mind.

Oswald took a deep breath.

Walter Lambert took a step back. He opened the door even wider.

Oswald stepped through and started down the corridor. He did not say a word. He did not look back. Lambert followed him, just a few feet behind, until they approached the penthouse door.

Lambert stepped past Oswald and came to a halt. He knocked, waited for a word from inside, and then opened the door.

He left it open as he started speaking, and then reached his hand back through the gap and made a beckoning motion.

Oswald went in, gun raised.

'What the hell—' Kennedy started, but Oswald was already pulling the trigger.

He barely heard the reports above the hammering of his own heart. He saw the impact of the first bullet, how the blood bloomed and grew, the way Kennedy staggered back and was stopped by the wall. From there on it was like fish in a barrel, one shot after another until the hammer clicked against spent rounds and the president was on the floor, the wall spattered with blood, his face barely recognizable.

Oswald closed his eyes for a second.

He opened his mouth to speak, and as he did so, he turned back toward Lambert.

His change of expression was so sudden and so strange that Lambert almost laughed. It didn't last long. Lambert pulled the trigger of the Secret Service-issue Smith & Wesson Model 36 four times, sending Oswald careering sideways toward the bathroom.

The sound of gunshots brought agents running from all quarters.

They found the president exactly where he'd fallen, and it was clear that it was too late.

Even Ralph Portman, the attorney general's private physician, could do nothing.

Both John F. Kennedy and his as-yet-unnamed assassin were dead.

72

The world converged on Atlantic City, and Mitch was there to witness it all.

The news had spread quickly, the streets filled with federal and police vehicles. Crowds of people spilled from hotel rooms, all of them in wide-eyed disbelief, unable to comprehend what had happened, unwilling to accept that such a thing could take place in twentieth-century America.

But it had happened.

The King of Camelot had fallen.

Following an endless stream of unclear statements from television channels and telegraph offices, it was Walter Cronkite who brought the news to the world with a CBS bulletin that interrupted an episode of *As the World Turns*.

'From Atlantic City, New Jersey, the flash, apparently official: President Kennedy died at 7.18 p.m. Central Standard Time, 8.18 p.m. Eastern Standard Time...'

Cronkite had paused, a moment of dismay overwhelming him. He looked down, quelled the wave of emotion that rose in his chest, and then removed his glasses.

'Vice President Johnson has left Atlantic City, but we do not know to where he has proceeded. Presumably he will be taking the oath of office shortly, and become the thirty-sixth President of the United States...'

The Democratic National Convention was cancelled.

The United States of America went into mourning.

The whole world stopped – unable to breathe, unable to think – and it did not revolve again for days.

73

Mitch disappeared. He went back to Washington and watched as the newspapers pulled apart every aspect of Oswald's life history. Lester called numerous times, begged him to come and write a feature, to outline the precise sequence of events that had taken him to Atlantic City, but Mitch refused.

He had done what he could. That much he knew. He was not going to be a vulture, picking over the bones of this tragedy and regurgitating whatever he found for a desperate public. He understood the emotional effect. He felt it too, even more so, perhaps, for he had been so close to all of it and had been unable to do a thing.

The inevitable questions were repeated over and over. Where had Oswald secured the police uniform? How had he gotten into the hotel where the president was staying? Once in the hotel, how had he accessed the stairwell that would take him to the penthouse? How did he get into the president's suite? Where were the multitude of Secret Service agents and federal officers whose sole duty it was to ensure – with their own lives – that no harm came to the president?

Lambert was investigated. Dempster, Franklin, so many others. All of them were hauled before a special commission headed by Earl Warren, the very man who had chaired the ethics committee charged with investigating alleged corruption in the 1960 Kennedy–Nixon election.

Such matters were now forgotten, as were the rumors of infidelity and illness, the criticisms of Kennedy's dealings with Castro and Khrushchev, the bitter words about his supposed mishandling of the Vienna conference and how this had instigated the raising of the wall in Berlin. All such things were consigned to history. Though future generations might perhaps pore over the details, for now it was all meaningless in the face of insurmountable grief, suffered first by a family, then a nation, and ultimately the whole world.

On August 31, Kennedy was buried at Arlington.

On September 7, the official report of Secret Service failings was internally released by the Warren Commission. The full investigation would take months, perhaps a year, and whether or not the information would ever be publicly released was a question that was asked and went unanswered. After Warren himself, the commission was made up of Senators Richard Russell, John Sherman Cooper, Hale Boggs and Gerald Ford, along with Allen Welsh Dulles, head of the CIA, and John J. McCloy, a former president of the World Bank.

So it was that good men and true, men of great wisdom and experience, were charged with the responsibility of uncovering exactly how the president had been murdered. If anyone could find the truth, then it would be these men of reputation and stature.

On September 11, just eighteen days after the death of his brother, Attorney General Robert Kennedy resigned his position and made a public statement.

'Despite the terrible tragedy that we as a family and a nation have suffered, I am proud to announce my intent to run as the next Democratic nominee for the White House. With everything I possess, I intend to uphold the legacy of my brother's presidency, to further the programs he initiated, and to follow in his footsteps in every way that I possibly can...'

74

Mitch saw Robert Kennedy's address on TV from the very same bar stool where he'd seen the president's announcement of the Civil Rights Bill just ten weeks before.

Ten weeks.

It was impossible to imagine that so much had happened in such a brief span of time. But it had, and the degree to which he himself had changed was immeasurable.

Everything he'd done, he'd done for Jean – for her memory, perhaps as some sort of amends for his betrayal – but knowing what he now knew of her, of what she herself had done, his feelings toward her were very different.

All these years, he'd hoped that one day she would forgive him. Now he wondered how long it would be before he could reciprocate that forgiveness.

Tom was busy in the back. Mitch thought of the other Mitch, figured he should head back to the apartment and feed him. Maybe after one more drink.

He stood up, walked down the bar and reached over for the bottle.

He was drinking too much. He knew it. To be honest, he didn't care. If he died, he would die oblivious.

He picked up the day's newspaper too, went back to his stool and leafed through it.

Déjà vu.

A moment of striking and inescapable déjà vu.

It was a small squib, easily overlooked, almost identical to one he'd seen before. Vivian Wheaton – beautiful, just twenty-six years old – found dead. Overdose. Believed to be suicide. Her parents were quoted as saying that they could never understand what had driven her to do such a thing.

She was pictured. Mitch stared at the picture, just as he'd stared at the image of Lee Harvey Oswald, and he knew. He knew as well as he knew his own name.

Back at the apartment, he rummaged through his overnight bag. He'd left it just inside the door. It had sat there unpacked since his return from Atlantic City.

He emptied it out onto the floor, the cat watching him as though this was yet another indication of a man who'd lost his mind. At last he found it – the unmistakable shape of the film canister inside the balled-up socks.

His mouth was dry. He dropped the canister. He picked it up. He felt nauseous.

He could not take it to a commercial film development facility. He needed help.

He called Lester at the *Tribune*.

'I need to develop a film,' he said. 'Now.'

Little more than an hour later, he stood in the darkroom and watched the image come to life. He saw the young woman's face grow from the white paper, and he knew there was a world of pain and hurt and unanswered questions just waiting to be unleashed.

He hung the photograph up on the line with a wooden peg, and then he went to fetch Lester, hurrying him into the darkroom.

'What the hell is going on, Mitch?'

Mitch had the newspaper article. 'See this girl... this one here. The suicide.'

'Yes, yes, I see it.'

Mitch took down the still-wet photograph.

'Look,' he said. 'Look right there.'

Byron looked at the photograph, then at the newspaper, then back to the photograph.

'Same girl,' Mitch said.

'Absolutely,' Byron replied. 'Where did you take this shot?'

'Atlantic City. That's the Crowne Excelsior.'

'Look,' Byron said. 'Mitchell... look...'

He pointed to another individual behind Vivian Wheaton. He was looking directly at the camera. The image was clear and unobstructed.

The face that looked back at them – a face so ordinary, so unremarkable – was now familiar to the whole world, and there was no mistaking it. He was in police uniform. He was smiling.

'Oh my God,' Byron said, his voice barely a whisper. 'Oh my God almighty...'

75

Mitch was standing in Jean's apartment. He'd got in the same way – up the fire escape and into the kitchen.

He didn't know what to feel, save the certainty that there was something here that he needed to find.

Jean had gone to Dallas looking for Kennedy, and she'd found something else.

Having seen the picture of Vivian Wheaton, remembering also Judith Wagner, knowing how they'd died... it was too much, too coincidental.

His breathing was shallow. He was lightheaded, nauseous. He felt things that were alien and inexplicable. Hatred, anger, a sense of injustice having been perpetrated – not just against himself, but against everyone.

The world had been lied to, and the lie would remain hidden forever unless someone told the truth.

Mitch closed his eyes. He breathed the musty air. No one had been here. Nothing had changed.

He walked through the living room, to the bedroom, the bathroom. He opened cupboards, looked under the bed, behind the chest of drawers. He took up the carpet and checked for floorboards recently removed. He looked and looked and looked and found nothing. There was not a single sign of anything having been moved or repositioned.

Where? he asked himself. *What am I looking for, and where will I find it?*

Back in the kitchen.

Under the sink, behind the pipes, in the icebox, the trash can, taking up the linoleum and then lying with his face as close to the ground as possible to see if there were any telltale bumps or raised sections that would suggest something hidden beneath.

Nothing.

Just nothing at all.

He felt frustrated with himself, with Jean, with all that had happened. He couldn't bear how he felt.

He glanced back toward the door, saw Mitch's food bowl.

He turned the other way, and there it was. The litter box.

Kneeling, he pulled the box toward him. He reached out his hand and his fingers touched the coarse gray sand. He knew. Somehow, he knew.

There, beneath a half-inch of cat litter, was a plastic-wrapped envelope. It wasn't large, perhaps five inches by seven, but it was perhaps the most burdensome thing imaginable.

Tentatively he removed the package. He brushed sand from it, took it to the kitchen counter.

He stood there looking down at it.

This was Jean's legacy. This was what she had left behind.

This was why she had died.

From the utensils drawer he took a pair of scissors. He cut along the upper edge of the plastic wrapping and slid the envelope out.

Opening it, he saw Jean's handwriting, unmistakable and clear.

A single sheet of paper, and on it she had printed several names.

ESTHER WHYTE
HOLLY WALSH
JUDITH WAGNER

VIVIAN WHEATON
AUDREY QUINN

The names went on, at least another half a dozen, and Mitch's mind unfolded at the seams.

It was inconceivable. It was utterly terrifying.

There were photographs too, names printed on the back.

The one that held his attention was a strikingly pretty girl, her hair tied back, her smile radiant and hopeful.

On the back, Jean had written *Holly*.

Beneath that she'd scribbled *Dallas*, *November*.

Mitch stood in the doorway of Jean's bedroom.

Was this where they did it? Or did they kill her elsewhere and bring her here afterward?

He had to move quickly, and he did, retching as he went. He found the toilet before he actually vomited, but he was crying too, and the pain that racked his chest burned fiercely.

He kneeled there, one hand on the edge of the tub, and he wept for Jean, and he wept for the child, and he knew he was going to do whatever it took to bring the whole shameful, sordid house of lies crashing down on their unworthy heads.

Even if it killed him – even if took his life too – he would do this one final, necessary thing.

Just like Jean.

Epilogue

Bobby Kennedy stood in the doorway of the East Room, watching as the last few items of his brother's personal effects were carried through in unmarked boxes.

He glanced over his shoulder at the sound of someone approaching.

Walter Lambert came through from the corridor and paused.

'You didn't let me down, Walter,' Bobby said, 'and loyalty always earns the greatest prize.'

'Thank you, sir.'

'Are we all done?'

'A few loose ends to tie up, but nothing significant.'

'I've been thinking about this Oswald character. I understand he was a Marine.'

'Yes, sir, he was. Perhaps not the model Marine, but a Marine all the same. Ironically, I actually met him.'

'Really?'

'Just before I came out of the navy, sir. I was doing a course in aircraft control and warning at Keesler Air Force Base. Oswald was in that class. Along with a whole host of others, of course, but he was there.'

'A hell of a coincidence.'

'Yes, sir. I guess you could say that.'

Bobby said nothing for a few moments. Then he turned to Lambert and said, 'I've been trying to remember the name of that journalist who came down here last year. The one from Washington.'

'Boyd, sir. Jean Boyd.'

'Yes, that's the one.' Bobby paused, frowned. 'Am I right in thinking that she ended up as yet another of my brother's little conquests?'

'Yes, sir, she did.'

Bobby made no effort to hide his distaste. 'And perhaps it's about time Dr Portman was retired, don't you think?'

'Yes, sir.'

'Not right away, of course. Let the dust settle.'

Lambert nodded.

Bobby smiled. He looked around the splendor of the East Room. 'Let's just appreciate a quiet moment or two before we begin the real business of running this country, shall we?'

'The calm before the storm,' Lambert said.

'Yes, indeed,' Bobby echoed. 'The calm before the storm.'

Afterword

Perhaps more than any other figure in twentieth-century world history, John Fitzgerald Kennedy has provoked interest, intrigue, curiosity, a litany of unanswered questions, and an endless catalogue of conspiracy theories. From his father's involvement with bootlegging, organized crime, and Hollywood (alongside a political career that was itself dogged by scandal and corruption), to the rumors of serial infidelity and drug dependency, Kennedy has been the subject of perhaps more books, television dramas, documentaries and exposés than any other US president.

Documents relating not only to the investigation into his assassination but also his tenure in the White House have been carefully and selectively released over the past decades. It is doubtful that the truth of what happened that fateful day in November 1963 will ever be known, and if it is ever revealed, it will be long after the death of anyone who was directly or indirectly involved. With time and perspective, opinions have changed markedly. A recent Gallup survey indicated that a mere 13 percent of those who were polled believe that Oswald acted alone.

Concerning John F. Kennedy's physical condition, it is known that he suffered many and various ailments. He was plagued with colitis, an inflammation of the inner lining of the colon, causing abdominal pain, cramping and diarrhea. Prostatitis (bacterial infection of the prostate gland) was another concern, precipitating chills, fever, burning and painful urination. He was perhaps most notably affected by Addison's disease, a rare disorder of the adrenal glands in which the body produces insufficient quantities of the hormones cortisol and aldosterone, resulting in fatigue, muscle weakness, depressive mood, loss of appetite, weight loss and increased thirst.

Alongside this, he suffered with degenerative osteoporosis, not only causing him consistent and significant discomfort, but also inhibiting simple physical movements. Reaching across his desk for paperwork, putting on his socks, standing for any extended period of time and other such routine functions could precipitate agonizing pain and subsequent immobility. It has been suggested that the corset he wore to ease the pain, which kept his back and neck straight, may have been a factor in his death. Had he not been wearing this support, he perhaps would have slumped forward after the first assassin's bullet hit him. The fact that he remained upright made him all the more visible as a target for the fatal headshot.

Kennedy was known to have simultaneously taken as many as twelve different medications. These included codeine, procaine, Demerol and methadone for pain, Ritalin as a stimulant, Meprobamate and Librium for anxiety, Tuinal and assorted barbiturates to help him sleep. He also received injections of thyroid hormones and a blood derivative called gamma globulin to assist in combating his propensity for infections.

During the Bay of Pigs, Kennedy also took steroids, antispasmodics, and antibiotics for urinary tract infections, and on at least one occasion he was administered an antipsychotic to treat severe mood changes that were believed to have been precipitated by the antihistamines he was taking for various allergies.

Hard though it may be to accept, numerous doctors – including those who personally attended Kennedy – have stated that the very considerable number and dosages of his medications 'did not in any way affect his ability to execute the office of President of the United States'. Yet Ritalin, as we now understand, can exaggerate existing psychotic conditions, and can also be the cause of additional psychotic traits. Amongst further side effects are libido disorders, disorientation, even hallucinations. Methadone is an opioid and a narcotic. Its side effects – diarrhea, fatigue, sleep problems, anxiety and mood changes – might necessitate the use of even further medications.

As for Kennedy's history of alleged infidelity, this subject has occasioned perhaps as much interest and raised as many questions as the circumstances of his death. 'If I don't have sex every day, I get a headache,' he famously commented to British prime minister Harold Macmillan.

Dozens of unsubstantiated reports and rumors have abounded, but there is evidence supporting the belief that Kennedy did have affairs and liaisons with the following:

Marlene Dietrich, ex-lover of Kennedy's father, believed to have been intimate with JFK when she was sixty.

Marilyn Monroe. Allegations and theories surrounding the suspicious nature of her death – ranging from the fatal dose of barbiturates having been administered by her psychiatrist, Ralph Greenson, to Robert Kennedy's presence in her home on the night of her death – continue to this day. A recently released letter to Marilyn penned by Jean Kennedy Smith, younger sister of the Kennedy brothers, reads: *Understand that you and Bobby are the new item! We all think you should come with him when he comes back East!*

Angie Dickinson, actress.

Judith Campbell Exner, introduced to Kennedy by Frank Sinatra. Exner would go on to become the mistress of Mafia boss Sam Giancana. She has stated publicly that she became pregnant with Kennedy's child and had an abortion

Ellen Rometsch, an East German prostitute and a communist

who came to America and ended up in a call-girl ring called the Quorum Club. Situated in a three-room suite at the Carroll Arms Hotel across the street from the Senate Office Building, the club was reported to have been frequented by many significant and influential political figures. Rometsch was deported, apparently under orders from Bobby Kennedy, for fear that revelations about her relationship with JFK might become public.

Mary Pinchot Meyer, married to a CIA agent, sister-in-law to Ben Bradlee, editor of the *Washington Post*. Meyer was a close friend of LSD guru Timothy Leary, and an outspoken pacifist. She was killed, execution-style, in October of 1964 while walking in Georgetown. Her murder remains unsolved.

Blaze Starr, stripper. As a congressman, JFK visited her Maryland strip club, Crossroads.

Gunilla Von Post, a Swedish socialite with whom Kennedy shared an intimate evening on the French Riviera just three weeks before he married Jackie. That intimacy was enjoyed again two years later, though just for one night. It is said that JFK called his father and expressed his wish to divorce Jackie and marry Gunilla. Joe Kennedy said that such an action would end his political career. JFK and Gunilla never met again.

Gene Tierney, actress.

Pamela Turnure, press secretary to Jacqueline Kennedy.

Mimi Alford, White House intern.

Priscilla Wear and Jill Cowen, White House secretaries. Wear and Cowen accompanied JFK on trips to Berlin, Rome, Ireland, Costa Rica, Mexico and Nassau. On one occasion, as Jackie was giving a tour of the White House to a reporter from *Paris Match*, she passed Wear's desk and commented, 'This is the girl who is supposedly sleeping with my husband.'

The list could go on, but it would serve no purpose but to fuel further theories, notions and assumptions.

Kennedy will forever remain an enigmatic myth, the fallen King of Camelot, the dynamic young leader of the most powerful nation in the free world, and yet in so many other ways a contradiction and a conundrum. Had he not died, who knows what would have happened. Would he have gone on to secure a second term, or would his faults and failings have been so widely exposed by the Republicans that he would have fallen at the last hurdle? Would his own party, fearful of what his continued behavior might bring down on them, have derailed the campaign in favor of someone they could more easily police and control?

Had Kennedy not died in November of 1963, would he now be remembered as he is, or would he have joined the ranks of the disgraced?

This question is another to which we will never know the answer. In our hearts and minds he will be forever young – smiling, confident, his beautiful wife beside him, greeting well-wishers and shaking hands as he departed Love Field and headed toward downtown Dallas in the presidential motorcade. Perhaps, when all is said and done, we remember him this way because that is how we wish to remember him.

We want to believe that for one brief and shining moment, there really was a Camelot.